THE SECOND LADY

The biggest of the group, a squat hulk of a man, General Ivan Petrov, chairman of the KGB, jumped to his feet. His broad Slavic face bore a grin.

'Ah, Vera Vavilova!' he exclaimed. He went to her, kissed one of her cheeks, then the other. 'My dear, you were superb. A performance without flaw. My congratulations!'

General Petrov was speaking again. 'So the last dress rehearsal is over.' He studied her. 'Do you feel you are ready?'

'I am ready,' she said.

'Very good.' He picked up his cap. 'We go now to the Kremlin to inform the Premier.' . . .

Three more days, she thought, after nearly three hard years.

At last, Vera Vavilova smiled to herself. A real smile this time.

Yes, indeed, she was ready.

The Second Lady

Irving Wallace

Arrow Books

Arrow Books Limited

An imprint of Random House

20 Vauxhall Bridge Road, London SW1V 2SA

First published by Hutchinson 1980
Arrow edition 1981
Reprinted 1983, 1986, 1987, 1988 and 1989

Printed and bound in Great Britain by
Mackays of Chatham PLC, Chatham, Kent

ISBN 0 75 299972 9

For Sylvia
My Lady
With My Love

'Oh, what a tangled web we weave,
When first we practise to deceive.'
SIR WALTER SCOTT
Marmian, A Tale of Flodden Field (1808)

1

Sitting there, she began to feel better. The ordeal was almost over.

The Louis XVI furniture in the Yellow Oval Room had been rearranged. She sat straight, alert, in the middle of the striped sofa, her back to the arched window and expanse of south lawn, facing at least twenty female and four male White House reporters, most of them in folding chairs, all of them relentless.

She had placed herself between Nora Judson, her press secretary and friend, and Laurel Eakins, her appointments secretary, which was supportive and comforting. But the burden had been on her. Since she had become First Lady, she had given only four press conferences in two-and-a-half years. This, at the urging of her husband ('more exposure could help us both'), was her fifth. Because of her long silence, the press had arrived with an overload of questions.

Although there had been no respite in the past hour, the questions had been mostly easy and frivolous. Was it true she had been on a low carbohydrate diet? Did she plan to resume her tennis lessons? Would she actively campaign for her husband in the primaries? Did the President confide in her and ask her opinion on matters of state? What novels had she read lately? Did she have an opinion on current women's fashions? Was Ladbury of London still her favourite couturier? What was her reaction to the recent public opinion poll naming her the most popular woman in the world today? And so on and on, without pause.

Now a corpulent woman with a Texas twang was posing

a serious question. 'Mrs Bradford, concerning the announcement that you will be attending the International Women's Meeting in Moscow this week, before accompanying your husband to the London Summit —'

'Yes?'

'— have you modified your views on the Equal Rights Amendment or on the subject of abortion? And will you speak of these subjects in Moscow?'

She felt her press secretary squirm uneasily beside her, but she ignored the warning and went ahead. 'I intend to discuss both subjects when I address the meeting. As to my views, they have not changed an iota. I still believe equal rights for women in the United States have been long overdue, and we are receiving more and more backing for it every day. On the matter of abortion, there is much to be said for either side.' She paused to hear her press secretary's sigh of relief, heard it, and continued. 'Nevertheless, I feel there should be no legislation against abortion. I think it should be a decision of individual choice, one made by every woman.'

'You will speak of this in Moscow?'

'Absolutely. I'll also try to evaluate, based on statistics made available to me, where the women of the United States stand on both subjects at the present time.'

Another reporter, tall, bony, was standing. She spoke with a modulated Boston accent. 'Mrs Bradford, can you tell us what else you expect to discuss at the International Women's Meeting?'

'Women in the American work force. Women in our armed forces. Oh, endless other topics. I'll have a full report ready when I return.'

The women's editor of the *New York Times* came to her feet. 'I understand you will be in Moscow three days. Can you tell us of any other activities, outside the meetings, that you plan to engage in?'

'Well, since this will be my first visit to the Soviet Union, I hope to find the time to squeeze in a little sightseeing — but I think Nora here is more familiar with my schedule.'

8

She looked at Nora Judson, and her press secretary took over quickly, efficiently, brightly.

With relief, Billie Bradford sat back for the first time. The day, especially from noon until now, had been so busy, so anxiety-ridden, that she had not realized until this moment how exhausted she really was. She felt dishevelled. She glanced down at her light blue cashmere slipover sweater and darker blue pleated skirt. Both were still fresh and neat. It was her hair then. She had worn her long blonde hair pulled back, tied with a silk ribbon around her chignon. But as always, some strands of hair had come loose and hung over her forehead. With a characteristic gesture, she brushed the strands into place.

Nora was holding forth to the press people about the First Lady's Moscow itinerary, and Billie Bradford was grateful. Pretending to be attentive to her press secretary, Billie let her mind drift back to the late morning of this crucial day and then forward across the afternoon to this very time. Before noon, she had disposed of all her personal correspondence, especially her letters to her father in Malibu and her younger sister Kit, telling both that after Moscow, and before her departure for London, she would have to be in Los Angeles for one day and hoped to see them both.

After that, she had stepped in the pressure cooker. There had been a long lunch in the Family Dining Room for the wives of the majority and minority leaders in the Senate and House, as well as for the wives of several important committee heads. Immediately following, she had received the winners of a painting contest sponsored by a national association of handicapped persons. Then, Ladbury himself, just arrived from London, had appeared for a preliminary fitting of new dresses and gowns she hoped to wear in Moscow and London. Without rest, assisted by her personal maid Sarah Keating, she had plunged into a search for an old college scrapbook that Guy Parker needed as research for the autobiography he was ghostwriting for her. Next, she had hastened downstairs, and made her way outside to the Rose Garden. The late August afternoon had been balmy, and it had been pleasant in the sun receiving the delegation of Girl Scouts and their leaders and passing out special awards to those who had performed outstanding community service.

With less than five minutes to spare, she had gone with Nora to the Yellow Oval Room upstairs, where the gathering of press representatives had been having tea while awaiting her arrival.

And now, after over an hour, she became aware that the press conference had just ended. Nora and Laurel were on their feet, on either side of her, and she hastily rose from the sofa to murmur her appreciation and say good-bye.

When the room was emptied, she remained standing, drained of energy. The smile, so long frozen on her classical pale features, melted to a straight tight line. It was done, the crucial day finished, and yet it was not.

There was one last act to undertake.

Pulling herself together, she left the room alone, went up the long corridor to the elevator and took it downstairs.

Minutes later she entered the West Wing, headed for the Cabinet Room and entered it. She was rarely apprehensive or nervous, but she was both right now. The large room smelled of leather and cigar smoke. As she had expected, there they were, the five of them, all seated at the near end of the rich mahogany table, still staring at the two television monitoring screens showing pictures of the Yellow Oval Room she had just vacated.

The biggest of the group, a squat hulk of a man, General Ivan Petrov, chairman of the KGB, jumped to his feet. His broad Slavic face bore a grin.

'Ah, Vera Vavilova!' he exclaimed. He went to her, kissed one of her cheeks, then the other. 'My dear, you were superb. A performance without flaw. My congratulations!'

Behind him, the others, Colonel Zhuk, her own beloved Alex Razin, and two she did not know, were also standing, voicing their congratulations.

Her heart stopped pounding. 'Thank you,' she said. 'Thank you very much.'

General Petrov was speaking again. 'So the last dress rehearsal is over.' He studied her. 'Do you feel you are ready?'

'I am ready,' she said.

'Very good.' He picked up his cap. 'We go now to the Kremlin to inform the Premier.'

When they left the Cabinet Room, she trailed after them, and watched them get into the limousine, and depart the fake White House, going through the gate in the high fence opened by the KGB guards. She stood and saw, far beyond the open fence gate, the distant golden cupolas and spires inside the Kremlin and the skyline of Moscow.

Three more days, she thought, after nearly three hard years.

At last, Vera Vavilova smiled to herself. A real smile this time.

Yes, indeed, she was ready.

2

The minute that he stepped out of his Georgetown apartment building, Guy Parker knew that it was not going to be his kind of day. When Washington DC was hot and humid, there was no city in the land more suffocating. By the time he turned into the alley and walked to the garage, he began to feel sticky all over. There were patches of perspiration from his armpits to his waist. His shirt clung to him like a vast bandage of adhesive. After unlocking his new Ford, he shed his seersucker jacket, loosened his knit necktie, then bent and got inside behind the wheel. He folded his jacket across the passenger seat and dropped his small cassette tape recorder on top of it.

After starting the car, backing out, and leaving the alley, he accelerated and drove as fast as possible toward The Madison hotel. His luncheon appointment was for 1.30. He did not want to be late because his guest was extremely busy and doing him a favour. Twice before he had arranged a lunch date with George Kilday, and each time Kilday had cancelled the date at the last moment because of a fast-breaking story. An hour ago, he had telephoned Kilday at the *Los Angeles Times* bureau in Washington, and he had been assured that this afternoon their appointment would hold. Parker was doubly determined not to be late, because the interview truly was a favour. The bureau chief had nothing to gain from seeing Parker, whereas Parker had a lot to gain from seeing him. It was all over town, at least among members of the Fourth Estate, that Parker was getting to keep a half-million dollars of the publisher's advance to the First Lady for her autobiography (the other half-million going to charities). Kilday might have had every reason to be jealous and sourly uncooperative. Instead, he had proved to be a nice person, an old-timer who liked to see fellow writers make it big.

Guy Parker reached The Madison four minutes early. Snatching up his tape recorder and coat, he turned the car over to the doorman. Inside the exquisitely furnished lobby, the cool air gave him immediate relief and fresh energy. He veered right past the reception desk and cashier's window and hurried to the unpretentious café. As he entered, he saw a waitress showing Kilday to a table. He went towards them, hailing Kilday with a wave, and Kilday waved back.

He did not know Kilday well, but had run into him perhaps a half-dozen times in the past two-and-a-half years in the time when Parker had been one of the President's speech writers, and the few times they had talked, it had always been brief and always politics.

He had known little about Kilday personally, except that he was a newspaperman respected among colleagues for his doggedness on a story and his almost religious regard for accuracy. Parker had not known there had been any connection between Kilday and the First Lady, until one early session when Billie herself had brought him up. They had been talking about the period after Billie had graduated from Vassar as a journalism major. Before her father's retirement, she had worked for the advertising agency that handled the company marketing her father's inventions. She had obtained a job with a New York public relations firm, and later been their representative in London for a short time. She had returned to Los Angeles determined to write a novel, and halfway through she had torn it up.

'And soon after, you got a job on the *Los Angeles Times*?' Parker had asked her.

'Not quite. Actually, my first newspaper job – if you can call it that – was on a Santa Monica throwaway paper at nothing-a-week. The money didn't matter. I really didn't need any. But it gave me access to many events and places

I would otherwise never have seen. Well, one day the editor assigned me to write a piece on a drug rehabilitation centre. Instead of doing it routinely, interviewing the director, I got an idea from something I'd read in a biography of Nellie Bly.'

'The one who tried to beat Jules Verne's around-the-world-in-eighty-days record?'

'The same. Verne's Phileas Fogg did it in eighty days in fiction. Nellie Bly did it in fact in 1889 and 1890. She went around the world in seventy-two days. Anyway, before that, while just starting out as a cub reporter on the New York *World*, Nellie Bly undertook a story about *insane* people who had been committed to Blackwell's Island and how they were being treated. But instead of doing the story in an orthodox way, Nellie disguised herself in ragged clothes, gave herself a deranged look, feigned insanity, and got herself committed to Blackwell's Island. As a patient, she saw the miserable conditions and the cruelty to the other patients first-hand. When she got out, she wrote two front-page stories about the experience. This *exposé* made her famous overnight. Well, there I was with a routine assignment to write a story about a drug rehabilitation centre in Santa Monica, and I thought of Nellie Bly, and I said to myself — why not?'

'You got yourself admitted to the centre as a drug addict?'

'Cocaine addict. And it worked. Quite an eyeful. Then I wrote the story first-person, patient's point of view. Well, I won't say it was a sensation — after all, it appeared in that small weekly throwaway cluttered with real estate and food market ads — but still, it brought me a little attention and some praise. Especially from my family. My father just loved it. In fact, he was so impressed that he mailed a clip of it to a friend of his who was an executive at the *Los Angeles Times*. The executive liked it, also the fact that it had been done by Clarence Lane's daughter — my father was quite well-known in those days for his inventions — and the executive sent it over to editorial. The managing editor called me in for an interview and decided to give me a try-out as a staff writer.'

'How did you do?'

Billie Bradford had laughed. 'My first assignment was a fiasco. I would have been hired and fired within forty-eight hours, if it hadn't been for George Kilday. He was a copy-editor. He saved my neck.'

'What happened?'

'Oh, I don't want to go into it. Just ask George Kilday. He'll tell you the whole thing. He's here in Washington now, the head of the *Los Angeles Times* bureau. In fact, you should see him anyway. He'll fill you in on a lot of things about my journalism fling that I don't remember. He has a real reporter's eye. Ask him.'

'I intend to, Mrs Bradford. But I want to ask you first. What happened on your opening assignment?'

So she had told him, told him what she could remember of that first time out.

Anyway, that had been some months ago, and that had been Parker's initial knowledge of Kilday's small role in Billie Bradford's life, and he had meant to meet with Kilday, and finally had recently tried, and now at last in his third effort Parker was sitting across from Kilday in The Madison café.

Parker immediately voiced his appreciation for the senior newspaperman's cooperation.

'Not at all,' said Kilday. The waitress returned for their orders, and as Kilday scanned the menu once more, settling for chicken noodle soup and a cheese and lettuce sandwich on wheat bread, Parker studied the bureau chief. He had shaggy white eyebrows, a prominent nose, a lot of jaw with two shaving cuts, all set on a short neck and stocky body encased in a crumpled greyish suit.

After Parker had also ordered, he indicated his tape machine on the plastic table between them. 'Do you mind?' Parker asked.

'Go ahead,' said Kilday. 'Myself, I don't use them. Find them a waste of time. Too much work transcribing, and most of it non-essential. But no, I don't mind talking to one.'

Parker depressed the record button and started the machine.

'How long have you been in Washington?' he asked.

'Transferred here the year before Billie Bradford moved into the White House.'

'About three-and-a-half years ago.'

'About. I'm mighty proud of her. She's giving the old House a new look. She's elegant as Jacqueline Kennedy. Smart and honest as Betty Ford. More creative than either. More political savvy than either. Certainly as much as Rosalynn Carter. Great instincts. To my eye, the best looker we've ever had there.'

'I agree,' said Parker. 'It's a joy working with her. Have you seen much of Mrs Bradford since she became First Lady?'

'Not much. I don't have much to do with the East Wing. I'm on the West Wing side. Presidential politics entirely. Still, she's been kind enough to have me to three or four state dinners.'

'I didn't know you had anything to do with her life. One day, not long ago, she mentioned you.'

'Did she? What did she mention?'

'How you saved her neck after her first assignment on the *Los Angeles Times*.'

'She told you that?'

'Yes. She said she owed a lot to you.'

'It was something anyone would have done. Hell, for a writer she was just a green kid out of college and a couple of publicity jobs.' He paused. 'What did she tell you?'

'Just the bare facts. She thought you might elaborate on them. It's colourful stuff for the book.'

'Go ahead.'

'Her first assignment for the newspaper,' said Parker. 'It was very important to her, and the managing director – I don't have his name –'

'Dave Nugent.'

'Thank you. Anyway, he gave her an assignment to interview somebody important –'

16

'Dr Jonas Salk. The polio vaccine man. Up from La Jolla to give a speech in Los Angeles.'

'Good. So she went out on the interview, got it. Salk was friendly. Gave her wonderful material. She went to her typewriter, wrote her story, handed it in to you to pass on to the managing director. You found the story appallingly bad, sophomoric, wrong lead, so on. Without telling her, you held it back. You knew if the editor saw it, he'd fire her. So you quietly turned it over to a close friend of yours who was on rewrite, a veteran named Steve Woodson –'

'Steve Woods,' Kilday corrected him.

'Yes, thanks. Woods. He rewrote it completely and handed it back to you at your request. You handed the rewritten story in to the managing editor. He liked it, and he gave her a permanent job. When she read the story in print, she was amazed at what had happened to it. She asked you, and you levelled with her. You told her that her interview had been awful. You told her exactly what she had done wrong. You told her you had given it to Woods to rewrite. You pointed out how he had changed the story to make it acceptable. She was a quick learner. The next time, and in all the times after, she got it right. That's Mrs Bradford's version. Is it substantially correct?'

Kilday had finished the last of his sandwich. 'Umm, I suppose so, substantially,' he said. He cupped a hand in front of his mouth, and behind it used a toothpick to clean the spaces between his teeth. 'Only one thing wrong with it. That's because I never told her the truth. There was no Steve Woods to rewrite it. He didn't exist. If he had, I wouldn't have showed it to him, wouldn't have wanted him or anyone else to know how poorly she'd done with her first assignment. Didn't want word getting out to the boss. No. The truth is I took her story home and rewrote it myself and handed it in. Never told her I did it. Didn't want her owing me. Just wanted to be her friend. So she never knew I did it. Didn't know then. Doesn't know to this day. So that part's no use to you. Can't put that part in your book. Just telling you as one writer to another. Now forget it.'

Curious fellow, Parker thought, drinking the last of his coffee. There weren't too many of these don't-want-no-credit people around any more.

'I appreciate that,' said Parker. 'So, after the Salk story, she was on the staff. She did about three years of big-name interviews.'

'Right. And one of the last was with a California senator named Andrew Bradford. That's when it began for her.'

'Yes, of course. I'd like to hear about some of the other celebrities she interviewed before she got to Bradford.'

'If you like,' said Kilday.

That moment, the café cashier came to their table. 'Pardon,' she said. 'Is either one of you Mr Guy Parker?'

Parker looked up, surprised. 'I am.'

'Call for you from the White House. Phone's next to the register.'

Puzzled, Parker put down his napkin, excused himself and crossed the room to the telephone.

The voice on the other end was Nora Judson's.

'I had trouble finding you,' she was saying. 'Then I remembered you were going to have lunch at The Madison.'

'With George Kilday. On the book.'

'Can you cut it short? Billie would like to see you as soon as possible.'

'But I'll be seeing her in an hour anyway for our –'

'No, that's cancelled. Her schedule is too heavy. I mean, she's leaving for Moscow tomorrow afternoon. There's no time to work with you on the book today. But there's something else she wants to talk to you about. If you can get right over – well, in fifteen minutes or so –'

'Okay, I'll try. It's just that it's been so hard to get together with Kilday –'

'See him another time. Please hurry, before everything piles up.'

With that she hung up. Parker replaced the receiver on the phone and wondered what he could tell George Kilday. But, as it turned out, he did not have to tell him anything. When

18

he returned to the table, Kilday was already standing, gathering up his cigarettes, matches, key ring.

'I know,' he said with mock exasperation. 'The White House. Something important's come up. It always does.'

'I'm sorry,' said Parker, as he glanced at the bill and laid down some notes. 'I'm glad you understand. You were being very helpful. Can we finish this another time?'

'Whenever you're ready, just call.'

They went out together and stood in front of the hotel. The street was an oven. Nevertheless, Parker decided to leave his car and walk to the White House. He could make it in fifteen minutes. He wanted the interval to be alone in his head. As Kilday ordered his car, Parker thanked him once more and was on his way.

Despite the heat, he walked rapidly in long strides. Across the street, two reporters emerging from the *Washington Post* building, hailed him. He saluted back but kept going. Several times, he caught his moving reflection in shop windows. What he saw of himself always surprised him. He looked so neat, so sure of himself, from the outside. This was deceptive. Inside he carried a tangle of anxieties and uncertainties.

It sometimes surprised him that he had become a writer. Although he was good at it, no question. People always told him that he looked like a writer, whatever that meant. He was almost tall, just under 6 feet. He was thin, lanky, sinewy. No fat whatsoever. His thick black hair parted at one side, his brown eyes set deep above the high cheek bones, his nose slightly Roman, sensuous lips (the women always said), a dimpled jut of a jaw.

Actually, there had never been a writer in his family. His father was a professor of political science at the University of Wisconsin. His mother was a psychologist. Parker had gone to Northwestern University, had become involved in American history with the vague notion that he might teach one day. His avocation had been voraciously reading suspense and mystery novels. This had heightened his desire to lead a more active and exciting life. Early in the Vietnam conflict, someone had promised him a chance to get into

19

army intelligence if he enlisted. Although he thought the American role in Vietnam immoral, he wanted an opportunity to act out his fantasies. He enlisted, went to officers' training school, and graduated to an intelligence desk in the Pentagon. For a while it was intellectually stimulating, but finally a sedentary bore. Also, more and more, some of the war information he had been privy to had begun to aggravate his sense of decency. Vietnam was an outrage, and he was becoming outraged.

He could not wait to leave the service, and when he did he wanted to put distance between himself and the military automatons and what they were doing to thousands of yellow people a half a world away. With his meagre savings, Parker went to Europe, to be alone, to think, to find diversion. It was his first trip abroad, and he felt sheepish confining himself to the popular cities and sights – London, Paris, Rome. But then he realized that they were popular because they were among the most interesting places to visit in Europe, and he felt better about staying on the beaten path.

When he returned to the United States, the Vietnam war had worsened and the protest movement was at its height. Some long-dormant activist sense in him was nudged, and automatically he made his way to San Francisco and joined an organization of the peace movement. The organization was lacking writers, so Parker began to write for it, mostly broadsides and pamphlets condemning the American government.

By the time the war ended, Parker found himself in Chicago and in need of a job. A large private detective agency had placed an ad in a Chicago newspaper seeking young operatives. Parker applied, and because his army intelligence background looked good on paper, he got the job. At first he liked it. He rather fancied himself as a Dashiell Hammett in his Pinkerton phase. Indeed, there was a fair amount of legwork, shadowing, illegal entries, placement of electronic equipment, but mostly it was a lowdown, seedy business monotonously filled with mean divorce cases, locating runaway children, investigating small-time money swindles. To make it more romantic, he had casually begun to write about it. He had written three factual articles, and sold all three.

Hearing of an opening in the New York bureau of the Associated Press, Parker dashed off a resumé and submitted it along with photocopies of his three published articles. In a week he was summoned to New York for an interview. After a half-hour chat with a senior AP executive, he was hired on the spot and sent to Washington DC to write light-weight feature stories and weekend mailers that gave him by-lines instead of a living wage. But he was utterly fasci-nated by Washington, and it showed in his stories, and soon the by-lines paid off.

One day there was a long-distance call from a man named Wayne Gibbs. He had read any number of Parker's feature pieces and had been favourably impressed. He was, he had said, an associate of Senator Andrew Bradford, who had just won the Democratic party nomination to run for President of the United States. Gibbs had a proposition for Parker. Could Parker fly into Los Angeles for the weekend, expenses paid? Parker could and did. The proposition was enticing. Supporters of Bradford wanted a book written and published about their candidate, a crisp, lively, easy-to-read biography of their nominee. A campaign biography to enhance their man's image. They already had a publisher. Now they re-quired a writer who could turn out the book fast. The money would be generous.

To Parker, the money sounded attractive, but there was something else that sounded even more attractive. This was mainstream stuff. Until then, Parker had gone through many convolutions in his attitude toward his country, toward American democracy. In the army he had gone along, finally been revolted by what he saw. He had run away from it, gone abroad. He had returned, become a dissenter, lashing out at his government's politics and corruption, wanting to topple the government. Then, at AP, seeing the government up close and more objectively, remembering the political sickness he had observed in Europe, he had come to the conclusion that, bad as it was, the democratic system in the

United States was still the best one conceived by the minds of men and the best one around anywhere. This conclusion was neither juvenile nor seen through red, white and blue filters. It was pragmatic. It was mature. If people were meant to live together in a society, this system was the best one to live under. The trouble was that the fat, sluggish giant was so flawed, and no outsider could do anything about improving it except by voting, which in itself offered few choices. But here, in Los Angeles, he had been give a rare opportunity to cease being a helpless outsider and step inside closer, much closer, to the main machinery.

Without giving it so much as a second thought, Parker quit the Associated Press and became a full-time political writer.

Preparing the book, he had met Andrew Bradford three times, once for dinner with his wife, twice for superficial research interviews. The book itself was more or less a paste-up job. He liked Bradford immediately, a man just under his own height, sturdier built, graceful. Bradford was forty-eight years old. He possessed a finely chiselled, handsome face, sincere, serious, attentive, direct. A fleck of greying at the temples, horn-rimmed spectacles, a clipped manner of speaking, all enhanced his authority. He also had a brain devoid of clichéing and stereotyping, quick, original, much superior to what one would expect from a politician.

Parker finished the book on time. It sold well at party rallies and banquets, and the paperback edition exceeded projected sales among curious independents. Parker's stock was fairly high. He was no longer a party drone. He had some visibility. Wayne Gibbs kept him attached to the election committee to lend a hand in preparing press releases.

The election came and went. After a nip and tuck beginning, the major polls had given Bradford a 6 per cent lead over his Republican opponent. Bradford won by 7 per cent. As President-elect, and before the inauguration, Bradford began to assemble his permanent staff. He remembered Guy Parker and the book. From San Francisco, he sent for Parker, just to be sure he was thinking of the right man. Before their interview was over, he hired Parker, and two months later installed him in the West Wing of the White House as one of three speech writers.

That had been two-and-a-half years ago. Parker enjoyed his role. He was in the centre of the action, an invisible man behind the movers and shakers, but he was there. Then, overnight, he wasn't there. Several prestigious New York book publishers, who were also party regulars, had suggested to the President that an autobiography by his wife might find a wide audience and enhance his own image as he headed toward re-election year. Billie Bradford had proved to be a colourful and enchanting First Lady. Somewhat reluctantly, a little embarrassed – she was only thirty-six years old – she consented to undertake the autobiography, on one condition. She wanted Guy Parker to work on it with her. At first Parker had resisted. He had regarded it as a demotion. To move from hard policy-making speeches for the leader of the free world to a frivolous, gossipy, tea-room confessional seemed a letdown. What convinced Parker that it was a good move was the half-million dollar share of the advance that would be his – and Billie Bradford herself. She was anything but frivolous, he learned fast. She was as serious as her husband, brighter perhaps, and never dull. She was a joy to be with. He respected her, adored her, and finally made the move from the West Wing to the East Wing with minimal resistance.

And there had been a bonus. Parker was placed in an office next to Nora Judson's office suite. She was the First Lady's press secretary who also had a hand in her social life and public appearances. To be able to undertake so many jobs, and do them well, was a measure of the young woman's energy and gifts. Parker guessed that she was about twenty-nine. He would have liked to regard her as a sex object. From her glossy dark hair, green eyes, pert nose, generous lips, to her bountiful breasts and shapely legs, she was a delight to the male eye. But the intellect was formidable. One rarely finished a sentence with her before she had concluded the task. She did things two at a time, to perfection. She could go from a press briefing to a hospital dedication to a state dinner without a fumble and without complaint. The problem had been her remoteness. She was always busy, or made herself busy, and she was otherwise a private person and preferred life that way. Parker had hinted at drinks or dinner together. She had ignored him. In five months he had not been able to penetrate the wall that separated their offices and persons. She had been correct. She had been pleasant. She had remained aloof. It was maddening, but her existence and nearness had been the bonus.

Parker had been busy, too. Laying the groundwork for the First Lady's much-touted autobiography had been a ten-hour-a-day occupation. The beginning of the assignment had been collecting material to read. He had located and read everything that had ever appeared in print on Billie Bradford. He had gone through a mountain range of newspaper and magazine clippings, making countless pages of notes. Then he had begun to travel outside of Washington, meeting and interviewing her relatives, friends, private school and college instructors, and classmates. He had even flown to California to spend two days with her father Clarence Lane, her sister Kit, her brother-in-law Norris Weinstein, and a nephew named Richie.

At last, lately, with hundreds of questions to ask, he had got to the flesh of the book. He had begun to interview Billie Bradford herself. She had set up a daily routine. One hour, usually every afternoon, to reply to his questions into his tape recorder. He had found her professional, forthright, fun, and the work wasn't work at all, except as he made it so in his absolute obsessive need for detail.

And here he was, this steaming afternoon in late August, heading for another interview session with — but no, not another today. He remembered. Billie Bradford had just cancelled today's session. She was too busy. This confused him, this cancellation, only the second one since they had begun. Yet Nora had made it clear the First Lady wanted to see him as soon as possible about something else. He wondered what else it could be.

He had come out of Lafayette Park, crossed Pennsylvania Avenue, approached the guard house, routinely flipped open his wallet to display his White House identification card. He passed through, went up the curving driveway to the North Portico entrance. He reached the red-carpeted main stairway, and with a nod to the portrait of Herbert Hoover on the landing, continued up the steps two at a time, past the portraits of Woodrow Wilson and Franklin D. Roosevelt. At the top, he was greeted by the person of Nora Judson.

'Did I make it in fifteen minutes?' asked Parker, winded. 'I hurried. I knew you couldn't wait to set eyes on me.'

'I was eaten up by worry,' said Nora. 'I was afraid you'd been hit by a truck – or your big ego.'

'What ego? It always shrivels in m'lady's presence.'

'We'll talk about that some other time.'

'Can we make a date?'

'No,' she said briskly, leading him toward the Yellow Oval Room. 'Anyway, you're right on time. Her press conference wound up ten minutes ago. The print media people have already gone. The television people are about through packing up.'

'She really couldn't keep our date?'

'She already had a tight schedule, what with leaving for Moscow tomorrow afternoon. Then Ladbury arrived from London – he was supposed to have been here yesterday – and insisted on being worked in for a last fitting before the London Summit next week. So I had to shift everything around. She still has the layout for *House Beautiful* to do. We couldn't postpone it again. She has to accompany the new French ambassador on his tour of the National Gallery. After that, Fred Willis insists on seeing her personally for a protocol briefing on the Moscow visit. Then she has packing to do. She won't let Sarah do it alone.'

'What does she want to see me about?' Parker asked.

'I have no idea,' said Nora. 'She wanted five minutes with you after the press conference and before the fitting. Here we are.'

They had arrived at the entrance to the Yellow Oval

Room, then stood aside as three members of a network television crew emerged carrying their equipment. When they had gone, Nora started inside, followed by Parker.

There was no one in the room except Billie Bradford. Her back was to them, her blonde hair down to her shoulders, as she reached for an arm of the sofa and slumped into it. Kicking off her shoes, she saw them.

'Oh, Nora, I wondered where you were. Hello, Guy –' She patted the sofa next to her. 'Here.'

Parker advanced and dutifully sat down. 'Hello, Mrs Bradford –'

'Guy, please,' she interrupted, making a face. 'For the tenth time, will you stop Mrs Bradfording me? I mean it. Here I am, seeing you every day on intimate terms, practically disrobing in front of you, baring psyche and soul, letting you see every skeleton in every closet – and you're still being formal. Let's change that right now, especially considering what I have to tell you. From this moment on, it's good-bye Mrs Bradford, hello Billie.'

She offered him her cheek. 'Seal it', she said.

He leaned over and awkwardly kissed her cheek. 'Hello, Billie,' he said.

She addressed Nora Judson, seated across from them.

'How did it go, Nora? How was it, the press conference?'

'You were wonderful, frank and open, no equivocating. They simply loved you.'

'I hope so. For Andrew's sake. I suppose I should do it more often.'

'You really should,' said Nora.

Billie turned toward Parker. 'I'm sorry about skipping today's exciting episode in the life and times of a First Lady. Where did we leave our heroine? Tied to a railroad track?'

'No, Pearl White, not quite,' Parker said with a grin. 'At the end of yesterday's session, you were in your third year of college and leaving for a school-sponsored literary tour of England.'

Billie's face suddenly fell. 'Yes,' she said. 'That was the

trip when I met Janet Farleigh. You've come across her name in your research.'

'Yes, of course. The English children's novelist. She's one of your best friends, according to what I read.'

'She *was*,' said Billie sadly. 'She died last night. Cancer. And I never knew. The British ambassador sent over a hand-delivered note this morning, informing me. The ambassador was one of the few who knew how close we were. It was quite a jolt, I tell you.'

'I'm sorry,' said Parker.

'I met Janet Farleigh on that student trip. I stayed with her. She was my hostess in London. She was ten years older than me, but we became the closest of friends. I hadn't seen her in some time. This White House stuff gets in the way of everything. I hoped to see her in London next week, but now – well, I will call on her husband and son.'

Nora was tapping the crystal of her wristwatch. 'Billie, I hate to bring it up, but we're running short.'

Billie aroused herself. 'Very well. I hadn't thought of it all day, running around like this.' She smiled at Parker. 'What were we talking about before, when you came in? Yes. About skipping today's session. I'm going to make it up to you. That's really why I wanted to see you.'

Guy Parker waited.

After a beat, Billie Bradford resumed more cheerfully. 'Tomorrow afternoon we're taking Air Force One to Moscow. It could be a long, dull flight. I have the choice of re-reading Tolstoi all the way or talking about myself. It's Anna Karenina those eight hours or Billie Bradford. No contest. I won. On the flight, I want to talk about myself to you. In other words, Guy, I'm inviting you to come along on Air Force One to Moscow. We can talk all the way there and back. Have you ever been to Moscow?'

Parker was flabbergasted. 'Why, no, but – well, thank you but this is kind of sudden – I mean, I'd need time to get ready – get a passport –'

'Guy, really,' she chided him. 'What's the big deal? I know your background – Vietnam intelligence, detecting – all that – you must be used to quick changes, moves. As to your diplomatic passport, we'll take care of that. Just pack up and let's go. You'll be occupied the entire trip. When I'm not keeping you company, Nora will. How's that?'

Parker glanced at Nora. 'That's fine Mrs – Billie,' he said. 'I'd better scramble and get my rucksack together.'

As he came to his feet, Billie said, 'Nora will give you details on takeoff time, and so forth. See you tomorrow.'

There had been a knocking on the door, and Nora moved quickly to open it. The chief usher took a half-step in. 'Mr Ladbury and Miss Quarles have arrived,' he announced.

Parker had just come up beside Nora, when the pair whirled into the room. Each was carrying an armload of clothes boxes. Hardly acknowledging the presence of Nora, ignoring Parker, Ladbury flitted straight for the First Lady, with Rowena Quarles at his heels. Parker had only a glimpse of them in their passage. Ladbury appeared a resurrected Aubrey Beardsley, straw-coloured fringe, hawkish nose, pale pinched features, lithe, slender, young, greeting Billie with a high-pitched, 'Darling! Countless goodies for you!' Behind him was the Quarles woman, his assistant apparently, definitely dyke, mean plump face, short and square body, tweeds (in this weather!).

Nora had Parker in the corridor and guided him toward the stairway. He gestured behind them, 'How come she's using a British couturier?'

'Oh, Billie knew him and liked him before she ever came to the White House. But once she was First Lady, it was political to Buy American, so she shifted to several New York designers. Actually, taking Ladbury on again was Fred Willis's idea. He thought the British would appreciate such a gesture for her London visit. Naturally, her Manhattan designers howled their protest, but Billie stuck to Ladbury for this time out.' As they neared the stairway, Nora added, 'I'll have your schedule, passport, everything in your hands by dinnertime.'

'Thank you.'

'You should be happy about the trip. Nice of her. She

won't sleep much, so you'll get a chance to talk to her most of the way to Moscow.'

'And to you,' Parker said.

Her reserve did not break. 'Me?' she said. 'I'll be busy with Tolstoi.'

He halted at the landing, caught her arm. 'Nora, dear, what have you got against me?'

Her eyes fixed on him coolly. 'Just that you're the same sex as my ex-husband.'

'Oh? Ex-husband? I didn't know.'

'Now you know.'

'Were you badly burned?'

'Third degree,' she said, and marched off.

It was five minutes before midnight in Moscow.

Not far from the massive Kremlin, at 2 Dzerzhinsky Square, stood a complex of old and new grey stone buildings referred to in the Soviet Union as The Centre, actually the headquarters of the Committee of State Security known as the KGB. On the third floor, behind his oversized desk in the main office of a spacious suite, sat the chairman of the KGB's seven directorates, General Ivan Petrov, staring out the grilled window into the dimly lit courtyard.

Surrounding him were the ornaments of leadership. The walls were panelled in mahogany. One wall held a framed portrait of V. I. Lenin. Below were the ornate sofas and padded chairs. On the floor stretched an oriental rug, one of the few offices with a rug. Filling the right side of his desk were six telephones, one directly hooked up to the general secretary of the Communist Party and the Premier, Dmitri Kirechenko, the others with direct lines to members of the Politburo, to the Ministry of Defence, to Petrov's six deputies on the same floor, and (with high frequency connections) to KGB offices in Soviet embassies around the world.

Yet, on this eve of glory, his thoughts were momentarily diverted to a slip of paper in his hands.

It had arrived minutes ago, this coded message from his agents in Washington DC. It did not seem of grave importance, but on this momentous day anything unexpected excited his suspicion. The message reported that one new name had been added to the passenger roster of those accompanying the First Lady of the United States to Moscow tomorrow.

Petrov set the slip of paper down on his desk and massaged the stubble on his broad creased face with dry hands. He could leave this for one of his aides when they came to work at nine in the morning. Or he could satisfy his curiosity right now. He pushed himself erect – automatically straightened the ill-fitting grey suit jacket on his short, blocky body – and went to the wooden index-card holder in a corner of the office. He found the letter P, and then the card marked, PARKER, GUY, with the cross-reference number. He telephoned the basement computer centre, and ten minutes later a messenger appeared with the manilla folder in hand.

Petrov carried the Parker dossier to his desk, lowered himself into his leather-covered swivel chair, and opened the folder. Who was Parker? Ah, there it was. Pentagon intelligence. Private detective. Political biographer. Presidential speech writer. Currently, collaborator with Mrs Bradford on her autobiography. There was more, but for Petrov this was enough.

Well, he asked himself, why was this Parker suddenly assigned to accompany the First Lady to Moscow? Maybe the answers were obvious ones. To provide the First Lady with companionship. To continue to work with her while she travelled. Or, more likely, to serve as a CIA undercover agent during the three-day stay.

Petrov tore free a piece of memo paper. He jotted a note to Colonel Zhuk, telling him of the new addition to the American party, ordering him to be certain that the KGB kept a close watch on this Guy Parker.

Shoving the note aside, he reminded himself once more that nothing must be overlooked in this eleventh hour. No chances could be taken now. There was absolutely no margin for error.

Unwrapping a Cuban cigar, Petrov's eyes lingered on his desk clock. After midnight. Moscow slept. Petrov liked to think that he never slept. In a twenty-four-hour day, this was his favourite time. Outside, the street was still. Inside, The Centre was quiet. Except for the wireless and decoding offices, and a number of other offices occupied by the night shift, he had the place to himself. It was ever a time to reflect and contemplate. Too few executives had such opportunity, which was a pity. Of course, he had such opportunity at the cost of sleep – small price. Sleep was the enemy of life, he had long ago decided, a waste in life, a surrender, an unwanted preview of death. There would be plenty of time, far off, for death and sleep.

His mind reviewed the exciting climactic day. The day's highlight in their secluded Potemkin compound, the last rehearsal of Vera Vavilova, had been successful beyond hope. Vera Vavilova had not been merely perfect. That would have implied imitation. She had been more. She had actually become the American First Lady, the embodiment and incarnation of Billie Bradford. A remarkable feat, almost metaphysical in its happening.

Yet, Petrov was aware, she was the product of men, of conscious effort, of diligent work, of creative genius. Perhaps his personal deputy, Alex Razin, deserved a small share of the credit. His effort, his work, had made the scheme possible. But he had been only a cog, implementing a stroke of genius. The real genius had been in the conception. This had been Ivan Petrov's own. Without his genius, there would have been no Second Lady. If this came off – and he was positive it would – it would be the most daring and magnificent espionage coup in world history. Unfortunately, world history would never know of it. The plot would for ever have to remain the most secret military and political event of all time. It was, Petrov reflected, like the perfect crime. If a crime could be found out, it would not be perfect. If it remained unknown, it might not have happened. The Vavilova undertaking presented the same paradox.

Still, happily, Petrov told himself, it was a reality known to a favoured few. The participants knew about it. Above all, the Premier and several members of the Politburo knew about it. Petrov was proud that he had been able to bring the Premier along with him for almost three years, from interest and hesitation to faith and cautious enthusiasm. Late this afternoon, receiving a report on the final rehearsal, the Premier had shown cautious enthusiasm. In three days he would have to make his fateful decision. To discard caution and proceed without reserve. Or to abort the project. Petrov refused to believe that the Premier would abort, knowing the progress that had been made, knowing the historic success that would result.

Once the project was undertaken, there could be no turning back. Once it was under way, success was inevitable. Then, and only then, secret though it be, Ivan Petrov would have his rewards. To add to the Order of Lenin, he would be crowned a Hero of the Soviet Union for some fictional feat. He would be elevated within the Politburo. He would be acknowledged as Genius by his superiors, peers, wife and sons. What more could a man on earth wish?

Puffing on his cigar, feeling pleased and mellow, contemplating the pay-off, Ivan Petrov allowed himself to revive and relive the plot, his role in it, from its inception. So as not to seem self-indulgent, Petrov pretended that he was reliving the plot to be certain it was airtight, without flaw, no tiny obstacle overlooked. With this serious motive imposed, he could permit himself the pleasure of once more celebrating his creative genius. Without difficulty he transported himself backward in time, three years backward to the memorable evening when the idea had first struck him. Three years backward. The past was the present.

General Ivan Petrov and his entourage were on a whirlwind tour of some of the major cities of the USSR. Petrov was seeking to streamline, and bring to a point of greater efficiency, the KGB operation in each city. He was in Kiev, below Moscow on the River Dneiper, Russia's oldest and third largest metropolis. After a hard day, with night-fall he was ready for vodka and a woman. Instead, he learned, to his dismay, the local KGB chief had arranged for him and his party to attend the theatre. Seats had been reserved at the Lesya Ukrainka Theatre, where plays were done in Russian and not Ukrainian, for a performance of *The Three Sisters* by Anton Chekhov. Petrov hated the legitimate theatre in general and Chekhov's plays in particular. He found these plays unbelievable, contrived, and boring. Nevertheless, he could not disappoint his host, a KGB veteran of value. So, reluctantly, he went along.

As his limousine took him up Lenin Street toward the intersection of Pushkin Street, Petrov sighted the grey façade of the Lesya Ukrainka Theatre with distaste. After he and his party left the car, they traversed the cobblestoned thoroughfare and made for one of the three entrance doors. About to go inside, Petrov's attention was diverted by a small crowd gathering near a glass display case to his left beyond the doors. Mildly curious, Petrov broke away from his party and, followed by a bodyguard, joined the crowd to see what was going on. Elbowing forward, he at last caught sight of the one who was the centre of the spectators' attention. She was a young woman, quite beautiful, rather Nordic, with short, pale blonde hair, smiling and hastily signing some autographs as she pushed through the crowd. This was commonplace, except for one thing. There was a familiarity about the young woman's face. At first, Petrov was certain that she was a well-known American woman on a tour of Russia and visiting Kiev. It bewildered him that her person was familiar yet her identity unknown to him. He did not remember seeing a dossier on her. Yet, she must be a foreigner of some small importance, since she was signing autographs and trying to escape from persons who had recognized her.

In a moment, shrugging it off, he had forgotten her as he rejoined his party and entered the weather vestibule of the theatre, walked a step behind his host through the lobby and into the foyer. Presently, fortified by a few stiff drinks, Petrov went down the green-carpeted centre aisle, sat in his plush gold orchestra seat, and prepared for a catnap.

But he was still awake when she came on stage. She was

playing a sister of Andrey Prozorov, the gambler. She was Olga Prozorova, the third of the three sisters, the one who wanted to return to Moscow. Petrov straightened in his seat and became alert. Despite her theatrical make-up, she was the young blonde he had seen outside, next to the theatre entrance, the one he had thought to be an American tourist. But there she was before him, a Soviet actress, not an American at all.

Petrov retrieved his programme from the floor and opened it, peering in the semi-darkness for the name of the actress who was playing the role of Olga Prozorova. There were printed the names of four actresses who portrayed this role on various nights. Petrov understood. This was a large repertory company. Then he made out that one of the four names had been lightly ticked by the usher.

Petrov squinted. Her real name was Vera Vavilova.

He looked up to locate her on the stage, focused on her face, and that moment realized the reason she had been vaguely familiar to him. She had appeared to be an American because she resembled an American woman whose face he had seen in many imported American magazines and newspapers that passed over his desk. Petrov had been following the American presidential election campaign, and the Democratic nominee and candidate, a Senator Andrew Bradford, had a glamorous youthful wife – Millie, Tillie, Billie, the exact name eluded him – who received much attention from the frivolous American press.

Petrov looked up at the stage once more. No question. The actress – he peered down at his progamme again – yes, Vera Vavilova, except for her hairstyle, was close to being a double for the American presidential candidate's wife. Petrov blinked. He had never before seen such an uncanny resemblance of one person to another, although he had read recently that such a thing does occur. Billie – he remembered her name now – Billie Bradford and Vera Vavilova could have been identical twins.

For some unaccountable reason, Petrov remained attentive during the rest of the Chekhov play. And for some unaccountable reason, when the play was over, Petrov found himself wishing to go backstage and congratulate Vera Vavilova. Learning of his desire, the theatre director excitedly escorted the great General Petrov and his bodyguard to the backstage area and the young actress's dressing room.

There were several of the company's actresses, in various states of undress, in the bright, small room. Petrov ignored them, and with the director went straight to Vera Vavilova. She was before the mirror, removing her make-up. The director, voice rising, introduced General Petrov with a flourish. Vera Vavilova slowly came to her feet, faced him calmly, and accepted his handshake. Petrov fixed on her up close. Yes, confirmed. The resemblance uncanny.

'Congratulations,' he said. 'I enjoyed your performance immensely.'

She dipped her head modestly. 'Thank you. I am more than honoured.'

He continued to stare at her. 'Excuse me,' he said. 'I am curious about something. Have you ever been to the United States?'

'The United States? Why, no.'

'Do you have relatives there, a sister, perhaps?'

'No, no one.' She offered him an attractive smile. 'I'm afraid my family is very provincial Ukrainian. My parents live in Brovari, a small village fourteen miles from Kiev. They have never been to Moscow, let alone to America. Except for my grandmother, I am the only one in our family to have travelled a little. Inside the Soviet Union. I received my training in Moscow.'

'Interesting,' Petrov said. 'Do you speak English?'

Their conversation had been in Russian. Now she replied in faultless English. 'Oh, yes, General, I speak and read English and French. In fact, I speak English with an American accent. I studied and spoke English for four years at the Shchepkin Theatrical School in Moscow. I had more than 1000 hours of it. My instructors always said I was a quick student and a natural mimic. My best instructor was raised in America. Can you understand me?'

Petrov nodded. 'Yes, very well.' He spoke a clumsy, laboured English. But he understood it effortlessly. Her accent was perfect. He could not define why he was pleased.

Two hours later, during his flight back to Moscow, the persons of Vera Vavilova and Billie Bradford came together as one in his mind, and as he snapped on his seat belt for landing his wild scheme was born.

By the time he had been deposited at KGB headquarters late that night, gone up to his office suite, undressed in his private bedroom adjoining his office, Petrov realized that all his speculations were fruitless unless something else happened two months from now, early in November. The United States election would be held then. If Senator Andrew Bradford failed to be elected, there was nothing further to be pursued. But if he should be elected, if he should become the President of the United States, then his wife would be the First Lady of America. And the Soviet actress, Vera Vavilova, would become a prize find. Petrov was eager to pursue his scheme. But he restrained himself. First things first.

Overnight, Petrov became an avid follower of the United States presidential election.

Because he was so busy, Petrov summoned Alex Razin, a KGB deputy in the First Chief Directorate, to help him. Razin had his offices on the floor above, the fourth floor, where he was one of those in charge of the First Department, the American Department, a section created six years ago in a reorganization of the KGB. Born and partially educated in the United States, trained in the Soviet Union, Razin was an expert on American history, social mores, politics, sports, current events. An attractive man, thirty-six years old, he had served the KGB loyally and energetically for over a dozen years. Petrov brought him down from the fourth floor and delegated to him the task of keeping his superior abreast on developments in the United States presidential campaign. Razin was delighted with the assignment. As part of his normal work load, he monitored all information on the election campaign and the behaviour of the rival candidates in order to build a KGB profile on the winner and next President. The new assignment gave an additional dimension to Razin's interest. Although Petrov trusted his deputy, he did not confide in him (or in anyone) the reason for his special interest in the outcome of the United States election. He merely ordered his deputy to place a one-page summary on his desk daily.

Once, in an early stage, when the Democrat Bradford and his Republican opponent were running neck-and-neck in the polls, Petrov discussed the tightness of the race with Razin. Petrov said, somewhat enigmatically, that the sentiment in the Politburo wanted Bradford to win. He wondered, aloud, what the Soviet Union could do to ensure a Bradford victory. He considered having the KGB intervene in the campaign – surreptitiously, of course – to spread scandalous rumours about Bradford's opponent, thus boosting Bradford's chances. Razin advised strongly against it. Far too risky. If such rumours could ever be traced back to the Soviet Union, it would have the reverse effect of labelling Bradford as soft on Communism and guaranteeing his loss in a close election. Because Petrov respected Razin's knowledge of the American mentality, he dropped the idea and never spoke of it again.

On election eve, a last poll announced that Bradford was in the lead. Petrov breathed easier. Still, throughout election day, Petrov was on tenterhooks. On the American election night, with Razin beside him, he spent four hours viewing the results by television satellite. He watched until the Republican candidate conceded defeat and congratulated his Democratic rival. Petrov could not hide his satisfaction. Andrew Bradford would move into the White House in January. His wife, Billie Bradford, would be at his side, mate and confidante and First Lady of the United States. In Russia, by a freak of nature, there existed a woman who was almost her double.

For the first time, Petrov permitted himself to transform fully what had been a wild scheme into what could be an espionage reality.

To what end, the scheme and the reality of it, he asked himself. He was not surprised to find that he had a ready answer. If, at an appropriate moment, and for a brief time, he could substitute for the United States First Lady her trained Ukrainian double, the Soviet Union would have the perfect conduit to the American President's secrets. If, during a global crisis and confrontation between the United States and the USSR – and at least three potential ones were brewing – this substitution could be made, and made to work, the Soviet Union would gain a political victory and international dominance.

The end objective, then, was clear. The difficulty was the beginning. There were, Petrov saw, three steps. He translated the steps into three questions: Could the deception be properly prepared? Could it successfully deceive? Could it win official sanction?

Petrov decided that there was only one way to gain his objective. Start with step one. Make basic preparations for the project. This meant the total cooperation of the actress in Kiév.

Petrov sent for Vera Vavilova.

It was a command, and she came at once. He had Alex Razin, his American expert, with him when she entered his office. Once again, he was surprised – and pleased – at her resemblance to the one who would be the American First Lady. From the corner of his eye, he saw Alex Razin's utter astonishment. Razin, perhaps the only person in Russia at this point to know anything about Billie Bradford, had been an important test. For Petrov, his reaction was reassuring.

Before the interview, Petrov had considered telling Vera and Razin the truth, what he had in mind, and then had vetoed the notion. Not yet, he had decided. Too early. So he had invented a cover story. It might not fool either of them. No matter. They would have to accept it for want of a better motive for this interview.

After she had been seated, Petrov stood up.

'Welcome to Moscow, Comrade Vavilova,' he said. 'You remember our meeting in Kiev?'

'I would not forget it,' she said.

'This is my assistant, Alex Razin,' said Petrov.

They murmured greetings.

'Very well,' said Petrov. 'I will come straight to the point. Have you ever heard of a woman named Billie Bradford?'

'No. I'm afraid not.'

'You will be hearing of her,' said Petrov. 'She is an American, and soon she will be a famous American. She is the wife of the new President-elect of the United States. She will be in their White House next year as the country's First Lady.'

Vera Vavilova was silent and uncomprehending.

'The reason I visited you backstage in Kiev,' resumed Petrov, 'is that you bear a striking resemblance to her. That also is the reason that I have brought you here.'

Vera Vavilova waited for further explanation.

'This resemblance, yours to hers, could be useful to your government,' said Petrov. 'We are planning to make a short film – one might call it a documentary of sorts – of the American First Lady, Billie Bradford, and it occurred to me that you could fill the role.'

'How interesting. I am flattered.'

'It is more than interesting. It is important. You would have to give up everything you are doing. You would have to dedicate yourself to the part. You would have to move to Moscow at once –'

'But Kiev, my roles in the repertory – the director wouldn't let me –'

'Forget that nonsense. We would take care of everything. You would be paid four times what you have ever earned. All of your expenses would be taken care of, and you would have your own comfortable living quarters in Moscow.'

'Merely to play Billie Bradford in a film? Where would the film be shown?'

'Never mind. Eventually you will be told more. But not yet. One other thing – are you married or do you have a lover?'

'Neither.'

'Good. Because this is a secret project, for the moment. We do not wish the project, or your involvement in it, discussed with anyone. If you agreed to join with us, you would drop out of sight entirely. You would not be permitted to tell your family or friends or anyone where you are or what you are doing. In return, I guarantee you this, you would rise in favour and one day become the foremost actress in the Soviet Union. Are your interested?'

'Do I have a choice?' asked Vera Vavilova with a smile.

'Of course.'

'I am more than interested. I am prepared to do anything on earth for my government.'

Petrov slapped his hand on his desktop. 'Excellent,' he said. 'Wait in the reception room. Mr Razin will bring you further instructions.'

No sooner had she left the office, than Petrov pointed his chair toward Alex Razin.

'Well, Razin, what do you think?'

'Of her? As you said – she is nearly perfect. Let her hair grow longer, eliminate the small cheek scar, shorten the nose slightly, and she *is* Billie Bradford.'

'No, I mean my story. Did she believe it?'

'Possibly.'

'Did you?'

Razin seemed amused. 'Not really,' he said quietly. 'But then, I have been with the KGB many years. I am sceptical about the film.'

Petrov laughed, and then grew serious. 'Oddly, there will be a film. But you are right. That is not our purpose. Just go along with me on faith. You will know the truth shortly.' He opened a drawer and sought a fresh cigar. 'We will begin at once. Under me, you will be in full charge. This – this film, it will take precedence over all your other work. You will not let her return to Kiev. Inform her theatre, her family – any innocuous story will do. Send for her personal effects. Arrange for a small villa in the VIP compound near the university. We will have her permanent quarters ready for her in a few weeks. But from today on she must be seen by no outsiders at any time. Tomorrow you and I will meet at length. Tomorrow the transformation of Vera Vavilova into Billie Bradford will begin.'

It began with the collecting of superficial data. Petrov gave Razin his assignment, and Razin, using KGB agents and connections in Washington DC and New York, began to assemble what was needed. In this early stage, what was needed were still photographs and television films showing Billie Bradford from head to toe, in order to study her physical dimensions, her gait, her gestures and mannerisms. Audio tapes would reveal her speech habits.

As Razin painstakingly gathered his information, Petrov quickly proceeded with another vital aspect of the project which he dubbed 'Second Lady'. Fifteen kilometres south of Moscow, on a high rise of land beyond the ring road encircling the city, Petrov commandeered five acres of virgin ground behind a forest of pine trees that lay off the main highway leading to Vnukovo airport. He had a private road built from the highway through the forest. Then, past the forest, he supervised the construction of a vast, cheaply made motion picture sound stage. Inside the stage he had reproduced the Red Room, the President's Dining Room, the Queen's Bedroom, the Lincoln Bedroom, the Yellow Oval Room of the American White House. The carpets and drapes, fireplaces, lamps and chandeliers, furniture, wallpaper and hung paintings were exact replicas of those seen in still pictures and television movies taken inside the American White House. Surrounding this entire stage, by order of Petrov, a high wooden security fence was built, with a gate leading out to the private road. Then, one hundred metres to the rear of the stage, Petrov had a small, square, two-storey house thrown up. It included a projection room. The moment the house was completed, Vera Vavilova was moved into it, to dwell inside as its lone occupant.

Meanwhile, Alex Razin had obtained the required data from the United States.

Billie Bradford's physical dimensions were impressive. She was 5 feet 6 inches in height. Her bust was 34 inches, her waist 23 inches, her hips 34 inches, her weight 110 pounds.

Her shoulder-length hair was soft and blonde (snipped samples retrieved by the KGB and included for Razin); her eyes blue; nose straight, 1¾ inches long, and slightly upturned; mouth 2¾ inches wide.

Vera Vavilova's physical dimensions were equally impressive. The day after she had been moved into her secluded house, Razin asked her to change into a bikini and had a KGB doctor take her measurements. She was 5 feet 5⁹/₁₀ inches in height. Her bust was 31 inches, her waist 25 inches, her hips 35¼ inches, her weight 118 pounds. Her bobbed hair was soft and light blonde; her eyes blue; nose straight, 1⁴/₅ inches long, and slightly upturned; mouth 2¾ inches wide.

Petrov summoned Razin. He had seen the figures. The discrepancies were minor, very slight – still, they were there. Vera Vavilova's hair must be allowed to grow to shoulder length and be a shade darker. Her breasts must be enlarged 3 inches. Her nose must be shorter by less than ⅕ of an inch. The small scar on her upper cheek must be removed. She must lose 8 pounds in weight, as well as 2 inches at the waist and 1¼ inches at the hips. Could this be accomplished? The surgeons at Moscow's Institute of Cosmetology promised it would be simple and easy. What did Vera Vavilova say?

'I don't mind losing the weight,' she said to Petrov and Razin in the living room of her secluded house. 'But I don't like the idea of plastic surgery. Nose smaller, breasts larger, for a mere movie. Why? Why is it necessary to be *exactly* like that Bradford woman? I look enough like her as it is.'

Petrov showed restraint. 'I repeat, it is necessary. You will understand this better at a later time.'

'Don't I have anything to say about myself right now?'

'I am sorry – no,' said Petrov. 'Not for this moment, at least.'

'You insist?'

'I must,' said Petrov. 'You will not regret it.'

Her nature was not a rebellious one. She had never protested at anything before. She felt she had gone as far as she could. She shrugged her shoulders. 'Very well. Whatever you say.'

A few days later, the cosmetic surgery was undertaken, and pronounced successful. It was followed by a strict regime of dieting – gone the potatoes and other starches – combined with daily calisthenics and gymnastics.

When the KGB physician measured Vera Vavilova again, her dimensions were precisely those of Billie Bradford.

At this time, in distant Washington DC, Andrew Bradford was sworn in as President of the United States, and Billie Bradford entered the White House as First Lady.

Two months later, for an American television network, Billie Bradford gave millions of viewers a short tour of the private quarters on the second floor of the White House, acting as a historical commentator, serious, humorous, witty. The show proved extremely popular, won high ratings, and enhanced the First Lady's popularity. From New York, a copy of the First Lady's television tour was air-freighted to Moscow. There, Petrov, Razin and Vera Vavilova saw it in her private projection room. After the screening, Vera Vavilova was ordered to watch the ten-minute film three times a day for six weeks. She was to study and memorize every nuance of the First Lady's speech, every gesture, every movement, to absorb the entire performance, to imitate and rehearse it in the duplicate White House rooms on the sound stage.

Between these labours, Vera Vavilova continued her lessons in voice and carriage. With an instructor playing tapes of Billie Bradford's speeches and interviews over and over again, Vera Vavilova worked to pick up the First Lady's slight Western American accent and to make her own voice deeper and throatier. She learned, too, to mimic the small lilt in the First Lady's speech and to imitate her infectious laugh. From other instructors, in front of a montage of film of Billie Bradford, the Russian actress caught the First Lady's stride in walking, her graceful pirouettes as she turned to hear someone, her poise when not in motion, her many gestures.

At the end of six weeks, Razin said to his charge, 'You will report on the White House set tomorrow morning at eight. We will begin shooting the film.'

'Then there really is a film?' she teased him.

He was charmed by her, but remained professionally serious. 'Very much so, and you are the star.'

Four weeks later, when the film was done, and Petrov saw the final cut, he decided the time had come for the crucial step. He could go no further without official permission – and a considerably larger budget.

Petrov telephoned Premier Dmitri Kirechenko for a special appointment the following day in the Kremlin projection room.

The Premier, usually suave and imperturbable, sounded edgy. 'The projection room? I have no time for movies. Can't it wait?'

'It is a matter of high priority.'

'Mmm. I'm booked the entire morning and afternoon.'

'The evening then?'

'Evening, evening – Garanin, Lobanov, Umyakov – they are joining me for dinner.'

They were high-ranking members of the Politburo. Anatoli Garanin, especially, was a friend of the KGB and its projects.

'Bring them, too,' said Petrov. 'I'll need little more than a half-hour of your time before dinner.'

The Premier sighed. He sounded worn out. 'Have it your way then. Seven-thirty tomorrow evening. Projection room.'

He hung up.

The following evening, Petrov was inside the splendid Kremlin projection room, seated at 7.28 p.m. in the front row of the half-dozen rows of deep red seats. He had brought Alex Razin along, and Razin was up in the booth giving minute instructions to the projectionist. At 7.34, Premier Kirechenko arrived, followed by his Politburo colleagues, Garanin, Lobanov, Umyakov. The Premier, as ever, was an imposing figure, 5 feet 11, solid as a marble statue, immaculate in a striped blue suit. His horse's face was adorned with rimless glasses, moustache neatly clipped, short Vandyke beard cut to a sharp point, a fleeting resemblance to an enemy of the state, Leon Trotsky. He found a seat, as did Garanin, partially bald and short, a scholarly type, and Lobanov and Umyakov, who looked like prosperous middle-aged businessmen.

Petrov was standing, welcoming them.

'We are here,' said the Premier. 'What was so vital?'

'A new project,' said Petrov, 'a superb one. If activated, it can change the face of the world. It begins with two short pieces of film.'

Seeing Razin hurrying down from the projection booth, Petrov sat, as Razin crossed in front of him, signalled up to the booth and settled behind the control panel.

The lights went dark.

The screen up front was filled with Billie Bradford gliding into the Lincoln Bedroom of the White House.

'You recognize her, Mr Secretary?' Petrov called over his shoulder.

'The new American First Lady,' replied the Premier. 'A feast for the eyes.'

From the screen, the image of Billie Bradford began to explain the stories behind the eight-foot rosewood bed and the American Victorian furnishings purchased by Mrs Lincoln. The footage ran on as Billie Bradford moved from the Lincoln Bedroom to the President's Dining Room. After ten minutes, the film clip ended, and the lights went on.

Petrov half turned in his folding seat. 'That was a recent television film of the United States President's wife taking American viewers on a tour of the family headquarters of the American Executive Mansion. Now, one more showing of the film.'

'Since when has my security chief become a film distributor?' The Premier laughed, and the Politburo members laughed with him.

'You shall see – you shall see my real purpose,' said Petrov.

The lights went out again, and the darkened projection room was instantly illuminated by a picture of Billie Bradford on the screen, entering the Lincoln Bedroom of the White

House, pointing out the historic pieces, telling the stories behind them. As she finished, and went on to the President's Dining Room, the Premier's voice called down impatiently.

'Petrov, what's going on? You are running the same film again. We just saw it.'

'I know,' said Petrov. 'Please bear with me a few more minutes. There is a reason for this.'

The clip featuring the American First Lady ran on, repeating exactly what had been shown in the initial clip. The Premier's mutterings of annoyance grew louder. The film ran out. It was ended. The lights came on.

The Premier was more than annoyed. He glared at his KGB chief. 'Petrov, are you mad? How dare you take our precious time showing the same film twice? If someone else had done that, I'd see that they were put in a mental hospital. You'd better have a good explanation.'

Unruffled, Petrov stood up and fully turned. 'I have,' he said.

'Well, dammit, man, out with it.'

Petrov did not waver. He addressed the Premier softly. 'You are sure it was the same film, Comrade Kirechenko?'

'You think I am blind? The very same film shown twice.'

'With the American First Lady in the first film?'

'Of course.'

'With the American First Lady in the second film?'

'Yes, of course,' said the Premier with exasperation.

Petrov waited a moment, and then said, 'Forgive me, but you are quite wrong, Comrade. The first film showed the real American First Lady – Billie Bradford. The second film showed a Soviet actress – Vera Vavilova – playing the role of the American First Lady.'

Petrov could see shock and bewilderment in the four faces staring at him.

The Premier broke the silence. 'You are joking?'

'I am not joking, not at all. The first film was the American President's wife, Billie Bradford. The second film was her Soviet double, an actress, Vera Vavilova, who impersonated the First Lady against a background we constructed to duplicate some of the inner rooms of the American White House. My deputy here, Mr Razin, will confirm what I am telling you. You just saw the President's wife in Washington DC. You just saw her double in Moscow.'

Garanin looked at the Premier beside him. 'Remarkable,' he said.

The Premier nodded. 'Incredible.' He sat up in his theatre chair. 'All right, Petrov. A neat sleight of hand. A perfect deception. What do you have in mind?'

'A bigger, more daring deception,' said Petrov softly. 'At some moment in the next few years, on the world political scene, there will arise a crisis, an inevitable confrontation between the US and the USSR. The confrontation, as we all are aware, will take place in Korea, Boende, or Iran. At that moment, they will back down or we will back down or there will be war. At that moment, to ensure our victory, we would want a secret weapon. What you have just witnessed on the screen can be our secret weapon. If we have a woman who cannot be told apart from the President's wife, if we can install our woman in the White House in place of the President's wife for a short time without detection, we have in place the greatest espionage agent in history. We would be privy to every design the American President and his chief of staff and his war-mongers have in mind. We would learn every plot and plan of the enemy in advance. Our triumph in any crisis would be ensured.'

For long seconds the room was quiet.

At last, Premier Kirechenko's voice ended the silence. 'Is it possible, really possible?'

'Do you mean, could she really do it?'

'Could she?'

Petrov nodded. 'She can and will, given the chance. You've seen the evidence. She *is* Billie Bradford. Let me tell you how it came about, how we prepared her, how we plan to prepare her further, how we intend to use her.'

Then, for three-quarters of an hour, Petrov expounded without stop and without interruption.

When he finished, he was almost out of breath. 'There you have it, Comrade Kirechenko.'

'But what do I have?' the Premier said in a low voice. 'I have someone who actually wants to undertake this risky enterprise in life. Isn't that what I have? A brief movie is one thing. But expecting her to sustain this for days – perhaps two weeks – and get away with it – it's preposterous. She would have to slip, reveal herself. A mistake in a movie, it can be shot again, corrected, but in real life –'

'Comrade Kirechenko,' Petrov interrupted urgently, 'she made no mistakes – not one – in preparation of the film. She would make none in real life. She could sustain it for several weeks. I'd bet my entire career on her.'

Kirechenko studied his KGB chief.

'It would be your neck, if she failed.'

'I know.'

'It would endanger your country, your countrymen, if she failed.'

'I know that, also.'

'And still you recommend it?'

'Absolutely,' said Petrov with assurance. 'Because she will not fail. I am that certain of her. She will totally succeed. She will reap benefits for us that could not be gained otherwise. She will lay open their strategies, secrets, disarm them completely. Dangerous? Of course it is. But then, all great, historic enterprises are, Comrade.'

'One slip,' said Kirechenko, 'could disgrace us in front of the world – lead us to the brink of war.'

'That is true. But if we bring it off – and we are positive we can – it might guarantee the dominance of the Soviet Union over the United States for generations to come.'

The Premier sat lost in thought.

Garanin leaned over and whispered to him, 'A priceless opportunity.'

Ignoring his adviser, the Premier raised his head and stared at his KGB chief. 'You are very persuasive, Comrade Petrov.' His gaze drifted to the blank white movie screen. 'And so was she, just now.' His eyes held on Petrov once more. 'What do you require?' the Premier asked.

'Two things. First, your permission to go ahead. Of course, the final option to proceed with the project or to abort it at the last moment will be your own. But, for now – your permission.'

'You have it,' said the Premier, almost inaudibly.

'And the money.'

'You have it.'

That had been nearly three years ago. Behind his desk, General Petrov came out of his reverie into the present. Tomorrow would begin the countdown. Actually, tonight, since his desk clock told him it was after one o'clock in the morning. Seventy-two more hours. The waiting was almost unbearable.

Restlessly, he rose from his desk. It was late, and he should try to get some sleep in the next room. Yet, he knew that his mind was too awake to let him sleep easily. His mind brimmed with the events of those three years. It had been, actually, a secret college he had set up, a college with a three-year course, one major subject, one student. The major subject had been Billie Bradford. The entire student body had been Vera Vavilova. Now, with graduation in sight, with the real world directly ahead, Petrov had a sudden urge to see the dean of the school. Alex Razin, alone, would know whether his student was ready for the real world. Petrov needed reinforcement, reassurance, that no area had been overlooked, that the graduate could cope. He wondered if Razin, a night person like himself, was still in his office.

Upstairs, on the fourth floor, in his monastic KGB office – shaded ceiling fixtures, pale green walls, bare parquet floor – Alex Razin held the scuffed brown leather briefcase straight on a corner of his crowded desk and stuffed red-lined beige file folders into it. He had told Vera that he might be late – and it was late – but she had insisted that she would remain awake for him. Now, preparing to leave his work to spend the night with her – their last together for three weeks – he saw one of his hands tremble.

Tension clung to him unrelieved. While he had prepared this dangerous enterprise under Petrov, with many others, the sole responsibility for perfection had been totally his own. On the human level, he, more than anyone else involved, had everything at stake. His student, the pawn in this super espionage endeavour, was not merely an agent but the one person he cherished and loved more than any other on earth. This realization had made his job doubly difficult. Vera's performance must be flawless, her immediate future safe, not only to achieve a cold war victory but to preserve her precious being for himself and themselves. The responsibility filled him with a chill of terror.

When the knock on the door came, and General Petrov unexpectedly appeared with the request that he wanted to review certain aspects of Vera's training phase one last time, Razin' felt a gust of relief. Although eager to enjoy the warmth of Vera's body before she was taken from him, he was relieved to have the excuse to examine their handiwork one more time. Like Petrov, he wanted to be certain, beyond all certainty, that every possible surprise had been anticipated. He did not mind being even later for Vera. If she fell asleep, he could awaken her and know that because of his vigilance she would be safer.

'I hope you are not too tired?' Petrov added, settling into the chair across from his deputy's desk.

'Not for this,' said Razin. 'I hoped for some reason to review our preparations just one more time. We cannot be too cautious. It just has to be absolutely foolproof.'

As Razin started for his file cabinet, Petrov said, 'Oh, it is foolproof, I am positive of that. I don't know why I want to do it again. Maybe I just want to indulge myself, have pleasure in a job well done – before she is out of our hands.'

Out of our hands. Petrov's last words sent another alarm through Razin. He opened the cabinet drawer, dug deep inside, and lifted out the file of three thick folders on Project Second Lady.

He brought them back to the desk, and lay them before Petrov. 'Everything is here,' Razin said. 'You will find a copy of every memorandum, progress sheet, note on what we had to do to, what we did, covering every week's activities from the day Kirechenko gave us the go-ahead and the special fund.'

Petrov took the bulging top folder and opened it on his lap. 'Let me just skim through this, the highlights. It won't be long. Do you have a drink?'

'Yes. But no ice.'

'Ice only dilutes it.' While Razin poured a drink of vodka for Petrov and one for himself, the KGB chief studied the earliest papers. 'I remember,' he said. 'We started with the White House, constructing most of the duplicate to an exact scale. Slow, costly, a real bitch.'

Razin pulled a chair up next to Petrov and peered over his shoulder. 'But authentic,' said Razin. 'Once we had the last remodel plans and all the most recent photographs, I thought it went well.' He sat back sipping his drink. 'The only thing that's ever bothered me about that was scaling down a few of the rooms to save costs and time. I've always worried that she might be disoriented when she actually got into the real rooms.'

'She's insisted that'll be no problem.'

'Maybe not,' said Razin.

Their architect and builders had duplicated almost the entire interior of the White House, ground floor, first floor, second floor. Three sides of the exterior had been flat walls (again, costs, time), but the South Portico and outside area of the Oval Office and Rose Garden had been made faithful to the original.

Razin was looking over Petrov's shoulder again. 'Then, you can see, we doubled the number of our agents and informants in Washington, and increased the number around the country. While construction went on here, we started intensive fact-finding over there.'

Necessary materials had been funnelled into Moscow by the crateful, an endless stream of vital information. For the most part, it had been relatively easy. More tapes of Billie Bradford speaking, for Vera Vavilova's voice lessons. More film tapes of Billie Bradford in action inside the White House and in public. Over and over they had shown Vera film and tapes of the American First Lady, and had Vera imitate and rehearse Billie Bradford's facial expressions, gestures, mannerisms. What was known was not taken for granted. More and more audio tapes were played to pick up and note not only the timbre of the First Lady's voice, but to learn her preferences for word usages, phrases, figures of speech, repetitions.

The real First Lady's physique was monitored on a week-to-week basis, to note a new crease in her forehead, to note a newly adopted hair style, to note even the smallest growth or loss of weight. For every change that occurred afar, a change was made in Vera Vavilova in Moscow.

Other aspects of the First Lady's physique, the ones hidden from outside observers, were also considered. Her insurance company was secretly invaded, and her application forms and policies found and copied in case they might contain a record of some hidden deformity or blemish. Her dental files and X-rays were stolen or bought off and copied. The office of the White House physician, Dr Rex Cummings, was visited and records of her physical examinations photographed to provide information on any chronic illnesses.

For months, there was a troublesome gap. Friends and acquaintances could be deceived by duplication of a clothed or semi-clothed Billie Bradford. But what about the doctor, or her husband the President, mainly the President, who would see her in the nude? What did the nude First Lady look like? This would have to be known if Vera Vavilova could be expected to carry off successfully her masquerade stripped down. Razin had mulled over the problems and had finally come up with an inspiration. He recollected once seeing, in an Italian men's magazine, five full-length colour photographs of Jacqueline Kennedy, then Onassis, utterly naked. The one-time American First Lady had been sun-bathing in the nude on the island of Skorpios, her Greek retreat. An Italian photographer, on a fishing boat offshore, had used a camera with a sharp telescopic lens to capture her in the buff. The pictures of Jacqueline Kennedy proved to be thoroughly revealing, clearly showing her small breasts and dark brown nipples, her full buttocks, the long growth of pubic hair covering her vaginal mound. Recalling those photographs, Razin reasoned that if he could obtain similar pictures of the newest First Lady, Billie Bradford, his problem would be solved.

Persistent rumours indicated that Billie Bradford, when in private quarters at a holiday resort, enjoyed swimming in the nude. Thereafter, Razin hired a photographer, with a powerful telescopic lens attached to his camera, to follow Billie Bradford carefully on all her vacations. The photographer had trailed the First Lady to Miami Beach and to Malibu, and on both occasions, whether she had swum in the nude or not, foliage or other obstructions had shielded her from view. Then, as luck would have it, during her second year in the White House, Billied Bradford had flown off to Sicily for a week's vacation. The guest of the Italian ambassador to the United States, she had a small inlet and private beach to herself. The third morning early, she had emerged from the beach house in a light blue robe, reached a ringlet of sand, and while standing had shed her robe. She had been stark naked, turning lazily on the sand, eyes closed, to enjoy the blaze of sun. Razin's determined photographer had been perched on the baking tile roof of a distant house, his telescopic lens pointed toward the nude First Lady.

When the frontal shots of the naked First Lady arrived, Razin had been elated. He had already arranged, the week before, to have a set of nude frontal shots taken of Vera Vavilova. They had been excellent, and had excited Razin. With both sets in hand, Razin had laid out the nude pictures of Billie Bradford in a row, and beneath them lined up the nude shots of Vera Vavilova. Then, with a magnifying glass, Razin had examined them, comparing one against the other. The full firm breasts of each were identical, the nipples just about the same. The navels and bellies could not be told apart. Moments later, Razin had found a difference in their naked bodies, one small difference, then another. There was the tiniest mark on Billie Bradford's lower right side. There was no mark on Vera Vavilova's side. Further, the spread of the triangles of pubic hair covering their vaginal mounds and rising to their lower abdomens were not the same. Billie Bradford's mat of pubic hair grew into a higher and wider triangle than Vera's. Razin summoned a physician to take the magnifying glass and study the photographs. He did so. The mark on Billie Bradford's body, not to be found on Vera Vavilova's, proved easy to identify. The mark on the American First Lady's body was a scar, the result of an appendectomy. The solution was to put Vera Vavilova into surgery and make an incision with a scalpel that would duplicate the First Lady's scar. As for the differences in the contours and growth of their pubic hair, the physician thought that, too, could be resolved. More hair would be implanted and added to the area above Vera's vagina.

It had been more simply said than done. Just before these decisions, Vera Vavilova had protested posing in the nude for photographs. Razin had overcome her resistance by convincing her that the nude art would serve an important purpose soon to be made known to her. But when told that she must undergo additional surgery, as well as a pubic-hair implant, Vera Vavilova had put her foot down.

Petrov had meant to tell her the truth about her role immediately after the Premier had given permission to proceed. But Petrov had kept delaying it, because he had wanted the project to remain a secret as long as possible. He knew that he could not continue to keep his real purpose a secret from Vera Vavilova and Alex Razin indefinitely. Too many demands were being made on them for the pair not to know the truth. Petrov had decided to tell them when the imitation White House, being constructed inside the new sound stage, had been completed. That time had come and gone, and Petrov had continued to withhold the truth. But when Razin had come to him with the need for more surgery and a hair implant, and told him that Vera Vavilova had balked at both, Petrov knew that he could no longer keep the truth from them.

They met late one afternoon, after a long day of rehearsal. They had settled down in the living room of Vera's private quarters, each with a drink.

Petrov had spoken to Razin first. 'Do you know what is going on? The purpose behind what we are doing?'

'I think I've guessed,' Razin had replied.

Petrov had swung toward his actress. 'And you? Have you guessed?'

'I know you're not making another film,' she had said. 'I suppose it is some KGB matter I don't understand.'

'You are close,' Petrov had said. 'Now you are so deep in it – now I feel I can trust you – so now I will tell you.'

He told her and he told Razin the entire plan, from the project's inception to this moment of truth. He left out nothing. He told it all. He admitted it might be futile, might never be required while Mrs Bradford was still in the White House. But the odds were that it would be used. Several major confrontations between the Soviet Union and the United States were looming, might come to a head in the following year. For that possibility, they must be prepared.

'When it happens,' he concluded, 'you will replace Billie Bradford in the White House as America's First Lady for a brief period. It would be the greatest role an actress has ever performed – and – the most dangerous.'

He had not been concerned about Razin. Because Razin was clever and would have guessed all but the details. It was Vera Vavilova he had been worried about. He had long ago assessed her toughness and loyalty. But how tough and how loyal he had not known. He would know now.

After his recital, he had expected her to flinch, frown, voice some doubts.

She had sat very still, face expressionless.

After an interval of silence, he had said, 'Well, Comrade Vavilova?'

'I will continue with the role,' she had said. 'I like it. I'll never have a better one.'

After that, she went into the hospital for the surgery and the implant.

No sooner had Vera been released from the hospital than one final package concerning Vera's body belatedly arrived from KGB operatives in the United States. The package contained several items – copies of Billie Bradford's dental X-rays and duplicate plaster models of impressions made of her upper and lower teeth. Premier Kirechenko's own dentist studied and compared these to Vera's dental X-rays and models.

'Remarkably similar in alignment,' the Russian dentist announced, 'except the rear molars.'

'The teeth in back?' asked Razin.

'Yes. Comrade Vavilova's are a bit out of line, so they don't match exactly.'

'Would anyone be able to see them or know the difference?' Razin wondered.

'Only a dentist.'

Razin considered this. When Vera replaced Billie, it would be for merely a short time, and she would probably not need a dentist. If she had a toothache, she would be forced to live with it. If for some unimaginable reason she had to see a dentist, it would be in a foreign capital and not in Washington DC, where Billie Bradford's dentist resided.

'Is there anything else?' inquired Razin.

'Just one major discrepancy clearly shown in the X-rays. Comrade Vavilova's teeth are all her own. No work has ever been done on them. On the other hand, Mrs Bradford's lower left first and second bicuspids and first molar have been drilled down and capped. It is the only obvious difference between the two sets of teeth.'

This troubled Razin. 'Could Comrade Vavilova's teeth in that area be made to resemble Mrs Bradford's?'

'By drilling and capping them, yes, certainly.'

Razin hated to tell Vera that she must lose three good teeth to caps, and he was uncertain of her reaction. To his immense relief, she was understanding and cooperative. By now she had become obsessed with playing her role to perfection.

All of those events marking the development of the project were now revived in Razin's mind as he sat in his office, beside Petrov, sipping his drink and watching the KGB chief reviewing the papers, flipping the pages, nodding, smiling, sometimes thinking, sometimes speaking.

It was at this point, Razin recollected, that Vera had been converted from a Soviet actress trying to portray an American to a person who lived as an American and thought like an American. She was allowed to speak only English, dress in American garments (except for imports from Ladbury of London), eat American foods. At breakfast, she drank canned tomato juice and ate boxed sugar-free cereals brought in from the United States and read the previous day's editions of the *New York Times* and the *Washington Post*. When she played records, they were American standards or current hits in the United States. When she turned on her closed-circuit television, she could see only videotaped American newscasts, American situation comedies, American talk shows, reruns of American movies.

She was inundated by material relating to Billie Bradford, but never overwhelmed by it. She was a quick study, indeed, clever, intelligent, and possessed of a fantastic memory. She educated herself by absorbing Billie Bradford's own education in grammar school, high school, college. She read Billie Bradford's examinations, term papers, school newspapers, yearbooks. In the person of Russian actors (who believed they were auditioning or rehearsing for a movie, each one working briefly before being replaced), she met the First Lady's old schoolmates, teachers, instructors, professors.

She was briefed on her immediate family, on her father, sister, brother-in-law, nephew, on her mother dead a decade, on the family dog, on her aunts and uncles and secondary relatives in Los Angeles, Denver, Chicago, New York. Slowly, the briefings expanded to encompass favourite shopkeepers, friends, and acquaintances from past to present. The studies broadened, widened, to take in her husband's campaign staff and workers, the White House staff, her husband's aides, his Cabinet, other department executives, congressmen, the Washington press.

Above all, she was drilled daily on the background, quirks, prejudices, habits of Andrew Bradford, her husband, and as much as could be found out about their intimate relationship.

Here, once more, Razin ran into a stumbling block that nearly forced Petrov to abandon the project. For over two years, Razin had tried to learn something, anything, about the sex life of the Bradfords. If Vera was to be substituted for Billie Bradford, she would have to know how Billie performed in bed with her husband. What was their behaviour? Did they engage in straight sexual intercourse, and if so, how often? Was Billie docile or aggressive? Did he or she prefer to engage in a wide variety of so-called perversions? Yet, in the first two years, assigning agent after agent to turn up a clue, Razin drew a blank. As time passed, Petrov began to realize that, without knowledge of this aspect of Billie Bradford's life, Vera would not have a chance of succeeding except by pure luck. And no margin could be allowed for luck.

In desperation, Razin tried to find ways to circumvent the sex problem. Perhaps President Bradford could meet with an accident that would disable him for a month. But then such an accident might also force him to postpone a conference and showdown with Kirechenko. This solution had not been a solution and had been dropped. Perhaps Billie, herself, could suffer an accident that would make sexual intercourse unlikely for three or four weeks. As this possibility was being debated, Razin had his big break.

A well-paid American agent for the KGB in Washington DC, in the White House itself, had overheard some secretarial gossip that suggested the young redhead who was Dr Cummings's nurse also served as the President's occasional mistress. Her name was Isobel Raines, and she owned a small bungalow (well beyond her means) in Bethesda, Maryland. The KGB put her under immediate surveillance, while running a check on her past. Soon enough it was learned that, whenever the First Lady was out of the capital, the President would have Miss Raines in his bed until dawn. Shortly after this information had been confirmed, the KGB had its dossier on Isobel Raines's previous activities. There was one unsavoury period. Five years earlier, Miss Raines had lived with a notorious Mafia boss in Detroit. The time had come for a visit with Miss Raines.

Two efficient KGB agents, members of the Rezidentura attached to the Soviet embassy in Washington, one named Grishin, the other Ilf, travelled to Bethesda to pay a social call upon Isobel Raines. The resultant conversation had been fairly frank. The KGB agents hardly bothered to disguise the fact that this was outright blackmail. Although stricken by the knowledge that her secret past in Detroit was no longer secret, and that any leak of her past would end her wonderful job in the White House, Isobel Raines proved staunchly loyal to the President and his wife. She would not, whatever the cost to her, discuss the bed habits of the President or what she had heard of his wife's behaviour. She admitted to a few sexual encounters with the President, but only 'when the First Lady was travelling out of the city or – or recently when she was ill and couldn't do anything with him'.

Reporting their visit with Miss Raines to Razin in Moscow, Grishin and Ilf asked how they should proceed. One line in their report had made Razin curious and given him hope, the line that the First Lady recently was ill in a way that excluded sexual activity. Razin contacted his agents in Washington, told them not to expose Isobel Raines, not to see her again until ordered to do so.

Now, in his office, seated beside Petrov, who had the old report in his hand, Razin recalled what had followed. Increasingly nervous about the lack of information on Billie Bradford's sex life, uncertain where to turn next, Razin saw his opportunity and seized upon it. Days before departing for the Summit Conference in London, while his wife was in Los Angeles, the President had enjoyed Isobel Raines in his White House bed. The following evening a presidential aide had been trapped with a prostitute. The President had summarily dismissed him from his post. At the next morning's press conference, when questioned about the aide, the President had lectured the reporters on morality in government.

This had not been lost on Razin in Moscow. Isobel Raines would be more fearful than ever. It was time for Grishin and Ilf to pay her another visit.

Isobel Raines had, indeed, been nervous and frightened. If she refused to talk, her own immorality would be made public, harming the President and destroying her own career. This time she talked. Not much, but a little, enough. She insisted that she knew nothing about Mrs Bradford's sexual behaviour with her husband. This was not the kind of thing the President would ever discuss. He had summoned her to his bed only because he needed sexual release and he could not have it with his wife at the present time. He had told Isobel Raines that his wife had some kind of problem, and her gynaecologist had ordered her to avoid sexual activity for six weeks, until he could analyse her tests.

Unwittingly, Isobel Raines had given Razin what he wanted. In the three weeks that Vera Vavilova would be playing First Lady, there could be no sexual activity between herself and the President.

The last obstacle to Project Second Lady had been removed. Petrov was thrilled, Razin was pleased, and Vera Vavilova was relieved.

All this, while Vera continued to learn and rehearse, working steadily from daybreak to nightfall. Soon her work became more feverish. For, even as she studied the people and events of her new past, she had to contend with fresh people and the events of the present. Africa had long been a vague bone of contention between the two world powers, and now suddenly Boende became a familiar proper noun in her vocabulary. Boende was an independent nation in central Africa. It was uranium rich. Both the United States and the USSR needed uranium. A democracy with an elected President named Mwami Kibangu, Boende had close ties with the United States. On its northern border, a huge rebel force — the Communist People's Army, led by a Moscow-trained leader, Colonel Nwapa – waited for the Soviet signal to overrun the country and take control by staging a revolution. The Soviet Union was prepared to supply the rebel force with arms. The question was – how strongly had Kibangu's government troops been armed by the United States? The stakes for the future were high. Not only ample uranium, but control of the heart of Africa.

As the confrontation worsened, Premier Kirechenko called in Petrov and consulted him. Reassured, Kirechenko made the first move. He suggested a two-way Summit Conference, delegations headed by the American President and himself, to meet at a neutral site as soon as feasible in the interests of world peace. President Bradford had no choice but to accept the proposal. Next came the technicalities, the most important being the selection of a site for the Summit. The usual preliminary haggling began. Helsinki, Geneva and Vienna were suggested, and each rejected by one party or the other for various reasons. Then Premier Kirechenko made a surprising and astute suggestion. Although the Americans had been allies of the British for many years, the Soviet Union had recently signed several important agreements with Great Britain and their friendship had never been warmer. To underscore his trust in the British, and at the same time to disarm right-wing conservatives in the United States, Kirechenko suggested that the Summit be held in London. Taken off-guard, President Bradford could offer no objections. And so the turf would be London. President Bradford then proposed a date. Premier Kirechenko agreed to it at once.

Then, a few weeks afterwards, almost as an afterthought, the Soviet Premier's wife, Ludmila Kirechenko, announced that, one week preceding the London Summit, she would invite female leaders throughout the world to attend a three-day International Women's Meeting in Moscow. The subject would be – woman's rights, today and in the future. Despite Billie Bradford's misgivings about so much travel and activity in so short a period, the subject of woman's rights was closely identified with her. There was no possible way for

61

her to decline the convention. She was among the first to promise to attend.

While the International Women's Meeting in Moscow had been arranged and scheduled solely for Vera Vavilova's benefit, her own preparations were not affected by it. She would play no role in the convention itself. But the London Summit that would follow it presented Vera with an overload of extra work. New names entered her life, ones she was supposed to know already and ones she must anticipate meeting and learn about. Added research flowed in to her. Suddenly, Vera had to be familiar with London – a city familiar to Billie Bradford, unfamiliar to Vera Vavilova. And a new cast of characters like the Queen of England, the British Prime Minister Dudley Heaton, his wife Penelope Heaton, the British foreign secretary Ian Enslow, the Boendi President Kibangu and his ambassador to England, Zandi, were introduced to her.

All of that had filled the papers that Petrov had been reviewing in Razin's KGB office.

Petrov was holding the last piece of paper in the last of the three files. It was Razin's final typed memorandum on Vera Vavilova's dress rehearsal nine hours ago.

Petrov returned the third file to the desk, tossed down the remaining half-inch of vodka in his glass, and shook his massive head. 'What a job. Three years work. Worth it, I hope.' He came slowly to his feet. 'Well done, Razin. No holes, no flaws. Looks perfect to me.'

'To me, too,' said Razin.

'The First Lady arrives tomorrow – actually, today. It's definitely out of our hands. It's all the Second Lady from now on. Well, thanks, and good night.'

After Petrov left, Razin put away his files and secured the cabinet. He closed his briefcase.

Something went through his head. As an atheist he had never prayed since becoming a Russian citizen, but what went through his head was a prayer learned at his mother's knee in America. So long ago. A prayer, a prayer for the safety of his beloved Vera.

It was 2.23 in the morning when Alex Razin reached the high fence and gate in the Moscow outskirts, and was admitted into the restricted area by two KGB night sentries. He drove across the gravel road that wound past the imitation White House – the last time he would see it whole since it was being torn down starting early in the morning – and followed the yellowish ground lights that led him through the darkness toward the square, two-storey wooden house in the rear.

After parking near the front door, he felt about in his jacket pocket for one of the three keys (Petrov had the third one) to the hideaway and let himself into the weather vestibule. Going through the living room, he went up the stairs to the bedroom and quietly entered it.

Vera had left two floor lamps on for him, and a crack of light was showing where the bathroom door stood ajar. The bedroom was large, comfortable, furnished in early American. Petrov had not stinted on the furnishings. He believed in the best for his star. He believed everything in the room should remind her that she was to be an American.

Razin squinted towards the queen-sized bed.

He had expected that she would be asleep by now, and she was. She lay on her side, partially covered by the blanket, her bare back to him. He could hear her soft, regular breathing.

He removed his shoes, and padded to the bathroom. In the fluorescent whiteness of the room, closing the door behind him, he spotted a sheet of paper by the side of the sink. It contained a pencilled message to him –

> Darling heart,
>> Before going to sleep, wake me.
>> Don't forget.
>>> I love you.
>>> For ever.
>>>> Vera
>>>> XXXX

Razin smiled to himself. Slowly, he began to undress. He thought about her, about the first time he had met her in Petrov's office, and the earliest times he had met her after that.

Of course, for him, it had been love at first sight. At least, he was certain of it by the third or fourth time he had been with her. But he had deliberately not allowed his deep emotional feeling for her to surface.

Many times he had tried to analyse the reasons for his inhibition. He did so once more. Although he had known many women, had enjoyed satisfying affairs with some, none of them had affected him like Vera. Most of the other women had much to offer, but all of them had been flawed in various ways that made serious commitment impossible. Maybe he had been immature in his hopes. Nevertheless, he had waited.

And then Vera had come along. Yet, from the start, he had not been able to act out his feelings for her. He had found her totally intimidating: her incredible beauty, her femininity, her cleverness, her assurance, her poise. Then there was the actress part of her, meant to be savoured only from a distance. That, and her new role, which made her unique, precious, an untouchable state commodity.

Also, in the beginning, he had questioned his own worthiness in measuring up to her. Certainly, on a physical level, she could have any man she wanted. She was a goddess. He was plain. He had no feelings of inferiority about his appearance, but he could be lost in a crowd; she, never. Continuing to undress, he sought himself in the bathroom mirror. Flat black hair combed back. Bushy eyebrows, narrow eyes, a somewhat bashed nose, thick lips, a dark thirty-nine-year-old complexion. 5 feet 10, broad shoulders, small waist. He needed glasses to read. He was smart, but suspected she might be smarter. His horizons were limited. He was a small wheel in a machine. He might be a bigger wheel some day, but never more. Her future was infinite.

And here they were, together, together for almost two years.

It had been the necessity of daily contact with each other

the first year, the closeness, that developed into intimacy. Her life, her survival, was dependent upon him. She had needed to know him as she had not known any other man. He had to know her as he had not known any woman, to be sure she would come through what was ahead, and because he was in love with her. To his surprise, he learned that she was in love with him. Each had found what was needed from another.

He remembered the day he had received the nude photographs of her, to compare her body to Billie Bradford's. He had tried to be clinical about those photographs. Inside, he had seethed with the desire to possess her, to love and be loved by her. Nevertheless, he had stayed at arm's length, had played the mentor.

Still, they had been drawn closer and closer to one another by their common purpose. After a day's hard work, instead of returning to his office or home, Razin had gradually begun to linger on, walking Vera back to her house, accompanying her inside to join her in a drink or two. They had relaxed together, sometimes continuing to discuss their work, more often sharing information about their pasts. The transition from drinks together to dining together had come naturally. As mutual trust had grown, they had begun to exchange confidences, aspirations, dreams.

It had not taken Razin long to realize that Vera's background was more disciplined than he had imagined. She had not become a consummate actress by accident. Her dossier, which he had read and memorized, gave little indication of the depth of her interest in – and experience on – the stage. He had believed her to be the product of two unlettered factory workers, people far removed from the world of the theatre, who had permitted their daughter to indulge her fantasy about becoming an actress.

In truth, as Vera revealed, she had always had acting in her blood. Her maternal grandmother, alive and retired, had in her prime often appeared in plays with the great Alla Tarasova in the Moscow Art Theatre. While her own mother had no such gifts, she had been (and still was) a regular theatre-goer and a fount of theatrical lore. She had encouraged and supported Vera's interest in acting from the child's earliest years. At the age of eighteen, with assistance from her grandmother, Vera had gone to Moscow for the reading examination at the Maly. There had been 800 applicants to the school, and of the twenty-five accepted Vera had been the most promising. Vera had spent four years in training – 6000 hours in all, one-third of them in Mastery of Acting classes dominated by the Stanislavski method. Upon graduation, she had been farmed out to the Kiev repertory company to gain real stage experience. There had never been a moment's question in Vera's mind that she would one day wind up as a star of the Maly Theatre or the Moscow Art Theatre and eventually become one of the People's Artists of the Union of Soviet Socialist Republics, with all the special privileges that came with such an honour.

When Petrov had discovered her, Vera had been suffering the first qualms about her future. She had been mired down in Kiev too long, by her standards, and Moscow had not yet summoned her to greatness. She feared that, young as she was, she had been overlooked or forgotten. And then Petrov had come and had offered the challenge and opportunity that exceeded her most fanciful dreams.

Once, Razin had dared ask her about the men in her life. She had frankly confessed to only two affairs, one a callow trainee at the Maly school, another a leading man in the Kiev company, each without emotional commitment and both ultimately disappointing. Men had simply not played an important part in her past. Her life had been dedicated to her art.

After that, he had wondered if men – or some man – could ever be a meaningful part of her life.

Then it happened. What happened took place quite naturally, in her kitchen, in the eleventh month of their platonic relationship. She had been at the stove, frying pan in hand, as he discussed an aspect of her Billie Bradford role from the doorway. Entering the kitchen, going past her, misjudging his step, he had brushed against her back. Doing so, he had halted, apologizing, and playfully kissed the exposed back of her neck. She had dropped the frying pan, whirled about, reached up, kissed him passionately on the lips, clinging to him.

No words followed. They moved out of the kitchen, holding each other, continuing to kiss all the way upstairs to the bedroom. He had helped her undress, stripped off his own clothes, embraced her, and carried her to the bed. All restraints had vanished instantly. They had joined flesh to flesh as if each was hungrily trying to recover a missing part of his or her body. They stayed tightly joined, writhing as one being, for an hour or more. At last, the uniting was consummated, and both were emptied and wet with exhaustion but overcome with wondrous fulfilment.

Never again, in the many months that followed, were they long apart.

Instinctively, they kept their secret – a secret within a secret – from General Petrov.

Perhaps Petrov knew, Razin sometimes speculated. Petrov was supposed to know everything. If so, Petrov never spoke of it. If he did know, Razin usually decided, it did not matter. They were doing their jobs well. Only that mattered.

Emerging from the pleasurable past into the present, Razin became aware of his clothes hanging on the bathroom door and of his nakedness. She had wanted to be awakened, and he wanted to wake her and make love to her this last time before her mission. The preparation period had ended. From morning on she would be a charge of the KGB and Politburo. Razin would not see her again, alone, until she returned.

Razin went into the bedroom, did not bother about the two lighted lamps, and crawled into bed beside her. The weight of his body made her stir. His hand slipped under the blanket to caress her naked breasts, her belly, her clitoris. She came around on her back, opening her sleepy eyes. For a moment, seeing her full face, she was Billie Bradford. She was the First Lady of the United States. She was here in bed with him. It was impossible. She had pushed away the blanket, reached out for his hard penis, and she was his Vera Vavilova.

The knowledge that they would soon be apart drew them together quickly. He sank into her as deep as he could go, to bring her as close as she could come. It was like their first time, hot and passionate and ceaseless. In a half-hour their bodies were slippery. The mindless animal copulation heightened until she began the long breathless groaning toward climax. She arched high, and he cried out as the semen spurted and spurted into her. Then they collapsed, arms hugging each other.

Finally, she freed herself to leave the warm bed for the bathroom, to douche and to towel herself dry.

In bed again, sitting, she took a pill from the end table and downed it with a swallow of water.

'Why the sleeping pill?' he asked. 'You don't need it tonight.'

'Billie Bradford does,' she said, sliding under the blanket. 'She always takes one. I hope my memory will be better than yours.' Under the blanket, she sought his hand. 'I love you, my darling.'

'I love you more,' he said. 'And keep that good memory of yours. I want you back safely.'

'I'll be back safely.'

'And we'll be married.'

'Yes. Now I've got to sleep.' She paused. 'Good night, Mr President. Or may I call you Andrew?'

They both smiled. They both had learned that this was one of Billie Bradford's little jokes with her husband.

Razin leaned over and kissed her. 'Good night, my heart.'

She turned on her side, drew the blanket over her shoulders, and in minutes she was sound asleep.

He lay back, his body sated, his mind alert and anxious. After a brief interval, he sat up, came off the bed, and made for the bathroom to find the package of cigarettes in his jacket. Lighting a cigarette, he shut off the lamps, returned to the living room, felt his way to an armchair, and dropped into it.

He sat musing in the darkness. He hated the project now. He hated his responsibility for her role in it and for her security. What had brought him into this strange undertaking?

The fact that he was half-American, he knew, that was what had brought him to this night.

His heart had never been fully into the project, never wanted it undertaken, never wanted it successful, until he had fallen in love with Vera. She had been the turning point. After his involvement with her, he knew it must succeed, could not fail, and he had sublimated his American side for his Russian side. As he had prepared to do grave damage to the country of his birth which he had always secretly loved, he had rationalized that his real loyalty must belong to the Russia he owed so much and to the woman he loved more than life itself.

Razin's father had been Russian, born in Sverdlovsk, an Olympic track star turned journalist, assigned by TASS to cover politics in Washington DC. Razin's mother had been American, born in Philadelphia, taken to Washington as secretary to a Pennsylvania congressmen. The Russian journalist and American secretary had met, fallen in love, married. Their residence was a rented house in Virginia, where Alex Razin had been born. He had attended grade school in Virginia, been a Cub Scout and played Little League baseball, and been a candidate for the National Spelling Bee. When he was twelve, his beloved mother, his warm, dear mother, had died. Three years later, when he was fifteen, his father had been offered a promotion and higher salary to return to the TASS home office in Moscow as an executive editor. His father had been fascinated by the United States, but bereaved by his wife's death, lacking companionship and friends, he had decided to go back to where he came from, to Mother Russia. It meant that Alex had to accompany his father – leave his school, his friends, the only home he had ever known – and go to a distant land where he knew no one beside his parent. Uprooted at fifteen, transported to an alien place filled with strangers, he had felt frightened and alone for many months. Fortunately, he had been bilingual; the Russian learned from his father had been his second language. Because he knew the language, because this was his father's homeland, Alex Razin eventually adapted himself to the new life.

He had wanted to become a journalist like his father. Then he thought he might be a historian. When it was time for college, he enrolled in the Moscow State Institute of History, Philosophy and Literature. In his third year, he was tapped by the KGB. His American background, his knowledge of English, brought him to their attention. They needed English-speaking agents. The KGB interviewed him and selected him for training. Razin's father encouraged him to go along. He was reminded that KGB agents were a special elite in the Soviet Union, with more freedom than ordinary Russians and with a salary three or four times higher than that of the average skilled jobholder. Razin went along. He was shipped to the four-storey school in Novosibirsk, and after intensive training he graduated at the head of his class of 300 students. Following an apprenticeship in several provincial cities, he was transferred to 2 Dzerzhinsky Square in Moscow, and had been there ever since.

There had been one happy interlude, he recalled. Four years ago, Petrov had ordered him to serve as a foreign correspondent in the United States, in Washington DC, ostensibly representing *Pravda*. He had been given no specific espionage assignment, only been told to keep his eyes open. Eventually there would be assignments. He was to do routine newspaper reporting, and wait. Razin was thrilled. In his heart of hearts, Razin had longed to return to America. He had never mentioned this to anyone, not even to his father. Now his dream was to come true.

From the moment that he set foot on American soil again, he was filled with joy. He was stimulated and excited as he had not been since he was fifteen. He could not breathe enough of the free air. He threw himself into his work with fervour. Guiltily, he entertained thoughts of defecting, but knew he could not do so with his father alive in Moscow.

Nevertheless, he was in America and determined to savour every day of it. His pleasure was short-lived. One morning, in the tenth month of his stay, he was arrested by the FBI and charged with espionage. He was accused of trying to obtain military secrets from a navy officer. He had approached a navy officer, he admitted, openly seeking information, not military secrets, for a story he was planning. He insisted he was completely innocent. The FBI thought otherwise. A few days after he had been incarcerated, he realized what was going on. In Moscow, an under-secretary in the United States embassy had been arrested and jailed in Lubyanka Prison for trying to help dissidents. The American government had to retaliate. Razin had been picked as the goat. A week after his arrest, he was flown to Bucharest and exchanged for the under-secretary from the American embassy in Moscow.

Back in Moscow once more, settled in behind his familiar desk in the KGB headquarters, he learned that his father had died of a heart attack the day before his return. He was both saddened and embittered. Had his father died only a few weeks before, Razin might have been a resident of the United States and an American once more. It was ironic, because now he could never return to his native land. His hope of living in the United States some day had vanished. He had been branded a spy and was banned forever.

He was not bitter at the United States for railroading him out of the country. That had been politics, with himself an accidental and minor pawn. He was bitter at the fates that directed his life. But he was a realist. He filed away his old dream of American citizenship. He threw himself into his work at the KGB, gave his total allegiance to Russia, and in the years that followed he grew in Petrov's esteem.

Even after he had met Vera, fallen in love with her, the dormant dream persisted in the form of a fantasy. If the Americans absolved him one day, re-admitted him, he could arrange to have Vera follow him. He could blackmail Russian authorities by threatening to reveal photographs of Project Second Lady to the CIA. This would force Russian authorities to release Vera, and permit her to come to him, and together they would enjoy golden America.

Tonight, thinking about it, the fantasy was hogwash. It couldn't happen in a million years. Tonight, he didn't even wish it could happen. Russia had been good to him. With Vera beside him, his mate, Russia would be paradise. All that mattered was Vera, her safety, their reunion.

Sitting in the darkness, he could picture her sleeping peacefully in their bed. In a matter of hours she would be leaving him. If he had done his work well, she would be back in bed with him in three weeks. If he had made a single mistake with her, he would never see her again.

It was too dangerous, the whole project. She could never get away with it. No one could.

In a cold moment of clarity, he saw that it could not work. The entire project must be aborted at once. He was tempted to phone Petrov, wake him, tell him it was impossible, tell him to drop it while there was still time.

An extended moment of clarity gave him Petrov's answer. This project was Petrov's obsession. He would never abort it.

Besides, it was too late. In hours, the First Lady of the United States would be on her way. . . .

In not many hours, she thought, she would be on her way.

Billie Bradford, wearing her lace-trimmed, sheer, powder-blue nightgown, made herself comfortable beneath the blanket on her side of the bed in the President's bedroom of the White House.

She did not want to be on her way, not this time. Usually, she liked trips, was invigorated by new sights and sounds. But right now the trip to Moscow was just too much. She had no stomach for the endless flight there, the three hectic days there, the monotonous flight back. Then the flight to Los Angeles, and the flight back. Then the flight to London, and the tumult of pageantry there.

All much too much. London would have been enough. Just right. But Moscow first made the rest unbearable. Yet, the Moscow trip could not be avoided. The subject of the gathering was woman's rights, and she was an ardent feminist. Refusal to attend would have meant a bad press and would have brought resentment from her sister feminists. Furthermore, Andrew had wanted her to accept. They were heading towards the next election year, and he wanted another four years in this draughty house, and he felt the trip would enhance her image, therefore his image.

Andrew had said that he would be late tonight, a meeting with his chief of staff, Admiral Ridley, and numerous aides, in the Oval Office. Probably another meeting on the Boende matter, and debates on dealing with the Soviets at the London Summit. Well, it was already late, and still Andrew was not here. She had wanted to wait up for him, to say a proper good night before taking off from Andrews Air Force base in the afternoon. But she was too tired to stay up much longer. She had better try to sleep.

She reached for her sleeping pill, and swallowed it with a water chaser.

The pill would not take effect for twenty minutes. Rather than wait for it to work, she decided to check her open luggage once more. Her maid Sarah Keating had done most of the packing for her, but she had better see that she had everything she wanted.

Throwing aside the blanket, she swung out of bed, and stepped into her fluffy white mules. She walked past the five open leather bags and the open wardrobe, inspecting the contents of each. She missed her cashmere maroon sweater and plaid skirt, and went into the dressing room to find both and pack them. This done, she realized that Sarah, as always, had forgotten to give her any reading. There probably wouldn't be any time for it, what with dictating more of her autobiography to Guy Parker on the plane and running around Moscow, but it always felt reassuring to have some books along. She glanced at the jackets of four recently purchased novels, suspense stories and mysteries, and selected three, then saw the two non-fiction books on the Soviet Union that Nora Judson had left for her. The Russian books were unread, and they should be read, at least skimmed, between here and Moscow. She put down two of the three novels, took up the two Russian books, and placed them in her carry-on bag.

She had been kneeling, and getting to her feet she realized that she had become drowsy. The pill was doing its work. She barely made it back to bed, snatching up her typed Moscow schedule on the way.

Half sitting, she tried to read it, but it was a blur. She dropped it to the floor, snuggled under the blanket, and sank her head deep in the pillow. She was beginning to doze, when she faintly heard the bedroom door open. That would be Andrew.

She fought her eyes open and struggled awake. She saw him in his striped pyjamas, a cognac in one hand.

From the end of the bed, he was peering at her. 'Billie? Did I wake you up?'

'I dunno. I'm up.'

'Sorry if I did wake you.' He had gone to the opposite side of the bed, was sitting on the edge finishing his cognac. 'Sorry to be so late. But Boende is a big subject and the admiral is long-winded and stubborn. We're having a rough time getting ready for Kirechenko. God, I'm tired.'

He put down his glass, turned off the bedroom lights, and got into bed.

She felt his feet touching hers. 'Umm, warm toes,' she mumbled.

'How are you feeling?' he asked. 'Ready for Moscow?'

'Suppose so.'

'Wish I hadn't told you to go.'

'Goodwill,' she said.

'Yes, it won't hurt, especially when we're having so many other disagreements with the Russians. They'll like you over there.'

'Hope so.'

She felt his soft hands on her breast, felt his hair against her chin, felt his tongue on her nipple.

'What I'd give to be in you,' he said.

'Won't be long.'

'Four weeks is long. Are you still bleeding?'

'Little. Not so much.'

'Can't wait. It's something to wait for.' He moved off her. 'Good night, darling.'

Billie Bradford said thickly, 'Good night, Mr President. Or can I call you Andrew?'

3

It was five minutes to eight o'clock in the morning in Moscow.

The four of them were assembled in the living room of Vera Vavilova's secluded house, their chairs drawn up before the large screen of her television set. Vera, her long blonde hair caught by a barrette in the back, was attired in a pink blouse, blue pants, and thong sandals. To her immediate right sat General Ivan Petrov, wearing a conservative dark blue business suit, the buttoned jacket too tight for his thick chest and bulging middle, his beady eyes fixed on the blank television screen. Next to him sat his aide Colonel Zhuk and his best friend in the Politburo, Garanin.

Petrov consulted the black face of his Japanese watch. 'She has arrived,' he announced. 'Turn on the set.'

Colonel Zhuk sprang to his feet, stepped to the television cabinet, and twisted a knob. Zhuk hovered, waiting for a picture. The image unfolded slowly. It showed a hazy view of the flag of the Soviet Union and the flag of the United States on flagpoles fluttering in the breeze against a menacing, clouded, drab, grey sky. Hastily, Zhuk adjusted the focus of the picture and raised the volume on a disembodied voice. In Russian, the voice was announcing that the official American party from Washington DC had already landed at Vnukovo Airport, and that the plane was turning off the runway toward the terminal. After the First Lady disembarked, and a brief welcoming ceremony, the honoured guest would be escorted by automobile the twenty-eight kilometres into Moscow.

As Zhuk went back to his chair, the screen was filled with another picture, that of the official hostess and a group around her looking off, apparently at the approach of Air Force One, which could not be seen yet.

Vera leaned forward and made out the Premier's wife, Ludmila Kirechenko, a stately, bosomy, grey-haired lady with the appearance of a retired opera mezzo-soprano. Vera could not identify the other figures until the camera reached Alex Razin, so masculine, so handsome in his brown suit. Vera had difficulty suppressing her smile of pleasure.

Petrov extracted a cigar from his pocket and absently unpeeled the wrapper as he concentrated on the television. A gigantic jet airliner, the rectangle of the Stars and Stripes painted on it, came into view. The plane rolled across the screen and halted. The airport workmen were pushing the portable metal stairs toward the plane and setting them in place against the exit door.

The door slowly opened. As it did, a band, unseen, struck up 'The Star Spangled Banner'.

Vera leaned further forward, and Petrov's eyes narrowed. An athletic-looking youngish man had appeared in the plane's doorway, and began to descend the steps, followed closely by another.

'Her Secret Service guards,' said Vera Vavilova in English. 'The first is Van Acker, the other McGinty.'

'And the woman behind them?' asked Petrov.

'Her press secretary, Nora Judson,' said Vera.

'Yes. Then – who is the tall man again?'

'Guy Parker.'

'Ah, the CIA,' said Petrov, with a smile.

Colonel Zhuk spoke hesitantly. 'We don't know that, Comrade. We only know he is the one assisting Mrs Bradford in writing her book.'

'CIA,' muttered Petrov, chewing the cold cigar in his mouth.

Vera's total attention was directed to the television screen. She watched Nora Judson and Guy Parker come down the portable steps before which a red carpet was being unrolled.

She had seen numerous photographs of them many times. Now, fleshed out, three-dimensional in person, they seemed more formidable.

'And there *she* is!' Petrov exclaimed, sitting up straight. 'See her? Billie Bradford. The First Lady.'

Vera's eyes almost bore through the screen, following the First Lady's graceful descent down the stairs. She was tall, statuesque, yet fluid. There was a sheen to her flaxen hair, captured in a neat chignon. The contours of her lovely face were perfect. White earrings matched the white rims of her over-sized sun-glasses. A patterned chiffon dress was moulded to her sinuous body by a slight breeze.

Vera's smooth brow contracted as she stared at the woman she had come to know better than herself. Momentarily, Vera's poise cracked. Billie Bradford was breathtaking. She was world famous. She was real. She was unique, one of a kind. There could never be another like her. No one on earth would believe there could be another. Vera felt the constriction in her throat. For the first time in almost three years, she suffered qualms and stage fright.

'She's too beautiful,' Vera gasped.

Petrov had transferred his gaze from Billie Bradford on the screen to Vera Vavilova beside him. He studied her.

'Too beautiful?' he repeated, covering Vera's delicate hand with his own hairy hand. 'No more than you are, my dear.'

Vera's eyes were on the screen. 'Do I actually look like that?' she said with wonder.

Petrov pointed past her. 'There is the mirror.'

Vera's eyes followed his finger toward the wall mirror. She surveyed her reflection in the glass. To herself, in these moments, she was still she. Not Billie Bradford. Simply the actress she had always known, Vera Vavilova from Kiev. She swung her head back to the screen. Billie Bradford was accepting a bouquet of red gladioli from a child.

The American ambassador to the Soviet Union, Otis Youngdahl, the wealthy well-dressed towering man, was advancing on the red carpet to greet the President's wife with a kiss on the cheek. He had Billie by the arm now and brought her forward to the Soviet group. He was introducing her to the Premier's wife, Ludmila Kirechenko. The two famous women were shaking hands, as Alex Razin materialized between them. Ludmila was speaking at length to Billie, and Alex was interpreting the Russian into English for the American President's wife.

Presently, Alex guided Billie Bradford to the circle of Russian dignitaries. He was translating the greetings and remarks of the Russians into English for the President's wife, and her responses from English into Russian. Alex Razin's hand was on Billie Bradford's forearm as he moved her around the circle, bending his head toward her ear as he continued to interpret.

Following them on the screen, Vera Vavilova felt a pang of jealousy. Her loved one was with the most beautiful and exciting woman in the world. He was close to her now, and would be even closer to her in the weeks ahead. He might confuse Billie with Vera herself – or worse, prefer Billie to Vera herself.

Vera turned back toward the mirror for one more glimpse of her own face, and realized that all she had been fancying was ridiculous. If Billie was the most beautiful and exciting woman in the world, then so was she. Alex was seeing only a reproduction of his Vera. She turned from the mirror, reassured.

More relaxed, Vera devoted herself to the television screen. Billie had been led by Alex to a battery of microphones. She was speaking graciously in English – how much she had always wanted to visit Moscow, how thrilling to be here, how much she looked forward to discussions with female leaders of other nations about the progress of woman's rights. The whole thing was uncanny, Vera thought, the way that other woman had been imitating Vera's speech inflections, Vera's facial expressions, Vera's gestures.

Vera watched hypnotized as the American President's wife and the Russian Premier's wife were being led to the black Chaika limousine, flanked by two yellow police cars and four helmeted, grey-uniformed guards mounted on motorcycles.

As Billie Bradford disappeared into the limousine, Vera turned to speak to Petrov. She was surprised to find him staring at her.

Petrov nodded toward the television screen. 'Does she scare you?' Petrov asked quietly.

There was no hesitation in Vera Vavilova's retort. 'No, absolutely not,' she replied firmly. 'Who is that imposter? *I* am the First Lady.'

Petrov snorted a laugh. 'Good. Better. Much better. Just don't forget.'

'I won't forget,' said Vera. And she could see that Petrov knew that she meant it.

Inside the extremely modern Palace of Congresses, located near the Trinity Gate entrance to the walled Kremlin, in the mammoth main auditorium, the leading woman in the Soviet Union, Madame Ludmila Kirechenko, stood at the podium on the stage delivering the closing address to the 2000 female delegates and their parties from ninety nations.

It was the third and last day of the International Women's Meeting, and Billie Bradford, for one, was glad of it.

She sat wearily in the centre of the second row, trying to appear attentive with the earphones on her head and a voice translating Mrs Kirechenko's concluding speech from Russian into English. On one side of her sat ambassador Otis Youngdahl and protocol officer Fred Willis. On the other side sat Alex Razin, Nora Judson, and Guy Parker. Directly in front of her and behind her sat Secret Service agents Van Acker and McGinty. Earlier in the final afternoon session, she had listened to the introductory Soviet speakers without the headphones. As the speakers' voices had boomed out over the 7000 loudspeakers concealed throughout the auditorium, she had preferred to have the nice interpreter and guide, Alex Razin, translate for her. But when the head delegates of France, Germany, Spain had taken to the podium, and Razin could not help, she had resorted to the headphones.

She tried to concentrate on Mrs Kirechenko's summation – the findings and recommendations on woman's role in the world and its future – but Billie's mind wandered.

One of her legs was going to sleep, and she moved and massaged it. She was bone weary. She, herself, had been the second to last speaker on the podium, reading a report on the progress of woman's rights in the United States in the past ten years, and near the end of it her voice had been reduced to a hoarse rasp. Nevertheless, the words had been right, and leaving the stage she had received enthusiastic applause.

Generally, the international meeting had been what she had expected. Mainly, pointless. Mainly, a Communist showcase. The central topic, the variety of subjects to be covered, had sounded impressive. But rarely, during the three days, had they been tackled head on. The majority of female delegates had handled their tasks like so many Chamber of Commerce puppets. The meeting, and all of the Soviet side-shows, had been tiresome, even boring. Moreover, like so many American visitors to the Soviet Union, she had felt cut off from the outside world, alienated from all that was familiar, constantly lonely and, separated from Andrew, vulnerable. She had never missed Andrew this much. The second she was back in her hotel, she would telephone him.

Mrs Kirechenko's monotone, followed by Razin's rapid-fire interpretation, droned on in her ears, and Billie tried to escape and hide inside her head. Her mind sought the beginning of these past three days, and she tried to conjure up what had taken place. The first morning in Moscow, after being settled in a special suite at the Rossiya Hotel, she had hoped to rest, perhaps resume her talks with Guy Parker for the book. She had not been able to give him as much time as she had planned to during the flight to Moscow. After their arrival, she'd hardly had time to shower and put on fresh clothes, when her over-zealous hosts had plucked her out of the hotel and into the streets for a whirlwind sight-

81

seeing tour of the city. By now it gave her a headache even to try to recall the kaleidoscope of sights – Lenin's Mausoleum and St Basil's in Red Square, the dark red Kremlin wall and its nineteen towers and gates embracing five cathedrals and four churches and two squares, after that the Tretyakov Gallery, the Pushkin Museum, the Marx and Engels Museum, the USSR Exhibition of Economic Achievements, Gorky Park – hit-and-run, a half-hour a site at most, the mind reeled then and it reeled now. And along the way, she could not remember the time, the day, a model child-care centre, a hospital, a fashion show. People were friendly, hospitable, sincere. The leaders, also, but their sincerity suspect. Yet, that was true everywhere. Mid-afternoon, first day, she had convened with other delegates in this auditorium. Endless welcoming speeches. Dull documentary films on the women of the USSR and the strides they had made toward equality. Then, with one short break for dinner, brief reports from forty countries on the status of women in their nations, and on into late night.

The second morning had meant more reports. The second afternoon and evening countless panels, seminars on job equality, voting freedom, sexual equality, and more and more of the same. The third morning, this morning, the representatives of twenty nations, each reporting on her hopes for future progress. This afternoon, lengthy statements from delegates of eight major nations on the future of woman's rights. Now, Mrs Kirechenko was bringing it to an end.

Thank God for the farewell banquet this evening. After that it would be over, and Billie could sleep. But not long, she realized unhappily. Tomorrow, airborne again to Washington. Then to Los Angeles to report on this meeting. Then to London with her husband and the Summit. Too much. Her brain cells were unhinged. She wondered if she possessed one muscle that didn't ache.

She became aware of a resounding silence in her ears. People around her, throughout the hall, were on their feet applauding. Mrs Kirechenko had finished, just as Billie felt almost finished. Billie put aside the headphones and rose to clap her hands.

Presently, she was inching up the aisle, two Soviet security men leading her and her own Secret Service men at her heels. She was jostled four or five times by other women delegates who wanted her autograph, and she obliged. In the lobby, photographers ran alongside her, their flash-guns winking on and off.

One brash middle-aged female, apparently a reporter from India, pushed toward her shouting, 'Why do you bow to the sexists with that transparent dress?' Billie kept her temper and her set smile and called back, 'Because I want men to look at me – not only as an equal but as a woman.'

Outside, at the curb with its four steps, two black eight-cylinder Chaika limousines were waiting for them on the cobblestoned street. As the chauffeur of the first car opened the rear door, Billie hesitated, and faced the members of her party who were gathering around.

'How are we for time, Nora?' she inquired. 'I'd like to do just a little souvenir shopping.'

Nora Judson looked up from her wristwatch. 'If it's not too long. You could have an hour.'

'Let's do it,' said Billie. 'I'll be in Los Angeles in a few days. I should take something for the family.' She spoke to her interpreter. 'Where would I go, Mr Razin?'

'I'd suggest the nearest Beryoska shop,' said Razin. 'It is a state-controlled store that sells only to foreigners with foreign money. A Beryoska shop will have the best choice of goods – furs, hand-cut crystal, handpainted boxes, wine.'

Billie wrinkled her nose. 'But that's just for foreigners. No, I want to see someplace where Russians themselves go.'

'Ah, then you want to see GUM, the state department store,' said Razin. 'It is just across Red Square. It has 1000 shops in its arcades, but you won't find much to buy of any value. You'll find material for dresses, some kitchen gadgets, children's toys. And you'll need roubles.'

'No problem,' said Ambassador Youngdahl.

'And the Russians go there?' Billie inquired.

'Oh, absolutely,' Razin promised.

'Then I want to see it,' said Billie.

'Let me call the store director,' said Razin. 'He can speed things up for you. He speaks perfect English. You go. I'll be right behind you.' Razin dashed back toward the lobby.

Ten minutes later, Razin came forward on the rear seat of the second limousine, where he was sitting with Ambassador Youngdahl and Guy Parker, and pointed beyond the windshield. 'There they are, waiting. Park right in back of them.'

Billie Bradford's Chaika was standing before an entrance to the spired, three-storey, marble and granite department store. Even as they drew up behind it, Razin opened the rear door of the moving vehicle and jumped outside, almost losing his balance. 'I'll bring the director,' he called back.

In a few minutes, Razin had the portly director by the arm and propelled him to Billie Bradford and the others, who were together beside the first limousine. Razin introduced the director to Billie Bradford, then to Ambassador Youngdahl and Miss Judson and Mr Parker. The director gave each a dip of a bow.

'Honoured, honoured,' the director said. 'Come inside, let me show you around.'

Billie spoke to Nora and the others. 'Nora, I'll need your advice. Do you mind? As for the rest of you, don't bother. Stay right here. The shopping will only exhaust you. Besides, I don't want to attract too much attention.'

'I'd better go with you,' said Ambassador Youngdahl, falling in step behind Billie.

Alex Razin and Guy Parker remained next to the cars, watching the group head into GUM's.

Razin said, 'Want to stretch your legs and have a smoke?'

'Not a bad idea,' said Parker.

'We can stay in sight,' said Razin, starting off. 'Just stroll back and forth in front of the store.'

He offered Parker a cigarette, took one for himself, and applied a lighter to both.

They walked in silence for a full minute. Parker was the

first to break the silence. 'You don't speak English English,' he said. 'You speak American English. Where did you pick it up?'

'In the United States,' said Razin, 'I was born in Virginia.'

'Really? That's surprising. You seemed so – so Russian.'

'I am Russian, half-Russian, on my father's side. My mother was American, from Pennsylvania. I – well, I don't want to bother you with my genealogy.'

'No, I'm interested,' said Parker.

'You'll be sorry,' Razin said with a solemn smile, and he proceeded to recount more on the background of his parents, his own growing up in the United States, and a censored version of his return to Russia with his father. He did not mention his training and job with the KGB. He stated that he was a full-time government interpreter.

'So now you know it all,' concluded Razin.

Parker nodded, as they walked. He accepted a fresh cigarette and the light. 'Odd,' he said. 'There's something so familiar about you, I could have sworn I met you in the United States. But that would be impossible, since you left at fifteen.'

Razin decided to tell him. 'Not impossible,' he said. 'I forgot to tell you. I was back in the United States four or five years ago for a short time.'

'As a tourist?'

'I was a Washington correspondent for TASS.'

'Well, that might explain it,' said Parker. 'We could have met. Around that period, before I became one of President Bradford's speech writers, I spent some months in the Washington bureau of Associated Press. Off and on, I covered the White House. We may have seen each other at a press conference.'

'Very likely,' agreed Razin.

'Did you enjoy working in Washington?'

'I loved it.'

'Why did you leave?'

Razin decided that there was nothing to lose. 'I didn't leave,' he said. 'I was thrown out.'

Parker stopped in his tracks. 'You were thrown out?'

'Exactly. I was railroaded out. Some of my people in Moscow had arrested one of your embassy people for collaborating with dissidents. Your government decided to retaliate. At random, I was selected to be the innocent victim. I was set up, arrested on some preposterous charge, then returned to Moscow in exchange for your embassy person. I'm afraid I'm *persona non grata* in the United States.' He shook his head. 'Too bad. I've always considered the United States my first homeland. I *was* born there. I loved it. Now I am afraid I will never see it again.'

'I'm sorry.'

Razin would never know what impelled him to say what he said next. He thought he had buried his fantasy. But here, with an American official close to the First Lady and the President, he could not resist reviving the hope for an option, perhaps one he and Vera might be able to pick up on some future date. 'I wish there was a person over there who could know the truth, and perhaps help lift the ban on me. It would be nice, but I suppose it is unlikely.'

The last had been a muted question. Parker did not quite answer it. He shrugged, as they resumed their stroll. 'Who knows what can happen? You never know. The political climate can change. Old decisions can be reversed.'

'If it ever does change,' said Razin, 'I would appreciate it if you kept me in mind. You are well connected. A few words from you in the right ears, it could mean much to me. Understand, I like my lot here. I am happy. But it would be good to know that I could see the United States again.'

'I'll remember that,' promised Parker. 'But this is not the time for it, as you know. The climate between our countries is not the best. If it were better now, there would be no necessity for a Summit in London next week. But the future? Who can tell what that will bring? I'll keep an eye open for you.'

'You won't forget?' said Razin earnestly.

'I won't forget.'

'I appreciate that,' said Razin. 'I know what I'm going to

say next is ridiculous, but if ever I can reciprocate, do any small thing for you, I'd be happy to oblige. I admit, I'm not very important. But I do have some good contacts.'

'Thank you,' said Parker. He smiled. 'I might call you on it – a case of your local vodka some day.'

Razin did not smile. 'Try me,' he said.

Parker was pointing toward the store's entrance. 'Isn't that Mrs Bradford?'

Razin squinted off. 'Yes. She seems to have found something to buy.'

Billie Bradford had emerged with the GUM director, both carrying plastic shopping bags, with Nora Judson holding a package and Ambassador Youngdahl following.

'We'd better meet her,' said Parker, starting ahead.

Razin went after him, thinking. Had he made a mistake, speaking his mind to the American? Had he been indiscreet? What if it got back to Petrov, his love for America, his desire to go there?

But then he knew it would never get to Petrov. It was obvious that Guy Parker had not taken him seriously. Parker had only pretended to. Parker, like all Americans, had been polite.

It really didn't matter, Razin told himself. The old dream of America was only a nostalgia for his youth. He was grown up now. Only one thing mattered.

He saw First Lady Billie Bradford climb into the limousine. He saw Vera Vavilova climb into the limousine.

That was all that mattered. Vera safely back in his arms.

Night had fallen over Moscow, but inside the floodlit Kremlin there was activity, especially in the large and airy office of Premier Dmitri Kirechenko, General Secretary of the Communist Party, Chairman of the Presidium of the Supreme Soviet, Marshal of the Soviet Union.

The four walls of the Premier's office, wallpapered in white silk, offered no more than two decorations – a framed portrait of Karl Marx and a framed portrait of V. I. Lenin. In the centre of the room under the glass chandelier stood a conference table covered in green baize. In a corner of the hexagonal office rested the Premier's L-shaped desk. The desk-top was devoid of knick-knacks or equipment, save three white telephones and a pushbutton console, a green desk pad holding an open typed briefing book, a square brass clock, a pen and inkwell, a calendar. A dark brown button-back leather chair accompanied the desk.

This moment of the evening, the chair was solidly filled by Premier Kirechenko, rubbing his Vandyke beard as he looked through his rimless glasses at his associates around him. Across from him, briefing books in their laps, sat General Chukovsky, Colonel Zhuk, Politburo members Garanin and Umyakov, and two specialists on African affairs.

'All right,' said Premier Kirechenko, 'I have your suggestions. I appreciate them. Now, so that there is no misunderstanding, let me sum up our position and let me sum up America's position before we go to the meeting in London.'

He lay back in his leather swivel chair, slipped off his rimless spectacles, closed his eyes, and resumed speaking.

'Boende,' he intoned, 'until now an insignificant country of thirty million in south central Africa. A year ago it became significant. Huge deposits of uranium ore were found and mined. We in the Soviet Union need uranium. The United States needs uranium. To maintain a façade of neutrality, Mwami Kibangu, President of Boende, in reality an American puppet, set a quota on what he would sell us, while at the same time he sold the United States three times as much. An intolerable situation.

'We know that Kibangu heads a government that lacks solid popular support. His government is an artificial democracy propped up by his American ally. On the other hand, our man, Colonel Nwapa, heads a people's underground army of rebels pledged to adhere to the principles of Communism. Our ties to Colonel Nwapa are close, and he has informed us that he is ready to move, prepared to overthrow the American puppet government. So much for the background.'

Premier Kirechenko opened his eyes, his glasses dangling from his fingers.

'So we arrive at the situation as it stands today,' he continued. 'Colonel Nwapa has the necessary manpower to succeed. However, he does not have the sophisticated armament that would assure victory. On the other hand, America's President Kibangu claims to be strongly armed with the latest new weapons, an arsenal supplied by the United States. He also claims to have a treaty with the United States that would supply him with added weapons should there be any threat against his government. So we face the big question. Are President's Kibangu's claims true? And the subsidiary questions. Has his government army been fully equipped with American weapons? Can Kibangu get help from President Bradford if the rebel forces should strike?

'If Kibangu's claims are true, the government army would crush Nwapa with no difficulty. If his claims are true, we would not dare to airlift armament from Ethiopia for the rebel forces, and Nwapa would be helpless to go forward without us. However, if the government claims are *not* true, if the United States has not built up Boende's defences, if the United States would not reinforce them in an emergency, then we would have the upper hand. We could rush Nwapa sufficient supplies, technicians, advisers to enable him to take over control of Boende in a single week. Nwapa would head the country. We would have all the uranium we require. Boende's uranium exports to the United States would be shut off. Our nuclear standing would be enhanced. Our dominance over our capitalist rival would be complete.'

Several of those across the desk nodded their agreement. Premier Kirechenko ignored them. He went on.

'This brings us to the Summit Conference in London. Our intelligence agents in the field have been unable to ascertain the Boende government's strength. At the same time, President Bradford's CIA has been unable to learn the rebels' strength. So we have been at a stalemate. The enemy prefers the status quo, to exploit the riches of Boende. We prefer a war of liberation to save the people of Boende. To break the stalemate, we decided on a Summit confrontation with America. We know President Bradford's plan. He will propose a treaty for us to accept and sign. He will propose the status quo, not only for Boende, but for all of Africa – a treaty stating that there will be no further foreign intervention in Africa, and no exporting of arms to any African state. How will we regard this proposed treaty? If the United States is bluffing as to its past and future support of Boende, and we are unable to prove it, then a signed treaty would be a clever and important victory for them. But if we learn beforehand that the United States is bluffing, we will reject the treaty, signal Nwapa to attack, and we will possess Boende, its uranium deposits, and our best foothold yet for gradual control of Africa.

'How could the Summit be won by us? It couldn't be won, it wouldn't be won, except for one unknown factor – a secret weapon in our possession that will assure us a resounding victory.'

Premier Kirechenko's chair creaked straight. He adjusted his glasses to the bridge of his nose.

'Gentlemen, several of you have seen the development of our secret weapon. All of you have now heard about it. This weapon will probe and dig the truth out of President Bradford, reveals America's real position and Boende's real strength or weakness. With this truth in our hands, we will know exactly how to proceed at the Summit. Gentlemen, I want each and every one of you to see the secret weapon in its full readiness before it is launched.'

His hand went out to his desk. His forefinger pressed a buzzer. His eyes fixed on the double doors leading from the reception room at the far side of his office. All heads turned to follow his gaze.

The double doors swung open. General Petrov entered gravely, stepped to one side, and gestured off.

She appeared. She came slowly through the doorway. She advanced toward the Premier's desk.

Her head was high, her carriage erect. She wore a beige silk blouse, low cut with a gold chain holding a tiny gold medallion at the cleft between her breasts, and a soft brown flared skirt. Her blonde mane was smooth, her wide spread sapphire eyes twinkled, and beneath the tilted nose her ruby lips wore a half-smile. Her sinuous body glided across the office.

She went past the group standing at the desk directly to the man behind it. She extended her hand and the man behind the desk rapidly stood up and solemnly shook it.

'Premier Kirechenko,' she was saying, 'I am honoured to meet you at last. I am Billie Bradford. My husband, the President of the United States, has requested that I convey his warmest greetings.'

The Premier responded with an uncharacteristic smile. 'Superb,' he said. He took her by an arm and pointed her toward his associates. Even those who had met her before were staring. Those who had never seen her were gaping.

'For those of you who are confused,' said the Premier, 'it is understandable. For the rest of you, here is the finished product. Gentlemen, meet the Soviet Union's greatest actress, Comrade Vera Vavilova. . . . Petrov, bring her a chair. All of you, sit down.' He waited for Vera to sit, then, settling in his chair, he said to his colleagues, 'Although you've known, more or less, what we were planning, I don't think most of you believed in the reality of it. But it is real, she is real. You can see for yourselves.'

Old General Chukovsky could not take his eyes off her. 'Amazing,' he muttered. 'Yes, I knew what you were up to, but I had my doubts.' He wagged his head. 'I have no more doubts.'

The Premier showed that he was pleased, as did Petrov nearby.

'Here is our secret weapon,' said the Premier, 'our strength when we go to the Summit next week. Her findings will guide us to victory.' Over his shoulder, he added, 'A brilliant job, Petrov.'

'Thank you.'

Premier Kirechenko's gaze had returned to Vera Vavilova. 'So you are ready, Madame First Lady?'

'I am, sir.'

'You are confident?'

'Absolutely.'

'Then I am reassured,' said the Premier. 'The future of the Soviet Union, indeed the future balance of power in the world, may well rest on your shoulders.'

'I am fully aware of the stakes, sir,' said Vera Vavilova.

Momentarily, the Premier displayed concern. 'Perhaps I am a fool to allow this. The risks are enormous. One error, just one, and we are lost.'

Vera Vavilova nodded. 'Premier Kirechenko, believe me, there will be no error. Not one. I shall fulfil my mission.'

'Then so shall we.' He rose to his feet, extending his hand once more. 'Good luck, Mrs Bradford. My regards to the President.'

Fatigued as she was, Billie Bradford had to admit to herself that the scene was impressive.

She and her party were seated near the centre of one of the four banquet tables stretching along the four walls of the dazzling Hall of St George situated in the Great Kremlin Palace. She had been placed between her interpreter, Alex Razin, and United States ambassador Otis Youngdahl. In the gilt chairs on either side of them were Nora Judson, Guy Parker, and protocol officer Fred Willis.

The Czarist hall, she had been told, was 200 feet long and sixty feet wide. Eighteen spiral zinc columns supported the vaulted ceiling from which hung six giant gilt chandeliers. Besides the chandeliers, 3000 lamps shone down on the squares of parquet flooring in the centre of the room. On this floor, three or four hours earlier when the farewell banquet of the International Women's Meeting had begun, excerpts from three ballets had been performed by members of the Bolshoi Company.

Billie Bradford glanced up at the balcony where an orchestra was playing a medley of lilting tunes from famous Broadway musical plays.

Her attention drawn back down to the table by the waiters

in white livery removing her plate that still held most of her fillet of beef, and her glass that was still half full of Moldavian red wine, Billie realized that she had lost track of time. She guessed it to be near midnight. But now, with the beef plates being removed, she knew that the dessert was next and with that the endless evening and day would be over.

Despite the many exotic meals she had been served on state occasions in Mexico City, Paris, Rome, in the White House itself, she had never been forced to partake of a dinner as filling as this one tonight. She tried to think of the first course and counted forward. The first course, my God, fresh caviar and vodka, fish puffs, more fish jellied, followed by venison with dill pickles, and a salad. Merely the first course. After that had followed wild fowl broth with quenelles, then cold kvass soup, whatever that had been. Next a baked white salmon. Next, sterlet or Russian sturgeon with Georgian white wine. This followed by the fillet of beef. She had survived by eating only half of everything. And still the dessert to come. She would have to remember to tell Andrew they were being pretty skimpy at the White House.

Recalling her husband made her recall her frustration in failing to reach him before dinner. While getting into her black velvet evening gown, she had phoned the White House for Andrew. She had got Dolores Martin, his personal secretary, instead. She had learned that Andrew was in a Cabinet meeting, and had left word not to be disturbed. Billie had been disappointed. She ached to talk to him, to dispel her loneliness and fatigue. Miss Martin had wondered whether she wanted the President to call her back. Definitely, she had replied. She should be in her hotel shortly after midnight.

Her thoughts were disturbed by the waiter. He was setting a dish of strawberry ice cream before her, placing a bowl of fruit near it, filling her coffee cup. Then she saw that he was pouring champagne into the crystal glass. She started to protest – she detested champagne, but too late, it was already poured, her glass filled near to the brim.

She realized that all heads were turning to the centre of the banquet table, perhaps a dozen seats away. She saw a

93

male figure was standing, his champagne glass held high, and she made him out to be Premier Kirechenko, to her surprise. Earlier, his chair had been empty, and his wife had hosted the evening alone. Apparently he had just arrived and was offering a toast in Russian. Billie felt Alex Razin's breath in her ear as he whispered a translation. The Premier was toasting the success of women everywhere, the jobs they would hold, the babies their husbands would have. Joke. Laughter. Then, more seriously, he toasted the forthcoming London Summit and a meeting of minds that would lead to peace on earth for ever.

Billie could see everyone was standing, joining in the toast. She quickly got to her feet, holding the champagne glass. Reluctantly, she touched it to her lips, took a sip, made a face. Aware that Razin was watching her, she said, 'I can't finish. I hate the stuff.'

Razin bent to her, whispering, 'Please, Madam, you must drink it. Not to do so would be a breach of etiquette, especially from you.'

She turned helplessly to Ambassador Youngdahl, who had been listening. He nodded. Past him, she sought out Nora Judson, who disliked champagne as much as she did. Nora was downing her glass of champagne. Shrugging, Billie closed her eyes, brought the champagne to her lips and in quick gulps swallowed the entire contents of the glass. It was more bitter than usual, and immediately she had a short coughing spell. At last, putting down her empty glass, she sat, relieved that the toast was over.

An amplified voice was announcing something in Russian. Razin translated. The finale of the evening would be more entertainment by Russian women.

Lights dimmed, spotlights caught and held on the ballet troupe in the middle of the hall, poised to begin twenty minutes more of vignettes from memorable ballets.

Despite her weariness, Billie tried to devote herself to the whirling, wheeling, leaping dancers on the floor. Gradually, she felt a bodily weakness overcoming her. She started to slump, realized it, and pulled herself together. Through bleary eyes, she followed the acrobatics of the dancers. About to nod off, Billie heard the music stop, saw the spotlights black out. Everyone in the hall was clapping. Billie tried to clap, too, but one palm missed the other. Relieved that it was over, she pushed back her chair attempting to rise. but Razin's hand gently held her down.

'Mrs Bradford, please,' he said in an undertone, 'there is one more entertainment to end the programme. Our world champion women gymnasts.'

Billie smiled foolishly, as the spotlights came on to reveal parallel bars and various other pieces of equipment on the floor. The Russian female gymnasts, all young and tiny birds, attired in leotards, appeared. Light as air, they bounced about, tumbled, balanced, spun on the bars, to bursts of applause.

As their graceful routine continued, Billie tried to focus on them. It was impossible. The six on the floor became twelve and shimmied into eighteen or more. Billie squeezed her eyes, for better focus, but lost sight of the troupe. Her eyes were pasted shut. Her head lolled to one side.

The next thing she knew, someone was shaking her awake. Ambassador Youngdahl had her by the shoulder, and the hall lights were on.

'Come on, Mrs Bradford,' the ambassador was saying, 'time to get back to the hotel and bed.'

His hand under her arm, he helped her to her feet.

'Sleep,' she mumbled from a deep pit. 'I got to – must – I must sleep.'

She was locked in a crowd pressing to the exit. Surrounded by her Secret Service agents and KGB guards, she shuffled forward.

She wondered if Nora, somewhere, was as sleepy. Once, she stumbled, but strong hands held her upright.

Embrace me, she thought, embrace me, dear sleep.

They were out of the elevator and in the third floor corridor of the Rossiya Hotel.

Billie Bradford had been awakened to leave the limousine

and enter the hotel. Briefly, at the entrance, in the lobby, she had revived. But now, in the corridor, proceeding slowly toward her suite, she felt faint again, her limbs almost paralysed.

The Secret Service men on the night shift, Oliphant and Upchurch, were on either side of her, each holding an arm, tightening their grips every time it appeared she would collapse. A few feet behind them, Guy Parker was assisting a groggy Nora Judson.

To Billie Bradford, it seemed an eternity, but they had finally reached the majestic double doors of the First Lady's suite. Near the suite entrance, Billie's personal maid Sarah Keating, replacing the usual Russian *dezhurnaya*, the woman who doled out room keys, shot out of her chair. Hastily, key in hand, she unlocked one door.

The maid studied her mistress with concern. 'May I help you get ready for bed, Ma'am?'

Billie tried to raise a hand to send her away. 'Not neces . . . necessary. You go. I'm fine, fine. I can undress myself.'

Guy Parker turned Nora over to Agent Upchurch, and came forward. 'Are you all right, Billie?'

'Perfect – perfectly fine. Just too tired, I guess.'

'Remember, we're off to the airport at seven.'

'No worry. Alarm's set.'

'Get some rest then. You certainly need it.'

Parker retreated to Agent Upchurch, who was propping Nora up. Parker took her free elbow, and together they continued around the corner to deposit their charge in her double room.

Holding on to the door frame, Billie watched Nora being led away. Nora blurred in and out of focus. 'Poor thing,' Billie said. 'Overworked.'

She pivoted to her open doorway.

Agent Oliphant still had her by the arm. He looked anxious. 'Can I help you inside, Ma'am?'

'No, no.' She pulled her arm free. 'Going right to bed.'

She weaved into the living room.

'I'll be right outside your door all night,' Agent Oliphant called after her. 'Just let me know if you need me.'

She bobbed her head and shut the door in his face.

The lights were on in her living room. She scanned the room. It rose up and down as if shaken by an earthquake. Dizzily, she started to traverse the rocking room, bumping into furniture, until she fell against the wall light switch. She snapped it off.

On rubbery legs she entered the bedroom, darkened except for the yellow lamp that illuminated the double bed. She willed herself to reach the bed. Halfway there, she halted, teetering, pushed off her pumps, unzipped her velvet gown and let it drop to the floor, managed to step over it. She tugged down on her panty hose, almost falling as she got them off. Naked, one foot in front of the other, she stepped on the small oblong throw rug not far from the bed. Her green nightgown was neatly spread on the bed. She groped for it, clutched it, with difficulty put her head through it, her arms through it, and yanked it down. A corner of the blanket was folded back. She tore at it, throwing it aside. One step. Another. She felt the edge of the mattress. She let go, and dropped like a stone into the bed.

With effort, on her back, she wriggled under the blanket, tugged the rest of it to her breasts. She forced her eyes open. There were several ceilings on a seesaw above her. The walls of the room were going round and round. She brought the bedside lamps into sight, held on them until they materialized into a single lamp. Beneath it ticked her travelling clock. It was jiggling too much too read. But then she had one glimpse of the time. Ten after something – twelve – ten after twelve, after midnight. Her cold hand fumbled for the base of the lamp, turned it off.

In the darkness, she lowered her head into the downy pillow. Delicious pillows the Russians had. She let her heavy eyelids close. From somewhere distant she heard a ringing. Maybe her phone. Maybe Andrew calling back. Andrew. She made a small effort at rising, but her shoulders, her spine, refused to help her. She gave up. To hell with the phone.

She lay motionless. She'd never in her life felt like this before. Pinned down. Helpless. Only her head felt movement. There was a pinwheel in her head. She must be terribly drunk, she told herself.

The pinwheel spun on.

A flash of clarity superseded the pinwheel. She could not be as drunk as this from what she'd been served. Had she been drugged? Should she call the ambassador? Should she call the Secret Service man outside the door? Her mind laboured for a decision, tried to hold on one, but it was slipping away.

The pinwheel was back, turning more slowly, receding, fading into a void that was filling with darkness. Her body sank and drifted into slumber. Her head blacked out and joined her body.

Billie Bradford was asleep.

The clock on the bedstand read 12.14.

Darkness.

The clock on the bedstand read 2.10.

Billie Bradford slept on, slept deeply, unconscious to the night.

She was still. The bedroom was still. Then something moved. The small throw rug, the four-foot oriental rug on the planked wooden floor beside her bed, moved. Slowly, eerily, one end of the rug began to rise, one inch, two inches, three, four, five.

The oak planks of the floor beneath the carpet, two planks, and one on either side, were rising higher. A big-knuckled hand and a sleeved arm materialized next to the rug, chunky fingers seeking the fringe of the rug, gripping it, pulling it aside to reveal the four elevated planks moving upward. The farthest of the planks had come a full twelve inches off the floor and was being lifted sideways and quietly lowered. Then quickly, silently, the other three planks, one after the other, were being pushed high, balanced, juggled to the side and set down.

The bedroom floor now had a gaping, irregular, squarish hole in it, an opening five feet in length, four feet in width.

A form, a shape, outlined in the dark, began to emerge from below. A slender male figure, black clad, pulled itself up through the hole, pushed itself to its knees, then unfolded and stood erect. Moments later, another shadowy male figure, bulkier, emerged from the hole and stood up in the darkened bedroom.

Both figures, on tiptoe, closed in on the bed, stopped, looked down at the sleeping woman. One nodded to the other. Simultaneously, as if rehearsed, both reached into their jacket pockets. One drew out a handkerchief, the other a hypodermic syringe. One nodded to the other again. In a flash of motion, the handkerchief whipped across Billie Bradford's mouth, cutting into it. The same instant, the hollow needle of the syringe slid into the flesh of Billie's arm. The pressure, the stab of pain, made her start, body heaving as she tried to struggle awake. Her unseeing eyes fluttered open, stared, showed terror, lost focus, began to close, eyelids drooping, closed tight, as her head sank back into the pillow. The lips worked, then relaxed. The handkerchief was knotted tighter. The hypodermic, emptied of fluid, was withdrawn.

She lay limp, totally unconscious.

The blanket was yanked off her. The two figures bent low, their arms going under her shoulders and her legs. The four arms cradled her, with ease lifted her out of the bed. The four arms carried her, the four feet treading softly, as she was hurried toward the opening in the floor.

Carefully, carefully, she was lowered into the opening. Four new arms reached up for her, accepted the transfer of the slack body, hands and feet dangling, from the ones above. Carefully, carefully, the new arms curled around her, drew her downward until the body and green nightgown disappeared from sight.

The pair of figures in the bedroom waited. Then one went to its knees, stepped into the hole, and climbed down out of view. Seconds later, the remaining figure crouched, stepped into the hole, and was gone.

The bedroom was emptied of life.

For a minute only.

The top of a head was growing out of the floor opening. The outline of a full head emerged, a full head and a female shape, pushing herself to the floor alongside, pushing herself to her knees, rising to her feet, adjusting her green night-gown, standing still, trying to adjust her eyes to the darkness.

She was ready. She moved rapidly, gracefully, without wasted motion, with purpose. She lifted one of the loosened oak planks, brought it to the hole in the floor, and with great care fitted it into the opening as if she was filling in a jigsaw puzzle. She picked up the second oak plank and coaxed it into place in the floor, covering another section of the hole. Next, the third and fourth planks. The gaping hole was gone, the floor once more complete. Bending, she retrieved the oriental throw rug, flapped it out straight, and laid it down flat across the wooden floor.

She scanned the bedroom in the now familiar darkness. As far as she could see, everything was in place. Nothing amiss. In the doorway to the living room, she cocked her head toward the main double doors. Silence. The American Secret Service agent, at his monotonous post in the corridor, had not been disturbed.

Smiling to herself, she went barefooted to the bed. She studied it briefly, plumped down on the edge, swung herself on it, made herself comfortable under the crumpled blanket. Stretching herself at full length in the still warm bed, she brought the blanket to her chin, and nestled her head in the indentation in the pillow.

She peered at the illuminated travel clock.

2.26.

She put her hand out for the sleeping pill, and found it next to the glass of water. Her predecessor had not been in shape to take it. She realized she should not take it either.

Satisfied, she lay back, tried to make out the ceiling. She listened to her heart, thumping hard but steadily. She was anything but sleepy. The adrenalin still pumped through her veins, her nerve ends pulsated, her body throbbed with the excitement of danger. There was no denying that she was keyed up, and on edge, exactly as she had always been while waiting in the wings for the moment she must walk onstage. She supposed it was a good sign to feel this way, so up and alert. It usually promised a perfect performance.

But she must come down, she must relax. Sleep was necessary. Her mind rummaged through the attic of the recent past. Kiev. The evening Petrov first came backstage. Moscow. The day she was summoned to the KGB. The day she learned the true part she was to play. The day she knew she wanted Alex, and the afternoon he first entered her. And the delicious last time, too. Her mind left the realities of the past three years, vaulted high in slow motion into the future. The project over, herself a heroine of the Soviet Union, a princess among commoners, darling of the elite. Herself and Alex.

She was conscious of her head emptying, pictures of yesterday and tomorrow fading, her limbs easing. She yawned. Sleep was creeping over her. She welcomed it. She must be awake at five. The curtain would be going up.

She turned on her side.

Tomorrow. She must remember her role, her identity, her lines. She tried to remember. She could not remember a thing. But the nearness of sleep muffled panic. She would remember, she would remember. The curtain was going up. The play would begin.

Last thing remembered.

Good-bye, Vera Vavilova.

Hello, First Lady of the United States of America.

4

It was like climbing a steep and endless staircase, her coming out of sleep.

But Billie Bradford was awake in her head, her eyes still shut. Behind her forehead and the thin band of ache that lay there, her brain was a quagmire. Her mouth felt dry, with an aftertaste of bitterness.

Her thoughts waded through the quagmire, at last reaching a memory of last night. The banquet, the exhaustion, the drunkenness. That was it, the heavy drinking. She had a terrible hangover, and no wonder.

She kept her eyes shut, hoping that her brain would clear, that the headache would go away.

After a few minutes, lying very still, she felt the headache dull and begin to recede. Her brain freed itself from the quagmire, began to work. She was becoming alert. She recalled where she was, the day it was, where she was expected.

She was to be up at five o'clock in the morning, to depart Moscow for home.

She opened her eyes, as she turned her head on the pillow to read her bedside travel clock. The clock told her it was four. Thank God, she had not overslept. There was still an hour before the alarm would go off. She could steal another hour's sleep.

She was about to curl up, close her eyes for more rest, when she was struck by something odd. The clock on the table next to her bed. It was different, not her trusty little travel clock encased in red leather. It was a big timepiece set in a walnut frame. How strange. Had her maid Sarah been in and substituted another clock for her own? It made no sense. She shifted her head on the pillow, taking in her bedroom. At once with a jolt, she realized that this was not her bedroom in the Rossiya suite. This was a different bedroom, utterly different, from the flocked wallpaper to the modern furniture to the headboard posts on her bed.

She sat up confused, puzzled.

Yet, other things were familiar, the wedding band on her finger, the green nightgown, her own fluffy mules on the floor, her light wool turquoise robe across the chair.

But the room, definitely not her own.

What had happened? Had she been too drunk last night to be taken to her room, and been put to bed in Nora's room instead?

That was possible, unlikely but possible.

Then she heard two voices, male, indistinct, reaching her from the next room. Someone, two persons, were in the living room. Probably her Secret Service agents, Oliphant and Upchurch. She determined to find out. And find out why she was in this different room.

She came off the bed, pushed her feet into her slippers, stood up holding her robe, and got into it. After tying the belt of her robe, she sought the spare comb she always kept in the deep pocket. It was there. She went over to the dresser mirror, combed out her tangled hair, pulled it back, surveyed herself. The hangover had dissipated, and she looked and felt almost human.

The buzz of voices in the next room alerted her again. Curious about the voices, still puzzled by her surroundings, she left the bedroom and went into the living room.

She did not see the persons who belonged to the voices at first. She saw only another different room, one she had not seen before, different and far more spacious and modern than the room she had occupied in the Rossiya Hotel yesterday and the two days before. Then she saw them, the owners of the voices, off to her left and slightly behind her. She was startled, because neither was one of her Secret Service protectors.

They appeared to be Russians, one familiar, one completely unfamiliar. What were they doing here? What was she doing here? She stared at them, trying to bring an explanation to the mystery. Then, from his armchair, one man noticed her, and nodded to the other, who glanced back at her.

The familiar one was her Russian interpreter for the past three days, Alex Razin. The other one, a short barrel of a man with piercing small eyes, she had never seen before. Both were on their feet now.

'Ah, Mrs Bradford,' the burly one said. 'We were waiting for you to awaken.'

Billie ignored him and addressed herself to Razin. 'What is this? What's going on?' Her gesture encompassed the living room. 'How did I get here? I don't understand.'

Razin stepped forward. 'I'll try to explain,' he began apologetically.

The burly one raised a hand to silence him. 'I will answer your question, Mrs Bradford ... Razin, bring her some coffee.'

Obediently, Razin hastened through the dining area into the kitchen.

'Come here,' said the burly one as he went to the nearest of the two light beige sofas flanking the fireplace. Bewildered, she followed him. 'I suggest you be seated,' he said.

She meant to defy him, but sat down, drawing her robe together at the knees. The burly one remained standing over her.

He resumed speaking to her in a low, hoarse voice. 'Understandably, you are confused.'

'I'm more than that,' said Billie indignantly. 'This makes no –'

'No sense?' interrupted the burly one. 'It will, it will. Let me introduce myself. I am General Ivan Petrov. You've heard of me?'

'No.'

He fished into his pocket, withdrew his ID card and held it before her. His finger underlined three large Cyrillic initials beside his photograph. 'KGB,' he said.

She stared at the card without comprehension.

'I am the chairman of the KGB, our security police,' he said, returning the ID to his pocket. 'I shall answer your questions. You ask where you are? You are in a guest apartment of the Kremlin. You ask how you got here? We removed you from your hotel last night and brought you here.'

'You – you *what*?'

'Removed you, brought you here,' Petrov repeated patiently. 'It was necessary. You wonder why –'

'Wait a minute!' Billie flared. 'Are you telling me you – you *kidnapped* me?'

Petrov gave a little shrug. 'I suppose it could be called that.'

Billie was astounded, almost beyond words. 'You kidnapped me, abducted me, in my sleep? It's impossible. How could anyone –' She faltered. 'Unless – unless I was drugged. Did you drug me?'

'Of course,' replied Petrov in a matter-of-fact tone. 'At the banquet, with the champagne.'

'Are you crazy?' cried Billie, her voice rising. 'You must be crazy, completely mad! When my husband hears –'

'Mrs Bradford, your husband will not hear,' said Petrov with an infuriating smile. 'I promise you, he will not hear.'

She was speechless, utterly confounded.

Razin had returned with a tray of coffee, cream, sugar, a plate of black bread and jam. He placed the tray on the glass-topped low table in front of her, avoiding her eyes.

'Mr Razin,' she said to him, 'tell me this isn't true. It can't be true.'

He did not respond, continued to avoid her eyes as he withdrew to a position at the rear of Petrov.

Her eyes again held on Petrov. 'I'm dreaming,' she said. 'Tell me I am dreaming.'

'You are not dreaming,' said Petrov flatly. 'It is true.'

'I must be going crazy,' she said, her voice touched with hysteria. 'This makes no sense. You kidnapped me. No one kidnaps a – a First Lady, unless they are insane. You must be insane. Do you know what this can lead to – do you know the consequences? Do you? What are you after? Is it ransom? Or blackmail? Are you trying to blackmail the President? It won't work. This is unbelievable, total madness. Tell me – what are you after? Let's be done with it. I have to be on my plane in a few hours. We're leaving at eight this morning.'

'It is long past eight in the morning,' said Petrov calmly. 'It is four in the afternoon. Your plane left many hours ago.'

'It wouldn't leave. The plane wouldn't go without me.'

'You are quite correct, in one sense,' agreed Petrov. 'Air Force One would not depart without Mrs Bradford. Nor did it. I assure you – Mrs Bradford is on that plane.'

She stared at him, uncomprehending.

'I see you are still mystified,' Petrov continued. 'Let me be blunt, tell you exactly what is happening. Then you will understand, and I can go. I have a busy day. If you have more questions, after I finish speaking, Mr Razin has been assigned to answer them.' He paused. 'Mrs Bradford, your husband and our Premier are conferring at a Summit Meeting in London next week. Much will be at stake affecting world peace. It is vital to us to know what your husband has in mind, what his private plans are in dealing with us. To accomplish this, we hoped to place an undercover agent in the White House, someone who might be privy to or have access to your husband's thinking. This is not an uncommon practice, one often employed by your own CIA. We were fortunate in having anticipated the need for such an agent. Almost three years ago, even before you entered the White House, we began to plan for such an agent. By chance, we happened to find someone here in the Soviet Union who looked exactly like you –'

'Exactly like me? Impossible. Persons are like finger-prints, no two alike.'

'Not at all impossible,' said Petrov. 'Believe me, very possible. The young lady we came upon could not be told apart from you. Same face, body, and she spoke perfect English. There were a few discrepancies, which were resolved.

We spent three years patiently training her to be your double –'

'My double?' Billie was aghast. 'I've never heard anything so wild – so absurd – A double for a public figure?' She shook her head vigorously. 'It could never work. Such a thing has never happened –'

Petrov beckoned behind him. 'Razin, to improve our credibility, tell her. You were a history student. Convince her.'

Reluctantly, Razin came forward. 'I'm afraid you are – well, wrong, Mrs Bradford. This undertaking we are discussing is not anything new. It is as old as history. There are countless instances in the past where doubles, for a variety of reasons, have successfully enacted the parts of their leaders. Napoleon had a stand-in named Eugene Robeaud. Your President Roosevelt sometimes used a double. Certainly you have heard how Sir Bernard Montgomery, the British general, employed a double named Clifton James during the Second World War. It has happened before.'

'Yes, and it is happening now,' Petrov said to Billie.

'It can't work,' Billie insisted.

'It has and it will work,' said Petrov.

Billie was shaking her head again. 'I just don't believe this.' She stared at Petrov. 'And me, what about me? What are you going to do with me?'

'Not a thing, Mrs Bradford, nothing at all. Your life is not in danger. Do you think we are barbarians? You are safe. We will keep you incommunicado in this Kremlin apartment for approximately two weeks, while our agent – let us designate her the Second Lady – while she acquires the information we need. On the last day of the Summit, after we are victorious, we will return you, fly you to London, exchange you for our double, and you will go home with your husband. No one will ever know it happened.'

'Never know?' Billie exclaimed. 'Do you expect me to be quiet about this? I'll expose you. I'll tell my husband, everyone – I'll shout it from the rooftops –'

'Don't try, Mrs Bradford, don't for your own sake,' Petrov said. 'Would you expect your husband to believe you? Anyone to believe you, give credence to your babblings about such a mad and insane — as you have called it — enterprise? You, yourself, told us you can't believe it. If you can't, who will? If you persisted in your fanciful, paranoidal story, without a shred of evidence, you would embarrass your husband before the world. You would end up in — Razin, what's the place called —?'

'Menninger Clinic, sir.'

'Yes, in a hospital for the mentally unbalanced. No use, Mrs Bradford. When you are returned home, you will have to remain quiet, as if it never happened. We have no worry about being exposed. The very audacity of our scheme, the unbelievability of it, will keep us safe.'

Petrov retrieved his cigar case from the coffee table and shoved it into the inner pocket of his tight double-breasted jacket. 'Now I definitely must go,' he said to Billie. 'Mr Razin will see that you have every comfort. I hope you will keep yourself occupied. Eat, sleep, exercise, read. We have English books for you, your favourite authors. We have videotapes of American films for you to watch on television. You will find two radios. You can listen to the Voice of America or BBC. Duplicates of your bags and travelling wardrobe are in the bedroom. You will come to no harm if you accept your condition.' Petrov's face grew threatening. 'Try to escape, or get word to the outside, and you will be deprived of your comforts and suffer. For you own sake, adjust yourself to your temporary fate, to this brief vacation, and all will go well for you. If you require anything, within reason, Mr Razin will provide it. I, personally, will look in on you from time to time.'

He walked to the door.

Billie cried out after him, 'You'll never get away with it!'

Hand on the doorknob, Petrov favoured her with a brief smile. 'Never get away with it?' he repeated. 'We already have . . . Razin show her.'

He was gone.

Alex Razin came forward, tentatively sat on the edge of the sofa across from her.

Her bewildered eyes met Razin's. 'Is this really happening?' she asked with disbelief. 'Can it be true?'

Razin nodded unhappily. 'I am afraid it is true, Mrs Bradford.'

She frowned. 'Are — are you part of this? You seemed so nice yesterday, the day before.'

'I'm no less nice today,' he said seriously. 'As to being part of this, the answer is yes and no. I am against the plot. I found it outrageous. But this is strictly a KGB operation. I am not KGB. I was forced to participate with them, perhaps because I am half-American. My mother was American. I was raised in the United States. My father, Russian, brought me back here after my mother died, when I was fifteen.'

'Why didn't you return to America?'

He hesitated before replying. He stood up, walked over to a radio set on a table, turned it on to a music programme. Then he twisted a dial until the volume was much higher. He came back to the sofa and gave her a sheepish smile. 'Just a precaution,' he explained. 'Now — your question. Why didn't I return to America? I wanted to, and still do. That is nothing I'd like you to repeat. Although I went to Washington once, as a journalist. I was compromised in a spy case, even though I was innocent. I was banned from the United States.'

'I could get you back — speak to my husband — if you'd help me.'

'Help you? How? You are in the Kremlin, inside a fortress. You are under guard. It is too dangerous even to contemplate escape. Believe me, I'd like to help, but —'

'Not to escape,' she said. 'Just to let someone know, the American ambassador —'

Razin cut her off. 'He wouldn't believe me. But suppose he did, how would he find you? If he came here, he'd find nothing. By then you'd be far outside Moscow. As for myself, if it was learned I had informed, I'd wind up in front of a firing squad. I tell you, any move to free you would be futile.'

'You're right,' she said weakly. She paused. 'Will they really let me go in two weeks?'

'I think so.'

'They won't hurt me?'

'They'd have no reason to. It is to their own interests to see that you remain alive and well. They may need more information from you – some things the – the Second Lady – may not know. After the Summit you will be safely home.'

She was brooding, her mind on her situation, on the reality of someone impersonating her. 'It can't work,' she said, half to herself. She looked up. 'Don't you see? It simply can't work. The minute she steps out of the helicopter on the White House lawn, my husband will know – he will know the other one is not me – he knows the real me too well – the moment he sees her, he'll know she is an imposter.' She hesitated. 'The other – other man who was here –'

'General Petrov.'

'Yes, Petrov. When I said he'd never get away with it, he said, "We already have." Then he said to you, "Show her." What did he mean? Show me what?'

Razin nodded, left the sofa, went to his briefcase, pulled out a small reel of tape. After turning off the radio, he carried the reel to the videotape machine, which was tied into a closed-circuit television set. He inserted the tape into the machine. 'He wanted me to show you this,' Razin explained. 'We just recorded this event from American television which came to us via satellite.' He turned on the television set. 'Your arrival today at the White House.'

Billie fixed her gaze on the television screen. There was the presidential helicopter from Andrews Air Force Base hovering over the White House south lawn, settling slowly on its tarmac. There was the movable ramp being rolled into place. There was the helicopter door opening. There was – she – Billie Bradford, emerging, standing, waving.

Billie, viewing this, gave an audible gasp.

On the screen, she, herself, no question. Her own hair, facial features, body, clothes. She was descending. She was on the lawn. A shot of her husband moving to the foot of the stairs. Andrew. She was in his arms. They were embracing. He kissed her, took her arm. There was applause off scene, as he kissed her once more and led her toward the press, photographers, battery of microphones. She was speaking briefly. The International Women's Meeting in Moscow had been a success. She would be going to Los Angeles tomorrow to speak to the convention of the Women's Clubs of the United States and give her report on what had been achieved in Moscow. While she had found Moscow receptive, friendly, fascinating, nevertheless, it was *so* good to be home.

From the sofa, Billie stared at the television screen. She had heard her own voice, inflections, seen her gestures. All faultless. All from a Russian imposter. She watched Andrew leading her to the South Portico and into the Diplomatic Reception Room. Andrew taking her into their home as his own, as his wife.

You'll never get away with it!

We already have. . . .

Billie sat stunned.

Razin turned off the television set and confronted her sadly. 'You've seen what Petrov asked me to show you. No one knows she is not you, not even your husband. I'm afraid Petrov was right. He did get away with it. I'm sorry, Mrs Bradford.'

Arms crossed on her chest, fingers clutching her ribs, she began to rock on the sofa, as if in mourning. The disgusting KGB had been brilliant. The substitution, the substitute, perfect, beyond suspicion. The KGB was firmly inside the White House. Her own position was hopeless.

Yet, her mind reached for hope, found one loose strand to grasp.

Tomorrow she would be in Los Angeles. The day after she would make her speech. Following the speech, she would have a reunion with her father, with Clarence, her father of a lifetime. If her husband had proved too insensible and inattentive to realize that he was dealing with another woman, not his First Lady but a counterfeit Second Lady, if he could be fooled, her father would prove quite a different matter. No one play-acting as Billie could ever deceive her father. He would see at once that something was wrong, and he would break it wide open and uncover the KGB plot.

Then something else heartened Billie. Because it might not even get to her father. The hoax might be settled tonight. Tonight, when Andrew and the imposter went to bed. The imposter could not know that she must abstain from sex for at least four weeks. The imposter might make the wrong move, try to have sex, and instantly Andrew would become suspicious.

If that did not work, then the confrontation with her father would do it.

Dammit, there was hope.

With difficulty, she brought herself back to Razin and pretended a smile of concession. 'Okay,' she said, 'first round to – to your people. But mark my work, it's not over. For your Second Lady, it is only the beginning – of deep trouble.'

After dinner in the President's Dining Room of the White House, the three of them moved to the subdued Green Room to watch television.

Vera Vavilova had been thoroughly briefed on this room, as well as the other upstairs rooms and she knew that whenever the First Lady watched television she sat on the striped settee against the west wall and beneath the 1767 oil portrait of Benjamin Franklin. Vera was sitting there now. On either side of her, in the two Sheraton mahogany armchairs upholstered in green cloth, were seated Nora Judson and Guy Parker.

Since this was the first day home for the First Lady, after the gruelling visit to Moscow, it was understood there would be no work this evening. It would be a time for relaxation and early to bed, since tomorrow they would take off for Los Angeles.

Television, they had all agreed, was the most desirable sedative. Best of all, the rerun of an old motion picture. So they had tuned in *Casablanca*, and for the past hour absorbed themselves in the adventures of Humphrey Bogart and Ingrid Bergman. Vera was aware that Guy Parker had seen the film three times before, and Nora had already seen it twice. Vera also knew that Billie Bradford had seen it once. Vera had never seen it, but had to pretend that she had, that it was not new but somewhat familiar to her. To maintain that pretext, Vera had twice remarked, after particularly good scenes, 'Wasn't that great? Even better than the first time.'

But while outwardly devoting her attention to the movie, Vera was inwardly rerunning scenes of this first day in the White House.

She saw herself inside the day, throughout the day, and she was elated by what she saw. From the minutes after she had alighted from the helicopter, and received President Bradford's – Andrew's – warm embrace, her confidence had grown. In the eleven hours since her arrival, she had successfully passed every conceivable test.

Actually, the testing had begun earlier, from the instant that she had set foot inside Air Force One she had felt she would be under close scrutiny. Soon, she realized, she was under no scrutiny at all. Everyone expected Billie Bradford to be on the plane, and she *was* Billie Bradford. The stretch of time on the flight had presented no problems at all. The real Nora Judson, so close to the First Lady, provided no challenge to Vera. This was because the real Nora had been soundly asleep in her seat the entire distance from Moscow to Washington DC. Alex had once told her that they would drug Nora, as well as Billie, at the farewell banquet, and obviously they had done so. Nor had Guy Parker been a problem on the flight. He'd had no reservations about Vera's being Billie. Early in the flight he had approached her, inquiring if she felt like taping some more reminiscences. She had pleaded exhaustion, and the need for sleep, and Parker had been understanding. 'You were out on your feet last night,' Parker had said. 'Grab what shut-eye you can while you can.'

In her mind, the biggest obstacle to overcome would be immediate acceptance by her so-called husband. Waves of apprehension washed over her until the helicopter set down on the south lawn of the White House and the aircraft's door was opened. As she descended to the lawn, apprehension vanished. She suddenly felt poised, assured, belonging. When she went into the President's arms, she was Billie Bradford. After that, except for one instant, things had gone easily. In the White House – despite its familiarity to her from her rehearsals – there had been a suspended moment of awe and trepidation. She realized she had successfully penetrated the real White House, America's main house, and it had taken effort to subdue her emotions and appear perfectly calm and comfortable in her surroundings. But then the actress in her had again taken over. She was Billie Bradford, and she was home. What had helped her further was that she'd had little time with the President. He was busy, distracted, eager to get back to his heavy schedule. She had not seen him the rest of the morning, afternoon, or this evening. A few hours ago, he had telephoned from the Oval Office to apologize for not being able to dine with her. He and his advisers would be having sandwiches brought in while they discussed the impending London Summit and Boende.

In the President's upstairs bedroom, she had supervised Sarah's unpacking. She had selected the clothes she would want for Los Angeles tomorrow and the day after, and left Sarah to re-pack. She had been hostess at a late informal lunch in the Family Dining Room for three senator's wives. She had been well prepared for them, and there had not been a single hitch. She had given her anecdotal impressions of Moscow, and listened while the wives discussed woman's rights and gossiped about other wives. By mid-afternoon, Ladbury had reappeared with his assistant Miss Quarles for a final fitting of the new wardrobe she would wear at the Summit. Ladbury had fussed, praying everything was right, for he had booked plane passage to return to London that evening. Except for minor adjustments, everything had been right. The wardrobe would be waiting for her in London.

Guy Parker had brought in the first draft of the speech she would be delivering in Los Angeles. She had made several suggestions to liven it up, and Parker had willingly agreed to the rewriting. She had also been tempted to revise some of his inaccurate comments about the life of Russian women under Communism, but constantly had to remind herself that she was not a dedicated Soviet citizen named Vera Vavilova but a patriotic First Lady of the United States named Billie Bradford. Since Billie often invited Parker and Nora Judson to dinner when her husband was occupied, Vera had dutifully invited Parker and Nora Judson to dine with her later.

After that, she had taken a nap. Awakened by Sarah, she had changed into sweater and pants. Before dinner she had ordered herself a drink, being careful to remember it could not be her favourite vodka straight but had to be Billie's favourite and usual Scotch and soda.

At dinner, by then more comfortable with Nora and Parker, Vera had felt relaxed. Nora had turned the talk to last night's farewell banquet in Moscow. Nora had felt hung over, leaden, all this day, and thinking about it, she had begun to suspect that she and Billie had been drugged at the banquet. Vera had laughed at such a far-out notion. 'The Premier of the Soviet Union drugging the First Lady of the United States and her press secretary?' she had chortled. 'Why? Really, Nora, that's too much. Let's just face the truth. You and I got pie-eyed drunk, probably because their drinks are twice as strong as ours.'

As the meal had progressed, Parker had brought up the subject of Billie's family, each of whom he had interviewed a short time before and whom they would all be seeing the day after tomorrow. Vera had launched into a sentimental remembrance of her mother, long dead, and her father, who had gone on alone in the many years since being widowed. She realized that Parker, who had some of this material on tape for their book, was probing for more. Vera had judged quickly that Parker's interest was purely professional and not tinged with the slightest suspicion.

After dinner they had come into the Green Room to watch the rerun of *Casablanca* on television, and now they were still watching it as the movie entered into its climax. Conscious of her companions, Vera forced herself to show more absorption in the film's ending.

It was over, at last.

Parker stood up. 'That was great, except for the damn commercials.' He went to the set. 'Want to see what's on the other channels?' he asked Billie.

Vera stifled a yawn and glanced at her gold wristwatch. 'After ten. Long day. I think I've had it.'

'Me, too,' said Nora.

Parker snapped off the set. 'What time are we leaving for LA tomorrow?'

'Between four and five in the afternoon, I think,' said Vera.

'Five after five,' said Nora.

'I suppose you'll be too busy to work tomorrow,' Parker said to Billie.

'We'd better forget the book until we're through with LA,' said Vera. 'We can go over my speech when we're on the plane.' She came to her feet, stretching. 'Good night to both of you.'

In the President's bedroom, alone, Vera slowly undressed. She felt self-congratulatory. She had managed the entire day without stumbling once. She was in the lair of the enemy, on her own without allies, and she had deceived them all, every one of them. Then, a second thought: not quite without allies. During her intensive briefings before leaving, she had been told that there were two in the White House who were friends and who knew her real identity. If possible, she was not to contact them, or any of the other KGB agents planted in Washington DC. In fact, she was to attempt no contacts until she was in London for the Summit – except if there was an emergency and she desperately required help. In such an emergency, she had been given an outside telephone number to call in Washington. The person who received the call would, in turn, notify one of the KGB contacts inside the White House, who would use a special password to identify himself or herself for Vera.

Removing her panty hose, she felt confident there would

116

be no such emergency and no necessity to contact any Soviet agent.

She went into Billie's dressing room, took a fresh peach-coloured nightgown out of a drawer, and pulled it on. With fascination, she inspected the wardrobe containing a long row of Billie Bradford's dresses and pants. Billie's taste in clothes was more frivolous, more provocative, than her own had ever been, Vera could see, and as long as her role was that of Billie she could indulge herself.

Presently, getting into the double bed, she felt aglow with her triumph. Thanks to Alex. He, her mentor, would have been proud of his student. This moment she realized that she had hardly thought of Alex all day. Of course, he would have understood that – understood her concentration, stress, inner excitement. He might not have quite understood how she revelled in her success as an actress and enjoyed exercising her power. No matter who she actually was, she was for the moment the First Lady of this land. Fleetingly, she wondered how Alex, himself, was faring in Moscow. He was now the mentor of the deposed First Lady. Then Vera wondered how Billie was faring, poor thing. She dismissed the last thought at once. There could only be one Billie to be concerned about – Vera, herself.

She reached for the bedside table, dropped her sleeping pill in her mouth, downed it with a sip from the glass of water. She picked up the schedule Nora had typed for her of her activities tomorrow. Her schedule was purposely light, because of her departure for Los Angeles late in the afternoon.

About to flip the page, she saw the President enter the room. She cast the schedule aside as he bent over to brush her lips with a kiss. He removed his jacket, unknotted his tie, and absently inquired about her trip.

'Was it enjoyable?' he wanted to know. 'Did our Russian friends treat you well?'

'Too well. They wore me out with their hospitality and vodka.'

He continued undressing. 'Did you see Kirechenko?'

'Only from afar. Don't forget, it was all women's time. I had several nice chats with Mrs K.'

'Really? How was she?'

'She looks deceptively housewifeish. Forget it. She's one sharp cookie.'

'So I've heard.'

He had taken off his blue boxer shorts, and he was nude. She tried not to stare. This was supposed to be familiar to her. Still, she took in his physique. He wasn't Alex, but for a man his age he wasn't bad. She wondered what he would be like making love. She would never know. By the time he would be allowed to have sex with her, he would have his own wife back.

Her voice followed him to the bathroom, where he had left the door open as he brushed his teeth. She recounted some of the highlights of her Moscow visit.

'What about today?' he called out.

She ran through her activities of the morning and afternoon.

He reappeared in his striped pyjamas. 'I'm glad you took it easy,' he said. He turned out her lamp, and went around the bed to his side. 'And now I lose you again for two days.'

'California, here I come,' she said, pleased with the expression Alex had taught her.

'In case I forget tomorrow, say hello to your father for me.'

He turned off his lamp and crawled into bed beside her. He drew her into his arms. He kissed her. 'I've missed you, Billie,' he whispered.

'I've missed you more, darling,' she said.

He caressed her cheek, her neck, and slipped his hand down inside her nightgown, covering and lightly massaging one breast. To her surprise, she could feel her nipples hardening.

'You're getting me excited, darling,' she said.

'I guess I shouldn't,' he said, withdrawing his hand. 'How is it down there?'

'Better,' she said, carefully.

'Good. It'll go away. I can't wait to get in there again. Maybe we don't really have to wait.'

'Well – doctor's orders.'

'I suppose so. I'll be counting the days, the hours.'

'Me, too.'

He fell back into his pillow. 'Christ, I'm whipped.'

'Did you have to work so late?'

'It's pretty urgent stuff, the African business. Boende is getting to be a big issue. The Russians are pushing us hard. It's going to be a rough Summit.'

She wanted to question him further, but restrained herself. She remembered Petrov's instruction: don't press him until you are positive he'll talk.

He volunteered no more. She kept her silence.

Under the blanket, his fingers touched her hand. 'Good to have you back, Billie.'

'Good to be back, darling.'

He turned on his side, away from her, and was soon snoring softly.

Her eyes open in the dark, Vera emitted an involuntary sigh of relief. She had survived her first evening with him. He had swallowed her hook, line, and sinker. It meant good fishing ahead. More important, their need for sexual abstinence had just been confirmed. The KGB was remarkable.

She turned on her side, her back to him, smiling into the pillow. She was home – what was the American expression Alex had taught her? – yes, she was home free.

Except for one thing. The reunion with Billie's father the day after tomorrow. That was her last test. After that, it would be a breeze. After that, performing as she had today, she would truly be home free.

They were an hour and a half out from Los Angeles, heading toward the sun sinking in the west, when Vera Vavilova summoned Guy Parker to join her on the sofa of the presidential suite.

She had not planned to work, she said, but they had finished with her speech and she did not feel like napping. A woman has a right to change her mind, she said. Now she felt like working. Yes, on the book. It would make the flight pass more quickly. Besides, the book had to be done.

Pleased, Guy Parker went for his portable tape recorder, pushed in a fresh cassette, and activated the tape.

'The last full session we had,' he reminded her, 'was on our flight to Moscow. Let's pick up from there.'

'I'm ready,' Vera said.

'Early on, when we started talking, you told me a little about your first real job on the *Los Angeles Times*. You told me how, in your early courtship, you brought your husband to the beach to meet your father. On the plane to Moscow, we were on the subject of your courtship with Andrew Bradford. But before we finish with that, I'd like to finish with your reporting career on the *Los Angeles Times*. Let's get back to that.'

'Gladly. I think I've already told you about my first interview assignment for the *Times*. How I almost blew it.'

'And George Kilday saved your neck. Yes, I –'

'Not just Kilday,' she said, 'but Steve Woods, the rewrite man he had redo my story. You know all that?'

'Yes.' He hesitated. 'I think maybe there's something you should know. I heard it from Kilday himself a few days ago. I promised not to repeat it. But what the hell – you should know the truth. It's a small thing, anyway. No Steve Woods rewrote your story. Kilday himself did it, rewrote it.'

She seemed annoyed. 'He told you that?'

'He did.'

She shook her head and smiled. 'Then the poor man must be getting senile. Because when I learned Woods rewrote the story for Kilday, I actually went to Woods to thank him, and he admitted doing the job.'

'Steve Woods admitted to you he had rewritten your story?'

'That's right.'

Parker tried to hide his astonishment. 'I see,' he said.

But he did not see.

Less than a week ago, George Kilday had said to him in

The Madison café: *There was no Steve Woods to rewrite it. He didn't exist.*

Now, Billie Bradford had just insisted that she had gone to Steve Woods and told him how much she appreciated his help. Maybe she did not like to be contradicted. Maybe her memory had betrayed her. In either case, it was unlike her.

'Well, that's cleared up,' said Parker. 'Let's go on.'

Cheerfully, Billie answered his questions.

After forty-five minutes, she stopped. 'I think we've done enough for now,' she said. 'I'm tired. I'm going to try to get in a catnap before we land in LA.'

Parker clicked off his tape recorder. 'Thanks for all the choice stuff,' he said.

'Thanks to you, Guy. See you later.'

Parker walked out of the suite and slowly up the aisle toward his suite.

He was definitely shaken. It was the first time, to his knowledge, Billie had lied to him.

He wondered what was wrong with her.

It had been a curious day in Los Angeles, but now it was over and they were winging toward Washington DC.

Guy Parker tilted back in his seat, peered out the window into the black night, looked across the aisle at Nora, and observed that she and many of the others on the staff were trying to catch some sleep. He unlocked his seat belt, stretched against the rear of his seat, and nursed his Scotch and water thoughtfully.

After a while, Parker set his glass down next to the looseleaf folder that held his personal journal lying on the pullout table in front of him. Ever since he had agreed to work with Billie Bradford on her autobiography, he had been keeping this personal journal. He did not know what motivated him to do so. It was a burden, writing up each day's events at the end of every day before going to sleep. Faithfully, he recorded what he had done and seen and thought during the day, often supplementing his work notes for the book with added observations and comments for his own eyes only. It seemed a useless exercise, this journal – still it might jog his memory to recall certain things he had failed to include in his work notes.

Only fifteen minutes before, he had finished writing down a summary of the First Lady's activities, and his own, from early morning until evening departure time in Los Angeles. The events of the day had fascinated him, and he wanted to review them. He took up the looseleaf binder, opened it to the pages he had just filled, and began to reread what he had written:

A really curious day with Billie in her native Los Angeles, her old stamping grounds.

This morning, at nine, she held three separate interviews in her Century Plaza presidential suite with feature writers from the *Los Angeles Times*, *Los Angeles Examiner*, and United Press International, about her visit to Moscow, about her feelings upon returning home to Los Angeles (always worth some new quotes, no matter how often she returned to LA), and her thoughts on accompanying her husband to the London Summit with the Soviets next week. Nora, who is not always at her most pleasant in the morning, was full of good humour. She thought the interviews had gone extremely well. Billie had proved surprisingly knowledgeable about Russia, and had been very sharp on all matters.

I accompanied the First Lady and her party down to the Century Plaza's Los Angeles Ballroom for her nationally televised report on the findings of the International Women's Meeting in Moscow delivered to delegates attending the Women's Clubs of the United States Convention. The place was set up for a huge lunch affair and every chair was filled. Everyone was on hand automatically. The First Lady has glamour and drawing power, no question.

There was a minor confusion, minor embarrassment, at the head table when Billie was being seated. Nora had briefed Billie that she would be seated between the president of the Women's Clubs of the United States and Agnes Ingstrup, her oldest friend in Los Angeles. One of these two women was already in place when Billie settled into her chair. Billie immediately took her arm, greeting her with, 'Agnes, dear!' The woman looked dismayed, saying she was not Agnes Ingstrup, but the Women's Clubs' president. That moment, Nora brought another woman to the table, saying to Billie,

'Here's your old friend Agnes.' Then Billie profusely apologized to the lady president, explaining, 'Sorry I was confused. There's too much going on.'

I had been place-carded next to Nora. They started to serve lunch, when I heard Nora emit a small groan. I wondered what was the matter. Nora said, 'I goofed. I should have told them, but forgot. Billie won't eat oysters. Look, as a starter they're serving oysters. Well, *c'est la guerre*. She won't touch them.' I cast a covert glance at Billie. She was gulping the oysters down. Nora couldn't believe it. I said, 'Maybe she's just being polite.' Nora shook her head. 'She's never been polite about that before, but thank God she's being a good sport.'

After those two minor fumbles, by Billie and by Nora, everything went smoothly. The meal was finished, and Billie was introduced. She rose, and with perfect poise, she delivered her speech. It was a wonderful speech, if I must say so, especially the part she insisted upon putting in, the part where she castigated the nations that had not yet given women the vote, including India and Pakistan who allow women to vote only in regional elections, not national ones. The speech was interrupted with applause throughout, and given a standing ovation at the end. A big hit. Nora was excited enough to grab my hand spontaneously.

As Billie was being hustled out of the hotel, she was told that there was a last minute change in her schedule, personally approved an hour ago by the President. Billie had been scheduled to be driven directly to Malibu, to have a few hours with her family before getting ready to return to Washington. Now, the family reunion had been postponed for a short time while the First Lady was taken to Dodger Stadium to throw out the first ball in an intra-mural charity baseball game between the Los Angeles Dodgers and the California Angels. In the limousine, Billie looked bewildered and protested. 'It wasn't on my schedule,' she said. Nora tried to placate her. The owner of the Dodgers had phoned Tim Hibberd, the President's press secretary, last night, inviting Billie to the game, saying the presence of the First Lady would help the charity event. Hibberd could not get to the President until this morning. The President thought this would be an unexpected treat for Billie, since her father had been a baseball fan and had brought her up as one, too. 'You'll have to stay just two innings,' Nora promised. 'Then we can go on to Malibu.'

I could see Billie was not happy about the matter. At last she sighed and gave her consent. All the way to the ball park, she sat bemused and uncommunicative.

At the stadium, we were effusively welcomed by the owner of the Dodgers, and escorted to one of several reserved front-row boxes. The loudspeakers announced the First Lady's arrival, and she was noisily cheered and photographed as she entered the box.

The California Angels had taken the field when Billie was led to a seat. The Dodgers' owner handed her a ball. She accepted the ball gingerly, rubbing the seams. The owner helped her to her feet and pointed to the Angel catcher whose round glove was beckoning. Billie just stood there, as if she was uncertain what to do next. I could hear the Dodgers' owner saying to her, 'I hear you have a great arm, Mrs Bradford. Now you can show it. Just toss the ball into his mitt.' Billie stood there, as if she hadn't heard him. The owner then gestured throwing the ball to the catcher. Suddenly, Billie nodded enthusiastically, reared back and threw the ball wild. A roar went up, and in minutes the game was underway.

However, for one I know to be an avid baseball fan, Billie appeared somewhat uninterested in the first inning. In fact, she seemed to give most of her attention to the occupants of the adjoining box. An elderly gentleman was speaking to his granddaughter, and through much of the first inning Billie leaned toward them to listen. Once, she spoke to them. In the last half of the second inning, Billie perked up and followed the play on the field. At the end of the second inning, it was time to leave. Billie and the others left their seats and climbed up the aisle toward the exit.

I lingered behind. I wanted to know what she had said to the elderly man and little girl in the next box. He was honoured to have exchanged a few words with the First Lady, of course. 'What did she say to you?' I asked. He beamed as he repeated her first words. 'Your grand-daughter is very pretty. I overhead you explaining the game to her. Do you mind if I listen, too?' He told Billie she wouldn't learn much from him that she didn't already know. Then she said, 'But I want to learn how to explain baseball to children.' Odd episode.

We were followed up Pacific Coast Highway by a bus-load of television crews and still photographers. Billie was withdrawn and preoccupied throughout the long drive. The house her father Clarence Lane owned was a two-storey frame structure, forty-feet wide, on Carbon Beach. As I recalled from my recent visit to Billie's family, it had a fair-sized living room with a wall of books, stone fireplace, and a glass picture window looking out on a wooden terrace and the blue ocean.

As the two limousines, the police escort, and the photographers' bus parked, and we left the cars, the front door of the house opened, and Billie's younger sister Kit burst out and flew into Billie's arms. The photographers were spilling to the ground, shooting or setting up to shoot. Billie and Kit made an attractive contrasting pair. Kit was brown-haired, pug-nosed, shorter. They continued to hold each other and talk animatedly, to give the photographers a chance to catch them.

Soon we started into the house, trailed by two pool photographers. By the time I got inside, Billie had already greeted her father and drawn him off into a corner for some privacy. They chatted warmly, at some length, while Kit poured and served coffee and English biscuits.

Eventually, after Billie passed out some of her Russian presents, we settled down around the coffee table, with the photographers kept at a distance. The talk was mostly about Billie's trip and the Russians, about London, about movies seen and books read, when the doorbell rang. Kit popped up and admitted her husband and son. I recognized them at once. Norris Weinstein, dentist, Billie's brother-in-law, and fourteen-year-old Richie, her nephew. Billie kissed her brother-in-law, stooped to kiss her nephew, then gripped him by the shoulders and held him off to study him. 'Good heavens, Richie, I can't keep up with you,' Billie said. 'I mean, how much you've grown in the year since I last saw you.'

Kit stepped forward. 'What are you talking about, Sis? A year? You saw Richie less than a month ago. Have you forgotten?'

Billie seemed rattled.

'Not even a month ago,' Kit persisted. 'Don't you remember? I had him East to look at prep schools and we dropped in unannounced to see you at the White House?'

Billie slapped her hand to her head. 'Where's my mind,' she groaned. 'Forgive me, Richie. When you get to be my age the brain cells go fast.' She brought Richie to her for another kiss. 'Of course, I remember.'

Norris Weinstein started for the door. 'You have one more visitor waiting to see you,' he called back. 'Just hold on.' He rushed out to his car, and a half-minute later he was back carrying a black bundle of fur. I recognized the small black Scottish terrier that Billie once told me about. She had left it with the Weinsteins because it was arthritic and needed the California sun. The dog's name was Hamlet. Weinstein dropped the dog to the tile floor. Billie squealed with delight, quickly knelt and put her arms out for the dog. 'Come say hello, Hamlet,' she called out. The dog made no move toward her. It stood stock-still, sniffing, then stiffly backed away, barking at her angrily. Billie tried to coax the dog to her, but it continued to bark. Billie rose, embarrassed. 'I raised him from a puppy,' she said to no one in particular. 'He's always jumped into my arms and kissed me. What's wrong with him?' She wagged a finger at the dog. 'Naughty boy, Hamlet. If you're not nicer, I won't come see you again.' She laughed with the others, and changed the subject. We talked for a half-hour more and then we had to leave.

It makes no sense, but of all the things that happened today, the incident of the reluctant dog sticks most vividly in my mind. I kept thinking of *The Odyssey*. Odysseus, gone seven long years from Ithaca, returning in the guise of a beggar, and who instantly recognizes him and greets him? His old and faithful dog. I mean, no matter how long the separation, dogs never fail to recognize the return of their masters – or mistresses.

As we were at the Los Angeles International Airport, about to board our plane for Washington, I was briefly alone with Nora.

'Well, things went smoothly, didn't they?' I said.

'Couldn't have asked for better,' Nora said.

'Only one thing,' I said. 'Wasn't it strange the way Billie's old dog snarled at her?'

'What are you saying?'

'I'm saying it was strange.'

'Nonsense,' said Nora. 'The dog had indigestion, that's all.'

'Yeah, maybe that's all,' I said.

Because Billie had come in so late from Los Angeles, the President left instructions for her not to be awakened until ten o'clock in the morning. She needed the sleep.

He went downstairs for a brisk swim in the White House pool, after that showered, dressed, had breakfast, and reached the Oval Office at eight o'clock, in time for the second to last full-dress meeting on Boende before the Summit Conference with Premier Kirechenko in London.

They were gathering around the Buchanan desk as Andrew

Bradford, feeling refreshed, dropped into his high-backed swivel chair. He ticked off those on hand: military chief of staff Admiral Sam Ridley, secretary of state Edward Canning, head of African affairs Jack Tidwell, the President's personal secretary Dolores Martin, with her shorthand pad. Bradford realized that only presidential adviser Wayne Gibbs was missing. The President was about to buzz for him, to find out what was holding him up, when Gibbs came through the door carrying a stack of bound position papers.

'Sorry to be late,' Gibbs apologized. 'I had to wait for these updates.' He began passing them out. Giving the last one to the President, he added. 'Tell the First Lady I watched her speak from LA yesterday and she was absolutely sensational. Never better. Her best yet. It has to do both of you a lot of good.'

'With election time around the corner, we'll take anything we can get,' said the President wryly. 'Which brings us to Boende, not only a national security matter – but a re-election factor.'

He opened the folder Gibbs had delivered and thumbed·through it.

'Okay, Boende,' the President resumed. 'In the light of this latest information, let's review the situation on both sides. Inside Boende, the government position, the rebel position. Considering the Summit, our position, the Soviet position. Jack, you're the African expert. You kick it off.'

The President sat back, twirling a pencil between his fingers, prepared to listen.

Jack Tidwell, who had come to the administration after a professorship in African history at the University of Alabama, was more than ready. 'Our man in Boende, President Kibangu, has the manpower but not the weaponry required. In a straight confrontation, with no outside help on either side, our intelligence – military and CIA – evaluates that Kibangu's forces could hold off Nwapa's Communist People's Army and maintain the country for us. Nwapa has no chance unless he has firepower and advisers from Russia. With the most modern hardware and Russian technicians,

Nwapa could easily take over the country for the Soviets. The Soviets would then control Boende's uranium deposits 100 per cent, as well as possessing a base from which to infiltrate and topple most of the other nations in central Africa. However, if we intervened with supplies, matched the arms the Soviets are prepared to give the rebels, then Nwapa would not dare to move. We would remain dominant.'

'Yes, I guess that situation has been clear for months.' The President swivelled his chair. 'Well, Admiral, what say you? Do the Soviets have sufficient armaments in place?'

Chief of staff Admiral Ridley nodded. 'No doubt they have. Not exactly in place, but close enough. They have built up a huge stockpile of arms in Ethiopia, all ready to be airlifted to Boende overnight.' He pulled several stapled pages from his briefcase and handed them to the President. 'Here is an inventory, the best we could get up, of Soviet arms in Ethiopia, ticketed for Nwapa.' The admiral cleared his throat. 'You'll find it a formidable list, I'm afraid. SA-2 Guideline missiles, SA-3 Goa missiles, SA-6 Gainful missiles, Soviet Sagger and Snapper anti-tank missiles, TOW missiles, AKM assault rifles, rocket artillery, 122 mm siege rockets, T-54 tanks, MIG-21 jet fighters, Antonov 22 cargo planes, and so on. I repeat – formidable.'

President Bradford scratched his face, as he considered what he had heard. 'And our armament position in Boende. Any change?'

Admiral Ridley shook his head emphatically. 'No change. No improvement. Our armament to Kibangu amounts to a defence built largely of newsprint and publicity and camouflage. We've told the world – the Soviets really – of tremendous sales and shipments to Boende. But in fact, we've given Boende a minimum of supplies, next to nothing. If the Soviets knew this, their native rebels could overrun the country in less than a week.'

The President waved aloft the Soviet arms inventory that Admiral Ridley had handed him. 'If our supplies matched these, you think Kibangu could put down any rebellion?'

'No question,' said Admiral Ridley. 'Of course, sending

over our best weaponry would also require sending over our own military technicians in considerable number. In some quarters, it might be regarded as total US intervention – which might not be a bad idea, considering the stakes.'

'Wait a minute, let me do some intervening of my own,' said the President's adviser, Wayne Gibbs. 'From a strictly political point of view, Mr President, arming the Boende government, pouring in our military personnel, would be suicidal for you. I received the latest poll reports from New York last night. Right now, the public opinion polls show 55 per cent to 29 per cent – the rest undecided – against United States intervention of any sort in Africa. Right now, 46 per cent to 34 per cent against our intervention in Boende even if Russia supports Communist rebels anywhere in Africa. As to heavy shipments of arms to support an ally in Africa, the public votes 48 per cent to 31 per cent against it. The voice of the people is clear. To them it smacks too much of the beginnings of Vietnam. Any move, Mr President, against the public will, and you endanger your own popularity. It could lose you a close election next year.'

The President appeared to concur. 'So, politically, the stance we plan at the London Summit is good. We support, vigorously support, non-intervention of any sort by the Soviets or ourselves.'

'Perfect,' said Wayne Gibbs. 'Get the Soviets to agree, and you've won the Summit – and re-election to the presidency.'

Secretary of state Canning raised his hand. 'I'm inclined to agree that our only position must be hands off Africa. If I've wavered before, I have no more doubts. Absolutely, non-intervention. Behind this is the strong feeling I have that the American public does not give a damn about Africa. The public cannot identify with illiterate black natives. The public can't see how controlling a small black republic can affect their lives. Nor can the public be made to understand the importance of uranium. So getting a non-intervention treaty signed by the Soviets would be a victory for us militarily and politically.'

Admiral Ridley made his concession. 'I think the matter is

out of our hands. It is really in the hands of Kirechenko and his Communist gang. The Russians believe we've given our Kibangu tremendous amounts of arms, and they believe we are poised to send in more. Very well. If they still believe that next week in London, they won't signal an attack. They will sign our non-intervention pact. But if they should learn the truth – our military weakness in Boende, our inability to move if they move – if they learn any of that, they won't sign the Summit treaty. They'll simply airlift their arsenal into Boende and tuck the country in their pocket. If you are determined, Mr President, to keep hands off, then the future is not in our hands but in Kirechenko's hands.'

'Correct,' said the President. 'So, gentlemen, it all comes down to their not knowing the truth about our situation. It comes down to maintaining secrecy about our intentions.'

'It comes down to that,' agreed secretary of state Canning. 'Our secret weapon is secrecy itself. If the truth gets out, is leaked, we've lost – and the balance of power could be tipped against us in the next ten years.'

'Unless,' said Admiral Ridley, 'and let me repeat it – unless you are prepared, Mr President, to intervene actively at this time. That would stop them, repulse them.'

'And stop me and repulse me,' the President said. 'I'd lose the election. We'd have a new President, and you'd all have to look for new jobs.'

'That's right,' said Gibbs.

The President placed his palms on the desk and pushed himself erect, with an air of finality. 'Gentlemen, we have no choice but to act as we are acting. Should there be a change in intelligence information, we can reconsider. But as of now, we must proceed as planned. We must pretend our side is strong. We must continue to deceive their intelligence. We must keep our mouths shut about the truth. There's the winning formula. Okay, that's it. We'll have one last meeting after we arrive in London, confirm our posture, and march into the Summit. Until then, let's subscribe to an old World War II slogan – keep your lips zipped. Thank you, gentlemen, and good day.'

By early afternoon, in the President's Dining Room of the White House, Vera Vavilova and Nora Judson had finished their light work lunch.

Still drained by the travel and activity of the past week, by the demands of the role she was playing, Vera slowly spooned her coffee until it cooled, and tried to be attentive to her press secretary.

Nora had the remainder of the First Lady's afternoon schedule in her hand and was reading from it. As she came to each appointment, she digressed from what was on the typed sheet to give her own evaluation of the importance of the meeting and background on the persons or organizations involved.

To Vera, the rest of the afternoon offered no difficulties or suprises. Another sitting for a cover portrait to appear on *Ladies' Home Journal*. Receiving a contingent of foreign students being shown through the White House. A meeting with her hardcover and paperback publishers down from New York, with Guy Parker joining them. Tea with the wives of senior diplomats of the Chinese embassy. Time off to answer the most pressing mail. A short rest before dinner. The President and herself hosting an informal dinner for Democratic party fund-raisers and their mates, eight couples invited.

Easy enough.

Nora opened the rings on her plastic-covered looseleaf notebook, pulled out the day's schedule, and handed it to Vera. 'You'll want a copy,' she said. 'And this, too.' She picked up a sheaf of clippings and teletype sheets and gave them to the First Lady. 'The first notices and reviews on your television performance from Los Angeles yesterday. They'll make you feel very good, Billie. You were a smash hit, as we all told you.'

Vera fingered the clippings and restrained a smile. The notices stimulated private amusement. During her entire acting career, as a student in Moscow, as a professional in Kiev, she had never received a tenth the number of reviews that lay before her right now from a single brief appearance. America was a factory of newsprint and publicity.

'Oh, one more thing,' Nora was saying. 'Just completed your schedule for tomorrow. . . . Since tomorrow is your last full day here before you leave for the London Summit the next morning, I thought you'd like a copy to glance at so that you can organize your free time for packing and whatever. I purposely kept your schedule light for tomorrow because of your four o'clock appointment. I didn't think you'd want to be doing much before that.'

She passed over a copy of tomorrow's schedule.

Sipping her coffee, Vera held the schedule above her cup and ran her eyes down it. She came to four o'clock, stopped, read it: '4.00 . . . Lv 3.45 for 4.00 major appointment with Dr Murry Sadek, at his office. Out and return 5.00.'

The innocuous line struck her like a spear of lightning.

She sat in quiet shock, features rigid, as she continued to stare at the words 'major appointment'.

She struggled inside to regain and maintain her composure in front of Nora. The computer in her head whirred, retrieving information on her doctors that she had been taught by Alex Razin. She had been thoroughly briefed on their habits, personalities, and appearances. Dr Rex Cummings, the White House physician, of course. Brown, Appel, Stoleff, Sadek, specialists. Yes, Dr Murry Sadek, Gynaecologist. She remembered. But her intensive briefings had not prepared her about seeing him for what Nora characterized as a 'major appointment'. What was that? Ignorance of the facts unnerved her. Was this to be a routine three-month examination and check-up? Or was it to be something that was ongoing and special? The word 'major' obliterated 'routine' and indicated 'special'. If so, what was it about? She could not walk into such an appointment, blindly, unaware of what she was supposed to know about her own body.

'Dr Sadek,' said Vera. 'I'd forgot about that.'

Nora looked up, surprised.

'And "major",' Vera went on. 'Why "major appointment"? Were you being emphatic because it was a doctor's appointment?'

'Billie, I put it in because you told me to – remember? – just before you left for Moscow. You said "major" to me, so I said "major" to you on the schedule.'

'Yes, I guess I remember. Well, I'm sure I was over-reacting. Anyway, whatever it was, it can be put off until I return from London. I'm too pushed and pulled right now. Outside what's on your schedule, I have a million last-minute things to do. Why don't we just postpone –?'

Nora interrupted her. 'Billie, the doctor insisted on this appointment. You wanted it so much, too. You saw Dr Sadek before you went to Moscow, and he wanted to see you again as soon as possible after. You couldn't make it before Los Angeles. You agreed to see him before you left for London. So he juggled his other patients around to squeeze you in tomorrow. Of course, I don't know if it's actually that important. Only you know. But when I confirmed today, his nurse said to tell you the tests were ready.'

'The tests. Oh, yes.' Vera's voice was hollow. 'I don't know what I was thinking of. Of course – of course, it's important. I'd better see him, after all.'

The puzzlement left Nora's face. 'I'm glad,' she said with relief. 'It would have been difficult –'

'Never mind. . . . Now about these other appointments tomorrow.'

They discussed them briefly. They had just finished when Nora's purse, on the floor beside her, began emitting tiny squawks.

Nora jumped to her feet. 'My beeper. Excuse me, Billie, I better see who it is.'

She hastened to the telephone and dialled the central number of the Signal Corps office in the building. At last she came away from the phone. 'It's Tim Hibberd. He wants me to attend his press briefing. Quite an honour from that chauvinist. I guess, since your speech yesterday, he's decided to recognize the women's East Wing.' She snatched up her purse. 'Unless you have anything else, Billie?'

'Thanks, Nora. You go on.'

'You have a half-hour to yourself before I return with the foreign students.'

'I'll be waiting in the Blue Room.'

The moment that Nora had departed, and she was alone, Vera's poise evaporated. She could feel her agitation grow. She left the table, went into the hall, and walked thoughtfully to the Blue Room. It had gone so well up to now. True, the visit to Los Angeles had not been smooth. She had committed a series of small slips and blunders, yet, consummate actress that she was, she had overcome them. She was confident no one had noticed anything amiss. Certainly, Billie's father and Billie's sister had accepted her unquestioningly. Only the dog, the sonofabitching dog, had known, but thank heavens he was a dumb animal. No, despite Los Angeles, she had managed fine. And London, situated far away from those who knew Billie intimately, should offer no problems, provided ' – provided she could surmount this new and unexpected obstacle. Only Dr Murry Sadek stood between her and a successful mission. The unplanned 'major' visit to her gynaecologist could lead to her ruination.

She entered the Blue Room, still thinking, turned a Bellangé armchair towards the white Carrara marble mantel, and slumped into it, staring grimly into the fireplace. She felt distraught, but tried to contain her feelings. She must not panic. She must consider her precarious situation, and act with calmness. Obviously, her only protection existed in somehow being forewarned of the reason Dr Sadek wanted to see her tomorrow. Why was she going to him? Why did he consider it important? What was it all about?

She had a mere and frightening twenty-six hours to learn the reason she was going to Billie's – to her own – gynaecologist. Would General Petrov call this an emergency? He certainly would. She had been briefed not to contact KGB agents in the United States, except if she was confronted with an urgent problem that might lead to a disastrous misadventure. Well, this was an urgent problem if ever there was one. She must take the risk of making contact to seek help.

Her mind revived the procedure to be followed in case of trouble. It involved two telephone calls, both outgoing. She would give the switchboard operator one number. When a voice answered she would ask for Mr Smith. She would be told she had the wrong number. Hanging up, she would give the operator the same number, except for a different last digit. When another voice answered, she would again ask for Mr Smith, and again be told she had the wrong number. This done, it would be a signal to the KGB that she needed help. It would mean that the KGB would contact one of their undercover agents planted in the White House. This residence agent would soon approach her and say, 'It is served at Disneyland.' She would tell him as quietly as possible, as quickly and briefly as possible, her problem. Later, another safe KGB agent would respond with a solution to her problem.

Vera's wristwatch revealed that there was still twenty minutes before Nora appeared with her tour of foreign students.

Losing no time, Vera left her armchair and stepped over to the telephone on the table beneath the Gilbert Stuart portrait of President James Monroe. The portrait was unreal, Monroe's eyes gazing over her head, so she did not feel observed. She raised the receiver to her ear, gave the number, asked for Mr Smith, and was advised that she had the wrong number. Hanging up, she repeated the procedure. Once more, wrong number.

She dropped the receiver in the cradle, and felt relieved. Her call for help had been heard. Somewhere, in some way, someone in this mansion, an ally, a friend, was being contacted, and he in turn would contact her. She was no longer alone.

How and when she would be reached, and by whom, she did not know. She only knew that in a mysterious way it would happen.

She circled the Blue Room thoughtfully, trying to formulate a condensed means of informing the White House agent of her appointment with Dr Sadek and what she must know before she kept the appointment.

Waiting for Nora's tour group, Vera knew that she would continue to dwell on her problem. It was too unsettling. She needed some distraction. She decided to go to her bedroom and change from her frilly blouse into a sweater, and then return. She had moved to the door, when the telephone behind her rang. It sounded loud as a siren. She spun and ran for the phone.

'Madame Bradford?' A man's voice with a French accent. 'Yes?'

'I am your chef Maurice in the kitchen.'

She remembered the pudgy Frenchman, a product of Lyons, who supervised and headed the White House kitchen staff. She had met him twice, and had found him amiable.

'Hello, Maurice.'

'I am sorry to disturb you, Madame. But I thought you would like to go over the menu with me for the dinner tonight.'

She had no patience for this. 'Not necessary,' she said. 'I trust you with the menu. Prepare whatever you think is best.'

'Pardon, Madame, but I thought the main course might amuse you. It is served at Disneyland.'

At first she did not understand, almost missed it, and then realized he had flippantly spoken the key code sentence. *It is served at Disneyland.* The French chef!

She tightened her hold on the receiver, brought the mouthpiece closer. 'I don't know, Maurice. That may be too unusual a dish. Perhaps we should consult after all. Please bring your suggestions to me this minute. I'll be in the President's sitting room.'

She hung up, feeling weak. Stirring herself, she hastily headed for the bedroom.

After sending her maid Sarah off to inform Nora that she would be a few minutes late, Vera changed into a sweater. She was straightening the sweater, when several short knocks brought her to the door. She admitted the potbellied chef without a greeting, closed the door carefully, gestured him to a chair. She dragged a free chair so close to him that its edge touched his thigh.

She leaned towards him. 'The menu for tonight?' she said softly.

He placed a yellow pad in her lap. 'My suggestions,' he said in almost inaudible croak. 'I listen to whatever you have to say.'

'Trouble,' she whispered.

'Go ahead, Madame.'

'An unexpected doctor's appointment made a few weeks ago,' she whispered. 'I must see my gynaecologist, Dr Murry Sadek –'

'Dr Murry Sadek,' Maurice echoed.

'– at four o'clock tomorrow afternoon. I will leave the White House fifteen minutes earlier. An important appointment, I am told. Some tests were taken previously. I *must* know why I am seeing Dr Sadek, what I am to expect. Without knowing, I could make a serious mistake.'

The beefy face beside her remained immobile. 'It is understood.'

'I must know everything,' she said.

'I will report.'

'And one more thing,' whispered Vera. 'It is likely Dr Sadek will give me an internal examination. He has examined the First Lady's vagina inside many times before. He is familiar with it. To a gynaecologist this could be as individual and telltale as is a fingerprint to a detective. After the pelvic examination with the speculum, he will palpate, examine inside by feeling with his fingers, pressing ovaries, so forth. I do not know how much a gynaecologist can tell by this, what differences he may feel from one female's organ to another. But it is possible he may realize that the size or texture of my vagina is different from the First Lady's, and he could become suspicious. Of the two dangers, this may be the lesser one, but the danger exists nevertheless. It would be better if Dr Sadek himself did not examine me. You understand, Maurice?'

'Perfectly, Madame.' He rose with a grunt. 'All will be taken care of tonight. By morning you will be notified. Do not worry. Have a good evening and dinner tonight. *Bon appétit.*'

'Thank you, Maurice.'

He took his yellow pad from her lap, bowed, and waddled out of the bedroom.

With the problem off her mind, in other hands, capable hands, the rest of Vera's day went swiftly. At dinner, she was even gay.

Only later that night, when she and Andrew were in bed, was she reminded of the problem. She had got into bed first and was waiting for Andrew to join her, when she casually brought up the subject of the Summit.

'Are you primed for the Russians?' she had asked.

'Not yet,' he had said, buttoning his pyjamas. 'But we will be.'

'Is it going to be a serious confrontation?'

'I can't say.'

'Can there be a compromise?'

'I hope so.'

He was being maddeningly cryptic and vague. She decided not to pursue the matter further.

'Will it be all work and no play in London?'

'Probably. I'll catch you up on the whole thing, Billie, once I'm sure where we're going.'

Now they were in bed together, lights out. He kissed her lips. He kissed the nipples of her breasts. He fondled one breast.

'You must be nervous about tomorrow,' he said.

'A little.'

He tried to reassure her. 'I wouldn't worry about it. Dr Sadek's the best there is.'

'I'm trying not to worry. I think any woman gets a bit apprehensive before she sees her gynaecologist. It's automatic. I'm not terribly worried.' She made a try for more information. 'Are you, Andrew?'

'Of course not.' He fell back on his pillow. 'Let's just wait and see. Whatever happens, happens. Let's trust the doctor. Good night, beautiful.'

'Good night,' she said weakly.

What had he meant? *Whatever happens, happens.*

It was frustrating, frightening, not to know.

Before her apprehension intensified, a second thought soothed her.

She *would* know.

This moment, the KGB was finding out for her. Its agents never missed. When they sought something, they found it. They were all-knowing. They had set out to put her in the White House, and here she was in the White House, in the bed of the President of the United States. They had set out to tell her why she was seeing Dr Sadek. By morning, they would tell her.

She felt safer, and ready for sleep.

5

It was a modern, ten-storey office building on 16th Street, one of the newer buildings in Washington DC and occupied during the day by professional people, attorneys, accountants, physicians. At this hour, midnight, the place was darkened and devoid of humanity, except for the illuminated lobby where the uniformed private guard perched on a stool at a tall narrow table set against a marble pillar near the glass entrance doors.

Two janitors in overalls, one moustached, middle-aged, husky, carrying a heavy-duty vacuum cleaner, the other clean-shaven, young, slender, carrying a wooden box of supplies, opened the doors and trudged into the lobby towards the check-in table.

The guard glanced from one to the other. 'Don't think I've seen you before. You new here?'

'Yup,' said the younger of the pair. 'First time. Kleen-up Janitorial Service assigned us to do extra work on some suites on the fourth floor. Last stop for tonight.'

'Funny,' said the guard. 'The building manager didn't give me no notice. Guess she forgot. Got a business card?'

The older janitor fumbled about inside a pocket of his overalls, at last pulled out a bent and soiled business card, passing it over to the guard.

As the guard studied the card, the younger janitor wandered off a few yards, whistling, then came back towards the table. The guard put the card down in front of him and reached for his telephone. 'Let me give your outfit a call, just to confirm –'

'You'll get the answering service at this hour,' the older janitor said.

'I'll just check anyway.'

As the guard's fingers touched the receiver, he suddenly jerked straight on his stool and winced.

The younger janitor had a snub-nosed black revolver jammed into the guard's back. 'Okay, now,' said the younger janitor in a hard, low voice. 'Do what we tell you and you won't get hurt. First, let's relieve you of that extra weight.' He reached around, tugged the police special from the guard's holster, checked the safety catch, and handed the gun to his companion, who pocketed it. 'Okay. Don't be a hero. Get off that stool easy like, and walk real natural to the first elevator. We'll be right behind you.'

The white-faced guard stepped off the stool and stiffly started for the first of a row of elevators, its doors open. The older janitor trotted ahead, and entered the elevator with his cumbersome vacuum and the box of cleaning supplies. The younger one prodded the guard. 'In you go.'

The older janitor punched the eighth-floor button. The doors closed and the elevator glided upward.

On the eighth floor, they emerged into the dim empty corridor. The younger janitor prodded the guard with his weapon again. 'To your right, to the ladies' room.'

Going into the lavatory, the older janitor set his equipment down inside the door and turned on the lights. He dug into the covered supply box, came up with two pieces of rope and a roll of wide tape. As if experienced at this, the two janitors proceeded efficiently, quickly. They yanked the unresisting guard's arms behind him, bound his wrists tightly. To silence the guard's protests, they slapped tape across his mouth. The older one pulled him into a booth, pushed him down on the toilet seat, while the younger one knelt and tied his ankles together.

Then the two janitors backed out of the booth. The older one said, 'Have a good night, mister. Some lady is sure going to be surprised in the morning when she comes in here to pee.'

Shutting the door to the booth, they picked up their equipment, turned off the lights, went into the corridor, and made for the elevator.

'Smooth enough, Ilf,' said the older janitor.

'You're good to have on a job, Grishin,' said the younger janitor.

They rode the elevator down to the fourth floor, came into the corridor, ambled around the first corner, and stood before the reception door to the suite. A small wooden plaque on the door read:

MURRY SADEK, MD
RUTH DARLY, MD
OBSTETRICS
GYNAECOLOGY

The hefty, moustached one, Grishin, bent, and picked the doorknob lock in fifteen seconds.

Entering the dark reception room, they abandoned their equipment, ignored the light switches, and found their flashlights.

'Pretty fancy here,' said Ilf.

'The First Lady wouldn't go to a dump,' said Grishin.

Beaming their flashlights low, they explored the suite. Waiting room. Receptionist's office and files. Dr Sadek's brightly decorated office. An examination room. Another. A laboratory. A bathroom. A third and fourth examination room. Dr Darly's office.

'Okay,' said Grishin. 'The files.'

Their flashlights led them back to the green files. In these cabinets were manila folders, each tabbed and labelled with a patient's name. While Ilf held both flashlights pointing downward on the second file drawer, Grishin searched and located the tab labelled BRADFORD, BILLIE L.

'Got it,' said Grishin with satisfaction. 'Let's have a look.'

He walked to the receptionist's desk, sat in the armless swivel chair. Ilf had set the flashlights down to hunt for something in his pockets.

'Dammit, hold up those flashlights so I can see,' Grishin ordered. 'You can find your Minox later.'

Ilf quickly snatched up the flashlights and illuminated the Bradford folder, as Grishin opened it.

There were about a half-dozen sheets of paper. Grishin scanned the first sheet, turned to the second and studied it. 'Just dates and notations on examinations from the time she started seeing Sadek two-and-a-half years ago.' Grishin frowned. 'All straight routine visits. Nothing unusual, nothing different, no emergencies far as I can make out.'

'Maybe the last page, her last visit, will tell us what's going on,' said Ilf.

'Yeah. But first let me finish with her other visits to see if there's ever —' He paused. 'Vaginal infection, last December —' He hesitated. 'No good. Cleared up three weeks later.' He flipped more pages. 'Nothing. Nothing. And here's the last entry, made two weeks ago — this should —' He stopped cold, was silent a moment, then muttered, 'What the hell is this?'

He thrust the page at the flashlights for Ilf to read.

'It's shorthand,' said Ilf.

'None I ever saw.'

'I guess it's the doctor's own,' said Ilf. 'Lots of people make up their own — wait a minute, there's a note on the side in red pencil. It says, "To be transcribed." '

Grishin brought the page before him. 'Why didn't that goddam nurse transcribe it, type it so we could read it? The rest are all typed.'

'It was too recent. Guess she didn't have time.'

'Well, it makes no sense in his crazy shorthand,' said Grishin. 'I can't make heads or tails of it. We're cooked.'

'Hold on, Grishin. I have another thought. I know someone who could make heads or tails of it. His nurse. She types it up, so she must be able to read it.'

'Meaning what?'

'Meaning we pay her a late-night social call. Make her translate what it says for us. If she refuses, we shove her around a little, until she cooperates.'

Grishin stared at his partner, and slowly shook his head.

'Ilfy boy, where were you when they passed out brains? How stupid can you get? We beat up Dr Sadek's nurse until she tells us what was going on at Mrs Bradford's last visit? That's hardly a covert operation. The nurse'll scream bloody murder to the police, to the White House, tell them about two thugs trying to find out about the First Lady. Well, I don't think the new First Lady wants that much attention. I know Petrov doesn't.'

'You're right,' admitted Ilf. 'Forget it.'

Grishin put the medical reports back in the file. 'We can't decipher the bastard's home-made shorthand, and that's that.' He handed Ilf the file. 'Put this back where it came from, and wipe off the fingerprints. Leave me a flashlight.'

As Ilf went off with the folder, Grishin felt around the desk, finally opened the middle drawer and found the receptionist's appointment book. He checked the appointments for the next day. Sure enough, Mrs Billie Bradford was written in for four o'clock. He dropped the appointment book back in the drawer and closed it.

He called into the darkness, 'Ilf?'

'I'm here with the files.'

'We struck out on step one. We better make it on step two. Bring me six other women's files.'

'All right.'

A few minutes later they were both poring over the files of six women who had seen Dr Sadek in the past year. They scanned the most recent reports in each one, discarding three. Grishin was studying the last entry in the fourth file when he looked up with a grin. 'Pay dirt.' He slid the white telephone toward him. 'Here we go.'

He punched out Dr Sadek's home telephone number. The physician's message service picked up.

'This is Mr Joe MacGill. I'm calling Dr Murry Sadek for my wife, for Grace MacGill. She's Dr Sadek's regular patient. She's pretty sick right now. I have to speak to the doctor.'

'Are you sure it's not something that can wait until morning?'

'Lady, I got a sick woman on my hands. She's in great pain. She needs help. This is an emergency.'

'Very well. Let me see if I can get the doctor. Can you give me the number you're calling from?'

'Uh – no, no I can't. Our home phone is on the blink. I'm in a phone booth. The number isn't legible.'

'This'll take a little working. Let me see what I can do. Please hold on.'

Grishin winked at Ilf and held on. There were static sounds on the phone. A sleepy voice broke in.

'Dr Sadek here. Mr MacGill?'

'Yes, sir. Calling for my wife, Grace MacGill. She's been a patient of yours for –'

'I remember Mrs MacGill, of course. Do you want to tell me what's wrong?'

'Well, she has terrible pains in the pelvic area, and cramps below the stomach. She says it feels just like last year when you put her in surgery – she says –' With Grace MacGill's medical chart in front of him, Grishin selectively chose, and purposely mispronounced, medical terms describing Mrs MacGill's condition.

Dr Sadek clucked. 'Yes,' he said, 'I think it best I look in on her tonight. You keep her resting, and tell her I'll be right over. Can you give me your address?'

Grishin read the address into the phone.

'I'll be there in three-quarters of an hour,' said Dr Sadek and hung up.

Grishin put his receiver in the cradle, offered Ilf a victorious smile in the subdued glow thrown by their flashlights, picked up the receiver once more. He punched out a number with familiarity.

The phone rang once and was answered by a male voice.

'G and I checking in,' said Grishin. 'Step two operative.'

'When?'

'Immediately. He's dressing to make the house call. You have the address he is leaving from. Here is the address he is going to.' Grishin read off the address. 'He expects to be there in three-quarters of an hour. Will you have time to be in place?'

'We will be in place.'

'Good luck.' Grishin ended the call and stood up. 'Ilf, check out this area to see that everything's in order. I'll get our cleaning equipment. Meet you at the door.'

A minute later, Ilf joined Grishin at the reception room door.

'Well, we got half of what the First Lady wants,' said Grishin. 'For the other half – hell, she's an actress, isn't she? Let's go.'

Upstairs, in the Green Room of the White House, at mid-afternoon, Vera Vavilova sat on the edge of the hard sofa pretending to be attentive to her press secretary while keeping one eye on the clock. As Nora rattled on about the first and second days of Billie's London schedule, Vera worried about the time. In an hour and twenty minutes, she would be on her way to Dr Sadek, and she still didn't know a damn thing. The passing minutes ticked loudly on the old clock, drawing her appointment with her gynaecologist closer and closer, and she knew no more about the appointment than she had known yesterday. She wondered when and how the KGB would contact her, and what the agent would have to tell her.

With each movement of the long hand on the clock, her confidence eroded slightly. But she continued to cling to her faith in the KGB just as her Russian mother retained (even in these enlightened times) her belief in God.

'So that takes care of the second day in London,' she heard Nora say. 'I don't think they're crowding you too much.'

'No. It sounds fine. That second evening. Do you mind going over that again?'

'As I said, the first evening is rest, adjustment to the time change. Which means the social festivities begin the second evening. Prime Minister Dudley Heaton and his wife Penelope Heaton are throwing the big formal reception and dinner for you and the President – and for the Kirechenkos, of course.'

'Where?'

'The Banqueting House in Whitehall.'

'I've never been there.'

'It's wonderful, Billie. A legacy from Henry VIII, who built an earlier banqueting hall on the site.'

'I can't wait to –'

The telephone rang, and Vera's heart leaped. That must be Maurice, she thought, Maurice the saviour chef. Nora started to rise to get the phone, but Vera was already on her feet. 'I'll get it, Nora,' she said. 'I've been expecting a personal call.'

She caught the phone at the fourth ring. 'Hello.'

'Is this Mrs Bradford?' The voice was high-pitched, with a touch of lisp and an artificial British lilt. She wasn't sure if it was the voice of a man or woman.

'Yes.'

'Fred Willis,' the voice said. 'Protocol.' Male, sort of. She saw him now and then, and should recognize that affected voice, but never did. He was going on. 'I must meet with you about the state trip to London.'

She sagged with disappointment. She had expected *the* call, with time running out, not this silly nonsense. 'Sorry, I'm tied up,' she said, more sharply than she had intended. 'We'll have to make it some other time.'

'Mrs Bradford, I must see you *at once*,' Willis said shrilly, his voice an octave higher and tinged with hysteria.

'I have to change clothes. I'm –'

'*Please*, Mrs Bradford,' he implored her. 'I'm downstairs.'

There was something about his tone that made her reconsider. 'Well, all right, but just for a minute.'

She put down the phone, angry at herself for bothering to see him.

Nora was already throwing together her papers and taking her briefcase. 'I gather you're having a visitor?'

'Fred Willis. I was afraid he'd come apart if I didn't see him.'

'That creep,' said Nora. 'But I guess he knows his job. I'll go now. Don't forget your doctor's appointment.'

'I won't forget.'

Vera watched her leave. When the door closed, she looked at the time once more and then at the dumb phone. What had happened to her informant? So far, the KGB had not let her down. In an hour she would be in Dr Sadek's office, uninformed and helpless. This was impossible.

There was a brisk rapping on the door.

'Come in, come in.'

Fred Willis bounced into the room. She was always taken aback by him. So ridiculous. Nora must be right. He was probably good at his job. He was a small, immaculate man. Hyperthyroid eyes, pointed nose, weak chin and mouth. He resembled an over-aged juvenile lead, and was attired like an Eton old boy.

He gave her a half-bow. 'I'm glad you could give me the time, Mrs Bradford.'

'Not much of it, I'm afraid.' She lowered herself into a chair and waited.

'I would not have troubled you unless it were important.' To her surprise, Willis was pulling a chair across the room and setting it up flush to her own.

He sat down, leaned into her, dropping his voice to a squeak of a whisper. 'It is served at Disneyland.'

She went blank for a split second until it had penetrated. 'Disneyland?'

'Correct.'

She half twisted in her chair to view him better. 'You?' she whispered. 'I must say, the thought entered my mind when you phoned, the urgency to see me, but I put it right out.' Fred Willis was the last one she would have cast in this role. How clever of the KGB, how deceptive. And how daring to have penetrated the Department of State and White House at his level. 'I didn't expect it to be you,' she added. 'But thank heaven you're here in time.' She tried to read his face. 'I'm listening.'

He spoke in a thin undertone. 'Your requests. The first,

148

the purpose of your visit to the specialist. An effort was made to learn, but the information was not available, simply not available.'

She recoiled. 'Oh, no. That's terrible. There must be something?'

Willis shook his head. 'Not a thing could be learned. However, this is not as serious as it sounds. Because we have been successful with your second request, which affects the first one. Fortunately, at four o'clock, you will not be meeting with Dr Murry Sadek.'

'I won't?'

'He been replaced by his associate, Dr Ruth Darly. Last night, driving to an emergency house call, Dr Sadek was involved in a serious automobile accident. His vehicle was hit by a speeding car that came out of a side street – the two occupants of the other car escaped – they were driving a stolen car, so they could not be traced. Dr Sadek was unconscious when the ambulance arrived. He was rushed to a hospital. He suffered a severe concussion, two fractured limbs, and other injuries. I am told he will survive, but he may be hospitalized for many months and may not work again. At any rate, his associate, Dr Ruth Darly, is taking over a few of his patients. All his appointments for today have been cancelled, all except your own.'

'Dammit.'

'Considering who you are, considering the fact that you are leaving the country, Dr Darly cancelled her own four o'clock patient to accommodate you.'

'Double dammit. But yes, much better than seeing Sadek.'

'Have you ever been examined by Dr Darly?'

Vera thought back on her medical briefings. 'No,' she said.

'Then you need have no fear,' said Willis.

'But I still won't know why I'm there.'

'With Dr Sadek it might have been difficult, awkward. With Dr Darly it should be easier. She doesn't know your case, except from Sadek's notes. She doesn't know your body at all.' Willis withdrew his ferret face, which had been close to her ear. He rose, smiled at her. 'Besides, Mrs Bradford, you are resourceful, as you have already proved, a divine actress. I venture to say you will manage nicely.'

Starting for the door, Willis called back loudly, 'We will conclude this briefing en route to London. By then I will know whether the Queen will be returning from Bermuda while you are in London. Good day, Mrs Bradford, a good, good day.'

At five minutes after four o'clock in the afternoon, Vera Vavilova, wearing little make-up and no jewellery, dressed in a simple blouse and skirt, sat quietly in the armchair opposite Dr Ruth Darly, who was at her desk. The folder with the tab imprinted BRADFORD, BILLIE L. lay before the gynaecologist unopened.

Upon leaving her Secret Service men at the door, and entering the suite, Vera had been cautious. Presumably, she was acquainted with Dr Darly, had been introduced to her long ago by Dr Sadek, had run into her several times afterwards, and now she had not wanted to greet the wrong woman. Luckily, a young nurse, treating her with great deference, had led her straight to Dr Darly's office.

Dr Darly welcomed her warmly, taking both of Vera's hands. She proved to be a kindly middle-aged woman, dumpy, stringy brown hair, apple cheeks, light down on her upper lip, pudgy hands, heavy legs, almost lost inside an overlong white jacket.

'Nice to see you again, Mrs Bradford,' she had said 'though I never thought we would meet professionally.'

'I was horrified to hear about Dr Sadek. The poor man —'

They had talked about Dr Sadek for several minutes, and they were talking about him now.

'Well, we can only pray he will get better soon,' Dr Darly concluded, rolling her swivel chair closer to her desk. She opened the folder, considered the reports, turning the pages until she got to the last one. 'Not transcribed yet,' she muttered, half to herself. 'Still in his shorthand. Fortunately, I'm the only one in the office, besides his nurse, who can make out Dr Sadek's innovative writing. Now, let's see what we have here.' She looked up. 'Have you been to the bathroom yet, my dear?'

'No.'

'Please go, while I read through this. Just across the hall. Leave the specimen bottle of urine in the lab.'

Vera left the office, went to the bathroom, and in a few minutes she was across from Dr Darly once more.

'Well, I think it's clear to me,' said Dr Darly. 'As you know, we have two matters to resolve.'

'Yes,' said Vera nervously.

'How have you been feeling since your last visit? I know you've been travelling a good deal. Have you been better?'

'Much.'

'All right.' Dr Darly brought herself to her feet. 'Before we get into this, let's have a look at you. Follow me, please.'

Vera followed her to the nearest examination room. 'You know what to do,' said Dr Darly. 'Remove your clothing. The hangers are over there. The gown is on the table. The sheeting next to it. Then get on the table. I'll be right back.'

Dr Darly shut Vera into the small room. Quickly, Vera began to undress, desperately wondering what the gynaecologist would be looking for. When all of her clothes were off, and she stood nude, she took the gown and pulled it on. The back was open and the gown came only to her knees. She found the piece of sheeting, larger than a bath towel, stepped up to the table, and sat on the end of it. She threw the sheeting across her lap. It covered her down to her calves. Sitting there, trying to make herself comfortable, she saw the door open and a young brunette nurse appeared. 'I see you're all prepared,' she said. 'Let me take your blood pressure.'

When she was done, she put aside the equipment. 'The doctor will be here in a moment,' she said. That instant, Dr Darly bustled into the examination room.

'Here we go,' she said, as Vera lay down on her back. 'Let's get you down a little bit lower.' She helped Vera squirm down further on the table. Vera lifted her knees, spread her legs apart, and Dr Darly helped her place her feet in the metal stirrups on either side of the table.

While Dr Darly adjusted the flexible light, she inquired, 'How's the bleeding, Mrs Bradford? Are you still bleeding?'

Bleeding! So that was it.

She had her first clue. 'Uh, I had been bleeding, yes, spotting. Irregularly, less and less. Five days ago it stopped entirely.'

Dr Darly nodded. 'Very good. It was what Dr Sadek hoped for.'

Dr Darly had a transparent disposable glove on her right hand. She accepted the warm plastic speculum from the nurse. She raised the piece of sheeting, peered between Vera's legs, and Vera knew that she was examining her outer genital area, labia majora, labia minora, for inflammation or sores.

Then Vera felt her labia being separated, felt the speculum being inserted into her vagina, felt the blades opening to spread her vaginal walls. She heard Dr Darly intone, either for herself or for the nurse, 'Cervix. Smooth, firm, pink. We took a cell sample last visit.'

On her back, Vera had been trying to develop the one clue she had to her condition. She had been bleeding – or Billie had – and now she was not bleeding. What did that mean?

She became conscious of the speculum deep inside her. Somehow, when she had undergone similar pelvic examinations in Moscow and Kiev, she had not given them a thought. She was a woman. Nature had given her, and every female on earth, a complex procreative system. Examination, from time to time, was obligatory and sensible. But this moment, the plastic instrument being removed from her vagina, seemed unnatural and dangerous. She was an alien, in an alien place, among *enemies*, posing as someone she was not, posing as the most important lady in the land. Could her vagina expose her, reveal that she was an imposter?

She shuddered.

Dr Darly said, 'Sorry, Mrs Bradford.'

Vera realized that the speculum was out and the gynaecologist's fingers were moving about, pressing her ovaries and internal organs – palpating was the American word – exploring for abnormalities.

She saw Dr Darly's smiling face rising. 'All done,' she said. 'Nothing to worry about.' She pulled off the glove and threw it in the covered basket by the sink. 'You can get dressed and then come to my office. We'll have a little talk.'

Relieved, Vera sat up, as Dr Darly left the examination room. She waited for the nurse to follow the doctor. Once she was alone, Vera discarded the sheet and gown and hastily began to dress. At the sink, she used the foot pedal to run the water and wash her hands. After drying them with a paper towel, she sat up at the vanity table, combed her hair back in place, and applied fresh lipstick.

She started for the gynaecologist's office, trying to keep herself alert, hoping she could carry off the act.

Dr Darly was behind her desk, on the phone. As Vera sat down, Dr Darly finished her call and swivelled toward her.

'Mrs Bradford, there's bad news and good news,' she said. She looked grave. 'Let's get the bad part over with. We had the report from the lab on your pregnancy test after you'd left for Moscow. Since you were here for only a day before you were off again, you obviously had no time to see Dr Sadek, and he didn't want to relay the report by telephone. Despite some sign in the first test, as often happens, that you might be pregnant, the latest test makes it clear you are not pregnant. I am sorry about that.'

Vera, who had been hanging on every word almost breathless, felt a wave of relief in her first knowledge of what the main part of this visit was all about. But she realized instantly that, as Billie Bradford, she must react in an expected way. Billie Bradford wanted to be pregnant and she was not. On the stage, in Kiev, Vera had always been admired for her histrionic ability to evoke tears at the director's command. This was how she must respond now. Disappointment, sadness, but not overdone. Immediately, her eyes moistened. She averted her face, fumbled in her purse, withdrew a dainty handkerchief, dabbed at her eyes.

Dr Darly was beside her, arm around her, trying to comfort her. 'I do know how you feel,' the doctor said sympathetically. 'But believe me, Mrs Bradford, it is a temporary setback. You and the President want a child, and I promise you that you will have one or as many as you wish. The main thing, I can assure you, is that you are healthy, fully able to be impregnated and bear a child, and you shall.'

'Thank you,' said Vera tremulously. 'Forgive me. I – I just want it so much.'

'And, I repeat, you shall have it.' Dr Darly was at her desk again, sitting. 'Now for the good news. The bleeding condition.' She reached for some test reports atop papers at the side of her desk. 'It was not serious, not at all. Excessive and prolonged bleeding – it was due, in your case, to that small polyp that Dr Sadek cauterized plus an emotional disturbance resulting from your own worry about it. I don't think you need know the details. All that is important is that it has totally cleared up. The condition has been resolved. As you, yourself, said, the bleeding ceased five days ago. My examination has confirmed this. You are as good as new.'

Inside, Vera felt as if a great weight had been removed. She felt light and wonderful. The mystery clouding her visit had been dispelled. Unprepared, she had survived this venture into the unknown. Yet, instinct told her, that while she might display pleasure that the bleeding had not been serious, she must still retain a touch of sadness over the failed pregnancy. She must be Billie Bradford.

Vera forced a partial smile, but kept her eyes and facial expression sad. 'I'm pleased to hear that, Dr Darly. I was concerned about the bleeding, of course.'

'Well, have no more concern. You are just fine.'

'Thank God.'

Vera was preparing to leave, when Dr Darly's voice held her in her seat.

'One more thing,' Dr Darly was saying, 'one extra bonus bit of good news.'

Vera waited, wondering what other good news could make her feel higher.

'I am aware from Dr Sadek's notes,' Dr Darly said, 'that

he told you and your husband there could be no sexual contact between you for six weeks – well, that would have meant, as of today, no sex for four more weeks. But now, I'm happy to say, I can modify that restriction. Your condition is so improved that you could resume your sexual relationship almost at once – but, to play it safe, certainly in four or five – let's say in five days. So you will soon have the opportunity to become pregnant again. That should please you.'

Vera felt her heart trip, begin to beat hard.

'Sex – in five days?'

'Absolutely.'

Vera tried to appear calm. But she knew that she was coming apart. She fought to steady herself. 'I – I'm very pleased. I can't wait to – to tell my husband.' She knew that she would never tell him about the five days. She would lie to him, maintain that they still had to wait four weeks. He must never know. Only that could save her.

'Oh, I'm sorry,' said Dr Darly. 'But I've already told your husband. I should have kept the surprise for you. He telephoned me just before your appointment, when you were on your way here. He couldn't wait to learn Dr Sadek's – or rather my – diagnosis. I told him I'd call him back after I examined you. And I did when you were getting dressed. He was a little unhappy about the pregnancy report. At the same time, he was relieved about the bleeding – and, well, frankly, delighted to hear he could resume a normal relationship with you in less than a week.'

Vera found it difficult to speak. 'As long as he knows,' she said under her breath. 'Thank you for everything, Dr Darly.'

Thank you for nothing, you meddling stupid cunt, she thought.

Leaving, joining her Secret Service guards, walking with them to the elevator, she suffered imbalance. She was dizzied by this unforeseen complication.

She sank into the rear of the White House limousine as if it were a tomb. She was aware of curious pedestrians, who had recognized her, gathering around the car for a closer glimpse. Several waved. For the first time, she ignored them, stared grimly ahead, as the car eased away from the curb and headed for Pennsylvania Avenue.

An icy, cold fear gripped her. Her situation had gone from bad to worse. Discovering the reason for the gynaecological examination had, for a while, seemed an insurmountable obstacle – but now she faced a far more formidable trap, an obstruction neither Alex nor the KGB had anticipated.

Sex with the President in five days. And she had over two weeks to spend with him before the exchange and escape.

For five years, six, seven – she could no longer remember exactly – the President had been going to bed almost daily with his Billie. He probably fucked her – or whatever the hell he did with her – three or four times a week. In bed, together, knowing each other intimately, each knowing every protrusion and crevice of the other's body, each knowing what the other liked and disliked. And now, Billie gone, herself in Billie's place with that other person. It was frightening. How did Billie behave in bed? How should she behave? How much foreplay? How passive? How passionate? How aberrated? Fellatio? Cunnilingus? What to do? What to expect?

Vera had experienced sexual relations with three men, and each of them had been individual, different, quirky in his own way. What were the President's quirks? What were Billie's?

This was a nightmare.

During her long training period, she recalled, Alex and the KGB had never ceased hunting for this one missing piece of information – Billie Bradford's bed habits. So confident had Alex been that he would acquire the information, that he had redoubled his efforts in preparing Vera for her impersonation. But as time passed, and the International Women's Meeting in Moscow had drawn closer, his confidence had flagged. Without the necessary information, the Second Lady Project could not proceed. All their efforts would have been wasted. Then, at the eleventh hour, their lucky break. The President had told his mistress that he and his wife could not engage in sexual activity for six weeks. Vera remembered the relief and exhilaration that she and Alex and Petrov had felt. With knowledge of Billie's sexual behaviour no longer an issue, the project had become obstacle-free and ready for launching.

Now, Vera was back where she had started from – once more requiring the knowledge that the KGB had never been able to produce – except that this moment her situation was worse then before. Because this moment she actually was Billie, with coupling time around the corner, and her ignorance total.

As the limousine spun on to the White House grounds, the South Portico ahead, Vera's mind centred on one picture projected in her head. Andrew Bradford, naked, with a pole of an erection, closing in on her, and she, naked, stretched out before him, paralysed, waiting – for what?

The pitfall was too enormous to grasp, to avoid, to survive.

Without carnal knowledge, she was lost. Only the sheerest luck could save her. One false move on her part, one uncharacteristic act or response, and he would be surprised, disconcerted, suspicious. He would be questioning. He would be doubtful. He would become aware that she was not what she seemed, not the familiar bed partner he had known so long.

You're not Billie. Who in the hell are you?

That could lead to the end – of the plot, of herself.

This was not simply an emergency situation. This was an even more desperate one. Only one thing on earth mattered to her now. To find out how to handle it.

The instant she was alone in the White House, she must contact chef Maurice or protocol chief Fred Willis. No, not them. It was the telephone she was supposed to use. Two calls to wrong numbers. Then a rescuer would appear – maybe Maurice, maybe Willis, maybe someone else. Whoever it was would pass the word to Petrov in Moscow.

Only one question, General Petrov, only one.

How does the First Lady of the United States fuck the President of the United States when they go to bed?

'How in the hell should we know?' General Petrov sputtered, handing the decoded inquiry from Washington DC to Alex Razin beside the desk.

Skimming the dispatch, Razin's expression turned from one of surprise to deep concern. 'This is unexpected,' he murmured.

'There is no room for the unexpected in an operation of such vital importance,' Petrov said angrily.

The door to Petrov's private KGB office opened, and Colonel Zhuk, Politburo member Garanin, and the KGB's head psychiatrist Dr Lunts trooped in, all hastily summoned to a meeting. Each greeted the KGB chairman, before taking his place. Petrov snatched the message back from Razin and glared at it.

'A problem, a serious problem,' Petrov grumbled. 'Our invincible lady, our Vera Vavilova, is in trouble.'

'But everything was anticipated,' said Garanin.

'Not everything,' snapped Petrov. He fixed his glare on his American expert. 'Comrade Razin overlooked one thing.'

'But we were assured there would be no sex for six weeks,' Razin protested.

'To be assured is not to be certain,' said Petrov. He saw the bewilderment on the faces of the others. 'Mrs Bradford had an appointment with her gynaecologist. The reason was unknown to Comrade Vavilova. Nevertheless she kept the appointment in the First Lady's place. She saw it through successfully. She learned that she had been suffering from vaginal bleeding. This was the reason she was not to have sex with the President for six weeks, meaning not for four more weeks from now. This meant Comrade Vavilova would have had time enough to fulfil her Summit mission, be exchanged, and returned safely to us, before the President would have sexual relations with her. Now Comrade Vavilova has learned that she is cured of her vaginal complaint, and that her gynaecologist has informed the President that he can resume the sex act with his wife in five days; exactly five days from today. Do you see the precarious position in which our agent has been placed?'

'Too clearly,' said Dr Lunts. 'It is unfortunate –'

'You understate, Dr Lunts,' said Petrov. 'This is a potential disaster. Five nights from tonight, when we are all in London, our Vera Vavilova must go to bed with the President to enjoy sex again. But she is ignorant of their previous relationship. How did the real First Lady perform in bed with her husband? Our Second Lady does not know. But she must know – or run the risk of being exposed. Either we learn the truth and help her – or we abort the entire project.'

'Can we abort on such short notice?' said Colonel Zhuk.

'Why not? A day or two before the President is to have sex with her, we get Vera Vavilova out of London and fly her back to Moscow – at the same time replacing her with Billie Bradford. It can be done. Only I don't want it to be done. I don't want Vera Vavilova back here until she has obtained the information the Premier requires for the Summit.'

'Bringing her back,' Garanin complained, 'three years of wasted work.'

'Worse,' said Petrov, 'it would leave the Premier unarmed at the Summit, leave him in the dark, possibly forcing him to capitulate to the capitalists. No, I can't have that. I won't have that. We *must* find out how the First Lady performs in bed with her husband and transmit our findings to Vera Vavilova.'

'How, possibly?' Razin asked no one in particular.

'That is why you are all here, to think of something.'

'Some secrets are impossible to penetrate,' said Razin. 'Sex between a husband and wife is such a private matter.'

'Not necessarily,' said Petrov. 'Perhaps one of them has visited a psychoanalyst?'

'Neither has,' said Razin.

'Or confided in a close friend?'

'Doubtful,' said Razin. 'Even if one did, we don't have time –'

'Then let us say only two persons on earth know how

Billie Bradford performs in bed with the President,' Petrov conceded. 'Obviously, we can't interrogate the President. That leaves us his wife. We have his wife here. Maybe we can get the information from her.'

'Unlikely, General.'

'Come now, Razin, your Billie Bradford, she is hardly a vestal virgin. I know from our profile of her some of her previous involvements.'

'Did she have sex with every man in her past?' said Razin.

'I don't know, ' admitted Petrov. 'We have no proof. And we don't dare to go to the various men.'

Dr Lunts spoke up. 'Has she ever committed adultery since marrying the President?'

'No evidence of that,' said Petrov. 'But I'm sure there are other possibilities.'

'What possibilities do you have in mind?' inquired the KGB psychiatrist.

'One is the direct route. Go to her. Tell her frankly what we need from her. Tell her that her future safety depends on her cooperation.'

Dr Lunts shook his head. 'Her profile indicates that she would never cooperate. Sanctity of marriage. Privacy. Puritanism. She would defy you to the end with silence.'

Petrov frowned. 'Then we should treat her as we would any obstructionist.'

'Torture?' said Dr Lunts.

Petrov shrugged. 'Why not?'

Razin quickly intervened. 'Begging your pardon, General, but any physical harm to her could not be explained when we return her to the Americans.'

'Who spoke of physical harm?' said Petrov innocently. 'There are other forms of persuasion. Starvation, for one.'

'It would leave its marks.'

'Drugs, then.'

'Not reliable,' said Dr Lunts. 'They would probably distort any normal response. Hypnosis would be just as untrustworthy, especially if she had strong resistance.'

Petrov had become progressively impatient. 'Enough of

this,' he said. 'I'll tell you simply what should be done. I say go in there and fuck her by force. We'll see how she behaves. We'll find out first-hand.'

'Find out what?' said Razin. 'Do you think she'll react to violent rape in the way she reacts to natural sex? Never.'

Dr Lunts supported Razin. 'He is right, General. Rape would not give you a dependable response.'

Petrov showed his exasperation. 'All I get from you nay-sayers is nothing. Not one constructive idea. Only *nyet*. Why have I assembled you here? Because I regard you as the best brains in the KGB. We must chart a course today. We must act on it. We must succeed. Or everything is lost.'

This was followed by silence, as all of them assumed postures of deep thought.

Razin, lifting a hand for attention, broke the silence. 'General Petrov,' he said.

'Yes?'

'There is one possibility. I – I think I have an idea. Please listen to me.'

He began to speak slowly, and soon everyone in the office was absorbed.

In her secured Kremlin suite – her jail, her prison, her camouflaged Lubyanka, why dignify it with any other name? – Billie Bradford, in grey T-shirt and white slacks, sat picking at the vomitous Russian breakfast of salami slices, cottage cheese with sugar, a heavy pancake topped with sour cream, yogurt, and black bread, on her tray. The food revolted her. Besides, she was not hungry. She ate what little she did merely to sustain her strength for whatever might come up.

She had been taken by surprise when General Petrov appeared a few minutes ago, actually cordial, the animal, announcing that he thought he might drop in to join her for a cup of coffee. He had disappeared into the kitchen to heat and pour his coffee.

She had been surprised by Petrov's arrival because she no longer expected any official visitors. In the last three or four days – she was muddled about the time that had passed –

there had been only one caller. The interpreter, Alex Razin, had come by the second day, for a brief visit, to drop off the latest American newspaper and magazines. He had inquired after her health and had departed. She did not count the daily visits, three times a day, of the two unspeaking, armed and uniformed, KGB guards. They brought the three meals – the breakfast; the lunch, usually red caviar on hard-boiled egg halves, oily lox, vegetable soup flavoured with bits of dill pickle, chicken Kiev; the dinner, usually pork or beef stroganoff on rice, cabbage rolls, ice cream with fruit sauce. They also delivered new videotapes, cigarettes, bottles of drinks, her laundry and cleaning. One guard stood at the door keeping his eyes on her. The other deposited the trays of food, inspected the suite, and they both left.

She had been alone for endlessly long periods. She had always, in her life, been able to cope with loneliness, but the unreality of this experience made it more difficult to handle. She had tried to divert herself from introspection by exercising, making her bed, puttering in the kitchen for an unwanted snack, dusting, reading, viewing the day-old American network news on videotapes, watching movies, listening to the Voice of America and BBC.

But for the most part, she lived inside her head. Over and over she kept telling herself what had happened had not really happened, that it was a mad dream from which she would awaken. When she admitted that it was not a dream, she tried to imagine how the enemy could have conceived this improbable caper, how the Soviets could have found and trained another woman to be her double. Then, as always, her imaginings brought her to that other woman, the bogus First Lady, and what that other woman was doing in her place and with her husband.

Not everyone would be fooled. Someone would find out. The thoughts always came to that. She had counted on Andrew's realizing the truth. Or Nora or Guy or Wayne Gibbs or one of the Secret Service men, *someone*. Certainly, her father. He would see something wrong immediately. He would sound the warning. The imposter would be exposed.

The scandal would be worldwide, beyond belief. She listened to the English radio news (especially taped for her) religiously, because she thought the exposé would top all the news for days. She waited hourly for her prison door to open, for Razin or Petrov to come in and admit they had been found out and that she was being returned home. Or Ambassador Youngdahl. He would come through the door to tell her the imposter had been arrested, that she could leave with him for the plane that would take her to the White House.

But no one had come with the news she expected.

Now, at last, one of them had come. The monster who had engineered the plot and her imprisonment. He might have the news of her release. Yet, he had appeared too self-satisfied to be the courier of his own defeat.

She looked up to see him walking from the kitchen with a steaming cup of coffee in hand.

General Petrov settled himself in the sofa across from her, put his cup and saucer on the coffee table, spooned the coffee, took a sip.

He knew, she decided, that his so-called Second Lady had failed, had been found out, yet he would not tell her. He was toying with her, the sadistic beast. She would never, never in a million years, give him the satisfaction of asking.

But out it came. 'It failed, didn't it?' she blurted.

'What?' He seemed genuinely puzzled.

'Your plot,' she said. 'My father – in Los Angeles – you didn't fool him?' she watched Petrov anxiously.

'Oh, that!' He threw back his head and laughed heartily. 'My dear Mrs Bradford, your father loves you, always has, always will. He was thrilled to see you in Los Angeles a few days ago. You two got along famously. And you and your husband, you've never been closer.'

She sat stricken.

It was as if every organ in her body was shrivelling.

Petrov eyed her over his cup of coffee. 'Really, Mrs Bradford, you didn't think, after all our endless months of preparation, our Lady would be found out? I'm sorry to disappoint you – but you are more popular than ever throughout America. Surely, you heard that your speech from Los Angeles was applauded everywhere?'

She had seen it on videotape, heard it on the radio, yet blotted it out of consciousness.

'You are not missed, Mrs Bradford,' Petrov said with a grin. 'How could you be when you are there, where you've always been in recent years, in the White House and intact, and soon in London.'

She bit her lip, knowing she was as crazy in her imagining as they were in their unreality.

'It still won't work,' she said doggedly. 'It won't work.'

'Do I have to repeat myself, Mrs Bradford? Do I have to tell you again it is working?'

'It can't go on, don't you see? Sooner or later your insane plot will unravel. End it before it ruins the Summit, destroys relations between your country and mine. Think of what would happen if you and your people found out that America had kidnapped Mrs Kirechenko, replaced her with an American woman agent posing as your Premier's wife, and that we held Mrs Kirechenko in captivity at Camp David. Don't you see the danger if that were found out?'

Petrov was amused. 'I respect your imagination, Mrs Bradford, but you miss the main point. It could not happen the other way around. You Americans do not have our mentality. You are not clever enough for such an undertaking, you are not audacious enough. Your CIA is clumsy, amateurish, crude. Your supposed democratic freedom – not real freedom, only licence – makes your people soft. They could not even entertain a scheme like this. As to our risking the Summit with our undertaking, yes, the gamble aspect of it has been carefully considered. If we win, we will have the power to maintain peace in the world. If we lose – well, to be honest with you, there is no contingency plan if we lose, because we cannot lose, we cannot and we will not.'

'We shall see,' Billie said stubbornly.

'Mrs Bradford, we've already seen.' Petrov gulped down the remainder of his coffee. 'The proof is plain in the progress we've made so far. Here you are. Outside of Razin and our

Politburo no one on earth knows you are here. Our Second Lady is in the White House. No one else knows she is there. I've already told you that your husband, your friends, your father and sister, accept her as you. Tomorrow, in London, the British will be welcoming the First Lady.' He paused. 'Mrs Bradford, if you have hopes there will be a slip, forget them. Accept your fate, be cooperative, and you will be back where you came from in two weeks or less. Cooperate with us and you will not be sorry.'

'Cooperate with you? What does that mean?'

'Don't be difficult. Don't try to escape or try to communicate with someone on the outside. Do answer all questions we put to you. In fact, I have several questions for you right now. They are not important. We know everything we need to know. But to verify what is in our files, we wish to hear what you have to say.'

'About what?' she said. She was aware that they had at last reached the purpose of Petrov's visit.

'About your husband,' said Petrov, unpeeling the wrapping from a cigar. 'About the President of the United States.' He meticulously clipped off an end of the cigar. 'Is he always as calm, as unruffled, as he appears in public?'

'You claim to know everything,' Billie said. 'Why waste my breath repeating what you already know?'

'We hear he has a terrible temper in private.'

'You do?' She smiled crookedly. 'How interesting.'

Her attention was diverted to the door behind Petrov. The interpreter, Alex Razin, had admitted himself. He gave her a short nod, and went quietly to a chair nearby. Petrov ignored him, his eyes narrowing on her.

'That, Mrs Bradford, is what I mean by being uncooperative.'

She compressed her lips and met his stare.

Petrov scowled. As he spoke, his voice became harsh. 'Young lady, I suggest you reconsider your attitude. You have much at stake. Your health, for one thing.'

'Is that a threat?'

'It is whatever you take it to be.' He busied himself lighting his cigar. 'Yes, it is a threat. Know this – we have the means to make you talk. I would prefer not to use them, but if I am forced to, I shall. This is no polite parlour game, Mrs Bradford. This is not a social visit. We are not equals, you and I. At this moment, you have no rights, no choices. If you remain obstinate, you will be punished.' He took a puff of his cigar. 'Very well, I'll give you one more chance to show your goodwill. Let us try your husband again. Is he interested in sex? Does he like to go to bed with you?'

She was immediately furious. 'It's none of your goddam business,' she spat out. 'How dare you!'

Petrov rose menacingly. 'Lady, everything is my business, you hear? I will ask you the question once more. If you refuse to answer me, I will see that you answer the guards. I will bring them in –'

Razin leaped to his feet, placed a restraining hand on Petrov's shoulder. 'General, please –' He tried to draw the KGB director away from the coffee table. 'You promised, sir, no – no force –'

'If she was reasonable,' Petrov said angrily. 'But she is a stubborn bitch –'

'Wait, please listen,' Razin protested. He had succeeded in moving Petrov away from the seating arrangement, leading him toward the door. Razin continued to speak to his superior in an undertone.

Billie sat immobilized on the sofa, watching, waiting, frightened.

She heard Petrov snort, and saw him jerk away, regarding Razin with contempt. 'Stop your whining. There is still too much of the American in you, I see. Weak and sentimental.' He puffed hard on his cigar. 'This once, all right. Talk to her alone. But don't try my patience too far, Razin.' Petrov glared at Billie, swung away and stalked out of the room.

After the door had slammed, Razin's attention remained fixed on it, until he slowly turned around and walked back to Billie and sat near her.

'I'm sorry,' he said.

'God, I hate him,' Billie burst out. 'He – he's subhuman.'

She looked at Razin gratefully. 'What did you say to him to make him stop?'

'I simply told him he does not understand American women. I told him torture would get him nowhere, in fact get him the opposite results. I told him you were a decent woman, a nice woman, and a sensible one, and that you would be reasonable – that it was his questions that were unreasonable.'

She favoured Razin with a smile of appreciation. 'Thank you.'

He stood up. 'I think we both could use a drink.' He paused at the radio, turned it on, raised the volume. At the sideboard, preparing a Scotch for her, a vodka for himself, he said, 'Most men here, men with the authority of a Petrov, they have no understanding of women in the Western world. I was raised by American women. As an adult, I dated them. I understand them. When I was brought back to Russia, I saw at once that the Russian attitude toward women was different. Men here, while they allow women in the work force, really regard them as chattels. To Russian men, women are to be treated as captives, servants, pliable sex objects. It was one thing I always disliked about Russia, one more reason why I always wanted to return to the United States.'

'If you care for the United States so much, how could you let yourself get involved in this plot?'

'Self-survival,' he said simply. He brought her drink and a napkin to her, then sat with his own. He raised his glass in a toast. 'Your health, Mrs Bradford.'

'I'll drink to that.' The Scotch warmed her. She took two more swallows before setting her glass down. 'I was alone with Petrov a while. I wondered if my – my, what? – double? – my double was getting away with her act. Petrov insisted that she was doing perfectly. No one had the slightest suspicion of her, not my husband, not my friends, not my father. It was hard for me to believe. Should I believe it?'

'I'm afraid so Mrs Bradford. It is true.'

'I still find that unbelievable. How could the woman, pretending to be me, have learned so much?'

'She's an actress.'

'An actress?'

'A brilliant one, who happened to look like you. I was commanded to work with her, because of my background, my knowledge of English. I hated the assignment, but I had no choice. Actually, coaching the actress was fascinating in one way. I was fascinated, not with her, but with the role she was playing.'

'She was playing me.'

'Exactly. And, ever since you came into the public eye, I was aware of you and fascinated by you.'

'But why?'

'I don't know. Perhaps because you were the prototype of the typical all-American girl, California version. You were wonderfully pretty, open, frank, bright, zestful. I went with such an American girl once, when I was very young.'

'I'm flattered,' said Billie.

Razin made a wry face. 'Don't be. I got too fascinated in cloning you. I did my job too well, to my regret.'

'So for me there's no hope on that score?'

'That our actress will slip up, be exposed? No, I wouldn't count on that.'

'Then my only hope is getting out of here on my own, getting to the American embassy.'

'Not a chance.'

'With your help it could be possible. As I promised you the first day in this room, I could get you into the United States.'

He stared down at the floor, turning it over in his mind. Almost imperceptibly, his head moved from side to side. 'No, even with my help, you'd never make it. They'd find out I was involved. They'd –'

'I'd die before telling them.'

'No,' he said flatly. 'Let's not speak of it again.'

With a sigh of resignation, she reached for her drink and finished it. 'To get back to Petrov. Those questions about my husband, our sex life. Did he really ask them to verify anything?'

Razin smiled. 'Of course not.' He hesitated, finally spoke. 'I'll tell you what it is. They have a problem, but they don't want you to know it. Something unforeseen has come up. I shouldn't tell you, but I will if you'll hold it in strictest confidence.'

Billie held up her hand. 'I swear.'

'You had an appointment with your gynaecologist this week.'

'My gynaecol –?' she repeated, puzzled. 'You mean – oh, Dr Sadek. I remember. Yes.' Then she said quickly, 'Your actress had to keep my appointment?'

'That's right. Unfortunately, your doctor met with an accident, so your double had to see his associate. She had to go through the examination, hear the verdict on your tests. I am sorry to have to tell you, Mrs Bradford, but you are not pregnant.'

The news gave Billie a sting of disappointment and pain. She sat very still, letting it soak in. She felt her eyes fill, but fought off tears. She was sorry for Andrew, for herself, too. But hopefully, hopefully, there would be a next time.

Razin was watching her worriedly. 'I know it is upsetting,' he said. 'Are you all right?'

'Never mind, I'm fine,' she said. 'Considering my circumstances here, maybe it's just as well.'

'As to your bleeding,' Razin said. 'Of course, your gynaecologist was examining another woman, and found her normal. But that tells you nothing about your own condition. Are you still bleeding? Because if you are, we can –'

'No bleeding,' she said. 'I'm okay.'

'Good. Anyway, when you had started bleeding a few weeks ago, you were ordered not to have sexual relations with your husband for six weeks. Petrov found that very convenient for your double.'

Billie sat up. 'How did they know all that – my bleeding – no sex for six weeks –?'

'I haven't the faintest idea. But the KGB knew it. Now they know something else. Your bleeding has stopped. You've been pronounced cured and healthy. The doctor says you and your husband — meaning your double and your husband — can resume having sex in five days from today.'

'In five days.' Billie nodded. 'I see. Now my double has to know what my husband is like and what I'm like in — in bed?'

'You've guessed it.'

Billie smiled to herself briefly, but when she looked at Razin she was serious. 'Mr Razin, I'm sure you know, I don't intend to discuss this subject in any way. I don't intend to help your actress.'

Razin was sympathetic. 'I can't blame you.'

'I'm glad you understand. I may be liberated, but not that much. I think some things have to be private.'

'I agree with you. But it presents one problem for me. I managed to get Petrov out of here, prevent him from having you harmed, by insisting that I might be able to gain your cooperation by appealing to your reason. Now I have to prove to Petrov my way was the best way. If I go to him empty-handed, he may take over your interrogation again. For your own safety, I must give him something, anything, some crumb. If I can do that, I'll have proved to him my way is better than his.'

She stared at him. 'What do you want from me?'

'Oh, anything, anything — no matter how minor — as long as it is true.'

Billie considered her answer. Obviously, what this man was saying to her was honest. If he could prove his manner was effective with her, it would keep Petrov off her neck. Yet, it revolted her to have to speak of Andrew's sexual behaviour to strangers — not just strangers, but criminals. This man beside her, while one of them, at least had some instinct of decency. Also, he was half-American. The choice was a poor one, but it was a choice.

She chose Razin over Petrov. 'Well,' she said hesitantly, 'this is — this is embarrassing, you know —'

'I don't want to hear anything that embarrasses you,' he said quickly, 'just some morsel that will keep Petrov quiet.'

'Well — my husband — I suppose you could tell them, my

husband – he doesn't like normal – normal sex – in our – relationship.'

There it was. Something for the bastards. It would keep them quiet. It might save her.

Razin seemed pleased. He leaned forward to pat her hand. 'Thank you. I know how difficult it was for you. But that's quite enough. You needn't say another word. This'll help both of us.'

'I – I appreciate your – your concern for me.'

He was on his feet.

'I'll do everything I can for you, Mrs Bradford. You can depend on me. Good day.'

6

Air Force One had taken off from Andrews Air Force Base in Maryland two hours ago, and now the four-engined giant jet was at maximum altitude over the Atlantic, its aluminium-and-steel frame hurtling toward London and the Summit Conference.

In a corner of the spacious conference room of the thirty-five-foot-long presidential suite, Guy Parker and the First Lady reclined in blue easy chairs opposite one another, with Parker's portable tape recorder resting on the table between them. Parker bent forward to see if the cassette had to be replaced, but he saw by the digital counter that there was plenty of tape left.

Satisfied, he sat back and concentrated on the task of getting more material from Billie Bradford for her autobiography. 'Okay,' he said, 'I think we have all we need on your courtship with the President and the wedding. What I'd like to tackle next is your marriage. But before going into the highlights, I'd like to know more of your personal relationship with your husband up to this point. I mean, intimate little things no one else would know. How you two get along from breakfast to bed. Don't hold back. Just tell me what you can as frankly as possible. You'll be able to edit it, of course, when I show you the first draft. But for now, be up front with me, Billie. I repeat, every intimate detail –'

That instant, he caught the expression on her face, and stopped in mid-sentence. She was aghast.

'Guy, are you crazy?' she said. 'You know better. Under no circumstances will I discuss anything intimate about

Andrew and myself. Not on your life. I thought that was understood from the start.'

Parker was taken aback. 'But you once –'

'No,' she said emphatically. 'Forget it.'

'Billie, I don't mean –'

'Please don't argue with me' She shook a cigarette loose from the pack on the table. 'Better move on to something else.'

Bewildered, he put a light to her cigarette, and finally settled back. 'All right, something else. Your husband's personality, as you see it.'

'You mean, like his moods and so forth?'

'His temperament, his humour, whatever comes to mind.' She exhaled a stream of smoke. 'Let me think –'

She began to recall things about her husband. All of it was flattering, most of it puerile. Parker half listened. The tape spun on.

Dull stuff, he thought. She was usually brighter, more insightful than this. She talked for ten minutes, while he waited patiently for a cue that he could pick up to lead her back to where she had side-tracked him.

'That's interesting,' Parker interrupted, 'about the President's being such a movie fan. He used to hang out with some of the movie crowd, didn't he?'

'A few were his friends.'

'I believe he was even dating an actress, a movie star, when he met you and began going out with you – and then, if I remember, he took you to a party, and the star was there, and the two of you met –'

'Not so, Guy. He had been going with this movie star, but she and I – no, we never met.'

'I thought I'd heard –'

'No matter what you heard, we never met.' The First Lady wriggled free of the easy chair and came to her feet. She stretched. 'Enough talking for now,' she said. She indicated the bedroom with its two single beds. 'I'm going to lie down for a while. We'd all better be rested for London. Thanks, Guy.'

Dismissed, he quickly shut off his tape recorder, picked it up, and made for the door.

'I'll try to find some time for us in London,' she called after him.

'I'd appreciate that.'

Outside the presidential suite, Parker moved from the forward part of the plane, past the next compartment where the four Secret Service agents, the four Air Force security guards, and the Navy nurse were seated, into the roomy compartment which was reserved for the White House staff. Across from the Xerox machine, Parker saw that one of the two electric typewriters was not in use. He considered using it to make some notes, then decided against it. He wasn't in the mood. He had too much on his mind.

He glanced about the compartment. Most of the oversized seats were occupied by staff members either dozing or reading. The chairs faced each other, separated by tables, and in one pair sat presidential adviser Wayne Gibbs and protocol chief Fred Willis engrossed in a game of gin rummy. Just beyond them sat Nora Judson, busily making notes on a pad at her table. The chair opposite her was empty. Parker thought of taking it. He had to unburden himself to someone from the East Wing. Perhaps Nora wasn't the best choice, the way she seemed to avoid him and be uncommunicative in his presence, but there was no other choice. Besides, he liked to look at her bosom.

Parker took the chair across from Nora. She did not raise her head. She kept on writing.

'Mind if I smoke?' he asked.

'It's a free country,' she said, continuing to scribble away.

He pulled his crusted brown pipe out of his pocket, filled it with tobacco, and applied a light with a match from the book of matches bearing the presidential seal on one side and imprinted Air Force One on the other. He sat listening to the hum of the plane's turbofans, reviewing his meeting with Billie, and in doing so he could feel his face set in a frown.

He considered opening up a conversation with the beautiful icicle across from him, and had just reconsidered and decided against it, when she looked up at him.

'What's got into you?' she said. 'You don't look too happy. Anything wrong?'

Her interest encouraged him. 'I'm confused,' he said. 'Your Billie is very confusing.'

Nora threw down her pencil and sat back, fingertips touching. 'Now what?'

'I just had a session with her. I wanted to go into her personal life with the President. You would have thought I insulted her. She wouldn't discuss it. Not a word. Not a thing. Yet – listen to this, Nora – when we started our talks two months ago, one of the first things she told me was that she would discuss her private life with the President freely with me, providing she could see it later. She promised she'd go as far as possible to spice up the book, try to make them both look human. That was two months ago. Now, a half-hour ago, she says no soap, she'd never dream of discussing their personal life. She tells me I should have known that all along.' He removed the pipe from his mouth. 'Don't you find that pretty odd?'

Nora gave a small shrug of her shoulders. 'What's so odd? In two months she could have changed her mind.'

'But so completely? And acting like we'd never discussed it before? I don't get it.' Since he had Nora's ear, he made up his mind to go on. He pressed against the table. 'Another thing. Maybe you can explain this one. Early on, when we first started our talks and were skipping around from this to that, I told Billie I'd read somewhere in my research that when Andrew Bradford met her, he was going out pretty steady with a famous movie actress. He started dating Billie, too. He escorted Billie to a dinner party and they bumped into the actress. A sticky moment. I asked Billie whether it was true, and, if it was, would she talk about things like that. I remember how she reacted. She laughed and said yes, it had happened, and it was a funny thing and she'd tell me about it when we got to it in the book. So okay, just now in the presidential suite, when it seemed appropriate, I brought up the whole incident, and she went cold on me. She insisted that she had never run into that actress at a party, had never met the actress at all, and just shut me off.' He put a light to his pipe. 'I tell you, Nora, I don't know what to make of it, such a blatant contradiction.'

Nora eyed him curiously. 'Do you have those so-called contradictory statements by her on tape?'

'Not exactly. This one I have.' He rapped his tape recorder. 'But not the first one. We weren't taping things in the beginning. Just talked away, feeling each other out.'

'I see. So you're simply trusting your memory.'

This annoyed him. 'I'm hardly senile, Nora.'

'No, but you're human. We all get mixed up sometimes.'

'I'm not mixed up. She contradicted herself badly. And while we're at it, let me tell you something else. Ever since she got back from Moscow, she's like another person, as far as I'm concerned. Our sessions used to be a pleasure. She was funny, lively, clever. Now – now she's simply dull – just blah. You wouldn't know it was the same person. I mean, there was one Billie I got to know. Then off she goes to Moscow for a few days, and now she seems a different Billie.'

'Oh, she's just worn out, that's all. Look the way the President has been running her around. She's whipped.'

Parker started shaking his head. 'No, it's more than that, Nora. It's as if she was brainwashed while she was in Moscow. I could give you at least a half-dozen other examples of her odd behaviour recently –'

Nora cut in on him. 'Don't bother Guy. I don't want to hear any more, because it's utter nonsense. I like you, Guy, in many ways, but when you become suspicious, fanciful, obsessive, it can be tiresome. I suggest you jettison that hugger-mugger stuff before we land in London. Stick to reality and to your job, and save the rest of your imaginings for a novel. I promise you I'll buy the novel. But I won't buy this. Now excuse me, I've got to go to the bathroom.'

This was the evening of their official welcome to England, the reception and dinner hosted by Prime Minister Dudley

Heaton and his wife Penelope for Premier Dmitri Kirechenko of the USSR and President Andrew Bradford of the USA and their wives.

This would have also been one of the most exciting evenings in her life, Vera thought, if she weren't so deeply worried. The knowledge that three nights from now she would be having sexual intercourse – or whatever he expected – with the President haunted Vera. Unless she heard from her KGB contacts in the next seventy-two hours, she would be in serious trouble. Fear of the unknown gnawed at Vera, and destroyed any prospect of pleasure.

When they had touched down at Northolt Airport last night, she should have been brimming with anticipation. She had never been to London, as Billie Bradford had, but Alex had thoroughly prepared her for what to expect. It was an experience she had looked forward to throughout her training period. But, despite all the pomp and ceremony in the floodlighted area at the air terminal, apprehension tagged along at her heels.

Ensconced in one of a fleet of gleaming Rolls-Royces, she tried to appear excited and curious the entire fifteen miles to London's West End, but inside she brooded. When her Rolls entered Brook Street, and pulled up before the revolving door of the reserved and majestic Claridge's Hotel, she made an effort at showing interest. In the richly carpeted lobby, surrounded by Secret Service men and British security officers, she had no more than a glimpse of the ground floor. To her left a small porter's desk and beyond it some sort of key counter, across from the porter's desk a single elegant elevator, straight ahead a broad lounge with a costumed orchestra and people drinking and waiters in knee breeches, and to her right the lobby sitting area next to a wide sweeping staircase.

The hotel manager, in tails, had guided the President and his wife from the ground floor up the carpeted stairs to the first floor. He directed them to the immediate left. 'Of course, you have the Royal Suite,' he had informed the President.

In the entry hall of the corner suite, the manager had been

eager to show her about their quarters. Tired as she was, Vera followed him. The entry hall led to the dining room, straight ahead, and to the living room to the right. They went into the dining room. The manager tapped the oval table. 'Regency,' he said. 'There are eight chairs. You may have more if you desire.' He indicated the brown double doors with gilt doorknobs behind him. 'These lead to a rather large adjoining suite of three bedrooms and two sitting rooms. We converted it into offices before your arrival, Mr President. When you have time to inspect it, you will find a small vestibule that leads into a sitting room which we have divided into a series of small offices, including one for your personal secretary. This leads into another sitting room which has been designated as your private office. The bedrooms in the suite, of course, have also been made into offices. Now, if you'll follow me, I'll show you your personal quarters.'

An opposite set of double doors, standing open, gave them access to the sitting room of the Royal Suite. It was magnificent, Vera could see. At her feet, soothing green carpeting. Above, a Wedgwood white ceiling with a single chandelier. She scanned the room. Armchairs, one red, one green. A curved green sofa, shielding an old, light brown grand piano, 'once owned by D'Oyly Carte, producer for Gilbert and Sullivan as well as chairman of our Savoy Group', the manager had explained. Floor-length windows would brighten the area in daytime. Vera's eyes continued to roam across the flower-filled room, held on a Victorian desk holding two telephones, moved to a white fireplace topped by a mirror. The manager was opening a brown door next to the fireplace. 'If you please, the bedroom.'

Vera preceded the President with trepidation. Two twin beds nestled side by side, each with its bedstand and lamp, one stand holding two grey telephones, the other a single phone. The footboards of the bed were one. The bedroom was pleasant, green shell-decorated ceiling and walls. A love seat. A gracious dressing table with two white lamps and a triple mirror. On the table rested a tray holding a bucket of ice and champagne and glasses. The President tested a bed and approved. Vera tried to smile.

Ahead, the bathroom, huge by any standard. All marble and more marble. In an alcove a bidet across from the toilet. In an opposite alcove, a graceful bathtub with inlaid trim. In between, a double sink. Tiberius would have been at home here, Vera decided.

'I hope everything is to your satisfaction,' the manager had said, ready to take his leave.

'Beautiful,' Vera had replied. 'Thank you.'

She had meant it, but the beauty did not alleviate the uneasiness that adhered to her.

The manager's parting words had been to the President. 'I remind you, your party will be occupying the rest of the first floor.'

After that, the President had wanted to see his personal office, and then left Vera to inspect the entire first floor, to make certain everything had been properly arranged and that the members of his staff were well situated. By midnight, with Sarah's help, Vera had unpacked, and shortly after finishing she and the President had gone to sleep, she restlessly. That had been yesterday.

Most of this day, while the President stayed behind to confer with his advisers, Vera had devoted to a scheduled sight-seeing tour of London conducted by their British hosts. A great deal of it – the British Museum, Westminster Abbey, a brief pause outside the Dorchester Hotel (where the Soviet delegation was housed), the Tower of London – was supposed to be familiar to Billie Bradford from her visit here as a student, and stay here as a public relations representative. Vera had been forced to pretend nostalgia. But it had been all new to her and had diverted the dark thoughts in her mind.

As Sarah had helped her dress in their Claridge's bedroom for the formal dinner, Vera kept visualizing the cosy twin beds as her Waterloo, and her moodiness returned. Soon, in the official Humber, seated between the President and the secretary of state for foreign and commonwealth affairs, the dapper, prattling, Right Honourable Ian Enslow, she had tried to be attentive to the historic sights Enslow was pointing out and explaining to them.

Now, their limousine turned into the wide vista of Whitehall. 'Just ahead to the left, on the corner, the three-storey brown building with the black metal, grilled fence at the front of the museum entrance, that's the Banqueting House,' Enslow was saying. 'We'll be turning into Horse Guards Avenue. A rather unprepossessing side entrance is used for major social affairs. The grounds behind the building are used for parking and the caterer's trucks – oddly, the Banqueting House has no kitchen. But the food, I promise you, will be first-rate.' They were wheeling into Horse Guards Avenue when Enslow exclaimed, 'Good heavens, the crowd! All of London and Fleet Street must be here waiting for the main attraction – you, Mr President, and your beautiful First Lady.'

They had come to a stop at the aisle formed by two rows of Metropolitan police extending to the plain door. The great throng of spectators, held back a short distance by a secondary line of helmeted bobbies, surged forward for a better look at the international celebrities. The British first secretary had stepped out of the car and was assisting Vera. A dozen photographers, holding their cameras over the shoulders of the police, were aiming their lenses at Vera. Vera parted her mink coat so that the imploring photographers could have shots of her gold lamé gown. Andrew Bradford emerged from the car, stood beside her briefly to allow the photographers to do their jobs, and then both followed Enslow toward the entrance to the seventeenth-century Banqueting House.

Passing through a small green entry decorated with floral arrangements, Vera found herself in a lobby beside a pedestal that held a bronze bust of James I. While the men removed their topcoats and Vera gave up her mink to cloakroom attendants, Enslow indicated the broad stone staircase leading up to the hall of the Banqueting House.

With Vera between the men, they started their ascent.

'You've never been here?' Enslow was saying. 'Quite an impressive old barn. Originated by Henry VIII for Anne Boleyn. Built and rebuilt many times. However, the basic Banqueting Hall was created by Inigo Jones – a jolly genius, that one – for James I. I don't expect you'll have much time to look around, but if you do – well, now – don't miss the Rubens paintings on the ceiling. Nine panels in all, commissioned by King Charles when Rubens was here in London on a diplomatic mission. The entire hundred-foot hall has been repainted amd remodelled for tonight's happy occasion. Here we are on the landing. Now, let's look in. The PM is waiting for this reunion, and the Russian Premier is already here.'

Caught between the British security officers who had formed a wedge ahead and the American Secret Service behind, Vera tried to maintain her balance and poise as they hurried through the hall doorway into the portion of the Stuart hall that had been partitioned off from the actual banquet hall to serve as a reception room. Vera passed between the giant white pillars on either side, heard the orchestra playing from the balustraded balcony overhead, and suddenly found herself surrounded by people.

Their host and hostess, Prime Minister Heaton, a smile pressed into his round bland face, and his elegant wife, taller than him by a head, were waiting. Vera remembered that she was supposed to have met them last summer, at a White House garden party for the pair. Vera sought to recall Alex's briefings. Heaton was Harrow, Balliol College, Tory, the Carlton Club, sherry, *The Times*. They were shaking hands, Heaton breathing in her ear his enjoyment of that garden party and his pleasure at having her here in London.

The place was swarming with guests, and the decibel level was that of 300 chattering magpies. Clutching her beaded purse and the President's arm, Vera was drawn into the crowd of formally attired guests by Enslow. Every few steps there were introductions, and the corners of her mouth and the ridges of her cheeks hurt from constant smiling, from having to appear interested and attentive. The most important introduction, the one over which they lingered longest, was to Premier Kirechenko and his wife Ludmila. The Russian Premier, Vera noted, did not look very proletarian tonight. His long aristocratic face, rimless spectacles, neat pointed beard, and tailcoat gave him the appearance of a wealthy Czarist minister. His rotund wife, in her terrible silk organza, looked fatter than ever. Vera had to alert her mind that as First Lady Billie Bradford she had never met Premier Kirechenko before and that she had become acquainted with Ludmila at the Moscow Women's Meeting recently. The President and Premier, she saw, struck it off immediately. She and Ludmila had little to say, since Ludmila spoke only a few words of broken English and Billie Bradford was supposed to have no knowledge of Russian. A heavy-set man with a potato nose and dark blue suit loomed up beside Ludmila and laughingly she introduced him in Russian. As Billie, Vera lifted her shoulders helplessly, not understanding, but as Vera the introduction had told her the proprietary man was Yankovich, one of their personal bodyguards, obviously KGB.

Soon Vera and the President were continuing through the jam of guests. Most introductions were fleeting and only fleetingly remembered. One made an impression. Vera met Mwami Kibangu, the President of the African nation of Boende. She knew, from her indoctrination in Moscow, that he was merely a capitalist tool. But the small, dignified black man proved intelligent, clever, humorous. Vera could not help but like him. As she prepared to leave him, she said with a twinkle, 'Now I must meet Nwapa – where is he?' Both Kibangu and Bradford laughed, and Bradford put his arm around Vera and said in a half-whisper, 'Shh, officially Nwapa does not exist – but he's what this dinner party is all about.'

Shortly after, the President had been drawn away from her to meet some British cabinet minister, and Vera found herself alone in the crowd. From a liveried waiter, she accepted a glass of white wine, then stepped over to a table to have some caviar.

As she did so, she noticed, out of a corner of her eye, that Ludmila Kirechenko was also alone, and had moved to a remote corner of the room to sit down on a love seat, probably because her feet were tired. It was a rare opportunity, Vera realized. She apparently had not been able to impress the KGB with the fact that her lack of knowledge about the sex life of the President and Billie was imperilling the entire project. Here was a chance to go over the head of the KGB straight to the rulers of the country. An anxious word to Mrs Kirechenko would bring the matter to the immediate attention of the Premier, who in turn would put pressure on Petrov either to help her at once or abandon the project. Yes, she told herself, it was the thing to do.

She veered away from the table of hors d'oeuvres and went rapidly through the milling guests to the person who could save her. She plumped down on the love seat next to Mrs Kirechenko, who seemed startled, then pleased. Vera cast about her to be sure that they were alone. They were, at least for the moment.

Vera pushed closer to the Premier's wife. 'I need your help,' she whispered. 'Please tell your husband – I –' She broke off what she was saying. She remembered that Mrs Kirechenko understood hardly a word of English. Quickly, Vera slipped into Russian. She began to explain her plight to the Premier's wife.

Before Vera could speak two sentences, Mrs Kirechenko bent toward her worriedly and interrupted. 'Do not speak Russian,' she cautioned. 'You do not know Russian. It is dangerous.'

Abruptly, the Premier's wife rose, left Vera, and became lost in the crowd.

Vera sat forlorn. Mrs Kirechenko had been right, of course. People in trouble did desperate things. Vera felt abandoned, and commiserated with herself. Then she realized someone had been behind the love seat, the KGB bodyguard Yankovich, who must have stationed himself there protectively when the two women had begun talking. She flashed him a foolish smile, but already his back was turned to her as he started to follow and stay with the Premier's wife.

Vera saw that the assembled guests were moving toward the doors that had been opened to the banquet hall. She saw her husband, standing in line with Kibangu, beckoning to her. She hastened to join them. The President, between Kibangu and herself, continued toward the double doors.

In an undertone, Bradford said to Vera, 'Quite a picture, the Soviet First Lady and the American First Lady cozily together on the love seat. What did you two talk about?'

'I haven't the faintest idea,' said Vera. 'It was hopeless. She knows about as much English as I know Russian. I wonder what she was saying?'

The President grinned. 'I suppose we'll find out eventually.' He dropped his voice. 'We have agents planted in that room, as I am sure they have. That's the game.'

Vera felt a flush of excitement as they went through the doors into the banquet hall. 'You mean we have an agent in there? Posing as a Russian? Working for us? Oh, Andrew, I don't believe you at all.'

Still grinning, he spoke under his breath. 'Look over your shoulder. The Russian with the flat hair and big nose. The one talking to the Premier's missus. Can you see him?'

She looked over her shoulder. She saw Yankovich having a last word with Mrs Kirechenko.

'You – you mean the Russian bodyguard?'

'Only he's not,' Bradford whispered. 'British MI6 planted him years ago. Now, let's forget it. Let's have dinner.'

Vera was engulfed with a wave of horror.

She had spoken to Mrs Kirechenko in Russian. She – the American First Lady who knew no Russian – had actually spoken in Russian, unaware that a British agent had come up behind her and might have overheard her words. What a fool she had been, what an unbelievable blunder she had committed. If Yankovich reported it to the British, she was dead. It could be a fatal error.

She glanced over her shoulder again. Yankovich was parting from Mrs Kirechenko.

'Here we are,' she heard her husband say.

He was holding out her chair for her. She sat down trembling, trying to think how to salvage her perilous situation. Prime Minister Heaton was to her left, directing a wine steward. To her right, the President was already engaged in conversation with Kibangu. Ignoring the Scotch salmon mousse set before her, she knew that she must act at once to avert disaster.

Unobtrusively as possible, Vera pushed back her chair, slipped out of it, and raising the hem of her gold gown a few inches, hastened back to the reception room. Except for a few stragglers lined up to enter the banquet hall, the room was empty. Then, to the left, she saw Yankovich heading towards the landing and the staircase. Wildly upset, she sought someone who might save her. Vera ran her eyes over the stragglers in line, and her gaze fell on Petrov's aide, KGB Colonel Zhuk.

She tried to remain calm as she approached him. Their eyes met. Her head made a slight signal, entreating him to follow her. She started for the door to the landing. She knew Colonel Zhuk had fallen out of line and was following her. As she reached the door to the landing, Colonel Zhuk darted in front of her and gallantly held it open.

It had to be casual and distant, she knew. She was the American First Lady and he a Russian security leader, someone she hardly knew.

'Thank you,' she said softly. 'The one going down the stairs, leaving the building –'

'Yankovich?'

'A British agent,' she said with a smile. 'He overhead me speak Russian to Mrs Kirechenko.'

'British agent? You are sure?'

'The President told me.'

Colonel Zhuk smiled back at her, but his eyes were cruel. 'Go back inside. Show no agitation. I'll handle this – if it is not too late.'

As she turned away, she saw Colonel Zhuk descending the stairway in great haste.

The orchestra in the banquet hall had just stopped playing when she returned to her seat, feeling conspicuous. The second she settle into place, Prime Minister Heaton, who had been listening to an interpreter speaking for Mrs Kirechenko on the other side of him, nodded, and rose to propose a toast. Vera turned her head. Her husband's eyes were on her, and he was frowning.

What came after that, she would have no memory of later.

The next few hours – the meal, with its borscht, its cold saddle of lamb, the conversation, the music – all had passed in a blur. She reacted to everything like an automaton. Her momentous blunder, her self-recrimination, played over and over in her head. This had become the big fear, the immediacy of exposure superseding her dread about the sex encounter. The sex thing was three nights away. But Yankovich was now, tonight.

The banquet seemed to last for ever. Vera was oblivious to most of it.

At last, some time before one o'clock in the morning, they were back in the privacy of their Claridge's hotel suite. No sooner were they alone in the bedroom, even before Vera could remove her mink coat, than the President turned on her.

'What in the hell were you up to?' the President barked. His handsome face was blotched with anger. Vera had heard about his occasional eruptions of temper. She had been briefed on them. But she had not seen one before, and she was taken by surprise.

'I – I don't know what you mean.'

'You damn well know what I mean,' he snapped, yanking off his bow tie. 'Walking out on us at the very start of the dinner. Just walking out, disappearing. You've never done that one before. It was a terrible display of bad manners. It's just not done, especially with the British.'

'I couldn't help it, Andrew,' she stammered. 'I – I had to go to the bathroom.'

'You'd just been to the bathroom before we got there.'

She tried to collect herself. 'Not that. I suddenly felt ill, nauseated. I had to pull myself together. I guess there was too much excitement.'

He had thrown aside his formal jacket. 'You could have managed,' he said. She could see that the steam had gone out of him, and his mind was already on something else.

She was contrite. 'I'm truly sorry, Andrew.'

'Never mind,' he said. 'I thought I should mention it.' He muttered to himself as he tried to get the studs out of his shirt.

'Let me help you,' she offered.

But he had managed to open his shirt and pull it off. 'Get yourself some sleep,' he said curtly. He dropped the shirt in a chair, and bare-chested he went to the bathroom and shut himself inside.

Vera stripped off her jewellery and began to undress. She would have to be careful about every move, she warned herself. He was high-strung, concerned about the Summit. He had probably taken the measure of Kirechenko and knew it was going to be a rough conference. Yet, he was not so preoccupied that he would overlook any unnatural behaviour on her part or fail to make such behaviour the target of his tension.

If his present mood continued, it was almost impossible that he would loosely discuss the American delegation's plans. Almost impossible, except for one thing in her favour. The resumption of sex three nights from now. That might do it, yet it might undo her. She had been too anxious tonight. Daring to convey her fears to the Premier's wife had been foolhardy. She had been naïve not to assume that the reception would be infiltrated by double agents. Needlessly, she had stuck her neck out, and any minute the axe might fall. She considered the paradox: she might lose her head – because she had lost her head.

She was in her nightgown. She padded into the sitting room trying to calm herself and prepare for bed. When she returned to the bedroom, Andrew was still not to be seen. The bathroom door remained shut. She wondered if she should wait for him. Actually, she did not want to talk to him any more tonight, not while he was in a foul mood.

She chased down Billie's usual sleeping pill with water and got into bed.

Sleep did not come at once, as she had hoped. Vera lay there for ten minutes, trying not to think. When she heard the bathroom door open, she closed her eyes and pretended to be asleep. The lights went out and the other twin bed creaked.

She must have dozed off, she realized, because the next thing she knew, she was groggily awake, roused by the persistent ringing of the telephone near him.

Andrew woke with a start, struggled to a sitting position, turned on a lamp, and groped for the phone.

'Yes? . . . Yes, it is.' He listened. 'Who? . . . Heaton, at this hour? . . . Okay, hold on, I'll get it.'

Hanging up, he got out of bed, and was putting on his blue silk bathrobe when he saw that his wife had been awakened.

'Prime Minister Heaton,' he explained. 'I've got to get to my desk. He wants me on the scrambler phone. Go back to sleep.'

Wide awake, she watched him leave the room, heard him unlock the connecting door to the adjacent suite that had been partitioned into the series of cubicles to serve as his temporary office. She could hear him speak to the Signal Corps night-duty man. Then silence.

Vera lay still, eyes open. The British Prime Minister calling the American President at 3.15 in the morning. What was this about? Vera would not allow herself to conjecture.

Eight minutes passed before Andrew Bradford returned, taking off his robe.

'Anything wrong, Andrew?' she asked.

'Plenty,' he said, cryptically. He reached the other side of the bed, sat down on it, rubbing his arms. 'Our best agent in the Russian delegation – they just found him – dead.'

'Dead!'

'Scotland Yard fished him out of the Thames a half-hour ago – multiple knife wounds – stabbed to death.'

'How horrible. Was it robbery?'

'They doubt it. His money wasn't touched. It appears to have been a political murder.'

'One of our agents?'

'British, but one of ours, yes. The British recruited him in Moscow years ago. He came here with the Soviet delegation, one of the bodyguards assigned to Mrs Kirechenko. He was at the affair tonight. Didn't I point him out to you? I can't remember. A fellow named Yankovich.' He shook his head. 'Bad loss. Not exactly an auspicious beginning for the Summit.'

He turned off the lamp and slid under the blanket.

'I wonder,' he said in the dark, 'who gave him away?' He yawned. 'Anyway, we'd better sleep. Good night, Billie.'

'Good night, dearest.'

Not until minutes later, when she heard him snore, did Vera dare think about what had happened.

The violence made her shudder.

She rolled on her side and snuggled deeper into the feathery pillow.

She felt light-headed with relief. She was safe, at least for three more days. Even that seemed less threatening right now. The KGB had protected her, as Alex had promised it would. It would protect her again.

Despite the fact that the President and First Lady and many of the key staff were away in London, Isobel Raines had endured an unusually busy day in the White House. There had been a steady stream of White House personnel dropping into Dr Rex Cumming's office with minor complaints and ailments, and as the only nurse in the office Isobel had been forced to work overtime.

Now, as she swung her BMW into the driveway of her house in Bethesda, she was pressed for time. She had made an early dinner date with her two closest women friends at a restaurant in Georgetown, and she did not want to be late.

She savoured these monthly dinners, the drinks and gossip, the chatting about life and the future. She did not want to miss any of it. By hurrying, she supposed she could still get in her bath before changing for dinner.

Isobel eased her car into the garage, set the hand brake, turned off the ignition. As she reached for the door handle, her eye caught something in the rearview mirror besides her own tousled red hair. When she had turned into her driveway, she had noticed a Ford with two nondescript men in it parked across from her house. She had paid no attention to the occupants of the Ford, assuming that they were waiting for someone in the house opposite.

She had been mistaken. The rearview mirror told her that the two men, or at least one of them, had been waiting for her.

One of them had stepped out of the Ford, crossed the street, and entered her driveway. He was a husky man, moustached, wearing dark glasses, and as far as she could make out a stranger. As he approached the rear of her car, growing larger in the mirror, she wondered if this was a hold-up. Not likely. It was still daylight. She kept her eyes riveted on the mirror with fascination. He seemed familiar, and at once she recognized him.

'Shit!' she exclaimed.

She started to open the car door to get away, but he was inside the garage, yanking at the passenger door on the other side.

'Miss Raines,' he called to her, 'I suggest you stay behind the wheel. I have to have a little talk with you. It's cosier here in the car.'

She had one foot out of the auto. 'Not now,' she said. 'I'm in a hurry. Leave me alone.'

He calmly sat down in the front seat. 'I need only a few minutes,' he said.

'No, I'm –'

'Miss Raines,' he said too quietly, 'stay put.'

She was half in the car, half out. She thought better of

190

leaving. It was no use. She had to face him sooner or later. She pulled herself back into the car and closed the door.

'All right, what now?' she demanded with irritation. 'The last time you promised you'd never —'

'Sorry,' he interrupted. 'I regret this call, but it is necessary. I have been requested to obtain a certain piece of information from you. Once I have it, I'll take my leave, and no harm done. I promise you I won't bother you again.'

'I heard that before. Who in the hell are you?'

'Who I am does not matter,' said Grishin. 'All that matters to you is what I know.'

She was perfectly aware of what he knew. Her old connection in Detroit with Da Costa. Her present position in the White House. Her occasional tumbles in the sack with President Bradford. Her two previous submissions to blackmail.

No matter what, she decided, this could not go on. They represented some foreign country, she had guessed from the start. Which one, she could not imagine — or maybe she could. To what purpose all these visits, she did not know. One thing certain. She could not continue betraying the President.

'So you've come to blackmail me,' she said.

'We only seek your cooperation,' he said.

'Well, I'm not cooperating any more. I'm sick of this. There's no end to it. I can see you'll never leave me alone. So I might as well stop it right now. Go ahead and leak what you want to about my past. What's the worst that can happen to me? I lose my job. There are other jobs somewhere. But I won't let you off free, either. I'll go to the FBI about you —'

'That would be inadvisable, Miss Raines.' His tone almost carried a note of regret. 'It would be bad for your health.' He paused. 'As to forcing us to leak your story, we wouldn't want to do that. We don't want to destroy you. Please reconsider. I promise you — this time I mean it — we will not be back. Answer one simple question, and it is over.'

She hesitated. He sounded sincere. Maybe he meant it. If she went along, maybe they would not bother her again. She reconsidered. It depended on what they wanted from her. She would see. 'The question,' she said, 'what is it?'

'It's about –' He was trying to find a way to phrase it. '– about the President's bed habits.'

Her anger surfaced. 'Don't you get tired of asking that over and over. My God, this is the third time.'

'We must know more.'

'You must also know I'm not going to tell you. It's no one's business. Anyway, that's not the kind of thing that can be explained.'

'Let me make it easier for you, Miss Raines,' he said quickly. 'Let me put it another way. Someone told us – we heard this from another source – that the President does not like – well, to be blunt, the President does not like normal sex.'

Isobel could not believe her ears. She suddenly burst into laughter. She kept on laughing. She tried to control herself. 'Who – who told you that?'

'Never mind. What's funny about it?'

Isobel had found a Kleenex in her purse and wiped her eyes. 'The thought of it, that's all. Because it's so wrong.'

'So wrong?'

'100 per cent wrong. Because he's straight as an arrow. You understand? Straight.'

'Do you mean –?'

She pulled herself together. 'You know what I mean. Now get out of here. Leave me alone.'

He nodded pleasantly. 'Thank you, Miss Raines.' He opened the door on the passenger side and left the car.

She watched his departure in the rearview mirror. She waited until the car across the street had gone. Then she got out of her BMW and started for the house.

There would not be time for a bath.

In the living room of her Kremlin suite in Moscow, Billie Bradford sat on the sofa, legs curled under her, trying to read an English edition, printed in Moscow, of Jack London's

The Call of the Wild. She was not particularly interested in the book, except as a time filler before dinner in two hours.

Alerted by the turn of the lock in the front door, she saw Alex Razin enter. She immediately closed her book, cast it aside, and lowered her legs. While she still classified him with the enemy, she did so uncertainly. She liked him. He was the only decent one on the other side. Besides, she wanted human company.

He dropped the latest newspapers on a table, and came towards her. 'How are you today, Mrs Bradford?'

She gave her usual answer. 'Frustrated and a bit bored.'

'I can understand that. Will you join me for a drink?' The drinking together had become part of their new daily routine for late afternoon.

'Of course,' she said. 'Only make mine double.'

At the side bar, pouring her a Scotch, himself a vodka, he inquired, 'Did you keep yourself busy today?'

'After a fashion. It was very depressing.'

'How so?'

He brought her the double Scotch, handed it to her, as he sipped his vodka.

She patted the sofa cushion beside her. 'Sit here.' He obliged her. She said, 'Listen to my tale of woe.'

'That bad?'

She drank down an inch of the Scotch. 'I started with the radio news in English. Mostly about my husband and Premier Kirechenko, their activities on their first day in London, their meeting at the Prime Minister's state dinner, some political speculation about the Summit and Boende, and a good deal about a Soviet bodyguard found floating in the Thames, stabbed to death.'

'Unfortunately true,' said Razin.

'Not a word about the First Lady, except that she accompanied the President to the state dinner. Then I turned on the taped television news. There I was, this time, in all my glory. Glamorous on Andrew's arm, in Whitehall, entering the Banqueting House.' She turned toward Razin. 'Do you know that vile little faker was actually wearing my new

193

Ladbury evening dress, the gold one? I couldn't believe my eyes. I could have killed her. And there were all those people, cheering her, greeting her, the spectators, press, guards, British escorts, and not one of them could see through her. Andrew least of all. It drove me up the wall. I simply can't imagine how she gets away with it. You know, Alex –' She stopped. 'There, I called you Alex. You'll have to call me Billie – if I *am* Billie.'

'Thank you, Billie.'

'You know, it made me feel so hopeless, so lost. As if I didn't exist. As if I'd become a non-person. Not anyone anywhere seems to know I'm on earth. No one needs me, misses me. Do you wonder that I got depressed? You have no idea –' Her eyes had moistened. She bit her lip, dumbly shaking her head.

Moved, Razin instinctively put his arm around her, wanting to comfort her. 'I can understand your feelings,' he said. Quickly, he withdrew his arm. 'Drink up,' he said.

They both drank without speaking.

He set down his glass, and for a while his fingers fidgeted with his trouser crease. 'There is something I have to discuss with you,' he said. 'Your mood makes it doubly hard for me.'

'I'm fine now,' she said. 'What is it?'

'It is something I shouldn't tell you, but I feel I must.'

Billie was becoming increasingly nervous. 'Tell me.'

'You remember the other day when I was forced to ask you in general terms how you regarded your husband as a lover? I hated to do it, but you knew the situation and you were kind enough to help me out. I had to repeat to Petrov what you told me. You were aware of that?'

'Yes.'

'Well, I repeated to Petrov what you had told me. The information was very general, in fact useless to them, except for one thing. It was a means of testing your veracity. Anyway, right after, the KGB went to other sources in America. To learn if you had been truthful about your husband. I'm afraid they now feel you were being untruthful. From what they've heard since, they believe you were lying about your husband.'

'Ridiculous!' Billie exploded. 'What other sources? Who else on earth could know how my husband behaves with me in privacy? Who, else could contradict me? Other sources? Whatever does that mean?'

'I can't say, because I don't know. It's not my business to know how the KGB operates.'

Billie's mind was still on the KGB's possible other sources. 'There is just no one they could have gone to,' she said, more to herself than to Razin. 'Unless they found some woman Andrew made love to before he met me. Or they think they've found someone he is making love to while married to me, some woman on the side. I doubt that. Or maybe it's true. I don't know. But supposing there were such a woman? He might behave differently with another woman than with me. It would tell them nothing about us.' She became conscious of Razin. 'Don't you agree? They are absolute fools.'

Razin threw up his hands. 'What can I say? I can only pass on to you, without their knowledge, that they believe you are lying, that you were untrustworthy in this matter – and therefore you may be untrustworthy in other matters. They met on this today. I heard about the meeting afterward. I made up my mind to prepare you. Billie, I care enough for you to tell you as much us I have. I must give you warning. In order to make you change your attitude, to make you truthful, they may be planning to punish you.'

'Punish me?' Billie said with disbelief.

'They can be ruthless.'

'Can you explain that?'

'I know of other cases. Suspects are tied up, interrogated endlessly. If they refuse to speak, they are kept without food and water. If they continue to resist, they are tortured. I am sorry to tell you these things, but –'

'Tortured? Despite who I am?'

'No matter who you are. They can pull out your finger-nails, burn your body, beat you, whip you, break your bones, defile and brutalize you. There is no limit. They are capable of anything, to teach their prisoner a lesson, to make their prisoner be truthful next time.'

Billie was aghast. 'They'd do this to me?'

'They might.'

'Alex, what can I do?'

Her question hung in the air, as he rose and walked to the radio. He turned it on to the music station, dialled the volume higher, and went back to her side.

'What can you do?' he repeated. 'There is not a thing you can do – except, perhaps, trust me. I won't have you tortured. I care for you too much. We are, in a way, fellow Americans.'

'Oh, Alex, you won't be sorry if you help me.'

'I've decided to take the chance. I am going to help you escape.'

She was overwhelmed with emotion. Spontaneously, she hugged him, kissed his cheek, thanked him. Embarrassed, Razin pushed her away.

'You must realize the risk – for both of us,' he said gravely. 'If we are caught, and I am implicated, I will be dead – and you, you will wish you were dead.'

'For myself, I don't care,' she said without hesitation. 'It's only you I'd –'

'Never mind about me. It is you I am concerned about.' He paused. 'Are you ready to take the risk?'

'I am, I am.'

'Very well.' He stood up. 'I have a plan. I have thought it out.'

'For when?' she asked, rising.

'Tomorrow. Get plenty of rest. Wear your drabbest clothes and flat-heeled shoes. Be prepared tomorrow at this time. I will see you then.'

He started to leave. As he reached the door, she hastened after him. She took him by the shoulders, looked him squarely in the eye.

'Alex, why are you doing this?'

He met her gaze. 'Because I love you,' he said, and with that he was gone.

The press conference for the British print media was being held in the drawing room of Claridge's ballroom off the hotel lobby. Nora Judson had invited twenty-four of the best-known and most influential British editors, feature writers, reporters in London, and none had declined. They were seated in the lyre-back chairs, writing pads on their knees, with Billie Bradford on a flower-bedecked platform facing them. Somewhat behind Billie, also seated in a lyre-back chair, was Nora, smiling, nodding and making notes, actually grading the First Lady (on a scale of 1 to 10, with 10 being perfect) as she responded to each question.

This encounter with members of the British press, whom most foreign visitors found snippy and snide, had proved to be as warm as a love-in. For over two years, the British journalists had been enthusiastic about the American First Lady from afar, but now, confronting her charm in person, their enthusiasm had been transformed into sheer adoration.

The proceedings were forty-five minutes old and, according to Nora's scoring system, Billie had earned a 9 or 10 for every answer she had given. From Billie's opening remarks (graded a perfect 10), which had been gracious and winning – really excellent, Nora decided, even if she herself had written them – to Billie's answer to the last question, things had never gone better.

Fortunately, Billie had been well briefed on the questions to expect, and every question up to this point had been anticipated. Nora flipped back through the pages of her notebook, reviewing some of those that had been posed. Had Mrs Bradford even been to London before? What had been her impressions the other times as contrasted with this visit? Did she play any role in the President's decision-making? Had she enjoyed her reunion with the Soviet Premier's wife? How did Mrs Bradford hope to spend her spare time in London? Would she be doing any sight-seeing on her own? Would she be shopping? For what? Had all her new wardrobe been done by Ladbury? What would she be wearing for tomorrow's reception at the Soviet embassy?

Nora beamed at Billie's grades. Her extemporaneous replies had been smooth as silk, yet lively, colourful, anecdotal, modest. Wonderful, wonderful, and in short minutes it would be done with, and Billie would have carried the day.

Nora raised her head from her notebook in time to see a tall, round-shouldered man in a brown suit, rising to his feet in the second row and introducing himself. '– of the *Observer*,' he was saying. 'A personal question, if I may?'

'Please,' said Billie Bradford.

'Since I know of your long friendship with her,' said the *Observer* feature writer, 'I'd like to know how you feel about Janet Farleigh?'

Nora's head swung toward Billie. To her surprise, Billie was smiling, as she embarked on her answer.

'I love her,' Billie was saying. 'I regard Janet Farleigh as I do members of my immediate family. As you remarked, ours is a long friendship. I met her on my first visit to London as a teenager. She was so kind to me, so wise. I was proud of Janet when she began writing her young adult novels and they caught on in the UK. I'll never understand why they've remained virtually unknown in the United States. I hope to change that, if I can. Anyway, I can't wait to see Janet Farleigh again. I hope to do so next week.'

Nora winced, and shut her eyes.

A ripple had gone through the press corps, followed by a low buzz of voices. Nora opened her eyes, and saw the journalists looking at one another in confusion.

A bosomy British lady in the back row had sprung up and introduced herself as the representative of the *Tatler*. She went on. 'Mrs Bradford, I'm not sure we heard you correctly. You said that you hope to see Janet Farleigh next week. Surely, you heard that Mrs Farleigh died of cancer two weeks ago?'

A hush had fallen on the room. Every eye was on Billie Bradford. The smile had left had face, instantly supplanted by a mournful expression. Nora watched her intently. Not an eyelash flickered.

'Forgive my unfortunate phrasing,' said the First Lady coolly. 'It is just that I can't accept Janet's passing. For me she continues to live. Of course, I was one of the first to be informed by her family of her untimely death. When I told you I hoped to see her – I meant I hope to see her last resting place – her grave – next week.'

A caustic voice was heard from the press corps, 'Don't waste your time looking for her grave, Mrs Bradford. There is none. What's left of her rests in an urn on the mantlepiece of the family flat in St James's Place. She was cremated.'

'Of course,' said Billie firmly. 'I was referring to that. I intend to pay a condolence call on the family next week. Any more questions?'

Listening, Nora was deeply shaken. She licked her lips and realized that her upper lip was damp. She searched her purse for a handkerchief, found one, dabbed at her upper lip. She stared down at her open notebook, quickly recorded the question on Janet Farleigh, and after a moment, marked Billie's grade. The grade was 0.

As Nora heard Billie winding up her answer to the last question, she leaped to her feet.

'Thank you, Mrs Bradford!' Nora called out loudly. To the press, she added, 'And thank you, one and all.'

As the journalists rose to leave, Nora grasped Billie by the arm and steered her toward the lobby. 'I'll be right with you. Let me get rid of them first.'

She waited until Billie had disappeared into the elevator, then stationed herself near the front door to say good-bye to many of the press members. In less than five minutes the drawing room had been emptied. Before shutting the door, Nora could overhear two of the male journalists, who had lagged behind the others, talking.

'Awkward little moment there, near the end, wasn't it?' one said.

'Strange,' said the other. 'Inexplicable.'

Nora pressed the door closed, and leaned back against it, trying to regain her equilibrium.

Inexplicable, she thought. Maybe, she thought.

Pulling herself together, she left the room, passed through

the lobby, hurried up the stairs, and entered the Royal Suite. She knocked on the bedroom door, and went inside.

Billie Bradford was seated before the mirror of her dressing table, fussing with her hair. She saw Nora materialize in the mirror, and spoke to her.

'Well, what do you say? How did I do?'

'You were never better,' said Nora, enthusiastically. 'Almost perfect.'

'Almost. Yes, almost.'

'No, really, you were on top of it, except for –'

Billie held up the palm of her hand. 'I know. The Janet Farleigh answer. My fault. I was inattentive. I let my mind wander. That'll never happen again. But not entirely my fault. The bastard tried to throw me with his question.'

'It was an innocent enough question, Billie.'

'You're being naïve. None of their questions were innocent. They're all bitches and bastards, the British press. The worst. I've heard about them. Don't ever get me into this again, Nora. No more press conferences.'

'No more, I promise,' said Nora.

Nora stood by lamely, watching Billie apply fresh make-up. She was bewildered. She wanted to tell Billie that the British press members this afternoon had been anything but bitches and bastards. They had been kind and loving. But Nora held her tongue. Billie was clearly upset and in no mood to be contradicted. She had even, indirectly, tried to blame Nora for the press conference. It was so unlike Billie.

'If you need me for anything –' she began.

'I don't,' said Billie. 'You can go. One thing. You can cancel my meeting with Guy. I've done enough talking for one day. I intend to treat myself to some shopping. Tell the Secret Service I'll be on my way to Harrod's in a few minutes.'

Although dismissed, Nora could not help but stare at Billie's face reflected in the mirror.

The face seemed hardened.

Billie looked in the mirror. 'What are you staring at?'

Flustered, Nora said, 'I – I was only admiring you.'

With that, she retreated and left.

In the corridor, she remembered to notify the Secret Service agent posted outside the door that Mrs Bradford would be out shortly to do some shopping. Then she walked slowly down the corridor, to the very end, to Guy Parker's single room. Lost in thought, she rapped on his door.

After a few seconds, the door opened and Parker filled it. His hair was rumpled and wet, not yet combed, apparently after a shower. He was bare-chested, a towel thrown over his shoulders. His handsomeness was not unexpected. She had found him attractive from the day they had first met in the White House. It was the reason she had always tried to avoid him.

He pretended shock. 'The elusive Miss Universe,' he said.

'With a message from Garcia,' she said. 'I'm to tell you the First Lady is cancelling you out for this afternoon. You're on your own.'

'How come?'

'Well, therein lies a story. It can wait.' About to turn away, she reconsidered. 'Or maybe it shouldn't. Hey, you want to earn some Brownie points? What about treating a colleague to a drink?'

'You've got a deal.'

'I'll be waiting in the bar,' she said.

'Claridge's has no bar. But they serve in the lounge off the lobby.'

'Put on your shirt,' she said. 'I'll be there.'

Fifteen minutes later, Nora was seated at a small table in a secluded corner of Claridge's lounge, half listening to the Hungarian orchestra which had just begun to play, when Guy Parker arrived to join her. He was wearing a tie and striped shirt and a suit now – definitely attractive – and she realized how glad she was to see him.

She held up her empty glass. 'Another – for a damsel in distress. Gin on the rocks. Make it a double.'

Parker beckoned the nearby uniformed waiter. 'Gin on ice, double portion. Scotch, J & B, on ice, also double.'

He studied her. 'You look like you've seen a ghost, Nora. What's wrong?'

'Who's says anything wrong?'

'You identified yourself as a damsel in distress.'

'Figure of speech.'

He examined her face again. 'Something's going on. Upstairs, when you told me Billie was cancelling, you added that therein lies a story. You also told me the story could wait, but maybe it shouldn't. What story, Nora?'

'Let a girl have a drink first, will you?' She indicated the waiter, with two glasses on a tray, advancing toward them. He served them and withdrew. Nora picked up her glass in two hands and gulped down the gin as though it were ninety degrees in the shade.

She set aside what was left of the gin, not much, she could see, and met Parker's steady gaze.

'Guy,' she said, 'a question.'

'Yes?'

'Tell me why you've been suspicious that – well, that Billie Bradford has changed. Why?'

'Oh?' He appeared surprised. 'I didn't know you were interested.'

'Maybe I am, maybe I'm not. Suddenly, I am.'

He was cautious. 'If you really want to know –'

'I do.'

'You won't bite my head off?'

'Not if you make sense.' Impulsively, she touched his cheek with her fingers. 'I'll be sweet to your head.'

'Okay. Here goes.' His suspicions, or at least his curiosity, had first been aroused after the return from Moscow, when they had been on the plane to Los Angeles. On her trial job at the *Los Angeles Times*, Billie had claimed to have talked to a newspaperman named Steve Woods. Parker had known that Steve Woods was non-existent. At the luncheon in Los Angeles, Billie was to be seated between one of her oldest women friends, Agnes Ingstrup, and the president of the Women's Clubs of the United States, and Billie had addressed the president as Agnes Ingstrup. At the luncheon, Billie had enjoyed oysters, which Nora herself said she never ate. At the baseball game in Dodger Stadium, Billie, a baseball fan, had spent most of her time listening to a grandfather explain the game to his grand-daughter. At her father's house in Malibu, Billie had not remembered that she had seen her nephew the month before, had seen her pet dog, Hamlet, turn against her. Earlier, Billie had pledged to Parker that she would discuss her personal relationship with the President and would also relate a funny incident about running into an actress that Bradford had been dating. And, as Nora already knew, a few days ago on the flight to London she had flatly refused to discuss either subject with Parker.

'Any single one of those instances might be explained as human frailty,' said Parker, 'but when taken all together, they add up to – suspicious. What do you think?'

'I think I need another drink,' said Nora. 'Another double.'

Parker ordered refills for both of them. He turned back to Nora. 'Well? Any reaction to my recital?'

'What does it all mean to you, Guy?'

'That, somehow, at least since Moscow, Billie's not been herself.'

He was waiting for some comment from her. She made no response. She pretended to listen to the music, but her mind was occupied with Billie. Their drinks came, the waiter went, and Nora began to down her gin.

After a silent half-minute more, Nora shakily put her drink on the table, spilling part of it. With great deliberation, using her napkin, Nora cleaned up the spillage.

Abruptly, Nora said, 'Billie had a press conference today, a little while ago, with the British press.'

'How'd it go?'

'She was in fine form, until near the end. Someone asked her about Janet Farleigh –'

'Janet Farleigh? Yes, I remember. Her old friend, the children's writer, here in London. The one who died a few weeks ago.'

'The one who died,' said Nora. 'Only Billie didn't know she was dead. Billie told them she was going to see Janet next week. When a member of the press reminded her that Janet was dead, Billie wriggled out of it, saying she meant she was going to see Janet's grave. One fresh reporter told her there was no grave, only Janet's ashes in an urn on the mantelpiece of the family flat. She wriggled some more and the conference was adjourned.'

Parker emitted a low whistle. 'What a doozy –'

'Double doozy, like double gin.' Nora lifted her glass and almost drained it.

'And the British press people, what was their reponse?'

'Like I told you, she got out of it. Well enough for the press. Not well enough for me. She's slick all right.'

He studied her once more. 'Nora, why did this one shake you up more than the incidents I had been reporting to you?'

'I don't know. I *do* know. Not only because this one just happened in front of me, but because the morning before we went to Moscow, in the White House – a few hours before she told you that you were coming along – remember?'

'Yes.'

'– she had got word of Janet Farleigh's death. She really came apart. It was a big thing, emotionally, not something she would be apt to forget.'

'Umm. How did she hear about Janet's death? A letter? Wire?'

'Not regular channels. The British ambassador sent over a personal note, hand-delivered.'

'Private.'

'Private, by hand. Just Billie knew and you and I knew.'

'What about obits?' asked Parker.

'None. Janet meant nothing in the United States.'

'But Billie *herself* knew.'

'Of course.'

'So how could she not know an hour ago?' Parker puzzled about it. He saw Nora finishing the last of her gin. 'Have another.'

Nora pushed away the glass. 'No, thanks. I'm a mile high.' She stood up woozily. 'Let's go up to your room.'

Parker signed the check, took Nora firmly by the arm, and led her to the elevator.

A few minutes later they reached his room. He unlocked the door, was about to turn on the light, when she pulled back his arm. 'No. Lamp's enough.'

He turned up the standing lamp near the bed. Nora shut his door, secured the chain. He watched her uncertainly. She walked toward him with care, so as not to lose her balance.

She looked up at him. 'I'm a little drunk, Guy. I admit it. Before I do anything foolish, answer me one thing honest – honestly. Do you have a letch for me?'

'A big one, Nora.'

'A serious one?'

'Real serious.'

'All right. I liked your face and body from the start. But I thought you were maybe kind of maybe egotistical – self-centred – expecting all women to have round heels for you. Later, I thought you were kind of a kook. Understand?'

He didn't, but he nodded.

She went on. 'I couldn't get involved with anyone that flawed. Guy, I had a husband. It was bad. He was selfish and spoiled. I finally shook him off. But everyone needs someone. So there was Billie. I could be devoted to her. But now – I don't know – now suddenly Billie's not there. Then you, you're there. I could see you better, a whole person. Nice, sensible, even sexy. I need someone I can believe in right now, Guy. Can I believe in you?'

He took her in his arms and kissed her. She felt the heat in her breasts, in her thighs. She felt his fingers unbuttoning her blouse.

With effort, she pushed away. 'You take off your things. I can take care of mine.'

He hesitated. 'Do you want to wait until you're sober?'

She had her blouse off. 'I don't want to be sober. I want to be high, higher than I am.'

As she unhooked her brassière, he turned away and busied himself undressing. Stepping out of his tight briefs, he turned back and saw her lying totally naked on the bed. As he advanced, his swollen penis began to rise. She was the most sensual sight he had ever seen. It was beyond belief. From the moment he had first met her, he had been undressing her in his mind, picturing what she was like nude. And here she was, glossy dark hair, green eyes fixed on him, ruby lips parted, milky white breast mounds with the brown nipples already pointed, the full thighs spread wide apart, the soft triangle of pubic hair visible.

She needed someone who needed her. So did he, so did he.

He was kneeling beside her on the bed. He lowered himself to kiss her mouth, touch her tongue with his. He kissed her neck and shoulders, massaging her breasts. He licked and kissed her nipples. He buried his head between her legs and kissed the moist vulva.

He was up on his knees as her fingers ran along his stretched penis. He was panting. She was finding it difficult to breathe.

'I'm ready,' she gasped. 'Love me, darling.'

His body sank down between her thighs, and resting on his elbows, he slowly slid into her all the way.

Twenty minutes later, they were both relieved and spent. Disengaged, he lifted himself off her, and lay back beside her.

'You're divine, Nora,' he said.

'You're not bad yourself, Parker,' she said. She kissed him. 'You're wonderful, you're incredibly wonderful. I never knew I could love fucking this much. Let's do it again some time.'

'Like tonight?'

'And tomorrow morning, too,' she said. 'You're a wonder boy. You're restored my faith in men completely. Do you have a cigarette?'

'I'm a pipe man, but I keep a spare pack around for the likes of you.' He opened the drawer of the bed table, fumbled for the package, extracted a cigarette for her and one for himself. He lighted each, and passed one to her.

'Another thing, Guy. An hour ago I wouldn't have thought

it possible. It was a horrible day. I was traumatized by Billie's blunder. I was in the dumps, miserable, and obsessed by the entire incident. Now I feel great, just great. No hangover from her or the drinks. You're a Merlin. You just made me forget the whole thing.'

Parker looked at her seriously. 'You can't forget it – it won't go away, you know.'

She blew a puff of smoke at the ceiling. 'I know,' she said. 'I'll tell you this. If I didn't know she was the First Lady, I would think she was someone else. But –' She stared at him. '– that's unthinkable, isn't it?'

He shrugged. 'Nora, all I can say is – you and I, we better start thinking about the unthinkable.'

7

The radio music was on louder than ever.

Billie Bradford stood motionless in the centre of the living room of her Kremlin suite awaiting Alex Razin's judgement as he circled around her, inspecting her attire. She had her long blonde hair drawn up in a tight bun at the back, to make her less conspicuous. She was wearing a short brown jacket, a striped beige blouse beneath it, a brown skirt, and serviceable flat-heeled shoes.

'Well?' she asked, anxiously, as Razin came in front of her.

'Fine,' she said. 'You look like a typical Western tourist, one of the wealthier ones, but that won't be uncommon. There will be plenty of them milling around in Red Square, snapping pictures of Lenin's tomb and St Basil's Cathedral. You shouldn't attract too much attention.' He glanced at his watch. '50 per cent of your chance for success in escaping will depend on timing.'

'And the other 50 per cent?'

'Luck,' he said.

Billie's frown deepened. 'And you think I can make it?'

'Most likely you will make it. Let's get back to timing, the one factor we can control. I have calculated carefully. You will emerge from this building and head for the Spassky Gate. I am allowing ten minutes for you to cross to the gate and exit. It will take another five minutes to cross Red Square, and walk unhurriedly past GUM's department store to the *voda* canteens on 25 October Street. There you will buy a drink –' Razin dug into his pocket for some coins and handed them to her. 'Here are several kopeks, to be on the safe side. Wait there after finishing your drink, and watch for a man carrying a blue suitcase. You will approach him. He will be expecting you. He will take you to the American embassy. From that moment on, it will be up to your ambassador.'

'You make it sound so easy,' said Billie.

'It might be. It might not. We shall see.' Razin consulted his watch again. 'We don't have much time, if you're to keep to the schedule. I will explain your route as simply as possible, and show it to you on a map I have drawn. We have fifteen minutes to go over the escape route. After that, I will leave you alone for ten minutes to memorize it. Then you must start, with no delays.'

'Where am I exactly? How do I start?'

'You are in the Supreme Soviet Building, in a suite of offices converted into these living apartments. Now follow me. I will show you where you start.' He preceded her into the kitchen. A few feet past the sink, he halted, and kneeled. 'There is an old trapdoor here, its outlines are lost in the design of the linoleum – Petrov overlooked it, if he even knew about it – but look here, two small notches.' He put the forefinger of each hand into the notches and partially lifted a square of the flooring upward. 'You see how easy it opens.'

Billie, intent on his every movement, nodded. 'Then what?' she asked.

'There are steps – really a wooden ladder – that will take you down to an underground room, a room that was used for cold storage in 1785. The walls are stone. It is extremely cold down there, and dark. Leave this lid off so you can have light from the kitchen. On the opposite side of the room you will find another set of stairs. Climb the stairs to an open hole. There was a second trapdoor. I've removed it. You will come up into another storage room, at ground level, used for furniture. There will be some light from two windows. There is only one door. Go to it and step outside. By outside, I mean out into the Kremlin street. Now I'd better show you the rest on my map.'

Razin lowered the trapdoor into place, and guided Billie back into the living room, gesturing her to the sofa. He sat beside her, pulling something from his jacket pocket. It was a folded sheet of paper, which he unfolded and flattened on the coffee table, smoothing it.

Billie peered down at the crude, pencilled map. Only one portion of it, on the right-hand side, was filled in with line drawings.

'The Kremlin is a mammoth place, as you probably know,' said Razin. 'Three walls in the form of a triangle. The inside covers twenty-eight hectares – that is sixty-nine acres. So as not to confuse you, I've pencilled in only the part that concerns you. This X mark shows where you are in the Supreme Soviet Building. The smaller x shows you where you will emerge. Actually you'll find yourself in a corridor, but right across from you will be a doorway to the outside. Am I being clear so far?'

'Perfectly.'

His finger traced a dotted line. 'Walk this way, along this building, parallel to the wall with arches. Now cross the street and go along the Administrative Building. At this point, at your left, is a spired tower with a red star on top. See it? This is the Spassky or Spasskira Tower, in English called the Saviour's Gate. There will be no more than one guard. Go past him into Red Square. He probably will not stop you. If he does, explain you were on a tour of the Armoury in the Oruzheinaya Palace and became separated from your tour group and expect to meet it at GUM's. The guard probably won't understand English. Point to GUM. The odds are he'll pass you through. Most of them are nice guys. And you are a pretty and innocent-looking American tourist.'

She tried to smile. 'I wish I was.'

'What?'

'A tourist. Pretty. Innocent.'

'At that point, you'll get by. Go right on. Stroll. All the way across Red Square, past the department store, to the street, right up to the *voda* canteens here. Buy yourself a drink. Wait for the man carrying the blue suitcase. Have you got it?'

'I – I think so.'

'If you have any questions, now is the time to ask them.'

She thought of several questions, and he answered them carefully.

'Very well,' he said. He took a second sheet of paper out of a pocket and laid it next to his map. The paper was blank. He handed her a pencil. 'Copy my map,' he said. 'I must destroy mine. I can't let you have anything in my handwriting.'

With an unsteady hand, she copied his map.

'There,' she said.

'Better carry it on you.'

She folded her sheet until it fitted into her jacket pocket. He picked up his map, tore it, and carried it into the bathroom. She heard the toilet flush. He returned empty-handed.

Billie got up, intercepted him, and facing him took both his arms. 'Alex, I don't know how I'll ever thank you.'

'Never mind. My time is up here. I have to go. Watch the clock. Remember, you have only ten minutes to memorize your route. Then leave at once.'

'I'm grateful beyond words,' she said. 'When I get home, I'll help you, I promise. You're the only thing that has made this nightmare endurable.'

'I'll remain in the Kremlin on other business until I'm sure you're safely out of here. If the alarm, the siren, does not sound, I'll know you're safe. Good luck, God speed.'

'Thank you, Alex.' She kissed him on the lips.

His eyes held on her. He was about to say something, but apparently thought better of it. Quickly, he left the room.

Once more alone, she returned to the sofa, sat down, removed the map from her pocket, laid it out and studied it, her eyes darting to the antique clock every few minutes. She tried not to think of the pitfalls ahead, the consequences of failure. The only diversion she would permit herself was the thought of a reunion with Andrew in London. Concentrating on her route, she saw that nine minutes had passed. She refolded the map, shoved it into her pocket, threw the strap of her purse over her shoulder, and headed for the kitchen.

Her heartbeat was accelerating as she lifted the trapdoor and shoved it aside. She backed down into the opening, got one foot and then the other on a rung of the ladder, and made a creaking descent.

The storage room, walls of rough-hewn stone, was almost unbearably cold. Shivering, Billie tried to get her bearings. In the shadows, at the far side, she made out what appeared to be rising steps. Reaching them, she saw the staircase was narrow and rickety. She climbed it on tiptoe, came up through the square opening into a dim, musty storeroom crowded with furniture covered with pieces of canvas.

At the door, she hesitated. Fear held her like a heavy weight. Her mind was clogged. She could not remember her next step. She tugged the map out of her jacket pocket, began to unfold it, then remembered. She pushed the map back in her pocket. The door would be unlocked, Razin had promised her. She would come out into a corridor. There would be an exit opposite her. She must go through it, turn right, walk along the building, cross a street, continue along the Administrative Building, see the Spassky Tower to her left, get over to it, and head for Red Square.

She wondered if Razin had allowed her enough time. Every afternoon, since she had been a prisoner, KGB guards had entered her suite to deliver lunch or supplies. The exact time they appeared was erratic. If they entered soon, and realized that she was missing or that the trapdoor in the kitchen had been removed, they would sound an alarm.

This thought impelled her to move faster. She took the doorknob and pulled. The door opened, Razin had kept his word. She was in a wide corridor, no one in sight on either side, and the exit across from her. She went through it and was outdoors at last, the air humid, the sky overcast. She saw the reddish wall ahead, a lesser tower identified on her map as the Senate Tower beyond which stood the Lenin Mausoleum, a group of four Red Army soldiers – visored caps, red shoulder tabs on their uniforms – in a deep conversation, and finally the walk to her right. She turned right – go casually, Razin had warned her – and started alongside the Supreme Soviet Building. She reached a street as a Russian truck rumbled past. Then she traversed the street. Another structure, the Administrative Building. Eyes straight ahead, purse swinging, she strode close to the building. Off and ahead, to her left, was the huge tower with the Red Star on top, Spassky Tower, her last trial before escaping this fortress.

About to leave the curb, a thin, shrill, distant sound pierced her eardrums. The sound rose higher, fuller, louder into a wail. It shrieked again and again, incessantly. Billie froze in place. A siren.

What had Razin said? He would know she was safe *if the alarm, the siren, does not sound*.

But it was sounding. She was unsafe. The siren was for her.

She was chilled and immobilized, uncertain which way to turn. She cast about to see if anyone was responding. No one was in view, not even the group of soldiers she had noticed when she emerged outdoors. For a split second she considered her options. To brazen it out and try to make the Spassky exit? To find some place to hide until it was quiet again? To scramble back to her suite?

Suddenly, as she teetered on the edge of decision, the entrance of the Spassky Gate exploded with life. A squad of uniformed Soviet soldiers, carrying rifles, catapulted into the open, swarming into the street.

Instinctively, Billie reacted. She had no choice now but to run, to get away from them, to hide. Her heart pounding, she spun back to the building behind her, hurried along it searching for the nearest door.

She heard shouts not far away. Looking back, she saw at least three of the guards point toward her, yelling at her in Russian. She plunged into the building, holding on to the strap of her flying purse.

Around the corner she went, slipping, regaining her balance, rushing past a row of office doors bearing incomprehensible plates with Cyrillic lettering. She searched for something that resembled a closet or bathroom door, could make out none. A new sound assaulted her. She heard the pounding of boots and clatter of guns in the corridor she had left behind. She slowed, tripped to a stop before the handiest office, its entrance an impressive double door. Her fingers snatched at the door lever, pressed down, and she pushed inside and shut the door behind her.

Breathless, she swung around to find out where she had landed. She was in a vast ornate room, a glass chandelier, massive fireplace, oriental rug, a line of gilded chairs against one wall. The room was empty, thank God, and then she saw that it wasn't, and her throat constricted. The farthest chair along the wall, next to another set of tall double doors, was filled by a stout, older lady in a print dress, who sat staring at her.

Attempting to catch her breath, Billie went toward the woman, trying to conjure up one useful Russian word from the few she had learned. It was impossible. She had reached the woman. 'Do you – do you understand English?' Billie gasped.

The stout woman blinked at her. 'I'm American, from Texas –'

Billie closed her eyes with relief. 'Thank God,' she whispered. She opened her eyes. 'Can you tell me – where am I? Do you know?'

'Why, yes – you're in the reception room of some Soviet office where the minister of culture is seeing people today.'

'You say you're an American?'

'All the way from Texas. I'm Mrs White from the Houston Museum of Fine Arts.'

'Listen,' Billie whispered fiercely, 'you've got to help me.'

Mrs White recoiled. 'But I don't –'

Billie grabbed her shoulder tightly. 'Do what I tell you. The second you leave here, go to the American embassy - Ambassador Youngdahl is a friend of mine – tell him I'm here in the Kremlin, being held prisoner – tell him someone else is pretending to be me –'

Mrs White's eyes and mouth were wide, as if she were being put upon by a lunatic. 'I – I – don't – don't understand you,' stammered Mrs White. 'Who are you? I –'

Billie had her by the shoulder again. 'Look at me. Don't you recognize me?'

'I – I think so. You're –'

'I'm Billie Bradford. Wife of the President. I'm –'

'What are you doing here like this?'

'Let me explain. I'm –'

One of the double doors next to Billie rattled.

'My appointment with the minister,' said Mrs White excitedly, trying to get to her feet.

The door to the inner offices started to open, did not fully open yet, but Billie could make out the secretary's hand as she spoke to someone in Russian inside her office.

Frightened, Billie backed away to the entrance, to avoid detection, cast Mrs White an imploring look, then quickly opened the hall door, stepped outside, shutting it.

She turned to run, and bumped squarely into two KGB guards.

She screamed, 'Don't kill me!'

Then, as the world slid from sight, and they grabbed her roughly, she lost consciousness.

If it wasn't happening to her, she would never believe it could happen.

Billie Bradford was fully conscious again. She was in a chair in her Kremlin living room. She could not move her arms or legs. She was tied to the chair. Her arms were drawn painfully together behind the chair, linked at the wrists by handcuffs. Her ankles were tightly bound by a strap or belt.

A short distance away, two powerful men in KGB uniforms were at the telephone. One was making a call. He had the twisted facial features of a gargoyle. He was identifying himself as Captain Ilya Mirsky, then jerking his thumb at his silent companion and apparently saying he was with Captain

215

Andrei Dogel. He was speaking in a flow of Russian, his thick upper lip curled back to reveal a row of steel-capped teeth. He was listening. He was hanging up.

Mirsky nodded to his companion and came toward her.

Mirsky stood over her. 'You are awake, I see.' His silver teeth disconcerted her. His breath smelled of onions. 'My English, it is not exact, but you will understand. You tried to escape. This we do not blame you. But how you escaped, this we must know.'

Billie sat pinned down, frightened by what she had dared do, by her failure, by her helplessness.

Mirksy's face was closer, while Dogel watched with no expression at all.

Mirsky said, 'I must ask certain questions. I must have your answer. You will answer.'

Billie offered no response.

'Questions,' Mirsky said. 'I must find who was – how say? – involved – involved with you in this escape? We see the floor of kitchen. We see your map, a good map. Who helped you, showed you the way, where to go? Who was the one to accomplice you? Is there CIA agent here in Kremlin?' He paused, 'Who was your help?'

Billie shook her head, compressed her lips.

Mirsky straightened, waited. 'You do not tell us, we do not leave. You tell, we go.'

She would not answer.

Mirsky said, 'We know you are big person. We do not care. To us you are small. You understand? If you do not give the truth, we take it from you. We make you tell. Who was your help?'

'No one,' she said defiantly.

'You lie!' Mirsky's fists knotted. His features had become menacing. 'One more chance. We are busy. Now – who?'

'No one,' she repeated.

'Whore liar!' he bellowed, his right arm swinging at her, the back of his hand hitting her across the cheek.

Stung, choking, she gasped, 'No – don't –'

'I say yes, you speak!' His rough flat palm whipped across

her face, then slashed back, his knuckles hitting her in the mouth. She moaned, almost falling over with the chair. Her tongue tasted blood. Tears began to well.

Through her moist eyes, she saw the front door behind them open. She could make out Alex Razin.

Mirsky had drawn back his hand to strike her again, when Razin roared out a word in Russian. Mirsky whirled about, stiffened. Razin rushed at him, shoved him aside. 'What in the hell is going on here?' Razin yelled.

'She tried to escape,' Mirsky said sullenly. 'We have orders –'

'The only orders come from me,' snapped Razin. 'I am the one in charge. No one else. Now release her.'

Mirsky tried to protest. 'But –'

'At once,' demanded Razin. 'Do you want me to call General Petrov? Take off those damn handcuffs. Untie her.'

Against their will, the two KGB guards obeyed. Mirsky went behind her to unlock the handcuffs. Dogel got down on his knees to undo the strap. Freed, Billie began to slump forward, but Razin caught her before she could fall. Over his shoulder, he said, 'Now, you fools, get out of here.'

Mirsky uttered one more token protest. 'But the commandant of the Kremlin guards –'

'Get out!' Razin bawled.

With as much dignity as they could muster, Mirsky and Dogel backed off and swiftly left the room.

Alone with Billie, Razin examined her face. Her eyes were closed. Blood was still trickling down her chin from her mouth. Razin got an arm around her back, another under her knees, and he lifted her off the chair and carried her into the bedroom. Gently, he placed her on the bed. He examined her face more carefully, his fingers probing inside her mouth to locate the source of her bleeding. Having found the cut on her inner lip, he went into the bathroom, gathered a bottle of alcohol to use as an antiseptic and a box of cotton swabs. He brought them to the table beside the bed. Using wet cotton, he wiped the blood from her cheeks and chin. Then, partially raising her, he removed her jacket, unbut-

217

toned her blouse and pulled it off, and washed the remaining blood from her throat and chest down to her brassière. After that, he worked his way on to the bed, until her head was in his lap. He relocated the lip cut, and stayed the bleeding with a swab of cotton. Finally, he applied alcohol to the laceration.

Cradling her head in one arm, Razin began to rock her back and forth. Her eyes gradually opened.

'You're all right now, Billie,' he said.

'Thanks to you. When they caught me, I was so scared. They were hurting me –'

'It's over with, Billie. No more hurting you. I won't let them. There's nothing to be afraid of from now on. You have my word.'

Her arms reached up and around him. She clung to him. 'You are so kind. Without you, I don't know what would happen to me.' She drew herself closer, huddling against his chest. 'My escape, it was close – but they found out.'

'I heard,' he said. 'I came right over. No one will harm you again.'

'You promise?'

'I promise.'

Her hands sought his head, brought it down close, and she pressed her bruised lips to his out of gratefulness and relief. His lips held on hers as he began to kiss her. He caressed her bare shoulders.

Because she was so alone, so afraid, so grateful, she responded to his tenderness, touching his face, stroking it. He drew her against him, his fingers gliding across her back. One finger touched the hook of her bra, releasing it. The bra loosened, and he lifted half of it away. The rising curve of a soft white breast, with its large circular pink nipple, was fully exposed.

'I love you, Billie,' he murmured from deep in his throat.

His head dipped down, his tongue seeking her nipple.

'Oh, no,' she groaned, her arms tightening around him. 'I need you, Alex, I need you, but please –'

Her nipple had grown to a point, and his mouth covered

218

it, as his free hand moved down to her waist, reached the zipper of her skirt, pulled down the fastener. Now his fingers had the elastic top of her bikini panties. He was pushing them down.

She was breathing in gasps now, when she felt his fingers reach her pubic hair. That instant, she came to her senses, wrenching free of him, trying to sit up, grabbing for his arm. She clutched his arm, and tried to pull it away. 'No, Alex, please don't. I've never done this. I can't.'

His arm was still. He searched her eyes.

'I mean it,' she whispered. 'I can't do this. I'm so grateful to you, but don't go on.'

Slowly, he removed his hand. 'I'm sorry,' he said.

'You know how I feel about you,' she said hastily. 'It's just that –'

'Never mind,' he said, separating himself from her and rising to his feet. 'I'll see that you are never threatened again. There was a mix-up. The Kremlin's KGB officer probably did not know you were a special case, and that we are solely in charge. Can I get you a drink?'

'No.'

'Then let me look in on the Kremlin officer. I'll be back to see that you're all right, before I go.'

'Thank you, Alex.'

After he had departed, Billie half sat up against the back-board of the bed, trying to sort out what had happened between Alex and herself. She looked down at her loose bra, open skirt. How had she permitted him to go this far? No, it had not been sex hunger, body hunger, although for a few heated moments there she had been carried away. It could only have been that she owed a debt, a big one, and wanted to repay him and maintain his goodwill. After all, he had risked his own life by helping her in the escape attempt. He had prevented her from being beaten and tortured short minutes ago. He, alone, was her only ally in this terrible place. She owed him so much. She had wanted to give him something back, some show of affection. When she had tried to do so, he had misread her gesture. Being a man, a human, he had wanted her entirely. This was understandable. Briefly, she had lost her control, that and not wanting to disappoint him. Yet, in the end, she could not give herself to him. She simply could not.

She considered Alex Razin. He was a decent man. There was no doubt about that. He had not forced himself upon her, pressed her to submit. This very minute he was with the Kremlin commandant to ensure her safety. Once he gave the order, no one would harm her again.

Suddenly another thought surfaced. Who was Razin to go to an officer on duty in the Kremlin and give him an order? Who was Razin to countermand the instructions given to the KGB guards who had been punishing her?

What had Razin said as he left the room? *You are a special case . . . we are solely in charge.*

We?

Petrov and himself? But Petrov was a general and the chairman of the KGB for all the Soviet Union. Razin was merely a civilian interpreter. What gave Razin such power?

Who was he, truly?

Her eyes fell on his sports jacket, hanging over the back of a chair. Before going to the bathroom to obtain alcohol and cotton, he had removed his jacket. A short time ago, leaving to see the Kremlin commandant, he had left his jacket behind and gone in shirt-sleeves. He would return soon to retrieve his jacket and to make sure she was all right.

Meanwhile there was his jacket. Perhaps it carried the key to his identity.

She came off the bed, her jaw and cheek throbbing, catching at the waistband of her skirt before it dropped. She ran the zipper up it. She slipped the brassière cup over her naked breast and hooked the brassière behind. Thoughtfully, she slipped her blouse on and tucked the bottom inside her skirt. All the while, her gaze remained on his jacket.

At last, she stepped over to the chair, dug one hand into a side pocket of his jacket. A comb, a pen, a loose button. Then the other pocket. A package of cigarettes, a lighter. She drew back one part of his coat. The inner breast pocket was bulging. She fished into it and pulled out his worn brown leather wallet.

She held it, wondering whether she would find out more about him and whether she really wanted to know. She decided that she did want to know. In the currency compartment there were roubles, high denomination bills. She unbuttoned the flap that covered a half-dozen cards encased in plastic. She began to flip them. One card, two, three, four, all in Cyrillic, incomprehensible. Next, a snapshot, a picture – of herself! She was astounded. What madness. She brought the wallet and photograph up closer. A waist-length picture of herself, all familiar except – except – except the embroidered peasant blouse. She did not own such a blouse. At once, the truth struck her, jarred her. This was not herself. This was her double, her actress double now posing as Billie Bradford in London. She studied the picture. Aside from the strange blouse, the woman was her exact likeness. And it made sense, being in Razin's wallet. He had admitted from the start working with her double. He probably loved the double, or else why keep her photo in his wallet? She reconsidered his attempt to make love to her – had he regarded Billie as a surrogate for his real love?

More slowly, she examined the remaining three cards. Unreadable. Only the heading of the last card, over a passport-sized photo of Razin, suggested something familiar. She tried to remember where she had seen that heading, the lettering, the Cyrillic initials before. She thought backwards, to her first meeting with Petrov. He had shown her his ID card, and had identified the initials as standing for KGB.

Here were the very same initials on the card from Alex Razin's wallet.

The Russian history and guide books Nora had given her had spelled it out in English. *Komitet Gosudarstvennoi Bezopasnosti* - K G B - KGB.

No more mystery. Alex Razin was an out-and-out KGB agent.

The rotten bastard.

Hastily, she closed his wallet and stuffed it back into the

inner pocket of his sports jacket. Blindly, she sought her package of cigarettes, found it, took one, lighted it, and sat down on the side of the bed to think.

It wasn't easy, thinking. She was still suffering aftershock from the full realization of Razin's identity. Finally, clarity came, and with it all the recent events during her imprisonment fell into place. Reality was hard to accept, but the truth of what had happened could not be denied.

So – Alex Razin, her benefactor, her friend, the half-American boy, the mild, sympathetic interpreter, was a KGB agent along with the worst of them. He had been the buffer against Petrov. He had tried to help her escape. He had protected her from being punished by the brutal KGB. But it had all been a vast charade.

Billie had seen enough films, read enough novels, to know the Good Cop and the Bad Cop routine. General Petrov had played the Bad Cop. To frighten her. Razin had played the Good Cop. To protect her and win her confidence. The escape had been the climactic part of the script, to make her believe in Razin completely, to soften her.

But to what end?

Her mind paraded possible motives, and fastened on one. If everything else had come clear, the motive was crystal clear. Billie's double in London, the Soviet imposter, the Second Lady, was in deep trouble. Her double knew everything about her except one fact, now the most vital fact. As long as the KGB had thought there was to be no sex during the Second Lady plot, there had been no problem. But now that a doctor had said Billie could resume sexual activity with Andrew in a few days, there was panic on the Russian side. That was the one area that the KGB knew nothing about. The performance of the Bradfords in bed was a closed book to them. Unless their Second Lady could be told what to expect from the President in bed, and what the President would expect from her, their whole plot would go down the drain.

The KGB's only hope of learning about Billie Bradford's sexual behaviour was to learn this from Billie Bradford, herself. Yet, how did they actually expect to learn this from her?

All at once, she realized what they hoped to do.

Her face tightened with determination. Never, she told herself, never in a million years would she let them find out.

How she behaved in bed with Andrew or any man? Never, never, never would they get the slightest hint.

Which gave her one bright hope – that her double would handle herself wrongly in bed, that Andrew would become suspicious of his so-called wife, that he would get the truth out of her and expose the whole KGB operation.

But then, thinking about it, that hope dimmed. Without knowledge, the Second Lady might play it wrong. At the same time, dammit, she might play it right and go on in triumph. It was fifty-fifty.

Yet, there was another hope. She had almost forgotten. Now, remembering, her heart lifted. The pudgy woman she'd run into in that reception room, when she had been trying to escape. That poor bewildered Mrs White from Houston, the museum woman from Texas. Billie had begged her, perhaps unclearly, to go to the American ambassador in Moscow and repeat what Billie had told her.

The question was – would she go?

It was late afternoon in Moscow, and still warm, and Mrs Louise White, of Houston, Texas, was perspiring after all the walking and activity during this strange day.

She halted on Tchaikovsky Street – such a romantic name – to consult her guidebook once more. Yes, the guidebook reassured her, she was on the right street. The address of the American embassy in Moscow was 19/23 Tchaikovsky Street. She realized that her destination could not be far away. She resumed walking.

Louise White had every reason to feel happy, yet she felt oddly disturbed. She had come to the Soviet Union on a charter flight with a group of art patrons, landing in Leningrad. The visit to the Hermitage had been a memorable experience. Yet, sight-seeing had not been the sole purpose of Mrs White's tour. Actually, she had been sent on a mission. The primary purpose of her trip was to meet with the minister of culture of the USSR in the Kremlin in Moscow. She was to discuss with him the possibility of obtaining a loan of thirty French Impressionist paintings in possession of the Soviet Union for exhibition in an important show the Houston Museum of Fine Arts was mounting in a year's time. The minister of culture had proved amiable and receptive, had promised to take it up with his superiors and have an answer for her a month from now.

For Louise White, it had been a successful and heady meeting, marred only by the peculiar incident in the minister's reception room. Leaving the Kremlin, she had decided to forget the encounter with the frenzied woman and her improbable claim that she was American's First Lady. Mrs White had rejoined her tour group, determined to enjoy her brief stay in Moscow, but somehow she had lost interest in the sights. The incident in the Kremlin nagged at her. The blonde woman who had burst in on her in the minister's reception room *had* resembled Billie Bradford. The woman had implored Mrs White to see the American ambassador for her. She had seemed desperate. Crazy or not, the woman's request did deserve attention. At last, Mrs White decided that, even if she was making a fool of herself, she must report the incident to the ambassador.

After being instructed in the use of a Russian telephone by her Intourist guide, Louise White had broken away from her tour group. She had found the telephone number of the American embassy in her guide book. She had located a telephone kiosk and dialled 252-00-11, after depositing a 2 kopek coin. When her call was answered, she had asked to speak to Ambassador Youngdahl about an urgent matter. Instead, she had been switched to an embassy staff officer, a Mr Heller. She had introduced herself, again invoked the fact that this was an urgent matter she must discuss with the ambassador. Mr Heller had told her to come and see him, and had given her directions to the embassy.

In five minutes, Mrs White had reached the American

embassy. It had been described to her as a nine-storey yellow-brick building, the windows protected by aluminium screens and the roof crowned with a maze of antennae and wires. She double-checked the address in her guidebook. This was it. Starting for the front door, she was intercepted by one of two armed KGB guards. Proudly, she displayed her United States passport. One guard looked at her passport photograph, looked at her and, satisfied, waved her on.

At the front door, she pressed the buzzer, was aware that she was undergoing scrutiny by means of a visual monitoring system. A hollow voice came through a speaker requesting her name, citizenship, business. She patiently replied. She was told to wait. After a minute, perhaps two, the front door swung open.

Mrs White stepped inside. A tall, thin, somewhat distracted young man in a tan suit met her and introduced himself as Mr Heller. If she would follow him to his office, they could discuss her 'urgent matter'. Mrs White firmly stood her ground.

'I'm here to see the ambassador only,' she said.

Mr Heller, with the air of one who knew his guest was going to be difficult, said to her as nicely as possible, 'I'm afraid that's impossible on such short notice, Mrs White. Ambassador Youngdahl is tied up with important appointments the rest of the afternoon.'

'What I have to tell him may be more important.'

'But he's busy.'

'I'll wait.'

'Mrs White, if you'll simply relate your business to me, I'll see that the ambassador hears about it.'

'No.'

'That would give us time to arrange a future appointment with him.'

'No.'

The bickering went on, but Louise White would not be deterred. In her home town, Mrs White was well known for her indomitable spirit and her fierce determination. If a ticket had to be sold, a donation for charity solicited, an endorsement sought, Mrs White was always the one given the assignment. For this very reason, the Houston Museum of Fine Arts had selected her to go to Moscow to talk the Russian minister of culture into the art loan.

Mr Heller was no match for her. After five minutes, rather than let the confrontation develop into a heated scene, he gave up. With a sigh, he told her to wait, and went to a telephone at the reception desk. He spoke to someone in an undertone. He nodded. He hung up.

The embassy officer returned to her. 'Very well, Mrs White. The ambassador will see you. But he can see you only briefly. He has another appointment in five minutes. His office is on the ground floor. I'll show you the way.'

In no time, Louise White was seated across the desk from Ambassador Otis Youngdahl. He was a lanky, white-haired Minnesotan. His hands nervously moved and straightened papers on his glossy desk as he offered Mrs White a smile and tried to be gracious.

'Well, now. What's on your mind, Mrs White?'

She glanced about her. 'Are you sure we're alone?'

'Of course we're alone.'

'No, no. I mean is your office bugged?'

The ambassador couldn't help but grin. 'Are you asking if the Russians have installed listening devices in this room? I seriously doubt it. But one never knows from day to day.'

'Then I can't speak to you. It would be too dangerous for me.'

The ambassador saw that this could go on for ever, and besides he was mildly curious about what nonsense this Texas tourist woman considered so serious and private. He decided to accommodate her paranoia. All this she could guess, as he abruptly stood up. 'Very well,' he said. 'We have a special safe room here, a sub-room where we hold confidential conversations.' The ambassador led Mrs White into an adjacent cubicle furnished only with a table and a half-dozen chairs. As he motioned her to be seated, he said, 'This area is shielded from penetration by electromagnetic waves. The walls are steel-panelled with a mesh of wires inside the panels to stop outside radio signals and baffle eavesdropping devices.' He sat down opposite her. 'Now do you feel you can speak?'

Louise White felt a surge of excitement. She nodded, pleased. She began to explain her reason for being in Moscow. She told of her appointment with the minister of culture in the Kremlin. Early this afternoon, she had gone to the Kremlin for her meeting.

'I was waiting in his reception room to see him,' she said, 'when it happened. It was unbelievable.'

She paused to recall to mind the entire incident. The ambassador prodded her. 'What was unbelievable, Mrs White? Please tell me what happened.'

'I was just sitting there, alone, minding my own business, when a youngish woman, a blonde, ran into the room, out of breath. She looked like she was running from someone, trying to find a place to hide. Then she saw me, and came right over. She asked me if I was an American, if I spoke English. She asked in perfect English. I told her who I was. She took hold of my arm, pleaded with me to help her. She said something like, "Soon as you leave here, go to the American embassy. Ambassador Youngdahl is a friend of mine. Tell him I'm being held prisoner in the Kremlin. Tell him somebody else is pretending to be me." I didn't know what to make of her when she stuck her face practically into mine and said, "Don't you recognize me?" I looked at her, and the fact is she did resemble someone whose face I had often seen on television and in the newspaper. She said, "I'm Billie Bradford, wife of the President." Before I could ask her more, I was called in for my appointment. That's when she turned and hurried out of the reception room. I didn't know what to make of it, but I had no time to think. I was busy with the minister. Afterwards, I joined my tour again. But the more I thought about her, the more I realized that she did look like Mrs Bradford. After a few hours, I decided it was my duty to report the incident to you. So here I am.'

Ambassador Youngdahl was silent a short interval, eyeing

her, considering her much as he might regard a person who had come off the street to tell him she had met a UFO pilot.

Now that the story was off her chest, it seemed more unlikely than ever and Mrs White squirmed uncomfortably under his steady gaze.

'Well, Mrs White,' the ambassador said, 'I hardly know what to make of this. When did the – the encounter with the young woman take place?'

'A little before two o'clock this afternoon.'

'And you thought she was the First Lady?'

'*She* said she was.'

'Well, of course, anyone could say that, as a joke, or because they were unbalanced.'

'True. But I must admit she did look like Mrs Bradford.'

The ambassador tilted back in his chair. 'Have you ever met Mrs Bradford – or seen her?'

'Only on television.' Mrs White felt rattled. 'I know this all sounds bizarre, Mr Ambassador. It was to me, too, at the time. But there she was.'

The ambassador nodded, continuing to hold his gaze on her. 'Uh, Mrs White, a personal question, if I may. Have you taken any medication while travelling?'

'What do you mean?'

'Like, well, any mood-changing prescriptions?'

'Of course not.'

'Did you have lunch before going to the Kremlin?'

'Our group did – yes –'

'Were cocktails served?'

Mrs White was affronted. She stiffened. 'Mr Ambassador, I was perfectly sober in the Kremlin, as I am right this minute. I'm here only as an American citizen, doing my duty. Shouldn't I have reported this?'

'Oh, you did the right thing, certainly.' The ambassador scratched his head thoughtfully and sat up straight. 'Mrs White, I can tell you only this much. The First Lady of the United States is in London with the President. I said hello to her myself yesterday. She couldn't come to Moscow overnight without my knowing it –'

Mrs White interrupted him. 'Mr Ambassador, I don't know what more I can say. This woman, she told me she was a prisoner. She told me someone else was pretending to be her. She told me to tell you. I've done what had to be done, and that's all.'

Ambassador Youngdahl forced a weak smile. 'And properly so,' he said, standing. 'It is certainly an unusual story.' He had her by the elbow and was leading her out of the safe room and through his office. 'I assure you, I will look into it further. I thank you for bringing this to my attention.' From the doorway he called to his secretary. 'You can show Mrs White out.'

As Louise White turned to go, the look exchanged between the ambassador and his secretary was not lost on her. They were saying to each other: tourist season is cuckoo time.

She felt angry, but by the time she was outside she felt righteous in her vigilance.

Then she wondered who that poor lady in the Kremlin really was and what had happened to her.

President Bradford's personal work area in Claridge's hotel in London consisted of a sprawling suite connected, by a small hallway, to his private suite. The work area was sub-divided into a circle of offices that surrounded the roomier space serving as the President's executive office. The most important of these satellite rooms was the one used by the President's secretary, Dolores Martin, which had one door that led into the hotel corridor and another that led into the President's executive office and a third that led to the other staff rooms.

Now, in the late afternoon, the sole occupant of the entire work complex was Nora Judson.

Since the President had wanted his own secretary to take notes at a meeting being held in a suite down the hall that had been converted into a conference room, Nora Judson had agreed to fill in for Dolores Martin for a few hours before having dinner with Guy Parker.

Nora sat at Dolores's desk, trying to concentrate on the

final draft of the First Lady's schedule for tomorrow, her mind constantly drifting to Guy Parker and the deep suspicions both of them secretly shared about Billie Bradford.

Trying to bring her mind back to Billie's schedule, Nora heard the unmistakeable ring of the President's special scrambler phone in his next-door office. This most likely meant a call from abroad. Nora leaped to her feet, ran through the open doorway to the President's desk, and snatched up the receiver of the white telephone.

'Hello. President Bradford's office.'

The voice on the other end said, 'Billie? This is Otis in Moscow.'

That would be Ambassador Otis Youngdahl, Nora knew, and she said hastily, 'No, Mr Ambassador, this is Mrs Bradford's press secretary, Nora Judson.'

'Ah, Nora, fine, how are you?'

'Very well, thank you. Could I –?'

'Actually, Nora, I was calling the President. Is he around?'

'I'm sorry, Mr Ambassador. He's locked up in a staff meeting. If it's important, I can transfer your call.'

'Not necessary,' said Ambassador Youngdahl. 'I was sitting here, after a long day, my feet on the desk, cold drink in hand, relaxing. Just wanted to chew the fat with him if he was free. Wanted to ask him how the Summit is going. But I can call him another time.'

'The Summit hasn't officially started yet. The first session begins tomorrow morning. But I'll tell the President you called.'

'Thanks, Nora, thanks. By the way, does Billie happen to be in the vicinity?'

'Sorry, but she is also out. She's attending a reception at the Boende embassy.'

'Well, that's okay, too,' said the ambassador. 'I just wanted to tell her something amusing that occurred today, something involving her name that would give her a kick. Hell, I can tell it to you, and you can pass it on to her when she comes in. Repeat it, just for laughs.'

'Glad to.'

Ambassador Youngdahl chuckled over the phone. 'Tell Billie, if she knows it or not, she's in Moscow right now, not in London. An American tourist from Houston cornered me today – forget her name, but nutty as a fruitcake – and bent my ear insisting that she saw Billie Bradford in the Kremlin this afternoon.' He started laughing, and proceeded to relate the American tourist's account of the woman who had burst in on her, claiming to be the First Lady, insisting that she was being held prisoner by the Soviets and that someone else was pretending to be her.

The receiver pressed to her ear, Nora's face had lost its colour. She listened to the ambassador with frozen fascination.

Although they were not to meet until dinner, Nora had located Guy Parker and implored him to join her earlier for cocktails.

They sat together now, in an isolated corner of Claridge's lounge, Parker drinking his first drink, attentive to every word Nora was speaking.

Nora had been repeating what Ambassador Youngdahl had told her about the American lady tourist's encounter in the Kremlin with a woman who claimed to be Billie Bradford. Nora was finishing, speaking in a low voice with great intensity.

'Then the woman who claimed to be Billie said someone else was pretending to be her, and then she ran off.'

'Someone else pretending to be the First Lady? Was it put that way?'

'According to Ambassador Youngdahl.'

'And the woman who claimed to be Billie said she was being held prisoner in the Kremlin?'

'Exactly.'

Parker downed more of his Scotch. 'Did the ambassador treat any of it seriously?'

'Not a bit,' said Nora. 'He thought it was funny. He kept laughing through most of it.'

'How did you react to what he was telling you?'

'How could I react? I finally forced myself to laugh with him. What else could I do?'

'Do you intend to repeat it to our First Lady here?'

'I'm not sure. On the one hand, I'd like to see how she reacts if I tell her. On the other hand, I don't want to put her on guard in any way. What do you think, Guy? Should I tell our Billie?'

'No, don't. My instinct tells me to forget about it.'

'All right.'

Parker stared at Nora. 'What do you honestly make of it?'

'It gives me the chills.'

Parker toyed with his glass. 'Of course, the ambassador may be right. The Texas lady could be another tourist kook of the kind he sees all the time. Maybe the incident never happened. Or if it did happen, maybe the woman who claimed to be Billie was off her rocker, another nut. On the other hand, considering our own suspicions, if it were true, it would certainly explain a lot of things.'

'A lot of things,' Nora agreed. 'But, Guy, how could this be true? Billie here, brainwashed, I can accept. Billie here, an imposter, just boggles my mind. How would the Russians dare to do such a thing? I mean, really, it's difficult to imagine their even considering it.'

'You're right,' said Parker. 'It does sound fanciful. But anything is possible. Especially in the light of our other evidence. This does support our suspicions.'

They had finished their drinks, and Parker ordered another round.

Nora searched Parker's troubled countenance. 'Guy, what can we do about it? I don't see —'

'We can tell the President,' he said flatly.

'The President?' Nora was totally sceptical. 'Go to him without hard facts? Without a shred of proof? He'd call them all cock-and-bull stories. He'd think us insane. He'd throw us out of here or put us both in the loony bin.'

'Maybe. Maybe not. It depends. What if it turns out the President himself has been harbouring his own suspicions about Billie? This would back him up, place him on the alert.'

'Guy, you can't *prove* anything, not a damn thing. Meanwhile, he's sure he has his own dear Billie, and maybe he has. If we lay this on him, when he believes in her, we lose all our credibility and his trust. And if he should repeat this to Billie, at pillow-talk time, if she is or isn't Billie, she'd fire me on the spot. And you, too. We'd be out of it.'

'Well, what are you suggesting?' asked Parker. 'What do we do?'

'We sit tight,' said Nora. 'We keep an eye on her while we can. We wait for a break, another and bigger *faux pas*. We wait for a real fact.'

Parker took his fresh Scotch and drank thoughtfully. He knew what had crept into his mind. Until now he had denied its entrance. It was the almost embarrassing desire to have some part in a government system that he had grown to respect and had wanted to influence and improve. It had been a motivating factor in joining Bradford's staff, becoming one of his speech writers. He had allowed himself to be drawn away from the centre of action when he agreed to become Billie's collaborator. He had been subverted by big money and Billie's charm. But now he was being drawn closer to the centre again. By accident, perhaps not by accident but by a keenness of observation, he had come upon something that might be a monumental threat to a system of life he held dear. He alone would awaken the somnolent giant. If he could not improve the system, he, alone, might help preserve the best part of it. He could not voice these sentiments, he knew. They would sound like a page out of the Boy Scout handbook. Even to Nora. Grown men did not think or talk like that.

He looked up at Nora. What had she said? *We sit tight . . . . We wait for a break . . . . We wait for a real fact.*

'Watchful waiting is too passive for me, Nora,' he said. 'I think I'm going to do more than that. I think I'm going to get on our Billie's tail. Wherever she goes from now on, I'm going to be a short step behind. I'm going to follow her like a guilty conscience.'

'I don't know. If you get too close, you might get hurt.'

'If I don't,' Parker said, 'we all might get hurt.'

8

The appearance of Billie Bradford, or the one who was supposed to be Billie Bradford, emerging from the elevator into
the lobby of Claridge's, was unexpected and caught Guy
Parker by surprise.

It was early afternoon of the following day, and Parker
had left his claustrophobic room over an hour ago to sit in
the lobby, scan the newspapers, reread some of his research,
perhaps take a walk, and pass the time between one o'clock
and four when he had an interview appointment with Billie.

He had spent the morning preparing to do what he had
told Nora he must do – keep an eye, a close watch, on the
possibly spurious First Lady. He had rented a car, an expensive dark blue Jaguar, a fast and manouevrable vehicle that
would serve him well in city traffic and on the open highway
once he got the hang of the right-hand drive. He had tipped
one of Claridge's top-hatted doormen generously to reserve
a parking place for him across from the Brook Street main
entrance. He had then sought Nora to find out the First
Lady's afternoon schedule, and had been disappointed to
learn that Billie would be going nowhere this afternoon,
would be seeing no one before meeting with him at four
o'clock. After that, since the President was busy, Billie would
be attending a musical comedy with Penelope Heaton, wife
of the British Prime Minister, and they would have a late
supper together with their party at The Mirabelle in Curzon
Street. Wherever Billie went tonight, Parker knew that he
would not be far behind.

Meanwhile, there had been nothing to do in the afternoon

but try to occupy the dull hours ahead until he worked with her. So he had been lolling in the lobby, reading, when he had just happened to glance up and see her leave the elevator.

It was really a surprise to see Billie Bradford alone, unaccompanied by her Secret Service men. He wondered how she had managed it, and then realized that it could be done, indeed had been done, quite easily. By traversing part of the maze of interlocking suites that wound around the first floor, she could avoid the Secret Service agents posted in the corridor, climb to the second floor, and take the elevator from there. That she did not want to be recognized or harassed was obvious. Her trademark tresses had been hidden inside a round wide-brimmed felt hat. Oversized dark sunglasses masked the upper part of her face, and the lower part was partially covered by the raised collar of a linen jacket. The camouflage might fool some people. It did not fool Guy Parker.

Hastily, he stuffed his research into his briefcase, bounded to his feet, and, keeping a short distance between them, he followed her out into Brook Street. As she made for the doorman, Parker passed behind her and strode swiftly toward the corner of Davies Street, then crossed over to his car.

He was in the Jaguar, swinging it out of the parking slot, just as he saw the flash of her leg disappear into the rear of a taxicab. Slowly, the taxi began to roll away. Impatiently, Parker waited for another car to come between them, and then he followed.

Her taxi turned right into Bond Street, right again into Bruton Street, and soon left into Berkeley Square. Parker did not have the faintest idea where she was going, but from her route it appeared her destination was somewhere in the West End. There was no difficulty tracking her through Fitzmaurice Place into Curzon Street, except for the change of traffic lights. Twice he had been forced to jump lights to keep her taxi in view.

Along the way, driving, he saw the posters holding the

Evening News and *Evening Standard* with their bold headlines about the opening of the American–Soviet Summit.

The Summit Conference had convened at the Soviet embassy this morning. Parker had heard a preliminary report on the first session from the President's press secretary, Tim Hibberd, at lunch. President Bradford had outlined a mutual non-intervention pact – no troops, advisers, weapons to be exported to any African nation by the United States or the Soviet Union. Premier Kirechenko had countered with his own version of such a pact. In principle, he had agreed to the proposal of no troops being sent to an African country by either major power. However, he had objected to any limitation on exporting weapons. He had insisted that some African nations required weapons for self-defence against more aggressive neighbours. Neither side had mentioned Boende by name.

To Parker's mind, the Russian posture seemed to be a stalling one. But stalling for what? There was one far-fetched answer. If Billie Bradford was not what she appeared to be, if she was – incredibly – a Soviet imposter, then Kirechenko had a reason to stall. He could be waiting for information on the President's secret plans from the Russian-made First Lady or from a brainwashed real Billie Bradford. The audacity of such a Soviet undertaking was what made his projection seem impossible.

Peering over the wheel of his Jaguar, Parker could see the taxicab veer to the right off Piccadilly to Hyde Park Corner and continue on to Grosvenor Crescent. The car between them had peeled off, and Parker had to take care not to get too close to the rear of the First Lady's cab. Another turn past some kind of private park and they were in Belgrave Square. The taxi circled the roundabout, slowing, and Parker, doggedly following, slowed too.

The taxi eased into a short two-way thoroughfare called Motcomb Street, and about a third of the way up Parker could see the driver point to the entrance of an arcade that bore the lettering HALKIN ARCADE, and the First Lady nodding. Since there was apparently too much traffic to let her

237

out in the middle of the street, the driver went on, then turned left into the intersecting Kinnerton Street, pulled to the left and stopped. Parker went wide of the parked taxi, crawled ahead of it by fifty feet and drew up against the curb. He shut off the Jaguar's engine and looked behind him. He could make out the First Lady paying the driver, waving off the change. As the rear door opened, and Billie stepped down to the sidewalk, Parker pocketed his car keys and opened his own door. She was striding toward the corner, back to Motcomb Street, and waiting to cross it. Parker started after her, and when she glanced around, he turned his back and pretended to study the window display of a shop bearing the sign QUALITY IRONMONGERS. When he looked in her direction again, she was crossing the street. He went after her fast.

From the corner, he could see her heading for the opening to the arcade. Dodging the traffic as he crossed to the other side, he wondered where she was going in this wealthy patch of Belgravia. He saw her disappear into the arcade, and he broke into a trot before she got out of sight altogether. Reaching the Halkin Arcade entrance, he squinted inside. The interior was lined with exclusive shops, rows of square white wooden planters outside, with glass lanterns above providing illumination. He picked up Billie at the midway point, just as she had reached her destination. He watched her open a shop door and enter.

When she was out of sight, he hastily went into the arcade to learn where she had gone. Approaching the shop she had entered, he proceeded cautiously. He must not be discovered by her. If he was, there would be no explanation. At last, he could make out the elegant storefront. The show window of the shop was framed in gold. A filmy powder-blue gown was on display. Above the window, against an oblong block of black onyx, the gold lettering read: LADBURY OF LONDON. He stared at the shop front.

Ladbury.

He had seen Ladbury in the White House last week, when the English dress designer and his assistant had come to deliver Billie's new wardrobe and make their final fittings and alterations.

What was Billie doing with him now? Why was she seeing him so surreptitiously?

Speculating on the reason for this furtive visit, Parker resumed walking rapidly, catching a glimpse through the glass display window of the back of her head. He hurried on to the opposite end of the arcade, took up a position behind a cream-coloured pillar, and kept Ladbury's entrance door under steady observation.

Inside the fashion shop, Ladbury, straw-coloured fringe, bow-tie, cotton suit, grey suede shoes, minced ahead of Vera Vavilova, showing her the way to his office in the rear. Directing her into his office, he closed the door behind him.

Once they were seated, he did not hide his displeasure. 'You know you are not supposed to be here,' he said, 'only unless –'

'Unless there is an emergency,' she cut in. 'Well, there is one.'

'How'd you get away? Are the Secret Service goons with you?'

'Of course not. I gave them the slip. I worked my way through the suites to Tim Hibberd's office and got into another corridor, and then up to the second floor elevator. It was no trouble.'

'You're sure no one knows you are here?'

'I'm positive. Quit fretting, and please listen to me. I'm in desperate trouble and I need your help.'

'I am here to help. Go ahead.'

'The President was to resume sexual relations with his wife tomorrow, tomorrow night.'

'Yes, I know.'

'Well, he told me this morning, he doesn't want to wait that long. To hell with the doctor's orders, he said. He's sure I'm all right. He wants to start sleeping with me tonight.'

'Did you try to put him off?'

'Have you ever tried to argue with a hard-on? As nicely as

239

I could, I tried to tell him we should wait the extra day. He wouldn't buy it. So finally I capitulated. I said good, I couldn't wait any longer, either. He left grinning.'

Ladbury's pinched face had become more wizened. 'So it's tonight, is it?'

'And what's worse is – I think he's ready to spill the whole thing – his plans about Boende – after we've had sex. I've been trying to get the information sooner. No luck. But tonight, afterwards, I'm sure he'll be ready to talk. He said to me this morning, "When I'm more relaxed tonight, I'll catch you up on politics." Well, "more relaxed" is his euphemism for consummating sex. If it worked, I'd have everything for the Premier.' She paused. 'But it probably won't work. I still don't know a damn thing about what he expects from me in bed. I simply don't know how Billie Bradford behaves in bed. One wrong move, and the President will realize I'm not handling myself like his good old wife. I don't know what will happen. If he becomes suspicious –'

'Vera, please calm down.'

'I can't! What have those idiots in Moscow being doing all this time? Why can't they come with up something? Now we've almost run out of time. Unless they give me something, I can't go through with it, I can't. Will you tell them?'

'I'll tell them,' said Ladbury, rising. 'Stay controlled. Wait. I'll be in touch with you, or someone will, by this evening, I promise you. Now let me call for a taxi.'

Guy Parker had returned to Claridge's shortly after Billie Bradford had returned to the hotel following her unscheduled visit to Ladbury's. He had hustled up to his room for his tape recorder, and then gone to keep his work appointment with the First Lady.

Now, seated with the First Lady in the living room of Claridge's Royal Suite, the tape recorder between them, Parker noted that they had been discussing Billie's first year in the White House for fifty minute. He had sought out his next questions and was preparing to pose the first of them to her, when he heard the main door to the suite open.

President Andrew Bradford, looking handsome, solid, un-ruffled, came from the entry hall into the room, deep in thought. He removed his horn-rimmed spectacles, stuck them in the breast pocket of his jacket, and headed for the improvised bar.

'Hi, Andrew,' Billie called out.

'Oh, hi, darling. Hello, Guy.' He bypassed the bar, and reaching them he pecked a kiss at Billie's cheek.

'You're early,' she said. 'How'd it go with the Russians?'

'As expected,' he said. 'Kirechenko was amiable, but we soon bumped heads. It won't be easy. Still, I think we'll make out with our treaty. I sat in on our staff post mortem, but decided I'd had enough.' He smiled at his wife. 'I left them arguing. Thought I'd spend some time with my wife, and rest up before dinner.'

'How nice,' said Billie.

The President unknotted his tie. 'What about you? Did you have a busy day? Been anywhere? Seen anything?'

'I'm sorry to sound dull, Andrew, but I've done nothing,' said Billie. 'I've been locked in all day. Haven't put a foot out.' She turned to Parker. 'I think that will be it for now, Guy. Thanks. Probably see you tomorrow. Check with Nora.'

Parker hurriedly picked up his tape recorder, mumbled his good-byes, and departed from the suite.

He wanted to see Nora. He walked to her room, knocked and announced himself. Her muffled voice welcomed him. He entered. She was at a spindly French desk writing letters.

He gestured toward the tray of bottles. 'Cocktails?'

'I'm ready,' she answered, putting down her pen. 'It seems all we do is drink around here.'

'Maybe with good reason,' he said, setting his tape recorder on top of the television set.

She watched him prepare the drinks. 'Anything today, Guy?'

'Something,' he said. He placed a glass before her, took a swallow from his own, put it down and went to the tape recorder. He pushed the reverse button, and waited a moment, pushed the stop button, pushed the play button and listened. He fiddled with the machine again briefly, until he had the tape in the right place. 'I was working with Billie,' he said, 'when the President walked in on us just now. I had the tape on, and it kept right on going. Want to hear some enlightening dialogue? Listen.'

Parker pressed the play button once more and turned up the volume. The tape spun. The President's voice: 'Did you have a busy day? Been anywhere? Seen anything?' The First Lady's voice: 'I'm sorry to sound dull, Andrew, but I've done nothing. I've been locked in all day. Haven't put a foot out.'

Parker shut off the machine and faced Nora. 'How do you like that?'

Nora was baffled by his question. 'What's wrong with it? She *has* been in all day. I didn't have a thing on the schedule for her.'

'You didn't? Well, she had something scheduled for herself. I was down in the lobby early this afternoon, and I saw her sneak out.'

Nora sat up. 'You're sure?'

'Positive.'

'Alone or with the Secret Service?'

'With no one. Just Billie by herself. And no limo. She grabbed a taxi.'

'How strange. Do you know where she was going?'

'I followed her. She went to Ladbury of London.'

'The couturier? He's her designer, but she'd have no reason to see him now. He came to Washington with her things for a final fitting last week. When we arrived in London, her clothes were ready and waiting here in the hotel. Why would she want to see him now?'

'Why would she see him now *secretly*, you mean?'

'I suppose so, yes. It makes no sense.'

'It makes plenty of sense if she's not the First Lady, and she's got to get in touch with a Soviet contact.'

'Are you saying that Ladbury could be a contact?'

'Why not? They've used similar ones before. Nora, I'm going to find out about this Mr Ladbury.'

'How?'

'By getting the President's help.'

Nora's brow wrinkled. 'You're really going to tell him?'

'I have to.'

'I don't know, Guy. But I do know what I'm curious about.'

'What's that?'

'If our Lady is not the First Lady, what is she seeing one of her agents about? What's her problem?'

'That, my dear Nora, is the big question.'

It was early evening in Moscow, and Billie Bradford, pacing her bedroom, was still turning the matter over in her mind.

She had thought about it last night, every aspect of it, until sleep overtook her. She had thought about it this morning after awakening, and she had thought about it in the shower, at breakfast, throughout the afternoon. Having no stomach for a full dinner, she had continued to think about it during a light repast of tea and biscuits.

Of course, Alex Razin was the key person in her thoughts. A glimpse at the clock reminded her that he would be arriving in fifteen minutes or so. His obligatory visit, his assigned visit. But with a difference. This time he was calling on her not in the afternoon but at night. She was sure that had significance.

Originally, she had looked forward to his visits. She had believed he was befriending her, wanted to soothe her. But now she knew that he was strict KGB, an enemy agent, and his assignment had actually been to make her trust his friendship, to disarm her, to gain her confidence. His purpose had become clear to her. To use her – to help his Second Lady and to destroy her own Andrew.

Razin – God, how she hated him since learning the truth about him. She did not want to see the bastard again, the filthy betrayer, the rotten KGB agent. But if she had to see him at all, she was glad it was this evening instead of in the afternoon. She had needed the afternoon to decide upon her stance, to determine how to deal with him. She had come closer to a decision, but had not fully arrived at one yet.

Ten minutes to make up her mind.

She strode into the living room, poured a stiff cognac and water, and for one last time revived her internal debate. She would examine every side of it – well, the two sides – and come to a final decision.

Perched on an arm of the sofa, sipping her cognac, she reflected on the central issue, for the KGB, for herself, the question that required an answer: since Andrew, her husband, would be going to bed with, making love to, the imposter tomorrow night for the first time, how was the imposter to act and perform without giving herself away?

Before Billie could consider an answer, she was diverted by an image in her head. The picture of her husband Andrew, naked tomorrow night, lying side by side with another woman, also naked, mounting the counterfeit of herself – she found the picture too disturbing to contemplate any further. With effort, she tried to erase it from her thoughts. After all, she told herself, Andrew did not know about the deception practised on him or realize what he was doing. It could all be dismissed as meaningless acrobatics. What was more important, these fleeting minutes, was her own role and her survival.

Obviously, the Soviets were desperate. They had to find out, and find out fast, how their imposter should behave with Andrew tomorrow. If the imposter performed by instinct, and performed as Andrew expected, she would win his gratitude and trust. She would most certainly learn the big secret she was after. Billie knew that Andrew, once sated by sex, once relaxed, had almost always discussed his presidential concerns with her. Feeling closer to his mate, he would unburden himself about his Summit worries. The following day, the imposter would relay this information to her Soviet superiors, and they, in turn, could score a triumph at the Summit.

On the other hand, by equal chance – the one possibility the Russians feared – the imposter might do everything wrong in bed. Should that happen, Andrew would know at once that this Billie was not his own Billie. Andrew was a creature of habit, in bed and out of bed, and instantly aware of change. If something was out of place, if someone reacted unexpectedly, it always gave him cause to wonder and to probe. His wife performing sexually in an unfamiliar way would absolutely arouse his suspicions. This might lead to an exposure of the KGB plot.

So it was fifty-fifty for the Russians if their imposter played it by chance. Intuition told her that the Soviets, if they had come this far, would not gamble everything on a fifty-fifty risk. The imposter must be prepared. The Russians must have the odds 100 per cent in their favour.

Then where did she, the real Billie Bradford, fit into all this?

She alone, here, possessed the information that they need-ed. And what they needed, they had to have tonight, for use tomorrow. How would they try to extract the information from her? Instead of Razin, the KGB might send in some of their bullies tonight to torture the intimate truth out of her. But she doubted that. Or they might send in some stranger to rape her. She doubted that, too, because it could give them only a distorted picture of her behaviour. Or would they send in Razin, after all, to undertake what had been his ultimate assignment, to play on her fear and loneliness to seduce her, as he had almost succeeded in doing yesterday? This, probably was their most likely plan.

Supposing seduction was Razin's assignment, how then should she react? Resist or succumb? Which was the better choice in her fight for survival? The dilemma remained evenly balanced in her mind and psyche, answered yet unanswered since last night. Now, with a few minutes left, a choice had to be made. No more equivocating.

To resist. If she refused to sleep with Razin, if she rejected him, the KGB would never know the truth. They would have to order Razin or someone else to rape her coldly or they would simply have to torture her. Either course would mean suffering fright and enduring pain, yet the satisfaction was that they would still not know the truth.

To succumb. She would emerge unscathed, except in her psyche. It was the quick way to survival, but they would have an approximation of her conduct in bed, information for their imposter, and somehow a victory. Yet, it struck her, this outcome was not inevitably so. Her submission to them could also trick them into a terrible defeat.

Yes, it was possible to do as they wished, and still convert their victory into their loss, and heighten her chance for survival. In submission, she could see, there remained another option for her. If she did sleep with Razin, she would be volunteering the act and she would be in full control. She could control his findings by misleading him, by acting contrary to her normal behaviour in bed. She could mislead Razin, and he in turn would mislead the Second Lady, who would then invite Andrew's suspicions.

There it was. So simple. An opportunity to help herself, as well as her husband. Yet, not so simple. One thing militated against it. Letting another man enter her, abuse her, cheapen her. Not once in her marriage to Andrew had she ever been unfaithful to him or even fantasized sex with another man. Only twice, before her marriage, had she had affairs with men, short immature affairs. Making calculated love to a barbaric stranger was not part of her nature. Worse, this man who would soon be here, an enemy on a destructive mission, was a person she despised. He was an enemy of her mind. He was an enemy of her body. He was an enemy of her husband, of her country, of every ideal she cherished. She was filled with revulsion at the thought of him inside her. Yet, as she had overcome her upset at the image of her husband in bed with another woman tomorrow, by realizing he was a victim of deception, and his act a mere exercise, she could now see that Razin's violation of her body could be reduced to a mere physical exertion. Sexual intercourse without love violated neither body nor spirit. The important thing was that this act might give her a means to reach her husband. Razin was the only conduit, through use of the imposter, to enable her to send a message to Andrew, an alert and a warning.

Which to do? Resist or submit?

Immersed in thought, she wandered to the bar, poured herself a second cognac and water, and drifted toward the bedroom, slowly sipping her drink. By the time she reached the foot of the bed, her mind was made up. She knew what she must do.

From that moment, she ceased thinking about her dilemma. She had come to her decision, and all that remained was to act upon it. With a glance at the clock, she began to strip off her clothes, article by article, until she was totally nude. Barefoot, she went into the bathroom, started the shower, adjusted it to warm, and stood under it letting the needles of water stimulate her skin. She soaped herself thoroughly, washed away the suds, turned off the shower and stepped out on the soft rose rug. She observed herself in the mirror as she dried, the high breasts, flat abdomen, soft triangle of pubic hair, generous hips, full thighs. Not bad, not bad at all. Dry, she found perfume, dabbed it behind her ears, between her breasts, and in her pubic hair. Doing so, her mind went to protection, some contraceptive device. She worried about this, then remembered her bathroom travel kit, one she always kept filled, even between trips, so that she would not forget anything. When she and Andrew had tried for a baby, she had placed her diaphragm in the kit against some future need. Could it still be there? She sought the kit – and, to her astonishment, there it was – her very kit, or one exactly like it. The KGB had overlooked nothing, had duplicated every possession she had brought to Moscow (presumably to make her return foolproof when she was exchanged, *if* she was exchanged).

She turned the kit upside down, dumping out its contents beside the wash basin. Apparently, everything in her original kit was also here. It was more than astonishing. It was frightening. She refused to speculate on how the Russians had done it. She put it out of her mind. A more immediate concern demanded priority. Sorting through the scattered toilet articles beside the basin, she found it, the good old diaphragm (or good new diaphragm) along with a tube of spermicide. With relief she prepared the diaphragm and inserted it into her vagina.

In a drawer, she poked through her nightgowns and selected the sheer white one, the short one that would fall not quite to her knees, and she wriggled into it. She went to her closet for her flimsy lace negligee, which she had not worn since her bondage, and she pulled it on. At the wall, she turned off the overhead light, put out a standing lamp, and left on the two dim ones on either side of the bed.

The double bed.

She drew back the spread, folded it, put it aside. She considered the thin blanket, tugged it loose, and brought it back toward the bottom of the bed. She puffed up the pillow.

Satisfied with her handiwork, she retrieved her drink and finished it. About to go to the living room bar for one more refill, she saw Razin appear in the bedroom doorway. Tonight, somehow, he looked bigger, more muscular than she had remembered. He was wearing a brown sports jacket, a shirt open at the collar, beige slacks. Her eyes went from his flat black hair and bushy eyebrows to his bashed nose and thick lips. He had wide powerful shoulders and a narrow waist. She had not inspected him this closely before.

The reality of his person, overlaid on her recent decision, gave her a moment of panic. She wanted to retreat from her decision, but she knew that she must not. She needed support. One more drink.

'Hi, Alex,' she said. 'I was hoping you'd come by.'

'I wouldn't miss the chance to enjoy your company,' he said, removing his jacket and tossing it on an armchair behind him.

'Here,' she said, handing him her empty glass. 'I could do with another cognac and water. Easy on the water.'

'I'll join you,' he said, accepting her glass and disappearing into the living room.

'Oh, and Alex,' she called after him, 'put on some music – loud enough for me to hear.'

As the music came booming in, Billie inspected the bedroom one last time, then made for the chaise longue. She stretched back on it, allowing her negligee to fall open revealing her abbreviated nightgown and part of the flesh of one thigh.

She tried not to imagine him naked. She must think only of her motivation and the end result.

He returned to the bedroom carrying two drinks. He halted to look her over. 'Very fetching,' he said. 'You are truly a beautiful woman, Billie.'

'Quite a compliment from you, Alex.'

'Too restrained,' he said, handing her the darker of the two drinks.

She lifted her glass. 'To you,' she said, 'for being such a wonderful man and for saving my life.'

'To you,' he said, touching his glass to hers, 'for enriching my life. I – I'm sorry it had to be this way.'

He lowered himself to the floor, at her feet.

'Even if it is this way,' she said, 'life doesn't have to stop, does it?'

'No, it doesn't.'

'So let's live a little. Drink up.' She could feel the strong cognac going down her throat, fanning out behind her breasts, heating her, dizzying her slightly. She looked down at him, while he drank. He seemed surprisingly young. She took another big swallow of the cognac, and kept the glass to her lips until it was empty. She set down her glass.

His eyes met hers. 'How are you?' he asked.

'Fine, never better,' she said. 'How are you?'

He finished his drink. 'Do you really want to know?'

'Of course, I do.'

He put a hand on her uncovered thigh. 'I'm insanely in love with you, Billie. I'd give anything on earth to have you.'

She took his hand. 'I've been thinking about it, too. I realize I was foolish yesterday. I want you, too. Very much. Let's not waste any more time.'

She felt almost a surge of relief. She was committed.

He scrambled to his feet, his hand grasping her hand

tightly and bringing her up off the chaise longue. He tried to embrace her, but she slipped away. 'I don't want clothes between us,' she said breathlessly. 'I want nothing between us. I want us together in bed.'

Moving toward the bed, she divested herself of the negligee, let it drop to the floor. About to do the same with the short white nightgown, she paused, and wheeled slowly to wait for him. His shirt was off, the ridged, muscular, hairy chest bare. He had already kicked aside his shoes and socks. His belt was open. The trousers came down, and he stepped out of them. He was wearing tight bulging white briefs. He bent to tug them off, and when he straightened to full height, the freed penis was rising, pointing at her. She tried to avoid looking at it, but couldn't help herself. It wasn't particularly long, but it was thick, my God it was thick. The ugly appendage was approaching her.

She whirled about from it, her back to him, and lifted her arms. 'Alex, help me off with this.'

His hands had the hem of the gown, drew it upward in one sweeping motion, over her loose blonde hair and head, and she saw it flung away. His hairy arms came under her arms, his large palms covering her breasts. She could feel him like the barrel of a pistol pressing against her soft buttocks. Heaven help me, she thought, and was momentarily afraid and nauseated.

He released her breasts. His arms scooped her up off the floor, carried her across the room, and deposited her on the bed.

His eyes were fixed on her nakedness. She wanted to cover her vagina, her navel, her nipples, wanted to hide her nudity, wanted to start all over with her clothes on and refuse to undress, but it was too late. She tried to keep her eyes off him, determined to remain in control and remember what she had planned, the purpose of this humiliation she was trading for freedom.

For fleeting seconds she welcomed Andrew in her mind, a quiet, neat lover, sweetly kissing her breasts, softly caressing her body, lightly rubbing her clitoris, gently rising above her to go between her parted legs. His lips on her lips, she warmly holding the sides of his head. His trunk lowering between her thighs, his erection finding her warm opening and sliding inside, his restrained, steady thrusting, her hips rising to his rhythm. No other movements except his thrusting. Passive, he, she, except for the constant thrusting. Then faster, faster, until he came with a gasp. No words spoken. She pulling him down on her, over beside her, and he reaching for her clitoris, and after a few minutes she coming with a shudder and an emission of breath. Then they would lie back, each silent, recovering, and he would offer her a cigarette, and take one himself, and gradually he would begin talking, wondering about her day, speaking of his day, office gossip, Cabinet meetings, other meetings, frustrations, hopes, secrets. At last, cigarettes out, they would sink into sleep.

Civilized, comfortable, warm.

How she wanted it tonight.

She felt the mattress beside her dip, the bulk and rough flesh of reality beside her, and memory vanished. Reluctantly, she opened her eyes to the stranger. Her heart thumped. It was time to begin.

Begin what? Begin how?

Her woeful inexperience gripped and held her. She summoned every resource of secondhand knowledge – movies seen, books read, tales heard – angrily trying to perform as a woman Andrew had never seen.

She arched the top part of her naked body toward him, her shoulders back, her firm globular breasts with big pink nipples still flaccid nearer to his face, all provocatively hot and wanting. His response was instantaneous. His hands caught her breasts underneath, his mouth kissed and sucked at the first nipple, until it hardened, and then the other nipple. She groaned, groaned more loudly, and she could feel his excitement, as her knees came up. His mouth left her. He began to leave her, shifting toward her knees. She knew where he was going. Not yet, she told herself, not yet.

She grabbed for his shoulder, fingernails digging in, and pulled hard, trying to bring him back to her. 'No, don't –

wait, Alex, wait!' she cried out. 'I like to do the other first. I love it. I want it.' She reached for the swollen penis, her fingers trying to encircle it, as she wormed her way from beneath him and pushed up higher against the pillow. She opened her mouth and brought it towards the penis.

This was going to be the meanest part, the part she had debated and dreaded. Fellatio was foreign to her, something she had never performed. She had kissed Andrew there several times but he did not like it. That was why she must do it now, transmit her love of the act to the imposter. But it revolted her, the idea of taking a male appendage in the mouth, especially this gross one. It seemed dirty and demeaning. Maybe not with someone you loved. But with this rotten bastard – it had to be done, it absolutely had to.

She closed her eyes, opened her mouth, and closed her lips on the distended head of his cock. She brought it deep into her mouth – it pushed at her palate, rubbed the inside of her cheek, flattened her tongue – as she tried to suppress gagging, and perspiration broke out on her brow. Incredibly, the thing was growing bigger, filling her mouth entirely, crowding against her throat. She was uncertain what to do next. Instinct told her to suck, to simulate sexual intercourse. She drew her lips back the length of it, then with a hand pushed it deep in her mouth again. Her head continued to go back and forth over the stiff shaft.

He was making little sounds in Russian, and gurgling something in English that sounded like, 'Good, so good, good.' Now he had a hold on the back of her head and was pushing it, pulling it.

She tore at his hands, jerked her mouth free, choking, coughing, 'Now, Alex, now, please.' She was working to position her body under his, spreading her legs as wide apart as possible, imploring him, 'Put it in me – let me put it in, let me. Oh, I love it so. Fuck me, fuck me good.'

She had the love muscle in both hands, drawing him down between her legs. She was eager to be done with it. In minutes it would be over with. But she must still perform, complete her act to perfection.

His cock strained in her hands toward her vulva, found the outer lips, and she let go. With great power he plunged into her, deep, deep into her. The soft walls of her vagina spread and stretched to accommodate him, and her inner thighs quivered. As he filled her, she realized with a small shock that a lubricant had not been needed, that her vaginal canal was hot and wet on its own.

She tried to understand her wetness, but immediately was shaken out of all thought. He was going now as if his cock was attached to a high-speed pile-driving mechanism. In and out of her, hammering faster and faster, ramming his cock inside her. She tried to hold his arms as her body trembled and her teeth rattled and her head began to be slammed against the headboard. She forced her heavy eyelids open briefly, and realized the dark face hanging over her was watching her, watching every expression and gesture, recording her behaviour. Christ, she'd almost forgotten. He was doing this to report to someone else. She'd almost forgotten her plan, her programme. She must perform for him in another way, impress her aggressive behaviour upon him. She must make this into something he would never forget, and would remember to report.

She tried to catch her breath. 'Alex, Alex – Jesus – you're tearing me apart.'

At first he did not answer. He continued fucking her, as her vaginal tunnel expanded. Panting, he said, 'Too hard? Want me slower?'

She dug her nails into his arms. 'No, goddammit, harder! I love it. I love you. Don't hold back. Give it to me harder!'

With painful effort she brought her legs off the bed, high in the air, hooked a leg over each of his shoulders, and locked her ankles behind his neck.

This sent him into a frenzy of jackhammering. He had her by the ass, lifting her as he pumped wildly. She felt like he was splitting her in two and she tightened on him before her brains were knocked loose. She battled to hold on to her senses, trying to recall and retrieve something of her plan. Her plan, her plan. Deceive him, try everything she had ever

253

heard or read. Immediately, she began to sway and buck, cling to him, ride the wild stallion, up and down with him, clawing at his chest, screeching obscenities she had never used before. A glimpse caught the crazy smile on his face, and she ripped at his flesh, screaming steadily as he impaled her against the headboard and pumped away like a madman.

She counted the seconds, the minutes, expecting him to come, but he did not come. She renewed her exertions, but her thighs and buttocks and legs felt dead. Still, she tried to drive him to a climax, rolling her ass, clamping her thighs, beating her fists at him, screaming and screaming, but he kept right on fucking her and would not come.

Then she felt something strange inside her, something she had never felt before with a man in her, it was like an explosive force rising low inside her, a feeling unsought, unexpected, unknown, the desire to have her vagina burst open and erupt. She felt herself beginning to drown in a flood of water, with the geyser in her vagina about to shoot a mile high. Then she knew, she knew for certain. She was losing control, she was on the verge of a mammoth orgasm. She wanted to cry because she did not want it to happen the first time in intercourse with this hateful oaf. And worse, far worse, it would spoil her plan. She could not orchestrate her moves if he gained control, if her body betrayed her to the monster and gave in. Her fingers grabbed the top of the headboard behind her. She bit her lip, and begged her battered senses to take over and not let her vagina surrender.

She tried not to respond any more. She turned her head sideways on the pillow, fighting to take her mind off his glorious lovemaking. It was impossible. It was too delicious, this going under. She was seconds away from total release. One more act, she begged herself, one more uncharacteristic, un-Andrew act to give him something new to record and report. Could she make it before blowing sky high? Dropping her legs, she reached in front of her, to either side of his perpetual-motion prick, she reached under and found his low-slung, swaying balls, those huge bags going from side to side, and she clutched them and massaged them and held on as perspiration clouded her eyes.

Whatever she had done, she had done right. For he began to bellow in Russian. His thrusts shortened, slowed, then speeded up. He squealed once, twice, merging into a long drawn-out shriek, as his movement ceased, he hung petrified above, yelling, shouting, as he came and came and came in his prolonged orgasm.

Then, as if in slow motion, he collapsed, going down like a punctured balloon.

Fascinated, she watched him roll over on the bed. She enjoyed triumph. She had averted her own climax. She had retained control. Now she must exercise control one last time with one final act left in her scenario.

She remained patient. He was resting next to her, still panting like an animal. A few minutes passed and his breathing began to sound normal. He was sitting up, grinning at her.

'It was good, Billie,' he said.

'Very good,' she breathed. 'But Alex, there's more. There's still me. Please finish it for me.'

'Finish it?'

'I'm almost there. I want to come. Please –'

He was uncertain. 'What do you want me to do?'

She raised her knees and parted her legs. She reached for the back of his head and urged it down toward her vagina. 'Kiss me between my legs. I'll come right away.'

'Oh, that?' he said. 'You like that?'

'Always, always –'

He moved part way around her, lowered his head between her legs, nuzzled his nose in the mat of her pubic hair, against her thickened clitoris, and began kissing her moist vulva.

She had never had this done to her, and to her surprise it was pleasurable. She felt his tongue inside her, circling inside her, and she lifted her buttocks and began shaking her thighs and tried to suppress a moan. It was excruciating trying to hold back – why was she holding back? Not to give him any satisfaction or dominance? – to hell with that. She allowed a prolonged moan to escape her, arched her back, curled her toes, let her ass go up higher and down and up again, emitted a throaty cry, and dissolved into a full orgasm.

He sat up pleased.

Groping for words, she tried to speak, failed, and silently nodded her gratefulness.

'Thanks, Alex,' she said finally. 'It was wonderful. Now shut off that music and let me sleep.'

She turned on her side, buried her head in the pillow, eyes tight. She heard him leave the bed, go to the bathroom, return. She feigned sleep as he dressed and softly hummed.

After a while he was gone.

The moment she heard the outer door open and close, she tried to rise. With difficulty, she forced herself out of bed. Every muscle in her body was aching. She stumbled to the bathroom, soaped and washed herself. In the bedroom, she turned off the lamps, ignoring her sleeping pill, and crawled into bed. The bed was still warm from their bodies, and the musky smell of their coupling hung over it.

Erotic fragments of what had happened passed in and out of her mind.

The First Lady of the United States. Je—sus. If anyone back home ever knew.

She suffered a wave of shame at what she had done. It made her feel unclean. And worse, she felt guilt at having enjoyed some of it. But she mollified both shame and guilt by remembering that she had engaged in this sacrifice to warn her husband, to save him and to save herself.

Razin, the bastard. All of them here, bastards. She'd fixed them good.

She smiled to herself in the darkness. She could visualize the interloper, her double, the imposter tomorrow night with her husband. She could see poor Andrew assaulted tomorrow night by a passive and tame wife gone mad – fellatio, scratching, cursing, legs around his shoulders, the whorehouse works – and in the end being encouraged to go down on her. It would be the most topsy-turvy, stunning evening of Andrew's life. She could imagine him wondering who this weird wildcat of a woman was, certainly not his own Billie, positively not his wife of seven years. Knowing him, she knew he wouldn't let it go at that. He'd find out the truth.

The other woman might be the actress, but only she herself, the genuine Billie Bradford, would know that she had pulled off the greatest act of the century.

Those bastards, the game was almost over for them. For herself, liberation loomed.

She would sleep well.

An hour later, in his KGB office in the quiet police building, Alex Razin brought a pad and pencil before him and tried to get his mind back on his work.

It was not easy. His mind did not want to leave Billie Bradford's bed. The pleasure of the marvellous sexual encounter still lingered. He felt really good. It was as if he had enjoyed Vera again. Not precisely true, he knew in his heart and loins. While it was wrong to make comparisons between women, and while Vera never failed to give him pleasure, this Billie Bradford had been even better, the best lay he had ever had in his life. A fantastic lay, an aggressive female without a single inhibition. It was a wonder the President of the United States was not a basket case by now.

Which reminded him that he had actually fornicated with the American President's wife. It had been the plan and the hope, but the fact that it had actually happened almost overwhelmed him. It seemed doubly astonishing to him that what he had regarded as a political assignment had developed into the high spot of his entire sex life.

He wondered if she was sexually insatiable, and would do it again with him. He supposed she wouldn't. Once she might excuse to herself, as an antidote to loneliness and repayment for his kindness, but twice she would not be able to justify to herself. Not to Billie Bradford, who was the First Lady of America and perhaps the world. He promised himself not to pressure her.

Besides, now that he had done his job, it meant Vera was coming home to him. He looked down at his blank pad.

257

Soon he would fill it with explicit instructions for Vera to follow when she bedded down with the President tonight. Once Vera satisfied the President, it was likely he would unburden himself about his work and secret plans. And once Vera passed the intelligence on to Kirechenko, her job would be done. She would quietly be exchanged, sent back to Moscow while Billie Bradford was flown to London.

The thought of Vera in his arms once more focused his thoughts on her.

Right now she must be in a panic. The President had changed the timetable on his wife. They would be resuming their lovemaking tonight instead of tomorrow night. And Vera was unprepared. How relieved she would be to get his decoded message with its explicit description of what the President would expect from her.

That Vera would soon be making love with the President gave Razin a twinge of jealousy. Vera would be giving Andrew Bradford a wonderful night. The thought of his beautiful Vera, the woman who would become his own wife, being mounted by another man, giving another man pleasure, cast a shadow on his own achievement this evening. Still, one had to be reasonable. Vera's unfaithfulness, like his own. was counterfeit, mechanical, an action performed in the line of duty. He would remain objective. If his message got through to Vera, if she gulled the President, the Soviet Union might have its Summit triumph.

Razin was suddenly aware that it was getting late, time was running out, and Vera must be desperate to hear from him.

He took up the black pencil to reconstruct his evening with Billie. He pulled his chair closer to the desk, and realized how weary his legs were. In fact, his whole body was sated and retained the afterheat of his extended love-making. He reminded himself to keep a cool head, not forget any detail of Billie's fantastic performance.

Actually, he told himself, the minute details were unimportant. It was the various acts in her performance that counted, that and her total attitude toward a lover and what she expected from her lover. Billie's overall attitude had been that of an unrestrained and sexually aggressive woman, one eager to engage in any variation of the sex act.

This analysis seemed sound. After all, he had the evidence first-hand. Yet, something about it niggled him. The Billie Bradford he had seen in bed this evening was a contradiction of the Billie Bradford he had known on a daily basis the entire past week. The sleek Billie of his acquaintance before tonight, with her neat blonde mane of hair, her clear young face, her genteel manner, simply was not the kind of woman he had experienced in bed less than two hours ago. From her general style and behaviour outside of bed, he would have expected anything but an unrestrained nymphomaniac in bed. In truth, he had expected her to be warm and fun, but relatively passive and entirely straight. She would give to a degree, yet she would not get her hair mussed. But going down on him for openers, clawing him, pouring forth obscenities, clutching his testicles, insisting that he go down on her, that had been utterly unexpected and unbelievable.

Razin dropped his pencil and leaned back in the chair to think.

Maybe it *was* unbelievable.

Despite the need for haste, he realized that he had better make haste slowly. Too much hung in the balance to allow for any error on his part. The message he sent to London could determine the outcome of the Summit – and Vera's fate as well. He would have to take a more critical look at the behaviour of his recent bed partner.

Was Billie Bradford's behaviour during sexual intercourse with him her normal behaviour and entirely honest? Or had it actually been a performance, contrived to mislead him into sending the wrong information to her double? He dimly remembered reading an American short story once – *The Lady or the Tiger?* The hero, a handsome youth, had committed the crime of presuming to love his king's daughter. Ordered to the public arena for judgement, the hero faced two doors and a dilemma. Open one door and a beautiful lady, whom he might possess, emerged. Open the other door and a ferocious, man-eating tiger emerged. Which door to open? Razin found himself facing a similar dilemma now. Had the woman in bed with him been a tiger? Or a lady? When you pushed the sex button on her, was she really a wildcat, as some women were, or was she just the opposite, a tame, compliant feline who had merely pretended to be a wildcat tonight?

He wondered if she had really made an effort to deceive him. He had regarded her as an uncomplicated, ingenuous all-American girl. Yet, he realized, there could be more there. There could be a more devious, more shrewd, more manipulative person behind the façade. Very few simpletons became American First Ladies. The ability to use others, for self and for one's mate, might be the common characteristic found in most First Ladies. Billie might not be above cleverly using him to destroy Vera.

Razin was uncertain now. He had to decide. There was no margin for error.

Restlessly, he pushed away from his desk and went into the adjoining office to his Billie Bradford file cabinet. He located the manila folder devoted to information on her sex life. It was a thin folder.

Leaning against the cabinet, he thumbed through the memoranda in the folder. There were the names of the two young men she'd had love affairs with before she met Senator Bradford. The information was sketchy and contained nothing about her sexual behaviour with them. Then there were his own notes on his questioning of Billie. These indicated, taking Billie at her word, that her husband performed with great diversity in bed. If this were true, Billie herself would have had to cooperate in these acts. This would certainly support Razin's own experience with her. On the other hand, the President's occasional mistress, Isobel Raines, contradicted his wife. Isobel Raines had indicated that the President was conventional in sexual matters. If this were true, more likely than not Billie would also have had to been straight with the President. This would make her behaviour tonight a sham and a lie. Two reports, completely at odds. Razin closed the folder and returned it to the drawer.

Unhappy, he walked back to his desk. He could see that time was indeed running out and that he must come to a decision quickly.

One last review of the evening's activity.

The case for Billie's having behaved honestly tonight. It had been obvious to him that she wanted sex, was open about it, loved it. She had asked him to undress quickly, and asked him to help her out of her nightgown. None of this had appeared staged. She had invited and welcomed the foreplay and responded like every woman he had ever known. She had insisted on fellatio as part of the foreplay, which had been unexpected from her only because he had romanticized her. Half the women he had slept with enjoyed fellatio. At this time, Billie's eagerness to be fucked, excited as she was, had been perfectly normal. She had expertly guided him to her vulva. Once he was inside her, she had reacted and cooperated as any practised lover would. Her vaginal wetness could not be contrived. She had performed with less inhibition and more aggressiveness than any female he had ever known, but in bed he had known only Russian women, and she was American, and members of the new breed of American women were celebrated for their forwardness in sexual matters. All the rest – her legs around him, her clawing, her mouthing of obscentities, her taking hold of his testicles – was hardly unusual, considering how well he had been fucking her and exciting her and how much she was enjoying it. That he had failed to bring her to an orgasm in intercourse had surprised him, but now, in retrospect, it was less surprising. Few American women, despite their boldness, had orgasms during the act. As an aftermath, she had begged him to perform cunnilingus to make her climax. He had done so, and her climax had been real. Yes, she had been quite a package of heavenly delights. Her behaviour had been such that Vera, he felt sure, could imitate it precisely. In sum, seen as a whole, seen as a participant, Billie's behaviour had seemed natural, normally responsive and real, without a single suspect move. If you played it by feel, relived it as a whole, Billie Bradford's performance could be trusted.

Or could it? If you examined it more closely, less by feel than by intellect, not as a whole but step by step, could it be trusted?

The case for Billie's having behaved dishonestly tonight. There had been something studied about each step she had made, from start to finish. The case against her rested on the presumption that she was as expert an actress as Vera. And why not? As First Lady in a White House glass bowl surrounded by cameras, she had to be gifted in theatrics – just as Jackie Kennedy had performed her role of cultural heroine and Betty Ford had played her role of earthy candour. This evening, Billie should have been suspect from the first moment he saw her. She had dressed – or undressed – herself for the role of seductress. The parted negligee had been meant to provoke, and the sheer short nightgown she had never worn before. She had been too ready, too eager, to climb into bed with him. Her record, well researched, had revealed no easy lay, no promiscuous past. In foreplay, her effort at fellatio had been crude and amateurish, exposing her utter inexperience at it. Most women, who had done it often, teased the tip of your prick with their tongues, kissed it, reamed it, before sucking. Billie, probably at a loss, had clumsily done nothing but take him in her mouth. Perhaps this was her style, perhaps this was the way she did it with the President. But Razin doubted it, doubted if she had ever done it before to anyone. As to their coupling itself, at no time had she laid back and allowed herself to enjoy it. She had pressed constantly to make him believe, to make him feel, that she was wild and uninhibited. All the scratching and clawing, perhaps some women did that sometimes, but thinking of it he had never personally known one do it except in teasing fun. Billie had played that part of her lovemaking, along with the uncharacteristic obscenities, as if she always reacted that way. Presumably with her husband too. Razin doubted it. Some of those Latin qualities, and the coarseness of language, would have been apparent to him in different ways during their daily meetings. No hint of these had ever been given. As for the clutching of his testicles, it had been difficult for her, awkward, and he could not visualize her doing it with the President. Nor could he visualize her making the President go down on her. Maybe a hand job but never a head job. All around, in their act, there had been too many contrivances of high-spots, as if these were quirks he would not forget and would remember to report to Vera. Only one thing he could be sure of. Her climax had been no fake orgasm. That had been real. But the rest? Suspect.

Both cases, for and against her honesty, had been heard. Now judgement.

Razin closed his eyes and thought hard. He opened his eyes. He had made his decision.

Swiftly, he picked up his pencil and began to write. What he wrote would be Vera's reprieve – or her death sentence. He did not falter. He wrote on.

9

In London, that evening, inside Claridge's, Guy Parker sat nervously in Dolores Martin's secretarial cubicle counting the minutes until he could see President Andrew Bradford.

Despite Nora's earlier entreaties that he wait longer until he had more positive information, Parker had determined to go ahead and confront the President with his suspicions. Ever since the First Lady's secret visit to Ladbury, Parker had been haunted by her deception. Failure to speak of it – in fact, to speak of the entire matter – to the chief executive would be a disservice to his country and its leader. Arranging the private meeting with President Bradford, on short notice, had not been easy. The President had been booked solid right up to minutes before his departure for a dinner engagement at nine. But Parker had been insistent. 'I know how busy he is,' he had told Mrs Martin, 'but this is something of a personal nature I must discuss with him at once. It is very relevant to the Summit. I must see him alone tonight.' Parker's urgency, added to his boyish charm, had finally persuaded Mrs Martin to abbreviate the last appointment and accommodate his own. She had pencilled him in for a ten minute meeting.

The buzzer on Mrs Martin's desk was sounding. She picked up the receiver, listened, hung up. She said, 'All right, Mr Parker, he'll see you now.'

Thanking her, Parker hurried into the executive offices. President Bradford, dressed for dinner, was at his desk initialling papers. Without looking up, he said, 'Sit down, Guy. Be right with you.'

Parker took a chair, stared uneasily at the top of the President's head, wondering if Nora had been right that he should postpone this talk. Perhaps he should back out of it while he still had time.

Then he saw it was too late to reconsider. The President had replaced his pen in its holder, set aside his papers, and was ready to hear what his visitor had to say.

'I – I'm sorry to intrude on you like this,' Parker said.

'Quite all right. I can spare ten minutes, Guy. I gather it is something important.'

'I believe it may be extremely important. I felt that I should discuss it with you as soon as possible. It is a matter that I feel affects you directly and has a bearing on the success of the Summit, so I had to tell you about it privately.'

The President appeared in a good mood. 'Okay, Guy, I'm listening. What's the mystery all about?'

'Uh, it concerns Mrs Bradford, the First Lady.' Parker was hesitant. 'I'm not sure I know how to get into the matter.'

'The easy way. Be direct. Get right to the point.'

'Very well, to the point,' said Parker. 'As you know, I've been working closely with your wife almost daily.'

'And I hear you're doing a good job with her book. Billie tells me it is excellent.'

'Thank you. Anyway, seeing her, as I do, regularly, I must admit something has been bothering me. Let me put a question to you first, Mr President. Since Mrs Bradford returned from the women's meeting in Moscow, have you noticed anything different about her?'

'Different about her?' The President looked puzzled. 'What does that mean? I haven't the faintest idea what you're talking about.'

For Parker, this response definitely ruled out the possibility that Bradford, himself, had become aware of some change in Billie. This would certainly make what he had to tell the President more difficult. He decided to lay out his suspicions as quickly and plainly as he could. 'Mr President, what I mean is that Mrs Bradford seems to have changed since her visit to Moscow. To me, observing her closely – before Moscow and since – she doesn't seem to be the same person in many ways. It is as if one woman named Billie Bradford went to Moscow for three days, and another woman named Billie Bradford came back.'

The President peered intently at Parker. 'What *are* you talking about, Guy? This isn't one of your damn speeches, you know. What are you trying to say? Speak straight.'

'Well, what I'm trying to say is that Mrs Bradford doesn't seem to be herself any more. Haven't you felt that at all?'

'I still don't understand you. Billie is Billie. She's my wife. What's different about her?'

Here goes, thought Parker. 'Many things seem different, at least to me. Her memory, for one thing. Her contradictions. Her general manner. Please bear with me.' Parker recounted the Kilday incident on the *Los Angeles Times*. He spoke of her failure, at the women's luncheon in Los Angeles, to recognize her old friend Anges Ingstrup. He mentioned the baseball game at Dodger Stadium, where Mrs Bradford had seemed neither interested nor knowledgeable. He brought up the visit to her father's home in Malibu, where Mrs Bradford forgot that she had seen her nephew only a few weeks before, and was rejected by her pet dog.

Before Parker could continue with his bill of particulars, he was sharply interrupted. President Bradford showed his irritation. 'Is that what this is all about, the nonsense you've been bending my ear with? My God, Guy, come to your senses. What do you expect of Billie? She's a fallible human being like everyone else. Everyone is occasionally forgetful. Human memories slip all the time. In crowds, under pressure, a person can become absentminded, fail to recognize a friend or acquaintance he's known a long time. I can vouch for it, because it happens to me. I can run into a staffer who's been with me for years and draw a blank. As to her dog – ridiculous – at his age his eyesight is failing.'

Parker refused to retreat. 'Please, Mr President, hear me out for a moment more. Once, Mrs Bradford referred to an awkward incident at a party, when she met a movie star you had been dating. She said she would tell me more about it later. Recently, when I questioned her, she insisted that she had never met this movie star. Perhaps you've already heard about the press conference Mrs Bradford held the other day. She told the press she hoped to find time to look up Janet Farleigh, although just before going to Moscow she had been informed that Janet Farleigh had died, and reacted emotionally. Don't you think that's a bit unusual, Mr President?'

'Not a bit,' snapped President Bradford. He was clearly annoyed. 'It just proves human frailty. I repeat, we all have memory lapses. We all suffer contradictions, saying one thing one day, another thing on the same subject another day. Every "for instance" you've brought up is easily explainable.' He paused, glaring at Parker. 'Is this really what you came here to bother me about? There must be something more on your mind. If there is, tell me and be done with it.'

Parker bent forward, his hands on the desk. 'Mr President, I'm saying – I have reason to say – I don't think your wife, the First Lady, is the same one you had in Washington a month ago.'

The President sat blinking at Parker for several moments. 'Are you trying to tell me you believe that she's been brainwashed?'

'No. I'm trying to tell you – but wait, first let me tell you of a long-distance phone call meant for you that Nora Judson picked up while you were busy elsewhere. The call was from Ambassador Youngdahl in Moscow. He said that an American tourist came into our embassy quite distraught with a message she'd had from a young woman who'd cornered her in the Kremlin. The young woman claimed that she was your wife, that she was Mrs Bradford, and that she was being held prisoner by the Russians – while an imposter was representing her right here in London with you.'

There it was, thought Parker, and where was President Bradford?

President Bradford had sat back, hooded eyes holding on Parker. He remained silent for long seconds. At last, he spoke.

'Guy, seriously – have you been drinking?'

'I've never been more sober, sir. I'm repeating exactly what Ambassador Youngdahl told Miss Judson.'

'Did the ambassador even pretend to be serious?'

Parker nibbled at his lip. 'Quite honestly, no, sir. He thought it was quite funny. He thought the tourist was another cuckoo.'

'And so do I,' said the President. His withering gaze held on Parker. 'But you take it seriously?'

'I do only in light of all the other slips, contradictions, lapses of the First Lady. She simple doesn't seem to be herself any more.' Then, almost pleadingly, he asked, 'Are you sure you've seen nothing different about her?'

The President's patience had worn thin. 'Nothing, not one damn thing. I breakfast with her. I see her, off and on, throughout the day. I sleep with her. I find her the wife I've always had. Does that satisfy you? To continue this discussion any further would be utterly ridiculous.'

Before he could be dismissed, Parker raised his voice in a frantic effort to save the day. 'Just one more thing, Mr President. One last thing. It happened yesterday. I was working with the First Lady late yesterday afternoon when you came in, remember? I heard you ask her what she had done all day. She said she had not stepped out of the hotel. Well, that was not strictly true. She lied to you. She had stepped out. I followed her. She –'

'Wait a minute there,' the President interrupted angrily. 'You say you followed her? Who in the hell do you think you are – following my wife around?'

Parker retreated slightly. 'I – I'm sorry, sir. I did it in your interest. I was worried and had to find out what she was up to.' He paused. 'She went to Ladbury of London.'

'And you find that suspicious? A woman going to her dress designer? And not telling me? Probably not telling me because she's afraid I might be miffed at the money she's spending on clothes. That's what this is all about? That's what you've used up my valuable time to tell me?'

'I've come to tell you I think Ladbury is a Soviet drop. And that *this* First Lady is involved with Soviet agents.'

'You can prove that?'

'I'd like to try,' said Parker evenly, 'and I'd like you to help me. I hoped I might persuade you to get British Intelligence to look into Ladbury's.'

'Look into Ladbury's? You mean raid it? Find nothing there? Create a public scandal? Antagonize the Russians just when we're in the middle of delicate Summit negotiations? Are you out of your mind?'

Parker stood his ground. 'I'm not crazy, Mr President, but what is happening around us may very well be. Please believe in my sincerity. I'm concerned about you, and if I didn't feel –'

'Never mind about me,' the President interrupted. He was plainly infuriated. 'Look after yourself. You'll have to if you keep this up.' He paused a moment to regain control of his voice. 'Listen to me, Parker. I hired you because I thought you were a bright, smart young man. I turned you over to my wife for the same reasons, and because I thought you had savvy and good judgement. But right now, I'm having my doubts. I think you've gone entirely off your rocker. You've been hallucinating. You've been stirring up trouble. And you're trying to impose this insanity upon me. But I won't have it. Stop right now while you're ahead. Had I let you go on two more minutes, I might have fired you. As it is, I'll give you time to come to your senses. I'm very tempted to tell my wife everything you've been saying about her here, just to prove to you –'

'Don't tell her, please don't,' Parker implored him, certain that if the counterfeit First Lady knew of his suspicions, his own execution would follow.

'You needn't worry,' said the President drily, 'I don't intend to tell her, because I know she'd have you removed on the spot. I don't want to see that happen, because you've been a good worker and deserve another chance.'

Parker nodded gratefully.

The President went on. 'One piece of advice. Keep your mouth shut. If I ever hear that you've repeated this cock-and-bull nonsense to a single soul, I'll have you thrown out of here. So you gather your wits about you fast as you can, and stick to your job. Do you hear me?

'Yes, sir.'

'And to restore us both to some semblance of sanity, let's agree this conversation never took place. Now that's enough, Parker. Be on your way, and don't ever bother me again with another word about this.'

'Yes, sir. Good evening, sir.'

It had happened in the nick of time, while the President was still occupied in some kind of meeting with Guy Parker, and just before she was to leave with Andrew for dinner. And before her own frayed nerves could unravel.

Vera Vavilova had been waiting what seemed an eternity for the news from Moscow. And Moscow continued to remain silent. Haltingly, she had tried to dress for dinner, numbed by fear, examining her alternatives. Not one alternative was promising. The best possibility was to plead illness. Returning from dinner, she could tell Andrew she felt ill – was suffering acute indigestion, an attack of the flu, a resumpion of vaginal bleeding. She might not get away with any one of these, she knew, because Andrew would immediately summon Dr Cummings, who would find nothing wrong with her. Even if the physician prescribed rest, Vera realized this meant only a day's postponement of the inevitable. Another possibility was to quit cold, instruct her contacts and let the Premier know she could not continue without information, and take off for the suburban airport outside London, the old RAF base that the British had turned over for the exclusive use of the Soviet Union, and return to Moscow to be exchanged for Billie Bradford. Yet, Vera did not want to quit, to be written off as a failure in her most challenging role. Such a chance to win glory might never come again.

There remained only one other option – face up to the inevitable, have intercourse with Andrew tonight, and trust her intuition.

Far too risky.

She had fallen into her deepest despair, when the telephone rang. The caller identified himself as the blessed Fred Willis.

'Are you alone?' he inquiried.

'Yes. For the moment.'

'I'd like to drop something off for you. It concerns your inquiry about what is served at Disneyland.'

Her heart leaped. It was like a last-second reprieve from death. 'Oh, Fred —'

'See you.' He hung up.

She waited nervously inside the front door, with one eye on the entrance to the President's work suite. If Andrew came in as Willis appeared, she'd have to think fast.

Three or four minutes later, she heard Fred Willis's voice in the corridor, speaking to the Secret Service men. She pulled back the door and greeted him. Willis stepped inside. Vera shut the door.

Willis was reaching into his trouser pocket. He whispered, 'Dangerous putting it on paper, but too detailed to pass on verbally.' He pushed a folded note into her hand. He smiled. 'All here. Exactly what you want. Read it privately and get rid of it.'

'Fred, I can't tell you —'

But he was already gone.

Glancing at the door to the President's office suite, Vera dashed into the bathroom. Safely locked inside, she hastily unfolded the note, which grew into a single sheet of typing paper with single-spaced typing in English that almost covered the page. Quickly she scanned it, beaming, carefully read it a second time word for word, committing it to memory. She was about to undertake a third reading when she heard Andrew's voice from the bedroom.

'Are you ready?' he called out.

'Give me a few minutes, dear,' she called back.

She turned on the sink tap full force, tore the KGB note into shreds, and dropped the pieces into the toilet bowl. She flushed the toilet, watching to see that every piece of paper disappeared. Satisfied, she removed her robe and resumed preparing herself for dinner.

She had been unusually vivacious throughout dinner, and she could see that Andrew was pleased with her. When they had returned to Claridge's and arrived at their suite, Admiral Sam Ridley, the military chief of staff, was waiting to speak to the President. He had drawn Andrew aside, addressing him in an undertone.

The President had nodded and returned to Vera. 'I'm sorry, dear, but something's come up that needs a little discussion. I'll have to go down the hall with the admiral. I won't be more than a half-hour.' He winked at her and leaned over, his lips close to her ear. 'Don't go to sleep on me. I've waited a long time for tonight.'

She had brushed his cheek with a kiss. 'I'll be up, darling,' she promised.

And here she was, drying herself from her bubble bath, noting that Andrew would be here in a short time, ready to bed down with her. Dabbing on perfume – Billie's favourite scent – Vera made a critical inspection of herself in the full-length mirror behind the bathroom door. What she saw was nothing to be ashamed of or even worried about. Her breasts looked wonderful, pointed straight out, no sag. She had held her weight down, and her stomach was flat and her hips beautifully curved yet firm. Briefly, she wondered how he would treat this body. Although fear had left her, and her confidence was restored, the wondering about him revived a certain anxiety. It was the familiar high-strung feeling that she had known since girlhood, the standing in the wings, poised for the curtain to go up or poised for a cue.

Quickly, Vera slipped into her flimsy silk nightgown, the light pink one. She walked into the bedroom, fiddled with the lights, leaving only his bedside lamp on. Turning toward her twin bed, she loosened the blankets, pushed the two pillows closer, picked up a novel and got into bed to await the last and most crucial hurdle of the perilous undertaking.

After a while, she saw that the half-hour had passed, then forty minutes, and fifty, since he had left her for his conference. It was no use trying to sleep or feign sleep. He would not permit it.

She opened the novel, determined to distract herself. But no use. Her head was elsewhere. She closed the book, set it on the table, lifted one pillow against the headboard, and propped herself up. The material she had received from Moscow on handling the President in bed had been general in some areas, specific in others, but overall it gave her an excellent idea of what to expect and what was expected from her. She wondered how this intimate material had been acquired, but of course she knew. Alex had seduced Billie Bradford. Alex had slept with the First Lady. Alex had written the instructions. Yet, the almost certain knowledge of this provoked no jealousy in her whatsoever. Billie Bradford would not have meant a thing to him except a job well done. Vera felt positive that his one concern had been to get her back to him safely. Recently, she had not thought about Alex much, but now she felt the old warmth and love for him and invoked his devotion to get her through this night. Speculating on her next action, for which she finally felt well prepared, she realized how eager she was to undertake it. The excitement it provided was probably far greater than what she might know if she was debuting in Moscow in *The Doll's House*.

She remembered, also, that what would happen tonight was only a means to the end that would follow. Giving herself to the President should bring the returns she expected. In a short time from now, he would be relaxed and talkative, and with gentle prodding from her, he could be depended upon to confide his secret Summit plans. Tomorrow, she would communicate them to the Premier. Her role in the victory would be ended. The day after tomorrow she would be flown back to Moscow, even as Billie Bradford would be flown to London. The exchange would have been made. The real Billie Bradford would resume her familiar role as First Lady. She, herself, in Moscow again, would undergo a second round of minor plastic surgery, to alter slightly her Billie-perfect face and restore it to her previous Vera face. Honoured and elevated, Vera would take up her stage career once more. The leading parts in the Moscow Theatre would be hers. And Alex, dear Alex, she could have him openly, marry or live with him as she wished.

She peered at the clock. More than an hour had passed. The President was extremely late. It had to be something important to keep him from what he desired so much. She must be patient, she told herself, and she must be giving and loving. For him, the experience tonight must be pure and it must be total. Above all, it must disarm him.

Five minutes later she heard the entry door open and close, and she heard the lock turn from the inside.

Andrew Bradford breezed into the bedroom, smiling at her, pulling off his suit jacket, casting aside his necktie, opening his shirt. He came directly to her and kissed her on the lips. 'My, you look beautiful,' he said. 'Sorry, I'm late. We had to bring some loose ends together, consolidate our talks strategy. I tell you, it was hard keeping my mind on the work, knowing you were here and that we could have our old times again.'

'I love you, Andrew. I've missed you.'

'Not more than I've missed you.' He had his shirt off. 'I'll be just a few minutes.'

'Hurry.'

He disappeared into the bathroom. He would be taking off the rest of his clothes now. He would move to the toilet. She heard the toilet flush. Then she heard the water from the tap. Then silence. Cologne, she guessed, Zizanie.

He returned to the bedroom on bare feet. As he emerged from the shadows, she could see he was wearing his blue boxer shorts. He had a nice solid figure, a little flabby here and there, but trim for a man of his age. He had unbuttoned his shorts, dropped them, stepped out of them, and started to the other side of the twin beds. She could see his penis, somewhat enlarged, swinging from side to side. It was not yet erect.

'Are you tired darling?' she said.

'A little. It was non-stop brainstorming down the hall.' He gave a short laugh. 'But not that tired.'

He was getting into the bed.

For an instant, the pulse at her throat jumped. Her confidence wavered. Alex's report had been definite enough, or so it had seemed, but suddenly it did not have anything exact. What were the interim details? What should happen in these next seconds? Should she move towards him? Or would he move toward her?

She started to slide under the blanket toward him, then stopped. Her directions had implied he would move first.

He did.

He had thrown the blanket further back, and he was beside her in her bed, reaching down for the bottom of her nightgown. She lifted herself up, as he indicated he expected her to, and then helped him draw the nightgown upward. She raised her arms to accommodate the flow of the nightgown over her breasts and arms. He tossed the nightgown on the floor.

He eyed her seriously a moment. 'You've got the most beautiful tits on earth.'

She pulled back her shoulders. 'They're all yours, only yours.'

'Oh, God,' he murmured, and bent to the breast nearest him, lips pressed to her flat nipple, kissing it, tonguing it, until it began to harden and rise. His lips moved to the other breast, curving his hand under it, massaging it, kissing it all over.

'Andrew, I –'

She closed her eyes and lay still, except for one hand resting on top of his head. He was kissing her navel and belly, one hand rubbing her pubic hair line, gliding downward, two fingers gently caressing her clitoris. She felt something press into her thigh, and opened her eyes to discover that he had grown fully erect.

Mouth near his ear, she forced herself to breathe harder. She was tempted to reach for his cock, but restrained herself. She remembered her instructions.

He was bringing himself to his knees, and she raised her legs and spread them apart. She was not completely aroused, not really moist, which worried her until she recalled that

275

she had earlier applied a sterile lubricant to help him.

He was coming down between her legs, one of his hands holding his stiff penis, guiding it toward her vagina. The tip of his penis probed, located the vulva opening, and he poked his erection inside her, pushing his torso closer until he had entirely entered her.

'Christ,' he said, 'how I've wanted you – how good this is – how good.'

'So good, darling.'

He was going steadily now, up and down, up and down.

She covered her eyes with an arm, her mouth half open in a pose of ecstacy. She wanted to shake her ass violently, go up and down with him, make him ride her harder, make him gallop with her, but once more she held back and confined herself to mild undulations.

She lifted her arm from her eyes. His features were distorted. His pumping quickened. She supposed he was enjoying himself. She hoped so. For herself, she wasn't really with it, only a silent partner to his solo.

For a fleeting second, Vera was again tempted to shake him up, give him a real pleasure ride. What fun to see his face, the face of the President of the United States, as someone fucked him out of his head. But the essence of the KGB report on Billie's sexual behaviour burned bold as cue cards in her brain –

Straight ordinary missionary position. Reactions mainly passive. Let him come to you. No foreplay except breasts and clitoris. Let him do everything his way. Respond normally and with pleasure. Make no aggressive moves. Doubt if he will bring you to orgasm by intercourse. If he does, do not overreact. When finished, he will probably give you an orgasm by hand. We do not know every detail, but this should suffice. Just let him run the show, and you go along, and let him know he is pleasing you. All your moves must be familiar, comfortable, expressive of married endearment. This is to be routine release, not big romance. The game is pleasurable cooperation in his man's world. Good luck.

Okay, good luck. Thanks, Alex. So Billie had been a dull fuck.

Vera felt the President arch, heard him gasp and wheeze, felt him going stronger, accelerating, punching into her harder, enlarging inside her, and then pubic hair flush against pubic hair he froze tightly to her, rasped something she could not make out, felt the sperm sputter deep into her. Ejaculation. Climax. Well, fine, she had gone the distance without a hitch.

Resting briefly on his elbows, he started pulling his slippery appendage out of her.

'Wonderful, Andrew, just wonderful.'

'Better than ever,' he breathed. 'You were better than ever.'

She lowered her cramped legs, and stretched. 'Oh, that was delicious,' she whispered, mocking Billie's sometimes husky voice, 'that was worth waiting for.'

He had rolled off her. 'There's more that's worth waiting for,' he said lazily.

She trusted the report completely now. 'You're too tired. You don't have to.'

His hand reached down between her legs. 'I want to. I want you as happy as I am.'

His fingertips found her distended clitoris, stroked it lightly, rubbed it harder, stroked her entire vaginal area, returned to the clitoris and glided back and forth across it.

As he continued the steady pressure, she moved her head on the pillow, from one side to the other, and rotated her ass gently – she knew her Billie by now – and she simulated controlled excitement.

Five or six minutes had gone by and she knew that she would not have a real orgasm.

The final problem. Billie came for sure this way. But how long did it take her? Ten minutes? Twenty? A half an hour? She must not miscalculate. He must tell her.

'Andrew,' she groaned, 'I'm sorry I'm taking so long.'

'You'll be all right in a few minutes. Just relax, relax, my darling, we have all the time in the world.'

Head to one side, a blink caught the time. Six minutes gone by. Two to go.

'Oh, Andrew, Andrew, I'm wet all over.'

'You're almost there. Easy does it. Don't think.'

Stupid idiot, she thought. Give him a big one. Now. Right now.

She went rigid, squeezing her thighs together, raising her ass, gave out a strangled cry, a long shudder – and collapsed in a heap.

Andrew removed his hand, smiling down at her. 'There you are.'

'Thank you, Andrew. Delicious from head to toe. Hold me, darling, hold me close.'

As his arms went around her, she smiled to herself. The best fake orgasm in history, she was sure. Move over Bernhardt, Duse, here lies an actress.

He was embracing her loosely.

Now transition, she thought, all's fair in love – now war. She had come through the long-dreaded ordeal unexposed, unscathed, apparently an utter success. But there was still the last act, the purpose of all the acrobatics, the pay-off. How to handle it? She had rehearsed it countless ways in her mind. She must get into it – not too fast, not too eagerly – yet, not too slowly, or else he might fall asleep. Be deft. Be natural.

'Andrew?'

'Yes, dearest?'

'The way I feel, I could do this every night.'

'I know. Me, too. I wish it were possible. But considering what we're up against with the Russians the next few days, we're going to be walking wrecks. It's high-tension time. Everything at stake. I can't say how I'll feel each night.'

She turned fully toward him. He had moved over to his bed and dropped his head into the pillow, and lay flat on his back staring up at the ceiling.

'What's so especially tense about this time, more than any other time?' she asked casually. 'It's always tense, I know.

278

But this meeting seems to be taking more out of you. I don't understand.'

'Well, I'll tell you the problem,' he said. 'Usually, we negotiate from strength. That makes it easier. But this time –' His voice trailed off as he lost himself in some thought.

'This time – this time what, Andrew? Don't leave me hanging.'

'Oh, sorry,' he said, bringing his mind back to their conversation. 'This time we have to maintain a bluff to win. Not easy. Complicated. I'll explain it all to you one day.'

She pretended exasperation. 'Not fair, Andrew. Don't treat me like a second-class citizen. You've always confided in me. I've confided in you. You're interested in what I do every day. Well, I'm just as interested in what you do. We're a team, Andrew. We share. So don't suddenly go chauvinist and relegate me to the kitchen. Tell me the problems you're dealing with. I want to share them with you.'

'I don't mean to withhold anything from you,' he said apologetically. 'It's just that I'm bushed and it's so late. But you've a right to know. Let me make it uncomplicated. I hope you'll settle for a capsule version for the time being. I'll expand on it another time. Will the capsule version do?'

'It doesn't even have to be a capsule version. I'll settle for a thumbnail version. I'm sure it has to do with that African place – Boende – and your disagreement with the Soviets. But what's the problem? Why are they making it so tough for you? I've got to know about anything that interferes with my sex life.'

He grinned. 'Right you are.' He thought about it and was serious again. 'The Soviets have that rebel Communist in Boende, Nwapa by name, ready to move in for a take-over of the country. But the Russians are unsure of us. If we've armed President Kibangu and the government, if we should be ready for them, if we should intervene, they'd be crushed. A defeat would affect Communist power all over Africa.'

'Well, have you armed him?' she asked almost casually – an interested-wife question, no big deal.

'That's exactly what the Russians have to know.' He

sighed. 'The fact is, we have not armed him.'

'You've not armed him?' she repeated.

'No, we've not. We're only pretending we have. That's my problem, maintaining the bluff.'

Vera felt a charge of thrill. Three years of effort had finally paid off. She had it all for Kirechenko, she had secured his victory.

Vera ran her fingers through Andrew's hair. 'Poor darling,' she said tenderly. 'No wonder you've been so troubled.'

He took her wrist and kissed her hand. 'And you've been so lovely.'

'Thank you, Andrew.' She wondered whether it would be pressing her luck to go on. She decided to try cautiously. She put on a puzzled expression. 'Just one thing I don't understand.'

'What's that?'

'Even if the Russians knew you were bluffing, and they made a move, couldn't you intervene fast, airlift supplies to the Boende government?'

'Yes, we could, but no, we can't. It would cost me any chance of re-election. I'll show you our latest private polls when we get home. So we can't move in to save Boende at the last minute.' He paused. 'Fortunately, the Soviets don't know that. If they knew, they'd have their rebels rolling over Boende and taking it in less than a week. They'd certainly refuse to sign our non-intervention pact. They'd break off the Summit.'

'You're sure they don't know?'

'Of course they don't. And they won't know. Which means a victory for us, the lion's share of Boende's uranium, an edge in controlling central Africa, an end to Communist inroads. So now you know what's been on my mind.'

Vera found it difficult to contain her excitement. She had learned all that was vital to learn. She had his big secret, the only Soviet on earth to know it. Until tomorrow.

'Andrew, we'll win, won't we?'

'You can bet on that. If we play our cards right, maintain our bluff, we win.'

You lose, she thought.

She yawned. 'Andrew, you don't know how much better it makes me feel, sharing things with you. At least now I can understand what you're going through.' She raised herself on an elbow. 'Good night, darling.' She kissed him. 'Thanks again for a marvellous evening, the best ever. Just forget your worries, and think of us. Now get some sleep.'

'Good night, sweetheart. We both better get some sleep.'

He pulled the blanket over his shoulder, and curled under it. She left her bed, took the sleeping pill, walked to the side of his bed, put out the lamp, and in the darkness felt her way back to her bed and got beneath the blanket.

She was lying on her back, waiting for the pill to take effect, when she heard his snoring. For herself, sleep would come slowly, she knew. She was too elated with success to shut out the joy of it.

She went over her next instructions. When and if she learned anything important, she had been told, she was to contact Fred Willis. He, in turn, would contact Ladbury, who would arrange for the meeting with Premier Kirechenko. At the designated time, Willis would see that she be provided with a car and driver without her Secret Service guards. She would be driven to Westridge, the abandoned RAF airfield ten miles out of London, the landing strip turned over exclusively to the Soviets for their air transports. At the airfield she would be escorted to the limousine where Premier Kirechenko and General Chukovsky would be waiting. She would pass on to them everything that she had learned from President Bradford. Immediately after, she would be placed aboard a Soviet jet and returned to Moscow, while Billie Bradford was being flown to London.

Kirechenko would have his triumph. Vera Vavilova would have her own. Curtain call after curtain call, a heroine of the Soviet Union.

She snuggled under the blanket. She had never been happier.

Vera Vavilova, heroine and legend.

That was something to sleep on.

10

It was late afternoon, getting later, getting more overcast, when Guy Parker once more drove up before Buckingham Palace, circled the Queen Victoria Memorial, came along the curb, braked his Jaguar to a stop, and let the engine idle as he searched the three entrances for any sight of Nora Judson.

For twenty minutes he had been driving around St James's Park, continually slowing before the Palace to pick up Nora. But she still had not shown herself.

He was supposed to have interviewed the First Lady in the morning, and had planned to devote the afternoon to following her if she left Claridge's. A short call and a scribbled note from Nora had changed all that. Nora's call advised him that the interview on the book had to be cancelled. The note from her, arriving after lunch, told him, 'The Prince of Wales is having Billie and Madame Kirechenko to tea at Buckingham Palace this afternoon. I am taking Billie there. Can you pick me up at front entrance around four o'clock? Please do.'

It was now 4.20 and no Nora. About to take another spin around the Memorial, Parker spotted Nora in the courtyard beyond the tall iron rails, hastening past the police guard house, toward the side gate, the north-western gate. She came through quickly, skirted a cluster of tourists, paused to look for him. He hopped out of his car, signalled her, and finally caught her attention. She hurried to the car, and got in.

Spinning the Jaguar into the stream of traffice, he glanced at her. 'How are you?'

'Our Queen is still with their Prince,' she said. 'I was

tangled up with the Palace press office. Sorry to be late. I asked you to pick me up not because I needed a lift, but because I wanted to hear what happened to you last night. Did you actually go in to see the President?'

'I did.'

'You told him what you thought?'

'Everything, every suspicion I had about the First Lady.'

'Well?'

'Well, you were right. He almost fired me.'

'Was he that sore?'

Parker nodded gloomily. 'Damn sore. He said I was crazy. He had an explanation for every slip-up she made. He warned me that, if I mentioned any of this to anyone, I was through.'

Nora puckered her lips thoughtfully. 'I suppose if you look at it from his point of view, his attitude is understandable. After all, he's living with her. She is his Billie, as she has always been, nothing different or changed.'

Parker halted the car at a red light. 'That's what made it difficult. To him, the same old Billie. That's what is so depressing. You and I know something is wrong, and there is nowhere to turn, no one who will believe us.' The traffic light showed green and he stepped on the gas pedal. 'I even advised the President what his next move should be.'

'Which was?'

'Have the British stage a raid on Ladbury's. Billie's secret visit makes it very suspect. I feel sure the Soviets use it as a drop. A sudden search might turn up the proof we need.'

'How did he react?'

'As expected.' Parker sighed. 'A man who thinks there is nothing wrong with his wife isn't going to think there is anything wrong with her visiting her dress designer. He just wouldn't consider my request. And he sure was mad as hell that I followed his Billie.'

Parker was suddenly aware of a movement beside him, and he saw that Nora was sitting up straight, her eyes bright with excitement.

'Guy, I've just had a great idea,' she said. 'It was so obvious we overlooked it. If the President needs a real fact to be convinced, I know how to get him one. Billie's fingerprints. They must be on file somewhere. Get them – somehow see if this First Lady's prints match hers –'

Parker interrupted her with a shake of his head. 'No go. You're on the right track, Nora. But a little late. I thought of that already – meant to tell you. I hoped to have the facts – if they supported us – to show the President. I phoned the White House, asked a close friend in the West Wing to locate Billie's prints in confidence and send them over to me on the next courier flight. A routine hunt for her prints was instigated. Will you believe what happened? The computer showed the prints on file in the FBI, in the California Motor Vehicle Department, and I forget how many other places. So my friend requested a set. You know what? Not a single set of Billie's prints was available anywhere. They were missing. Gone. Someone did a good job. So there we have another suspicion, but no facts.'

'Dammit.'

'You can say that again.'

They had turned into Brook Street and were approaching Claridge's.

'What's next, Guy?'

He heaved his shoulders. 'I suppose I'll keep trailing Billie and see if anything happens.'

'Don't bother any more today. Billie won't be back from Buckingham Palace until later. She won't be going out tonight. Wants to catch up on her correspondence. Wouldn't you like to spend the evening with me?'

He hardly heard her. 'No,' he said, slowing the car. 'I mean yes, I'd like to – but –' Deep in thought, he edged the Jaguar against the curb, some yards before the hotel doorman, and stopped it. His face lit up, and he slapped the steering wheel. 'You know what?' he said. 'It just struck me – what I should be doing.'

'What?'

'Visiting Ladbury's myself. Have a look around. Maybe invite him to dinner.'

'I'd think twice about that,' Nora said worriedly. 'If your hunch is anywhere near right, you could be getting into trouble.'

'What do you mean?' Parker made light of it. 'The First Lady's ghostwriter paying a visit to the First Lady's dressmaker? Absolutely normal. Absolutely innocent.'

'Well, I don't know. When do you intend to do it?'

Parker held up his wristwatch. 'Right now.'

He brought the car up in front of Claridge's entrance. The resplendent doorman hurried forward to open the Jaguar door.

Nora leaned over and kissed Parker. 'Guy, be careful.'

'I'll try. I want to see you again. Maybe even tonight. Hang around.'

'I'll be waiting.' She touched his sleeve. 'Guy, be *very* careful.'

She stepped out of the car, and he drove off.

Although the traffic was heavy at this hour, Parker reached Motcomb Street in less than fifteen minutes. He found a space a block from the Halkin Arcade and Ladbury's shop, locked his car, and covered the distance on foot.

At the elegant entrance to the dress designer's shop, he paused momentarily to collect his wits. At last, he grasped the door handle, and the door swung inward. As he crossed the threshold, a bell somewhere above him announced his entrance.

Standing on the deep plush off-white carpet, Parker surveyed the showroom. No salesperson was in sight. The room itself was richly and tastefully decorated. In the forefront, on a pedestal, a mannequin was draped in a black velvet cocktail suit and green scarf. Behind the mannequin rested a long glass case displaying jewellery. The walls on either side were lined with expensive clothes. Rectangular slots held sweaters and blouses. Dresses, skirts, suits, pants, were hung in alcoves. To the rear were two full-length mirrors, and a scattering of valuable antique chairs. Half the rear wall was covered with live vines that had climbed up several trellises. The other half of the rear wall featured a spiral staircase to the second floor, as well as an opening into a corridor that apparently led to fitting rooms and offices.

Parker had almost a half-minute alone – the chic casualness, the air of aloofness, amused him – before someone materialized from the back. This was the mannish, heavy-set woman that Parker remembered seeing in the White House, Ladbury's assistant, Rowena Quarles.

She planted herself in front of Parker, eyeing him as she might an intruder. 'Yes? May I help you?'

'I'd like to see Mr Ladbury,' Parker said politely. 'I'm working for Mrs Bradford. She suggested I see him.'

'Mrs Bradford?'

'Billie Bradford. The First Lady, the American First Lady. I believe she is one of Mr Ladbury's clients.'

Miss Quarles hesitated. 'She sent you?'

'Yes.'

'Well, Mr Ladbury may be tied up. But let me see. Who shall I say is calling?'

'Mr Parker.'

'If you'll wait a moment, Mr Parker.'

She disappeared into the rear corridor. Parker wandered about the intimidating room, coming to rest before the glass case with its dazzling jewellery.

From the corner of an eye, he saw the slender young man with a startling yellow fringe of hair on his forehead and a springy step approaching him quizzically.

'Mr Parker?' he inquired in a falsetto. 'I'm Ladbury.' He offered a drooping hand. 'Mrs Bradford sent you?'

'Not exactly,' said Parker, releasing the designer's hand. 'But, in a way, yes. I'm Guy Parker, and I work in the White House. I'm assisting Mrs Bradford in writing her book. What she had really said was that I might interview any people she knew in London. She may have mentioned it to you.'

'I've not heard a word concerning interviews,' said Ladbury. 'But I think I did hear her mention something of a book she was doing when I visited the White House recently.'

'Well, here I am about the book. I had hoped to catch you with a little free time to discuss her taste in fashions. What she doesn't like, what she does like, how you met her, an anecdote or two. Perhaps you could even join me for a drink or dinner? I know it is short notice, but –'

'You're most gracious, thank you,' Ladbury interrupted. 'I do understand what you're about on that book. I adore Mrs Bradford, and I'll be only too glad to cooperate, Mr Parker, but I'm afraid not now.' He consulted his gold Patek Philippe watch. 'It's a bit late. Almost closing time. We'll be shutting down in a few minutes. After that I have a long-standing dinner appointment. I am sorry. But look here, why don't you ring me in a day or two? We'll set up a proper meeting when we can speak at leisure. Perhaps over lunch. How's that?'

'In a day or two. Fine. I'll call you.'

Rowena Quarles had emerged from the rear corridor. 'Telephone, Mr Ladbury!' she called out. 'Paris!'

'Be right there!' Ladbury called back. He turned to Parker. 'Oh, dear, do forgive me for being abrupt, but I have been expecting this call for hours. Sorry about today. We'll make up for it.' He spun away, then said, 'Remember me to Mrs Bradford. I must see her while she is in London.'

Parker started for the door. At the door he halted, glanced around. Ladbury had vanished into the corridor. Once more, Parker had the room to himself.

What were Ladbury's last words?

Remember me to Mrs Bradford. I must see her while she is in London.

But Ladbury had seen her here in London. Parker, himself, had watched her enter this shop.

She had lied about it. Now Ladbury had lied about it.

What was going on?

His suspicions rekindled, he was tempted to find out the truth about this shop.

He gazed across the room toward the corridor. Certainly, Ladbury must have his office back there.

Parker made up his mind.

He took the doorknob, opened the front door. The bell

above sounded loudly. Without moving, Parker closed the door. He remained inside the shop.

Turning, he moved as quietly as possible, abetted by the deep carpeting, to the rear. He squinted inside the lighted corridor. It was empty. Trying to hold his breath, he entered the corridor. From a midway point, he could hear Ladbury speaking on the telephone. Parker continued into the corridor. There were several curtained rooms to his left. The fitting rooms, he guessed. Treading softly, he moved on further up the corridor until Ladbury's voice on the right could be heard distinctly as he addressed a colleague in Paris. Almost directly across from what must be Ladbury's personal office was one more curtained room. Parker separated the curtains and slipped between them.

He was in a medium-sized, attractively decorated, feminine dressing room. At both ends, tall three-way mirrors. Straight ahead, the wall was an open wardrobe filled with women's gowns, the floor-length formal gowns taking up most of the rack. Quickly, Parker crossed to the wardrobe, pushed apart the formal dresses, stepped through them to the very wall, letting the dresses fall back together in front of him. Pressed uncomfortably against the hard wall, shielded by the dresses on their padded hangers, Parker was sure he could not be seen by anyone happening into the dressing room.

He gave his full attention to listening. Coming from the office on the other side of the corridor, Ladbury's voice was partially muffled, but still audible.

Parker stood motionless behind the dresses, feeling suffocated by them, deeply conscious of the rashness of the risk he was taking. Should someone find him there, there would be no acceptable explanation and the consequences would be horrendous. If Ladbury's shop was, indeed, a KGB contact point, his captors would eliminate him immediately. If it was legitimately only a couture house, his captors would turn him over to the local bobby as a common thief or trespasser. The President would learn of his arrest and fire him promptly. He would be disgraced and helpless after that. He was beginning to have doubts about his suspicions and his amateur sleuthing, and was considering giving up his surveillance and leaving the shop while it was still possible, when the front doorbell rang out. He went rigid against the wall, but cocked an ear.

Faintly, he could hear the front door close, then open again, the bell ringing again, the door closing once more. Over this he could hear Ladbury's voice. '*Attendez, attendez,*' Ladbury was saying into the phone. Now he was speaking to someone in his office. 'That must be them. Here, Rowena, take the phone. Your French is better than mine. Tell her she'll have her bloody shipment next week for certain. Don't go on at length. Get rid of the miserable woman. We have business here . . . I'd better go see if they've arrived.'

Parker peeked between the dresses, and beneath the ankle-length dressing room curtain he could make out the patent leather loafers of Ladbury emerging into the corridor. Apparently, Ladbury was looking toward his front door. In his high-pitched voice he called out to someone, 'Ah, there you are, right on time! Come on back to the office! Oh, Baginov, let's close the shop. Be a good fellow and secure the dead bolt on the front door. The spare key is in the pocket of the velvet suit model, the black velvet outfit on the mannequin. Don't want any bloody customers coming in on us now . . . . There, that's a good fellow!'

Ladbury seemed to be waiting outside his office for the new arrivals. Then, beneath the curtain, a pair of brown suede shoes came up to Ladbury, followed by a pair of thick-soled black cowhide shoes.

'Gentlemen,' Ladbury greeted his visitors shrilly, 'I hear it's good news.'

'The best,' an American voice with a pseudo-British accent and the slightest lisp replied. The lisp sounded vaguely familiar to Parker, but he could not immediately identify it.

'Front door secure,' a bass voice with a faint Russian accent reported.

'We won't be bothered now,' said Ladbury. 'Come into my office. I've some excellent sherry.'

From his hidden post, Parker listened. For a short interval, he heard nothing. He wondered whether Ladbury had closed his office door.

To Parker's relief, Ladbury's voice suddenly could be heard again, drifting toward him as if from some distance. 'Here's to a momentous success,' said Ladbury. Apparently, the silence had taken place during a pouring of drinks, and now the four of them were toasting the good news. Parker tried to speculate on the reason for the celebration. If it was some kind of Soviet victory, what was an American doing here? If it was some kind of American or British triumph, what was a Soviet doing here?

Ladbury could be heard again. 'So our lady delivered?'

'Not yet, but almost,' the American said with his small lisp. 'She simply informed me she has what we want. She will meet the Premier at the assigned rendezvous at eleven o'clock tonight. At that time, she will make her report.'

'Do you want us to transmit this much?' Ladbury inquired.

'I think not,' said the American. 'Let's wait until it is done.'

'But the exchange – the timing –?' This was Ladbury.

The Russian voice at last. 'There will be no exchange. After Vera passes on the information, her usefulness is ended. Then the other will be returned.'

An extended silence.

Ladbury broke it. 'So our friend Vera is to be liquidated?'

'It is necessary,' said the Russian, who Parker remembered had been addressed as Baginov when he arrived.

'I suppose so,' said Ladbury regretfully. 'Too bad. Clever woman. That will happen after she sees the Premier?'

'Tonight,' said Baginov.

'You have a safe place?' wondered Ladbury.

'Everything has been arranged,' said Baginov.

'What if the body is found one day?' said Ladbury. 'It could –'

'Not to worry,' said Baginov. 'It will not be identifiable. Not even the face. Acid.'

Another silence.

'When will we transmit?' asked Ladbury.

'You will be here from eleven o'clock tonight,' said Baginov. 'Fedin will join you with the code. On the other end, they will be ready to act.'

'Settled,' said Ladbury.

Parker could hear the barely distinct sounds of shuffling – chairs or feet – and peeking out he glimpsed the movement of shoes, four pairs of them, one pair belonging to the Quarles woman, leaving the office. Shortly after, the sound of the front door closing. All the lights went out, obviously from a master switch.

Parker remained stationary behind the rack of dresses. He did not know whether he was alone in the shop. Perhaps one of them had stayed behind. To be detected now meant certain death. Still, he could not continue too long in hiding. Sooner or later he would have to leave his position. In fact, the sooner the better.

He decided to remain where he was fifteen minutes longer. If one of the four had stayed behind, any movement he made might be heard.

This waiting gave him the first opportunity to absorb what he had overheard. What he had overheard, stripped of all his suspicions and fancies, came down to the bare facts that the three men he had listened to were acting covertly. They had a female agent named Vera. She had uncovered some secret information of enormous value. She was delivering it to 'the Premier' tonight. Since there was only one Premier in London at this time – Soviet Premier Dmitri Kirechenko – this was undoubtedly a Soviet operation related to the Summit, and the three men in Ladbury's had been KGB agents. Certainly Baginov was one. Certainly, Ladbury. And an American with a slight lisp. Their female agent, Vera, having found what the Soviets needed to know, was to be killed immediately after delivering the information to the Premier. Not only killed, but disfigured.

There was no denying it any more, Parker knew. Every bit of it supported his suspicions. This Vera was unquestionably Billie Bradford's double. She had obtained vital information from the President. She was passing it on to the Premier. She must now be disposed of, and any evidence that she was a perfect double for the First Lady be destroyed, so that should the corpse be found there would be no clue to the Soviet plot. Then 'the other' – meaning the real Billie Bradford – would be returned, and perform as if nothing had happened.

The enormity of the plot dizzied Parker. The fact that it was so near success compelled him to leave his hiding place.

There had been no sound from anywhere in the shop for over fifteen minutes. Parker parted the hanging gowns and stepped out into the darkened dressing room. One hand held out before him, as if sleepwalking, he went in the direction of the corridor. His fingers touched the curtain. He pushed it aside and was in the corridor. There, a narrow sliver of light shone from the shop. He followed it cautiously into the main body of the shop. Several similar lights, inches above floor level, were serving as night-lights and aiding his progress. The front portion of Ladbury's place was partially illuminated by an arcade lamp. Outside, it was early evening.

At the front door, Parker halted. He was not surprised to find himself trembling. He tried the door. It held fast, secured from inside and out by the dead bolt. He would have to find a way to break out. At once, he remembered the spare key Ladbury had earlier ordered Baginov to use. Parker returned to the velvet suit on the mannequin. There were two pockets. One was empty. The other produced the key.

With shaking hand, he unlocked the front door, stepped outside, locked the door again.

He stood in the arcade staring at the key. If he kept it, the key would be missed later. He realized that he had better find a locksmith, make a duplicate, and return the original. He would have to consult the London telephone book, locate a locksmith who was open at this hour, perhaps one with twenty-four-hour service. As he headed for his car on rubbery legs, he had a flash of recall. When he had left his car in the intersecting street to follow the so-called First Lady, he had seen a shop that resembled a hardware store. In fact, it was an ironmonger's shop. Maybe that would do.

He picked up his pace until he neared his car. From the corner of Kinnerton Street he could see what still resembled a hardware store and, better yet, the lights were on. Reaching it, he glanced at the display window. There was an array of household gadgets, kitchen appliances, as well as a stand of shiny new padlocks. In the store itself, there was only a balding clerk, who seemed to be totalling the cash register.

Parker went inside, and approached the clerk. 'This key,' he said, brandishing it, 'could you possibly make me a copy while I wait?'

'Make what?'

'A duplicate. I desperately need another key.'

The clerk frowned. 'I was just closing. I'm already late for dinner. But – well, see here, you are an American, aren't you?'

'I am. I –'

'Very well,' said the clerk, taking the key. 'My wife has American relatives. Good lot. I'll be only a minute.'

He went to the rear with one key. Five minutes later he was back with two keys.

Parker thanked him, paid him, and was off, quickly retracing his steps to Ladbury's shop. At the front door, he looked about him. The arcade was empty of pedestrian traffic. Without wasting a moment, Parker inserted the original key and let himself inside. He went to the velvet suit on display and dropped the original key into the correct pocket. Turning back, he gazed outside. All clear. He opened the door, went through it, firmly shut it, and then locked it using the duplicate key. He dropped the key in his jacket pocket.

Swiftly, he made for his Jaguar. Once behind the wheel, with the motor idling, he sat back to catch his breath.

With wonderment, he reviewed his activities of the past hour. How had he managed it? He had managed it because it had been unplanned, spontaneous, and he had been a callow amateur. A real professional would have been caught and executed. What he had overheard, presuming he was not misleading himself, was almost too astonishing to accept. Yet, dammit, he had known it all along. But now he *knew* it. There was a second First Lady named Vera. She was real. She had been brilliantly planted, and was to extract information from the President of the United States. For her achievement – actually, for knowing too much – she was to be executed and mutilated this very night. Then, clearly, Moscow was to be notified, and the real First Lady sent to replace her here in London.

This had to be told. The Soviets and their Vera had to be exposed to someone. But to whom? Who on earth would believe him? Parker had found them out, yet he sensed that they still held the trump card. The Soviets could effectively return the real Billie without worrying about her exposing them. Who would know she had not been the First Lady in London all along? If she chose to expose the Soviets, who would believe her unbelievable story? The President? The CIA? The British Prime Minister? No one would believe her. Physicians would say overwork, mental pressure, cracked under strain of her position. Psychiatrists would say nervous breakdown, hallucinations. No one would ever believe her. She would never dare speak of it. The Soviets were safe and they knew it.

And Parker, himself, who would believe him now? He dared not voice what he had just overheard to a soul. Except to Nora – and – the idea came to him this instant – one other. Yes, one other should know – told directly – perhaps indirectly. That would be the way to go.

His hands stopped shaking. Gripping the wheel with one hand, he shifted gears with the other. He had to see Nora immediately. He would need her help. There was still something to be done – before the Summit was lost.

When Guy Parker reached the Royal Suite on the first floor of Claridge's hotel, he found Secret Service agent Oliphant on guard.

'Is Mrs Bradford back from Buckingham Palace yet?' he inquired.

'Not yet.'

Pleased, Parker asked, 'Is Nora Judson around?'

Agent Oliphant jerked his thumb toward the next-door suite. 'In her office.'

'Thanks.'

Parker went to the nearby doors where an officer from Scotland Yard was on duty. Showing his pass, Parker went inside through a small foyer, through Dolores Martin's small office, past the abbreviated hall that connected this suite with the Royal Suite, until he came to Nora's cubbyhole. Her door was half-open and he could hear her on the telephone. He went inside, shut the door behind him, and pulled a chair to her desk as she hung up.

Immediately, Nora swivelled toward him, a worried expression on her face. 'Did you go to Ladbury's?' was the first thing she asked.

'Did I? And how I did. You won't believe what happened.'

Lowering his voice, he proceeded to tell her everything that had taken place, from the moment of his hiding in the wardrobe across from Ladbury's office to the conversation between a Soviet agent and an American, right up to his escape.

Throughout his recital Nora's eyes had stayed widened, her clenched fist covering her open mouth, as she heard him out with absolute amazement. When he had finished, she sat dumb-founded, absorbing the full import of what he had told her.

'Well?' he said.

'Well what? What can I say? You know I've been with you this past week, been as suspicious as you've been. But this is different. This is like – proof.' She shook her head. 'Then the First Lady really isn't the First Lady, really isn't Billie.'

'Her name is Vera something-or-other.'

'Forgive me, Guy, but I can't handle this. My mind is blown. How did they manage to pull it off?'

'Not important right now. They did it. That's all that matters.'

'And Billie – where's Billie?'

'In Moscow, probably. They indicated they'd send her here – or send someone here – once Vera has delivered our secrets

295

and then been eliminated. Our job is to see that the secrets aren't delivered.'

'Guy, you've got to go to the President at once.'

'Again? He wouldn't believe me. Or if he did, he'd say this isn't proof at all. The President? My God, he'd throw me out, fire me. Then I'd be totally helpless.'

'You're right, Guy,' she conceded. 'That won't work.' She raised her hands in a helpless gesture. 'But what will?'

He came to his feet, and moved around the desk to stand over her. 'There's one possibility, maybe a long shot, maybe not. I got the idea coming back here. Look, our main job is not to expose this fake First Lady. There's no way to do that yet. What we have to do is stop her from turning our Summit secrets over to the Russian Premier. She'll be spilling the whole thing to him late tonight. That's what we've got to prevent.'

'But how?'

'By letting her – this Vera – know the truth about herself. What's in store for her once she finishes her assignment. I'll need your help, Nora.'

'Anything.'

'Okay, listen to me.'

He bent down and, mouth close to her ear, he began to whisper to her.

When he had outlined his plan, he straightened up. 'What do you think?'

'Can it work?'

'It has to. Have you got a better idea?'

'No. Okay. Let's do it.'

'Good girl. When will she be back?'

'She should be here any minute.'

'Is there a chance she'll go straight to the bedroom?'

'I doubt it. She always looks in to see me first. For any important messages or phone calls.'

'You're positive?'

'Oh, yes.'

Parker nodded. 'Then let's get ready for her.'

They left Nora's cubbyhole and entered the short hallway that joined the work area with the Royal Suite.

'Is the door to her living room locked?' Parker asked.

'Only at night.'

Parker tried the door. It opened. He left it open, and retreated a few feet, taking a position next to Nora. Neither spoke. They waited. Every few minutes Parker checked his watch. Six minutes, then eight minutes, passed. Parker was becoming increasingly restless, when he heard the door in the adjoining entry hall rattle. He brought his finger to his lips.

They recognized the First Lady's voice, saying something to the Secret Service guards who had accompanied her back from Buckingham Palace. Apparently, she had come into the dining room, because her voice was clearer now. 'I don't know whether we'll be leaving the hotel tonight,' she was saying. 'The President will let you know.'

Parker heard the door close. He heard the rustle of her approach, barely discernible. 'Nora, are you there?' she called out.

Once more, Parker put his fingers to his lips. Nora nodded nervously, maintaining her silence. Parker mouthed one word to her. *Start*, it told her.

Before the First Lady could get to their hallway, Parker began speaking to Nora in a loud but conversational tone. 'Yeah, she's a Russian spy. Hottest gossip since we came here. Heard it from one of the President's aides. He didn't know too much. The Russians have a female spy right here in London. She's supposed to have penetrated the President's inner circle.'

Nora spoke on cue. 'No kidding? Do you really believe it?'

'I don't know. I can only tell you what I heard. They even found out her name, or part of it. Her name's Vera.'

'Who is she?'

'Haven't the faintest idea. I don't think my informant knew.'

He paused. If the First Lady on the other side of the wall

had actually been Billie, she would have walked right in on them, admitted she'd overheard them, would have wanted to know more. But if the First Lady was this Vera, she would have stopped in her tracks, not come any nearer. She would be outside, very quiet. Listening for more.

He was certain that she was outside, very quiet, listening for more.

'How could your friend have heard this much?' Nora was asking.

'Again, I don't know. But from something he let drop I would sort of guess one of our agencies bugged a clandestine meeting of some of their agents.'

'What are our people going to do about it?'

'Well, until they have positive proof, there's not much they can do – or, I gather, have to do. This Vera has dug up some information on the Summit for Kirechenko. Nothing can be done about that. But, as for the Vera person, she's out of our hands.'

'What do you mean by that, Guy?'

Articulating the next carefully, Parker replied, 'I mean the word is there won't be any Vera after tonight. According to my friend, once Vera relays her secrets to the Premier, she will promptly be liquidated by the Russians themselves.'

'They'd kill their own agent?'

'Well, look at it this way – why not? What do they need her for? Once she's passed over the information, she could be a danger to them walking around free. She knows too much. For them, they're much better off having her dead.'

'They'd really do it?'

'They're going to do it tonight. Or so I'm told.'

'Good God, what goes on in this world?'

'I know what should go on. You should join me for a drink and dinner.'

'Let me look and see –'

They were interrupted by the First Lady's strident voice from the next room. 'Nora, are you here?'

'I'm here, Billie!'

The First Lady came briskly into the hallway, pretending she had just arrived. 'Any important messages?'

Unobtrusively as possible, Parker tried to examine her face. Her face was ashen. All blood seemed to have drained from it.

'The President sent word he'll be tied up until ten. If you want to wait, he'll join you for dinner in the suite. Otherwise, you can go ahead and eat earlier.'

'Thank you, Nora. I'll see. I'm utterly exhausted. I'm going to lie down for a nap. Don't disturb me under any circumstances.'

They watched her leave them, crossing toward the bedroom. They listened to her locking herself in.

Nora whispered, 'Do you think she heard us?'

'She heard every word.'

'What'll happen next?'

'I won't even try to guess. Only one thing I'm sure of. She'll think twice before she turns over her secret information.'

'And then what?'

'She might think of defecting. Anyway, I intend to encourage her.'

Nora frowned. 'You'd have to tell her you've found her out.'

'She might be glad.'

'On the other hand, she might get you killed.'

'All the more reason for us to enjoy a last supper.'

'It might be hers, too.'

'I'm not so sure of that. Let's wait and see.'

Alone in the bedroom, standing before the mirror, Vera Vavilova involuntarily shuddered. She was not sure whether the tremor came from fear or rage, or both.

The conversation that she had just overheard between Guy and Nora had shaken her up as nothing else had since the project began. How had Guy Parker's source, his friend the presidential aide, learned so much? And from whom? Guy had mentioned bugging. It was possible a government agency had bugged Ladbury or Willis. It could have been a CIA operation. Or maybe Fred Willis was performing as a double agent, although she doubted it. She was tempted to put her contacts on alert, but then she realized that it wasn't necessary. There had been no hint that the mysterious 'Vera' was actually the First Lady. Besides, before the enemy could expose her, she would be gone, on her way to Moscow tonight and safe. Or would she be on her way? If Guy had it right, she would be dead tonight, after delivering the secrets to Kirechenko, she would be coldly executed. It was incredible that she had trusted those ruthless bastards. Those dirty, double-crossing bastards. Her own countrymen, her supporters, allies, her own people rewarding risk and ingenuity with death. Well, she wasn't their submissive pawn any longer. She had power of her own now, and she would use it.

She stared into the mirror. She knew what had to be done. The only problem was that damn First Lady face in the mirror. That was her handicap, wearing the most recognizable face in the world. It impeded free movement, and she needed free movement more than ever in these minutes.

She had confronted difficulty after difficulty to get to this point. She had overcome each through sheer will, brilliance, and with aid from allies. But now she had no allies anywhere. She was completely on her own, and up against the greatest personal crisis of all. She would overcome it, as she had the others, she decided, because this time she was armed.

How to get where she was going unnoticed?

She concentrated on the problem, surprised at her new calm, and further surprised when the solution came to her so easily.

First, two telephone calls had to be made. Then she would be on her way.

She sought and located the small leather-covered address and telephone book, a duplicate of the one that Billie took along on her travels. Under the F tab she found, 'Farleigh, Janet'. All right, Janet was no more, but Vera had learned – after the press fiasco – that Janet's husband, Cecil, and seventeen-year-old son, Patrick, still lived in their old flat in Castlemain House, alongside Green Park, where Billie had once stayed with them. Holding the address book, with the Farleigh phone number before her, Vera sat down on the bed and read the instructions on her grey telephone: *To call the operator lift hand set.* She lifted the hand set. An operator's voice came on immediately. She read off the Farleigh home number.

One ring and the call was answered. A husky young voice answered. 'Hello, there. Patrick Farleigh here.'

'Patrick? This is Billie Bradford, an old friend of your mother's.'

'Billie –?' The young voice sounded awed.

'Yes, Billie Bradford. My husband and I are here from the States for the Summit Conference.'

'I know. I've seen you on the telly. I read in the papers you might be calling on us. I'm sorry my father's not in –'

'Never mind. I wanted to speak to you, too. I wanted to offer my heartfelt condolences. I loved your mother. Everyone loved her.'

'Thank you,' said Patrick. He sounded choked.

'Another reason I'm phoning,' said Vera. 'I need your help on a little matter. I wonder if I might stop by, look in on you for a few minutes? Will you be there?'

'Oh, certainly I'll be here. When did you mean? Tonight?'

'Right now. I could be over in maybe ten or fifteen minutes. Sure you don't mind?'

'I'd be highly honoured.'

'See you shortly,' said Vera, hanging up.

So far, so good. Now, the next call, the big one. From a rack near her bedstand hung four London telephone directories. She bent over to read their spines. The orange one read A–D, the pink one was imprinted E–K, the green one L–R, and the blue one S–Z. She pulled the first one, the A–D one, upward from the rack. On the cover was the heading, LONDON POSTAL AREA. She opened the directory near the back, turned the pages until she found the listing for the Dorchester Hotel and its telephone number. She jotted it down on a pad. Lowering the directory to its place, she glared at the phone number on the pad and gradually her expression became malignant.

Sitting on her bed, she lifted the hand set. An operator's voice responded. Vera gave the Dorchester number. After what seemed interminable ringing, her call was picked up. It was a switchboard operator at the Dorchester. Mustering some authority in her voice, Vera asked to be put through to Premier Dmitri Kirechenko's suite. She knew that she would not get the Premier, but rather some buffer person, which was good enough, because the person would quickly relay her message.

A person with a gruff voice had answered in Russian. He had said, 'The Soviet delegation.'

She recognized the voice. She said in Russian, 'Is this General Chukovsky?'

The voice on the other end was wary. 'Who are you? What is your business?'

With sadistic pleasure she replied in Russian, 'You do not know, General? This is Vera Vavilova.'

'Vera Vav –' He sounded as though he was going to explode. 'No! It is not permitted. You must never call.'

'But I *am* calling,' she continued calmly in Russian. Then, sharply, 'Please put me through to Premier Kirechenko.'

The voice on the other end hesitated. 'I cannot. Impossible. He is busy – occupied. Then he must rush to dinner. After that – after – later – you will see him as arranged.'

'I am changing the time of our meeting,' she said firmly. 'Not later, but earlier. In fact now, I intend to see him now. I am leaving for the Dorchester immediately.'

'You cannot! It is dangerous for you if you come –'

She interrupted coolly. 'It is more dangerous for you if I do not come.'

With that, she cut off his sputtering by hanging up.

Until now, it had gone without a hitch, as Billie Bradford might have said, thought Vera Vavilova.

Vera had made no attempt to slip out of the suite. Instead,

she handled her initial move openly and according to strict procedure. She had summoned her Secret Service agents, Oliphant and McGinty, to inform them that she was leaving the hotel to call upon the family of a friend who resided at Castleman House located at 21 St James's Place. She had requested one of the American delegation limousines as soon as possible. This had been arranged. The agents had escorted her downstairs and into the limousine. Together they had driven to Piccadilly Circus going east, backtracked via the Haymarket to Pall Mall, past St James's Palace, and into narrow St James's Place, an attractive dead-end street.

Now they were parked before Castlemain House, where Janet Farleigh's husband and son still resided. It was a seven-storey structure, the front lobby hidden behind glass walls speckled with gold stars. Vera had to pretend that she had seen it before.

Agent Oliphant stepped out of the car. When Vera half rose to follow him, McGinty deterred her. McGinty explained, 'Oliphant wants to case the place first. He'll only be a few minutes.'

Vera sat back impatiently, as Oliphant went inside. Through the glass she could see him engaged in conversation with a porter standing behind a counter to the right. Presently, Oliphant came out, held up his hand to indicate that they should wait. He strode past the garage beside the building, inspecting it, then reached a cramped alleyway leading to the rear. He plunged into the alleyway and was out of sight.

Five minutes later he returned to the limousine. He spoke across Vera to McGinty. 'I'm sure it's secure enough. There's a back lawn enclosed by brick walls on the sides and by an iron railing set in concrete at the far end. No exit or entrance in the back railing. Nothing to worry about. You patrol the street in front, McGinty. I'll go in with Mrs Bradford.'

Troubled by the knowledge that there was no rear exit, Vera left the limousine and preceded Oliphant into Castlemain House. There was a staircase on the left side of the lobby. As they started for it, Oliphant said, 'The Farleighs have the rear flat on the second floor.'

'I know,' said Vera, but she was grateful.

'There's an elevator,' he added.

'It's a lift here,' she corrected him. 'I prefer the stairs.'

Reaching the flat, Oliphant stationed himself beside the front door.

Pressing the bell, Vera said to him, 'This is a condolence call. I'll be at least an hour, maybe an hour and a half.'

Oliphant inclined his head. 'I'll be right here.'

The door opened, and the sole occupant of the flat at the moment, Patrick Farleigh, admitted her and closed the door. Despite her haste, Vera tried to maintain some social grace. She kissed the gangly young man on his pimpled cheek and held him off to study him. 'My, how you've grown, Patrick,' she said.

Awkwardly, he asked her to please have a seat, and she said unhappily that she could spend only a short time with him but did want to know how he and his father had been since their bereavement. Then, to make him more comfortable, she sat down in a corner of the nearest oversized armchair. She made Patrick talk about himself, his schooling, his interest in being a writer as his mother had been.

At last, with the formalities behind her, she decided to get straight to the point.

'I'm enjoying this, Patrick, and I'd like to find out more about you, but we'll have to do that another time,' she said. 'I mentioned to you, on the phone, I needed your help about something.'

'Yes, of course.'

'Actually, I have another appointment that I wish to keep privately. I mean, I prefer that no one knows about it. Nothing naughty, mind you, just someone I have to meet on my own. Unfortunately, privacy is not one of the privileges a First Lady enjoys. Everywhere I go, I have to go in an official limousine, and with the Secret Service tagging along. I've told the Secret Service I'll be in here with you for an hour or more. That was only to deceive them, put them off my track. I'd like to let them think I'm in here with you, but meanwhile I must slip out and make my way to my private meeting alone. Do you mind?'

'Not at all. I find it rather exciting.'

'Is there a way I can leave without my Secret Service men seeing me? There's one man outside in front. Maybe there's a service entrance – a tradesmen's entrance – in the back somewhere?'

'No. The tradesmen's entrance is in front.'

'If I remember correctly the rear is surrounded by brick walls and an iron-rail fence. Is that true?'

'I'm afraid so.'

Vera's heart sank. 'There's absolutely no exit in the back?'

The boy was silent, and then he looked pleased with himself. 'Oh, you know, there is a way, if – if you don't mind the inconvenience.'

'What do you mean?'

'You go down to the back garden. There are several ladders stacked on the lawn. Some builders are making repairs in the daytime. They leave the ladders when they go home. I could set one up against the metal railing, and drop another on the other side. You could climb up one and down the other, if you're game.'

Vera came off the chair and embraced Patrick. 'You *are* a darling. Of course, I'm game.' She hesitated. 'But when I come down the ladder on the other side, where will I be?'

'There's a wide asphalt footpath between our building and Green Park. You can simply walk up to the first major street.'

'Will there be taxis?'

'By the hordes. The street is Piccadilly.'

'Wonderful.' She kissed the young man again and he blushed. She had one more concern. 'Will the ladders be there when I return?'

'I'll see that they are.'

'You're marvellous, Patrick. I'll be back in an hour – remember, I'm supposed to be with you during this time – and then I'll go out to my Secret Service agents and the limousine.' She took him by the arm. 'Now, will you show me the way to your special exit?'

The taxi curved around the island in the street and brought her up in front of the Dorchester Hotel.

Vera Vavilova opened her purse and paid the driver the fare, adding a handsome tip. She extracted a handkerchief from her purse before closing it. She had a worn a cloth coat with a high collar to mask her giveaway face, but the collar only partially covered her features. The handkerchief, she hoped, would screen the rest.

A doorman had the taxi door open and touched the brim of his hat as she stepped out. She hurried into the revolving door, pushed it, and in the reception area she walked hurriedly past the reception desk into the mammoth lobby. Several seated Arabs raised their heads from their newspapers to appraise her, but she kept the handkerchief to her face as she searched for the elevators. She spotted them off to her right and swiftly entered the first one.

The elderly operator closed the doors and inquired, 'Floor, ma'am?'

'Premier Kirechenko's floor, please.'

The operator appraised her doubtfully.

'I am expected,' she added.

'Yes, ma'am. Number eight, ma'am.'

The elevator rode upward smoothly, until the light above the door blinked on number eight and it halted. She stepped out and then stood still, uncertain of where she was going.

The operator indicated the direction. 'To your left and then right, ma'am. Watch for the Terrace Suite.'

Vera nodded her thanks, started walking, turned into the long corridor illuminated by electric candles set in brass-trimmed boxes bracketed to both walls. She continued up the corridor slowly, made an inquiry of a passing maid, and at the second intersecting corridor turned right. Almost immediately she came upon a group of four men deep in conversation standing in front of a door with the lettering HARLEQUIN AND TERRACE SUITES.

As Vera started for the door, one of the plainclothes men swiftly left the group to bar her way. 'No one permit enter without pass,' he warned her in broken English.

That moment, another member of the group, whose back had been to her, turned around and she recognized him as Colonel Zhuk. His surprise was evident. Taking her by the arm, he led her aside. In an undertone, she told him that the Premier was expecting her. Colonel Zhuk nodded and preceded her to the door. He opened it and called inside in Russian that the visitor could be let through.

Vera entered, and was confronted by three more armed KGB guards planted before a steep staircase. Smiling at the guards, she gripped the railing and ascended the steps. At the top landing she saw another door bearing the lettering TERRACE SUITE. Beside it stood two KGB guards. She inclined her head to them, then rang the bell.

The response was almost instantaneous. In the doorway stood one of her country's leaders, the one she recognized as Anatoli Garanin, of the Politburo.

He looked at her with a twitch of annoyance. 'Comrade Vavilova? You were not to see the Premier until later, much later.'

'I telephoned,' she said curtly. 'I must see him now. It has been arranged.'

Garanin shook his head. 'I don't know.' He signalled her inside. 'Please wait here in the guest foyer. I will speak to the Premier.'

She had waited there no more than a minute, feeling determined and righteous, when Garanin reappeared and beckoned.

He led her into a living room, a grand one, luxuriously furnished.

'The Premier has consented to see you briefly,' said Garanin. 'But I must tell you he is angry.'

'So am I,' said Vera.

Garanin appeared to consider her disrespectful. 'Remember, he is the Premier.'

'Remember, I am the First Lady,' she said.

Garanin scowled. 'He will be with you in a moment,' he said, and he left the room.

Alone, impatient, Vera wandered about the impressive living room. There were costly drapes carrying a floral print that featured Chinese figures. There were French doors and a wide terrace overlooking the treetops of Hyde Park. Elsewhere in the room were three sofas, antique chairs, a French desk.

Pirouetting, she realized that Premier Dmitri Kirechenko had soundlessly materialized from a bedroom. He was tieless, wearing formal shirt and trousers, busily inserting his cufflinks. His long bearded face and rimless spectacles concentrated on the French cuffs. He advanced toward Vera without looking up at her.

'You take great risks, Comrade Vavilova,' he said quietly. 'Very unwise of you.'

He had spoken in Russian, and she realized that he preferred to conduct the entire conversation in Russian. She also decided, no matter what his awesome position, she must not crumble before him, nor play the servile subject. She steeled herself with the reminder that she had power, too.

She said, 'I am used to risks, Comrade Kirechenko. Everything I do for you involves risks. I would not have come here if it were not of vital importance.'

'Understood.' He seated himself at the French desk. 'Bring up a chair. Let us talk now.' He waited as she complied, and then he resumed. 'Do I congratulate you? I am told you have fulfilled your assignment and obtained what we want.'

'I have.'

'I hope it is significant.'

'Very.'

His eyebrows shot up. 'Excellent. A moment then while I summon General Chukovsky.'

She said emphatically, 'I do not want him here. I will speak only to you alone.'

She thought her audacity might anger him. But as he pulled his hand back from the buzzer, he soberly eyed her in a new way. Perhaps, she thought, with new interest.

'Whatever you wish,' he said, faintly amused. 'Comrade Vavilova, we have worked almost three years on this project. We have expended countless hours of energy and an enormous sum of money to bring you to this moment. Now the moment is here. This will be the meeting we had planned for late tonight.' He squinted at her through his rimless glasses. 'You have everything we need, you say?'

'Yes, everything.'

'From the President himself?'

'Yes, first-hand.'

'You believe what you heard from him? He did not suspect you, try to outwit or deceive you?'

Vera smiled. 'He spoke the truth. We were in bed. We made love. He was grateful.'

He looked her over. 'I imagine he was.' If there had been levity in his tone, it was gone now. 'All right, I am ready. Tell me what the United States plans to do at the Summit. Tell me what you found out.'

'No,' she said.

Apparently, he did not believe his ears. 'What's that?'

'No, I won't tell you what I found out.'

Premier Kirechenko was visibly taken aback. 'You won't tell me?'

'No, I won't,' she said flatly.

He stared at her, bewildered. 'What the devil is going on here? Am I crazy or is it you? Did I hear you correctly? You refuse to deliver the information?'

'Exactly.' She braced herself. 'I will not hand you my death warrant.'

His bewilderment seemed to increase. 'What are you talking about? What death warrant? Speak lucidly, and don't try my patience any further.'

Vera spoke in a rush. 'I know what you are up to. I heard it all from a reliable source. From the moment I tell you what I know of the American plans, I am as good as dead. Once I deliver their secrets to you, once I leave here, I am to be executed. Because I know too much. I am to be wiped out by your KGB. Tonight, in fact.'

He looked astounded. Either he is the better actor of the two of us, she thought, or he truly doesn't know what the KGB has in mind for me.

'What?' he was saying. 'What kind of drivel is that? Where did you hear such a thing?'

'From a White House source who heard it from one of the President's aides.'

'White House source?' he repeated. 'What would you have to do with such a person?'

She drew back her shoulders. 'Sir, I must remind you, I am the First Lady of the United States.'

He snorted. 'Of course, of course, I quite forgot.' His flinty eyes bore into her. 'You have been duped by your new White House friends,' he said. 'By some means, they may suspect you. They wish to prevent you from passing on to me anything you have learned. They are clever, using you this way. But surely you, yourself, are too clever to be duped. You are on our side. You are one of us. We are in this together against them. So let us stop this drivel and move ahead. Simply give me what you know. You will be rewarded beyond anything you can imagine for your patriotic effort. So speak out now.'

She tightened her lips, and was silent for long seconds. She spoke at last. 'I do not trust you.'

She could see he was making an effort to restrain his temper. 'Comrade Vavilova,' he said softly, too softly, menace cradling each word, 'you are insolent. I may be forced to teach you to trust me. I have the means to extract the information from you before you leave this room.'

Vera was almost reckless in her bravado. 'Of course, you can do anything you please with me. Which supports everything I have been saying. You are surrounded by brutes, by torturers, by executioners. But you will not order them to help you this time. Punish me, kill me, and the American secrets die with me. I am not afraid of you.'

Premier Kirechenko sat stone still across from her, staring at her. All that could be heard was a clock ticking somewhere. Abruptly, that stone façade broke. His body slumped back in his chair. His glasses came off, and his stern face split into a broad grin. 'You win, Comrade,' he said, almost cheerfully. 'You are a strong woman, and I respect strong women. Yes, of course, you are quite right – Petrov's plan was to execute you after you left me. Foolish, I knew it was foolish from the start. I was against it, but Petrov insisted, and I let him prevail. After that, I put it out of my mind. But I admit it was a crude mistake. I will rectify it. I will rescind the execution order. Here and now, I guarantee your safety.'

He looked pleased.

But Vera was shaking her head. 'Your word is not enough,' she said. 'I need a foolproof guarantee.'

'Well, what would satisfy you? How can I guarantee your safety?' Absently he picked up a pencil and doodled on a Dorchester Hotel pad. 'What could it be? Do you have anything specific in mind?'

'Not yet.'

He put down his pencil. 'Here's an idea. Perhaps it will do. A visa to a neutral country. We would change your appearance one more time and arrange for you to enjoy permanent residence in – let us say Sweden or Switzerland – with an ample pension fund deposited in your name in either country. How does that sound?'

'Not too promising,' said Vera. 'I would still be vulnerable. Petrov's bloodhounds would find me. You would fear blackmail from me, and you and Petrov would have me found and killed. It must be something better, something that would make me truly safe.'

They both sat there, each thinking about it, both trying to come up with an acceptable solution.

At least two or three minutes had passed when Premier Kirechenko stirred and leaned toward her. He seemed fascinated by something, some new idea. 'I've just thought of a possibility,' he said, 'rather daring, but workable, one that might satisfy you in every way.'

'Tell me,' she said eagerly.

'You know, except for the suspicions of some White House people – and these suspicions need not be taken seriously because no one could actually ever prove you are not the authentic First Lady – except for that, you have successfully deceived everyone imaginable in these past weeks, haven't you? The President, his staff, the politicians, Mrs Bradford's closest friends, the press, all have accepted you as America's First Lady.'

'Completely.'

'Well then. How would you like to continue to be the First Lady for life?'

'For life?' She had no comprehension of what he was leading up to.

'Yes, for as long as Bradford remains in the White House, the rest of his term, his next four-year term, and after that remain the former First Lady, honoured wherever you go, a celebrity for as long as you live. Wouldn't you like that?'

Vera had not really thought about such a possibility, or rather about the pleasure her First Lady role gave her. Not thought about it? Simply not true. She *had* thought about it. She had thought about it frequently. From time to time, these past weeks, she had entertained fantasies about going on with her role. Sometimes, she would forget altogether that she was a spy and a Soviet citizen. She would see only golden America wrapped around her, America with its riches, luxuries, easy living. And herself, as America's First Lady, and her possessions of power, respect, fame, the most famous female on earth. Even marriage to the President, later the ex-President, was pleasant. Andrew Bradford was relatively undemanding, easy to live with, even attractive in some ways. Of course, she could never love him as she loved Alex, and she would have to forfeit Alex, but still power could never be bought without some sacrifice. As for her acting career, it would be lost, but in her real-life role she would always be in the limelight and before cameras and the public. Oh, she had fancied it all in these past weeks. It looked even better to her now, especially now, when she could never live safely in the Soviet Union again, or safely anywhere in the world. Her part in the plot had made her a threat to her masters.

Her only invulnerability lay in her role as First Lady. Was the Premier hinting he might convert her fantasy into reality?

'What are you suggesting?' she said warily. 'How could I possibly be First Lady of the United States for life?'

He bent closer to her. 'By being the *only* First Lady, Comrade Vavilova. By our eliminating the other First Lady. If we liquidate Mrs Bradford, you would be the one remaining American First Lady in the world. For you, that would be the ultimate guarantee of your safety. Could there be a better guarantee?'

It shocked her a little, the casualness of suggesting the sudden death of an international figure. The ruthlessness of it appalled her.

'I don't like the idea of killing,' she said.

'Self-preservation is what counts in this world. Her life for yours. She will die anyway, some day, heart failure, stroke, cancer. We are merely speeding up nature. A quick and painless end to an unknown actress, while the First Lady lives on. What do you say?'

'I don't know what to say.'

'You wanted a foolproof guarantee? Here it is. Don't you agree?'

'I agree it would be foolproof.'

'Once done, it would allow you to tell me what you've learned and still know you are safe.'

'I suppose so.'

'Then it shall be done. We will quietly do away with Mrs Bradford.'

'When?'

'Immediately. Let us say within twenty-four hours.' He paused. 'She will be dead and buried. You will give us what we need. Have we made a bargain?'

Vera shivered. She must push Billie, the vibrant, beautiful Billie Bradford, from her mind. She must consider no other thing except her own survival, and her fantasy come true.

She nodded. 'I am ready to make the bargain – but on one condition.'

'Yes?'

'I must have proof you have killed her.'

'You are difficult, Comrade Vavilova. You remain suspicious.'

'With good reason. My life is at stake.'

The Premier appeared to consider this not unreasonable. 'Very well,' he said thoughtfully. 'You shall have indisputable proof. I will have photographs taken of her corpse after the execution. I will have them flown here. You will see them. Would that satisfy you?'

'It would.'

'You shall see the photographs tomorrow.'

'One thing –' She had exiled herself to real First Ladyhood, to an American life, too quickly. It would be lonely without anyone who had been close to her. Meaning, without Alex. True, she had been ready to sacrifice him, for her own safety, for power and wealth. But if she could have him at no cost to herself, why not? It was possible she could have all this and Alex, too, now that she had bargaining strength. 'You say the proof will be flown here?'

'By courier on a special aircraft. You will be notified when you can see the proof you require.'

'I should like to designate the courier,' she said.

'Whomever you wish.'

'Alex Razin of the KGB.'

His eyebrows went up. 'Razin? Your mentor?'

'And friend. I trust him. In fact, I would have him admitted to the United States, so that I could have someone, not far, to talk to from time to time.'

'You could complicate your American life.'

'I won't,' she said. 'It must be Alex. He must bring me the photographs proving Billie's death. When I see them tomorrow, and am assured she is gone and I am the only one, I will give you the information you need. I will do my part. But first you must do yours.'

'I will do my part.' He rose to his feet. 'By morning Billie Bradford will be dead.'

11

An hour and a half ago, Guy Parker had caught a glimpse of Vera, as First Lady, leaving the presidential suite with her Secret Service guards. A third Secret Service agent, posted at the door of the suite, had told him that she was going to visit friends. Parker knew that she was not going to visit friends. Now that she had heard of her impending execution, he had no doubt that she was off to see someone high up in the Soviet delegation. Parker wondered how she would manage it. He also wondered how she would get the Soviets to rescind her execution. She must have some bargaining leverage now that she possessed American secrets. Maybe her Soviet superiors would permit her facial surgery and defection. Or maybe, with or without her information, they would kill her anyway.

All this time, Parker had gone from the hotel corridor to Nora's office and back to the corridor, an eye on the elevator, watching to see whether the First Lady would return.

He had about decided that Vera had been liquidated, when he saw her emerge briskly, confidently, from the elevator, accompanied by her guards, and start toward her suite.

Quickly, Parker ducked out of the corridor and into Nora's office. By the time he reached Nora, she was busy on the intercom. The moment she hung up, he said, 'Our Vera is still alive.'

'I know,' said Nora, finding pad and pencils. 'She wants to see me. She wants to dictate some changes in her schedule.'

He took Nora by the arm. 'It means —'

Nora pulled free. 'I know what it means. Right now, I've got to get in to her.'

She started for the connecting hallway between the two suites. Parker chased after her. 'See what you can pick up for us.'

Nora nodded and disappeared into the Royal Suite.

Parker put an ear to the door, but the voices beyond it – Vera's and Nora's – were too muffled for their words to be understood. Impatiently, Parker began to pace the short distance between Nora's cubicle and the hallway that joined the two suites. He speculated on Billie's stand-in, Vera, and what she planned to do. Then he tried to consider what else he might do to entrap her. He thought that, at the first opportunity, he might try to enter her bedroom to seek something that would implicate her. But he knew there would be nothing useful there, not in a room occupied also by the President of the United States. The only option open to him was to continue following her whenever she left the hotel.

As Parker's pacing brought him to the connecting hallway once more, the door from the presidential suite suddenly opened and Nora came through it. He looked at her questioningly. She said in an undertone, 'Had to cut our work short. Fred Willis, the protocol person, just burst in unannounced for an emergency meeting.'

'That's odd.'

'I suppose it is .... Oh, Guy, I didn't shut her door completely. Will you please –' She saw his face and stopped. 'Are you – are you going to try to listen in?'

He went to the First Lady's door, open half an inch, and placed himself behind it. A familiar male voice floated through the crack. Something about the voice caused him to stiffen. It was a strikingly familiar voice, a pseudo-English accent combined with a slight unforgettable lisp. In the living room next door, it must be Fred Willis speaking. Yet, it was the same accented, lisping voice he had overheard earlier from his hideout in Ladbury's shop. Could it have been Willis conspiring with Ladbury and a Soviet agent? It had to be. The voices were the same.

It hit Parker with a real jolt. Fred Willis, a Soviet agent? Could it be? But then, it had to be someone in the White House. It always was someone. So why not Willis?

Parker remained stationary. He strained to hear the conversation in the living room. It was not easy. He could not see them, but he guessed that they were somewhere near the dining room that separated him from them. Also, their conversation was not at a normal pitch. It seemed to be hushed, confidential. Vera's speech did not quite reach audibility. However, Willis, more excitable, his voice more high-pitched, erratically crossed the sound barrier to touch Parker's ears.

'– just came to me,' Willis was saying. ' . . . you to know . . . going through with it.'

Vera was replying, but she could not be understood.

Willis again, the words rising, fading.

'– will be transmitted . . . an hour from now at the usual place . . . you . . . informed tonight.'

Gently, Parker closed the door. He turned away to find Nora staring at him. Taking her by the elbow, he led her into her office.

He spoke close to her ear. 'Fred Willis is one of them.'

'I can't believe it. How –'

'He is, Nora. I'm positive. Willis was reporting something to her. In an hour they're transmitting information, probably to Moscow, and they will keep our Vera informed. I intend to find out what it's all about. I'm going.'

'Where?'

'Ladbury's. I have to get there before they do. Wait up for me. I'll be back –' He paused at the door. '– I hope.'

He was striding at a brisk pace toward Ladbury's shop.

It was a chance, Parker knew. Maybe the person he had originally overheard at Ladbury's had not been Willis at all, only someone who sounded like him. Yet, the similarity between the voice he had heard at Ladbury's and Willis's voice just now speaking to the First Lady – to Vera – was striking. He could not ignore this lead. If his assumption was correct, someone would be at Ladbury's shortly to transmit a message from a wireless secreted on the premises.

It was dangerous coming here a second time. He was really pushing his luck. But it had to be done. He had the goods on them, perhaps enough to have them seriously investigated. But he had no one to go to. The President would not listen to anything so bizarre. If the President wouldn't believe, neither would his aides or the CIA. The entire matter was in Parker's own hands, his and Nora's. If only they had something concrete to offer, one shred of proof, they could block whatever plan Vera had of passing her information on to the KGB or the Premier.

He had come abreast of Ladbury's shining entrance. Scouting both ends of the arcade, he could see no one, except one young couple strolling and window-shopping some distance away. He stepped forward, extracting the duplicate key from his pocket, inserted it, twisted it in the lock. The door opened. As he entered, the bell above sounded. Quickly, he closed and secured the door.

The night lights were on in the showroom, but the illumination was poor. He considered detouring, going upstairs to hunt for the possible wireless set, but finally dropped the idea. Too time-consuming. And too much possibility that he might be caught upstairs with nowhere to hide. Better, his already proved listening post.

Cautiously, he made his way to the corridor, and went into it. At the farthest fitting room, across from Ladbury's office, he shoved aside the curtains and entered into total darkness. With one hand extended, he felt his way across the room toward the opposite wall. He groped, made contact with the rack of dresses, parted them, stepped between them and eased himself behind the section of formal gowns.

If the transmission was occurring at 'the usual place' – if that had meant Ladbury's – it would be happening in twenty minutes. There was not a thing he could do but wait.

He stood there in his suffocating hideout, smothered by the voluminous dresses, shifting his weight from one foot to the other. Time crept. The wait seemed interminable. His back began to ache. He was invaded by small doubts. Perhaps he had been mistaken about Willis. Perhaps he had chased a ridiculous false lead. Perhaps he should get out of here. And go where? There was nowhere else to go.

He waited.

His self-doubts had surfaced again, and he was trying to fend them off, when the silence was shattered by the ringing of the front doorbell. Parker's spine went rigid against the wall.

He listened. He thought he could hear the shuffle of feet approaching. The lights came on in the corridor, filtering into his fitting room. Peering out between the dresses, he detected a pair of patent-leather loafers beneath the curtains. Undoubtedly Ladbury.

The office door across the way opened and the office lights were switched on. The office door closed. Dammit.

Parker despaired, and waited.

Suddenly the front doorbell again. Heavier shuffling. He had a flash of shoes. Two pairs. Cloddish shoes. The office door opened and again closed. Goddam. Was this it? Being shut out?

That instant, the front doorbell rang a third time.

Quick footsteps. Under the curtains he could see the brown suede shoes. The office door wide once more. The stream of light from inside the office. This time the light from the office was not shut off. Parker's heart leaped. Ladbury's door remained open.

Parker held his breath waiting for the first to speak.

The high-pitched voice with the lisp, Willis, if it was Willis, was speaking. 'Ladbury ... Baginov ... Fedin. Okay, all present and accounted for. Let me have your full attention. This is important. I have the word from on high. The whole game plan has been changed. We're instructed to move fast. Fedin, you'll have to get right on the wireless the moment we break up.'

'I am ready.'

'What's going on?' It was Ladbury's voice. 'What's

changed? I'm told our lady saw the Premier earlier. Is that true?'

'She saw him,' Willis replied. 'I don't know any details, except that she found out she was slated for liquidation.'

'My God, how could she possibly?' Ladbury wanted to know.

'No idea. Anyway, she's blackmailing the Premier. She wants a guarantee on her life or she won't hand over her information.'

'A guarantee?' Ladbury repeated. 'There's no way —'

'She got it,' the Willis voice interrupted. 'It'll all be clear to you in a minute. Of course, the liquidation of Vera has been countermanded by the Premier himself. She is not to be touched.'

'That I have heard already,' growled Baginov. 'More I do not know.'

'I'll tell you the rest,' said Willis. 'You sit tight, Baginov. It's your partner my orders are for. Fedin —'

The response was a wordless snort.

'Fedin, you are to transmit this in the latest code to General Petrov in Moscow.' Willis articulated each word. 'The First Lady Billie Bradford is to be executed before morning.'

A shudder shook Parker's body. He grasped several of the dresses and retained his balance.

'What?' Ladbury exclaimed. 'Billie executed? I can't believe it. Are you sure?'

'I am positive,' said Willis testily. 'We have a First Lady here. We don't need another.'

'Ahhh,' Ladbury exhaled. 'So that's Vera's guarantee.'

'It is,' said Willis, 'and rather clever. I'm told the Premier thought of it himself . . . . Now, Fedin, here is the whole bag entirely. Better write it down.' A silence, then Willis resumed. 'Billie Bradford executed before morning. You've got that? After she is finished, before she is defaced, her corpse must be photographed to indicate clearly she is dead. Alex Razin has been ordered to bring the package of photographs here. A special plane is to be assigned to take Razin to Westridge, your temporary air base. The new First Lady will be standing by to inspect the photographs. Once she is satisfied – well, that part has nothing to do with your message. You will go ahead with what I've told you. Is that perfectly clear?'

'Perfectly,' said an unfamiliar voice that Parker supposed belonged to Fedin.

In his hiding place, Parker stood stunned. The horror of what was taking place blotted out all rational thinking. When he had heard that the Russians had replaced the American First Lady with one of their own, he had believed himself immune to further shock. But now he found himself shaken beyond anything he had known in any previous experience. The immediate problem was to absorb this as a reality. That the Russians would kidnap the First Lady, replace her, murder her, was almost beyond belief.

And tonight, it was happening *tonight*.

He stood stock-still behind his barrier of female garments listening for more. There was no more. The lights went out in the office across the way. He could see shoes moving beneath the dressing room curtains.

A receding voice, probably Baginov's, said, 'We're going right upstairs to transmit. You have today's code, Mikhail?'

'In my briefcase,' said Fedin.

'One more thing,' Willis called. 'Find out exactly what time Razin will be landing at Westridge.'

'Let you know later,' said Fedin.

Another voice, Ladbury's. 'Both of you, turn out the lights when you're ready to leave. Be sure to lock the door. You have keys?'

'I don't,' said Baginov, 'but Fedin has one.'

'Stay in touch,' said Ladbury.

In the fitting room, Parker heard the bell ring and knew that Ladbury and Willis had gone. He heard the two Soviet agents tramp upstairs. He heard no more.

Although eager to leave, Parker held back. He would give himself five minutes. He could not make out the time on his watch, so he counted seconds in his head. At last, he shook himself, pushed between the dresses in the wardrobe, and tiptoed into the corridor. He went down the corridor, past the stairs, glancing upward. He could see a dim light above. He headed for the front door. He turned his key and the dead bolt retracted. Opening the door an inch, no more, he placed his foot on the rim of the window display, hoisted himself up, clamped a hand over the bell to muffle it, and with his free hand pushed the door back far enough to allow for his exit. Releasing the bell, he dropped down to the floor, eased himself outside, closed and locked the door.

The air was fresh and cool, yet for Parker everything was oppressive.

By now he was frightened, both by what was going on and by his own helplessness.

Hurrying to his car, he pondered his next action. He needed help. Whom to turn to? The same record played back in his head. There was no one. To convince someone in authority that what he had overhead was true, to convince them to stage a major confrontation with the Soviet Union, to have them accuse the Russians of the plot and the murder of the First Lady, was impossible. Even if possible, it would take too long. Billie would be dead. If only he and Nora knew someone in Moscow they could risk trusting, and could contact . . . .

By the time he had arrived at the hotel, he had thought of one possibility. The odds against it were mountainous. But if taken step by step, in haste, it might work, it just might. Besides, there was no other direction to go. Overlooking the odds, he concentrated on what had to be done. It had to begin with Nora. He parked his car and hurried into the hotel.

Nora was not in her room. He wondered whether she could be with the First Lady. Then he remembered the First Lady would be dining out. Nevertheless, he asked the Secret Service agent posted in the corridor whether Mrs Bradford was still out to dinner. He learned that the President had cancelled dinner, and Mrs Bradford had eaten alone in the suite and was still there. Parker went on to Nora's office. He found her having a drink and waiting for him.

When she saw him, she almost collapsed with relief. 'You're alive,' she gasped. 'Thank God. I couldn't imagine what had happened. Or rather I could. I pictured you stretched on a rack, while they extracted what you knew.' She came out of her chair and hugged him. 'Oh, I'm glad you're back. Now I know what it's like for those who sit and wait.' She paused, searching his face. 'Guy, what did happen to you?'

'I'm not important,' he said curtly, leading her back behind the desk. He pulled a chair over to her. 'What I have to say is. Listen to me, and no interruptions. And believe every word I tell you.'

He addressed her in an undertone, revealing everything he could remember hearing in Ladbury's. When he had finished, Nora was speechless and pale.

Gradually, she found her voice. 'They'd kill her? It – it can't be?'

'It *is*,' he said.

'Guy, I know you refused this last time – but you've got to reconsider – you've got to go to the President once more.'

'I have reconsidered. But what could happen? He'd say, "So you were hiding behind some dresses and you heard all that? Now you want me to protest to the Premier? You want me to invade Russian to save my wife – when my wife is here with me this minute? Well, I don't believe one goddam word you say." '

She was nodding sadly. 'You're right. Okay, no more of that. What about Ambassador Youngdahl? I mean, he is in Moscow. He might treat us more seriously than he did that lady tourist.'

'No,' said Parker. 'It doesn't play. Youngdahl would insist on checking with the President first – presuming he believed us. But suppose we did get him to act – where would he go? Would he go to the Soviets and tell them to release the First Lady? They'd say – what First Lady? Are you mad? What if he tried to find her on his own? Where could he go? Even presuming he got a lead – they could move her.' He shook his head. 'No, Nora, none of that makes sense. But something else does. At least it makes a little sense. And it would involve Ambassador Youngdahl, but in a lesser role and in a role that would not tell him what's going on.' He paused. 'It comes down to one thing. Whom do we know in Moscow?'

'We met endless people when we were there.'

'Can you remember one? There were so many introductions, handshakes, forgotten names. But there was one, at least one I remember well. I don't know whether we can get to him. Or if we get to him, whether he'd lift a finger. But it so happens he wants something badly from me. We could give him what he wants – if he'd give us what we want. He was the one who was closest to Billie when we were over there.'

'The interpreter,' she said quickly.

'Exactly, Nora. Alex Razin. I told you they mentioned him at Ladbury's. He's the courier who's supposed to bring the package containing the pictures of Billie's corpse. My guess is – he'd know where Billie is. He's their American expert. Somehow, he's involved. The question is – is he on their side or ours? Does he know Billie is to be killed? Does he know the contents of the package he'll be asked to carry? My hunch is – he doesn't know. If he doesn't, if we can reach him before Billie is harmed and before he leaves Moscow for London, we might have a chance. Because we can promise Razin asylum in America, the one thing he seems to want more than anything else in life. I say it's worth a try.'

'How do we get to him?'

Parker jerked his thumb in the direction of the President's office. 'The President's scrambler phone to our embassy in Moscow. We get a direct line to Youngdahl.'

'The trouble is the scrambler phone. Only the President and First Lady are authorized –'

'You're the First Lady's right-hand,' Parker interrupted. 'She asked you to act for her. You get the ambassador and I'll come on with the rest of it.'

She stared at him a moment. 'All right. I think Mrs Martin is still here. We'll need her help.'

Nora left her chair for the next office. Parker followed

her. Dolores Martin's grey hair and head were bent over some handwritten notes she was transcribing. A cup of black coffee rested at her elbow.

Nora said, 'Mrs Martin, thank God you're still here.'

'I'll be here until dawn,' she said grumpily.

'Mrs Bradford asked us to see you. She wants me to call Ambassador Youngdahl in Moscow for her. She wants me to use the scrambler phone.'

'She should have told me about it.'

'You'll have to forgive her, since she's tied up. She said you'd understand if I made the call for her.'

'Well, I suppose it's all right.' She got up with a muttered complaint about her back. 'I'll unlock the phone for you.'

Mrs Martin led them into the President's temporary office. There was a white telephone on his desk near two black ones, and it had a small padlock in the dial. Mrs Martin located her key, opened and removed the padlock. She picked up a pencil and jotted a number. 'That'll get you the Signal Corps operator here. Identify yourself, and tell the operator whom you want and where. Let me know when you're through.'

She left them, shutting the door behind her.

Immediately, Nora sat down at the President's desk, drew the white phone to her, and dialled the number. A Signal Corps captain answered. Nora identified herself and announced that she had to speak to Ambassador Otis Youngdahl at the American embassy in Moscow. Following instructions, she hung up and waited.

She observed Parker standing over the desk composing a message on a sheet of paper. 'What are you going to tell him, Guy?'

'A message for Alex Razin,' he said. 'You'll hear it soon. I don't know whether it'll work, but we've got to give it a try.'

The telephone rang. Nora snapped up the receiver. 'Hello.'

Parker lowered his head and put his ear to the receiver close to Nora's. He heard Ambassador Youngdahl's tinny voice. 'Hi, Nora. They said it was you. I was expecting the President on this line.'

'He couldn't get to the phone. Neither could Billie, and Mrs Martin is away from her desk. They wanted me to buzz you for them. I presume it's urgent. Did I wake you?'

'Naw, I stay up late. What's so urgent?'

'There's a message they wanted you to pass on to someone in Moscow. They spelled it out for Guy Parker –'

'Who?'

'Guy Parker, one of the President's speech writers – he's helping Billie with her book – you met him a few weeks ago when we were in –'

'Yes, of course. I remember the young man.'

'I'll turn the telephone over to him. He'll pass on the President's message.'

'One second. Let me find a pencil.'

Nora handed the receiver to Parker. 'He'll be right on the line.'

Standing at the President's desk, Parker took the telephone to his ear, and continued writing alterations in the message he had prepared on a note pad.

Ambassador Youngdahl's voice came back on. 'Hello. Parker?'

'Yes, sir.'

'I'm ready. What is it the President wants done?'

'Mr Ambassador, do you remember when the First Lady was in Moscow last month? The Soviets assigned an American-born Russian interpreter to her. A man named Alex Razin.'

'Razin, Razin? I'm not sure –' There was a silence. 'Yes, I think I can picture him. Rather tall, black hair brushed to one side. Spoke excellent English. He sat beside Billie at the –'

'That's the one,' said Parker. 'Do you think you can run him down?'

'Our Intelligence should have him on file. I'll check with them tomorrow.'

'Not tomorrow, sir. It has to be tonight. Right now.'

There was a pause. 'It's that important?'

'I believe the President and First Lady feel it is that important. Anyway, I'm merely repeating their instructions.'

'Very well,' said Ambassador Youngdahl. 'I'll get Intelligence right in on it. Once we locate Razin, what do we do with him?'

'Give him a message.'

'Give Razin a message. Okay. What's the message?'

Parker had been drafting it, and had it on the note paper. The message had to be cryptic enough to excite no suspicion from the ambassador. Yet, it had to be clear enough to be understood at once by Alex Razin. And it had to be strong enough to inspire Razin to act at once, assuming he knew where Billie Bradford was being kept.

'The message,' said Parker. 'I'll read it to you slowly so that you can get it all down.'

'Go ahead.'

'Tell Alex Razin the following: "The First Lady needs your help desperately. She has personal concern about KGB execution taking place Moscow tonight. Your person Vera would remain permanently in place. First Lady hopes you can and will intervene on her behalf. In return for helping her you will be guaranteed entry to United States. If possible, report results to me in London Claridge's hotel via the American Ambassador in Moscow. Signed, Guy Parker." ' He paused, 'End of message.'

'I don't understand this at all,' a puzzled voice came back.

'Alex Razin will understand.'

'Is this a code or what?'

'Sort of.'

'Well, whatever you say. I'd better read it back to you.'

'Please.'

Haltingly, Ambassador Youngdahl read it back word for word.

Parker found it letter perfect. 'That's it exactly, sir,' he said.

'Soon as we locate Razin, I'll have someone deliver this to him.'

'No,' said Parker. 'The President wants you to deliver it yourself, personally.'

'Me?' said Ambassador Youngdahl with surprise. 'Isn't that somewhat irregular? Are you sure he wanted me to deliver it?'

'The President emphasized that he wanted you, yourself, to deliver it to Razin.'

'It really must be important. Well – I suppose I could take it to Razin.' He hesitated. 'I'd have to be very careful, you know.'

'Understood,' said Parker. 'I must also emphasize that the President wanted the message delivered at once.'

Parker heard the ambassador's sigh. 'I'll do my best,' he said.

Although late night in Moscow, the older building facing Dzerzhinsky Square was dotted with lights. The night shift of the KGB was busily at work. Some of the lights, however, did not represent the night shift, but illuminated the offices of tireless agents who worked both the day and night shift, and Alex Razin was one of these.

At this moment, Razin was feeling in a particularly good mood. He had finished the last of an overload of paper work, and would have a few hours to relax at home, enjoy a drink or two, catch up on his reading, and get some well-deserved sleep.

He fell back in his swivel chair, hands clasped behind his head, and soothed by the pale green walls he allowed his mind to caress Vera once more. He had missed her terribly in recent days, but now their separation was almost ended. Through the usual grapevine he had heard that tomorrow would be the crucial day at the Summit in London, and that Premier Kirechenko would be dealing with the Americans from strength. This certainly meant that Vera had survived her sexual test (with his own perceptive collaboration), had obtained information on the American strategy, and passed it on to the Premier. It also meant that Vera, having concluded her assignment in triumph, would be returned to

Moscow in a day or two in exchange for Billie Bradford. He would be relieved to have Vera safely in his arms again, and to be free of his responsibility of caring for Billie. He had decided to tell Vera that he wanted to be married at once, and to have her for ever and to father their children.

There was nothing on earth, he felt, that could mar his cheerful frame of mind, not even his awareness that Billie Bradford had recently become more morose and depressed. Her growing depression was understandable, and he knew its source. He had continued to see the First Lady daily on a social basis since their night of lovemaking. They had not repeated their coupling, nor had either of them ever mentioned it. But he sensed that Billie, after her aggressive performance in bed, had expected results from it. Vera would imitate her performance. The President, to say the least, would be suspicious. The Red plot would unravel. She would be freed. She would have outwitted him, outwitted all of them. At each visit from Razin, she had greeted him expectantly. When he had offered no word of hope, she had fallen into longer and longer silences. Hours ago, when he had seen her, she had seemed in the pit of despair, drinking too much, refusing to eat. But tonight he could not feel sorry for her, because he knew that in a day or two she would have what she wanted. She would be released, reunited in London with her husband, back in the White House in her First Lady role. He wished that he had been able to console her with this news today, but he was not empowered to do so. In fact, her imminent release and exchange was still only gossip, not yet official. But he sensed her freedom was near.

He had risen to pack his briefcase when his telephone buzzer interrupted him. he reached for the phone.

The speaker was General Petrov's male secretary. 'General Petrov would like to see you immediately on an urgent matter.'

Here it was, he told himself, word of the exchange of the First Lady for the Second Lady.

Pausing briefly before the wall mirror to comb his hair, Razin left his office, clattered down the stairs, entered

General Petrov's ante-room. The KGB chairman's secretary pointed him on inside.

Coming into the room, Razin saw Petrov studying what appeared to be a lengthy wireless message. Quickly, Petrov turned the message face down on the desk, and indicated a chair. Razin took it, eyes on the general, wondering whether the urgent matter was what he was expecting to hear.

'Razin,' Petrov said, 'I'm afraid you aren't going to get any sleep tonight, unless you can sleep on a plane.'

'A plane, sir?'

'I have an immediate assignment for you. I need a courier to deliver a package by hand to London tonight. You are to deliver the package.'

'But am I allowed to enter England?'

'Your destination, Westridge airport outside London, is temporarily Soviet soil, just as the Soviet embassy in London is considered our own territory. In a sense, you will not be setting foot in England. Except for British air controllers, and two uninterested British immigration agents at the depot entrance, there will be only Soviet personnel on hand. One of our people will meet you and accept the package, then you will board your plane and return to Moscow.'

'An immediate turn-around?'

'Immediate.'

'But, General, if I may – couldn't any ordinary courier handle this job?'

'Of course. But Premier Kirechenko requested you by name. So that's it.'

'Yes, sir.'

'You will follow these instructions. I have arranged for a private military aircraft to fly you to England. You will be the only passenger on the plane. Your plane will be standing by at Vnukovo airport, and leave with you in precisely three hours. Meanwhile, go home and have your dinner. Then wait for me there. I'll come by to give the sealed package to you. My driver will drop me back here and will take you straight to the airport. Do you understand?'

'Yes, sir.' Razin knew better than to ask what this was all about. 'I'll be waiting for you, sir.'

Leaving Petrov, Razin was confused about the purpose of the unexpected trip, but decided not to give it another thought, simply to follow orders as he had always done.

He climbed the stairs to his office, finished packing his briefcase, took it along with his light raincoat, and made his way out of the building to the public parking lot a few minutes away off Furkosov Alley.

The weather was cool. With one hand, he buttoned his raincoat as he walked, turned into the lot, found his black Volga sedan, bent down and got into the driver's seat. He laid his briefcase on the passenger seat, pulled out his ignition key, and started the car. He allowed the Volga to idle a minute, switched on the headlights, and looked over his shoulder to back out. Just then, he saw a tall, expensively dressed man hurrying in his direction. Unable to recognize the stranger, Razin was about to shift into reverse when the tall man came alongside the car on the passenger side, opened the door, pushed away the briefcase, and settled into the front seat.

'Alex Razin, I presume?' said the stranger in English.

Razin peered at his visitor, instantly recognized him, and did not try to conceal the surprise in his voice. 'Ambassador Youngdahl. What are you –?'

'I have a private and personal message for you,' said Youngdahl crisply. 'Let's get out of this parking lot. Find some empty back street for us. I think it would be much wiser.'

Razin hesitated momentarily, puzzled, then curiosity overtook him and he decided to cooperate. Releasing his handbrake, Razin pulled out of the parking slot and wheeled the car toward the exit.

At the first red light, Razin glanced at the imposing, elderly American ambassador.

'A message for me?' Razin inquired.

'Apparently an important one. I don't understand the message. I'm told you will.'

With the change of the light, Razin shifted gears and drove up 25 October Street. The thoroughfare was desolate, empty of vehicles at this time of night. Razin slowed past the side streets, searching for one to his liking, found a dark, cobblestone street barely lit and turned into it. There were trees and weeds along the curbs and several weathered highrise apartment buildings. After about fifty metres, with no sign of life anywhere, Razin pulled his Volga over to a curb in front of some temporary plywood fencing protecting a construction site. Applying the brakes, he shut off the motor, and half faced the American ambassador.

'Who is the message from?' Razin asked.

'A man who accompanied the presidential party to London. His name is Guy Parker. Apparently, you met him when –'

'I remember him,' Razin interrupted. 'He was writing the speeches for the First Lady. Also, a book for her. What does he want of me?'

'I don't know,' said Ambassador Youngdahl. 'He told me to give you a message that he dictated to me on the President's scrambler phone.' Youngdahl had reached under his topcoat and into the inner pocket of his jacket and withdrawn a slip of paper. 'I only know that I was to deliver it to you personally, and that it deals with a matter of some urgency. Here it is.' He handed the paper to Razin. 'You'll find my phone number on the attached card should you want to contact me at any hour.' Youngdahl lifted the door handle and pushed the door open. 'I'd better leave you here. I'll find my way back to my car. Good luck, Mr Razin.' He stepped out and was soon lost in the night.

Ten minutes later, Alex Razin was still seated behind the steering wheel of his car in the same place and in the same street.

He had read the message from Guy Parker three times. The first reading had confused and disconcerted him. His second careful reading had chilled him. His third reading had brought the blood to his hot throbbing temples.

332

There had been a series of shocks, one after the other, and they had affected him like a concussion.

Only now was he coming out of his stupor into a state of outrage that was settling into deep agitation. With difficulty he was trying to organize his mind and think logically.

He had translated Parker's deliberately obscure message into something he could totally understand. Parker's message had told him that Billie Bradford was going to be killed tonight. The mention of Vera's name, startling in itself, told him that she was not returning to Russia and would remain in her present role. Finally, it told him that, if he could save Billie, he would be allowed into the United States and be given asylum.

At the end of Razin's second reading, all the terrible implications in the brief message had begun to sink in and register on his mind. To begin with, there was the horrifying news that America's First Lady was to be murdered immediately. From the beginning to the end of their plot, Billie's liquidation had never been part of the plan, a violent act never even considered. Why was the inhuman deed now a necessity? If Premier Kirechenko had ordered it, he was either insane or a cold-blooded savage. If the execution was carried out, and word of it ever leaked to the West, it would lead to a break in diplomatic relations between the United States and the Soviet Union that might escalate into a suicidal nuclear war. Millions and millions would die because of one woman's senseless death. America's fury would be beyond comprehension. The USSR's image to the world would be that of a homicidal barbarian. Why the risk? It was almost impossible to imagine. Was it being done to clear the deck for Vera to play First Lady safely for the next five years and give the KGB a spy in the White House and later a spy in the upper echelons of American society? Or was there another motive for murder, one more compelling, that he could not fathom from this distance? Yes, there was probably a more immediate and powerful motive to drive the Premier to an act of butchery that would dispose of the most famous and beloved woman in the United States.

What was equally surprising, and less understandable, was that the Americans – or at least one of them, a minor bureaucrat named Parker – had actually found out that the real First Lady was a captive in Moscow and that a Soviet agent named Vera was successfully performing as her double. And that he, Razin, was somehow involved. And that now, with the two First Ladies known, the real one was to be eliminated. How had Parker found out? Not important at this point. But why had Parker not exposed it at once, gone to the President, gone to the military or the CIA, brought the Soviet Union to a showdown? Yet, no one else seemed to know about the plot, because the Summit appeared to be moving to its conclusion quietly and without any undue alarm.

Then, the one line in Parker's message that touched Razin's own life, shook his life and turned it upside down. *It would mean your person Vera would remain permanently in place.* Parker could not possibly have known of Razin's secret relationship with Vera. Yet, unwittingly, he had touched Razin in a sensitive spot. There was no questioning Parker's conclusion. It was true. If Billie Bradford was secretly executed tonight, she would still live on in the person of Vera Vavilova. America and the world would know only one First Lady, and that would be Vera. From the London Summit, she would return to the United States. She would remain in the White House for the rest of the President's term, and throughout the four years of his next term, and then remain his wife until death parted them. And Alex Razin – she would be lost to Razin for ever.

It was a loss so wrenching that Razin could not contemplate it further.

The full realization came to him: Vera's fate and his own fate were completely linked with Billie Bradford's life or death. If Billie died, his relationship with Vera died, also. If Billie lived, his love and future with Vera lived. Replaced and freed, Vera could join him in going to the United States. Parker's message had promised the reward – the lifting of the ban on him and permanent American residence.

There could be a perfect future for both of them. Razin's mind sped ahead. If he could intervene now, protect Billie, rescue her, return her to London – and beforehand arrange with Parker to have Vera and himself whisked to a clinic for plastic surgery, and get them admitted to the United States, they would both be safe and have their life together. And Billie would live, possess her own life again.

Was it possible?

Dostoevski had faced a firing squad, in this same Moscow, prepared for execution, when saved by a last-minute reprieve. Could America's First Lady, also prepared for execution, be saved by his own last-minute intervention?

Once more, he asked himself the question. Was it possible?

He answered himself with a question of his own. Why not?

Certainly, it was possible – but barely possible. By chance, circumstances offered some hope. For one thing, while the execution order had been secret, he had found out about it, unknown to his superior. For another, there was a plane waiting twenty-eight kilometres outside Moscow to take him to London to deliver a package. Why could not Billie Bradford be the package?

For a moment he wondered why Petrov had not confided in him the plan to eliminate Billie and to keep Vera on as America's First Lady? Perhaps because Petrov had learned of Razin's love for Vera. Or perhaps because the fewer people who knew of a murder, the better for the murderers.

Razin forced his mind to concentrate on the next steps. Petrov would be going to the Kremlin soon, if he had not done so already. He and his trained thugs would forcibly remove Billie. In the limousine she would be bound and gagged. She would be driven out to the suburbs, to one of the isolated wooded areas. From behind, she would be shot in the head. She would be further disfigured to blot out her identity for all time. She would be buried in an unmarked grave. She would never be missed, because she would live on in London and Washington DC.

The obvious first step was to get to her in the Kremlin before Petrov got to her.

But no, he told himself, that was too fast, too unthought-out. She might be spotted, both of them caught, before they ever arrived at the airport. Reaching Billie in the Kremlin was the second step. Before that he must hurry home to make necessary preparations. Only then did he dare take Billie out of the Kremlin and try to escape with her. They would go to the airport. There the plane would be standing by for him and his package. He would telephone Ambassador Youngdahl before departing. Then board the plane for London. Two hours later Operation Vera would be successfully concluded.

Maybe, maybe.

It was all so easy to plan, so difficult to act out. One false move and the First Lady would be as dead as she was supposed to be. And Razin, himself, would be dead, too.

He came out of his private speculations, and found Parker's message on his lap. He separated the ambassador's card from it, shoved the card in his pocket, held the message while he opened his car door. He pulled out his cigarette lighter, snapped it on, watched the flame lick out, and applied the flame to the slip of paper with the message. The paper flared red. As it scorched his fingers, he dropped it into the street. Soon it was ashes.

He ground out the ashes with his shoe, shut the car door, and turned the key in the ignition.

No more time for thought. Time only for action.

He knew the enemy.

Time, itself, was the enemy.

12

It seemed unreal to Alex Razin, twelve minutes after leaving the Moscow ring road, when he steered his Volga into the yard next to his four-room house, that he was seeing his home for the last time. The old wooden house, painted a subdued green, a light showing in the front window, was a *dacha* inherited from his father, who had received it as a gift from the State. Here Razin had been brought by his father when he was a boy and here he had lived comfortably to his middle years. The only other occupant was his Uncle Lutoff, now in his seventies, his thin frame hunched and twisted from arthritis, who was his father's older brother.

Having parked, Razin hastily left the front seat and strode to the rear luggage compartment of the car. Unlocking it, lifting the lid, he saw that it was roomy enough.

He hurried to the house, and as he ascended the narrow steps, the front door opened, and there was Uncle Lutoff waiting to welcome him as he did every night.

'Dinner will be ready in ten minutes,' Uncle Lutoff said.

Razin brushed past him into the house. 'Forget it, Uncle,' he said. 'No time for dinner tonight. I have to leave for London right away. You can help me. Do we still have that old trunk that used to be around? The large one Father took along from America?

'I am sure it is in the store room.'

'Find it. Empty it. Drag it in here. Call me, if you need help. Dust it off. Do we have a hand drill? If not, a chisel and hammer will do. Bring them here.'

Uncle Lutoff nodded, and limped away toward the store room.

Razin continued on into his bedroom. With an eye on the clock, he discarded his light suit jacket. He sought and found his wool-lined dark leather jacket, the one with the deep pockets (one still holding a small flask of vodka), and pulled it on. Next, he went to his dresser and yanked out the top drawer. Feeling under the shorts and socks, his fingers touched the box of cartridges and then his hand covered the familiar PM pistol. Taking them both out, he placed the cartridges on the bed, and examined the 9 mm Makarov pistol. Professionally, speedily, he stripped it down. It was in excellent working condition. He put it together again, and loaded eight rounds of cartridges into the magazine. Remembering something more, he searched the top drawer again, with no result, but in the second drawer he found it. He held his expensive silencer. Quickly, he slipped it on to the barrel of the Makarov. After pushing the safety catch up, he dropped the gun into the second jacket pocket.

At the bed, he retrieved his worn wallet from his suit jacket. He flipped through it, confirmed that his KGB pass was there, and he slipped the wallet into the hip pocket of his trousers. One more item in his suit coat, the diplomatic passport that Petrov had given him. Yet another thing he'd almost overlooked, the card from Ambassador Youngdahl with his telephone number. Razin recovered both and stowed them on his person. Since he was not returning, was there anything more? Somewhere there was a frayed snapshot of his mother, and the last portrait of his father. But there was no time. He would have to sacrifice them for Billie.

About to leave his bedroom, one more thing came to mind. He opened his closet, reached for the upper shelf and brought down a folded brown spare blanket. He carried it into the living room, where Uncle Lutoff had just finished dusting the five-foot, brass-trimmed black trunk. Razin tossed the blanket near it, knelt, opened the latches of the trunk, raised the top and peered into it. The trunk was spacious, but not quite large enough to hold him. However, Billie was considerably shorter and slimmer than he. He estimated that she could fit into it. She would be cramped, suffer some discomfort, but then her stay in it might not be long. At least he hoped not.

He stood up with the blanket, shook it out, and laid it inside the trunk to serve as a liner. Closing the trunk, latching it, he turned it on one end.

'Did you find a hand drill?' he asked his uncle.

'No, but I have a chisel and hammer.'

'They'll do.'

He took the chisel and hammer from his uncle, positioned himself above the trunk, with one hand held the chisel against the lid and with the other hand held his hammer over the chisel. He slammed the hammer down against the chisel, trying to drive its point into the trunk. But the trunk was sturdy, its surface giving only slightly. Razin hammered hard again, then a third and fourth time, and at the fifth blow the chisel penetrated the trunk tearing a jagged hole through it. Encouraged, Razin moved the chisel around the end of the trunk, laboriously hammering away until there were a half-dozen holes in the trunk. Pleased, he backed away. Anyone inside the trunk would require added oxygen. The holes would allow Billie to breathe.

Pocketing the chisel, Razin handed the hammer to his puzzled uncle. He dug out his wallet, extracted half of his rouble notes and placed them on the trunk. He went to the living room desk, found a piece of scrap paper and a pen. On the paper he printed the date and scribbled a note. The note transferred all of Razin's personal property and effects to his Uncle Lutoff. Razin signed it. He gathered the note and roubles together and pushed them into the old man's hand.

'Yours, Uncle,' he said. 'Everything I have – just in case something happens to me.'

'No, no,' protested Uncle Lutoff, 'please, nothing must happen.'

'Put that away, and help me,' Razin ordered, grabbing one strap of the trunk. 'Let's get this into the luggage compartment of my car. I'm in a terrible hurry.'

Because, at this late hour, the Kremlin parking spaces were only one-third filled, Alex Razin was able to leave his parked car in an advantageous spot for his purpose. On the way through the Kremlin, although the scattered guards knew him, he still routinely flashed his KGB pass.

Arriving at the suite that held Billie Bradford, Razin paused to chat with the familiar KGB guard. 'How are you, Boris?'

'Fine, Comrade Razin.'

'How's your son?'

'Fever's down. Another week and he'll be back at his sports.'

'Glad to hear that.' Then, Razin added casually, 'Anybody been by to visit our guest this evening?'

'Couldn't be quieter.'

Razin felt a surge of relief. His one abiding fear had been that Petrov might have arrived here before him. That would have been the end of the First Lady and of all his hopes. Fumbling for his key, he tried to behave as unconcernedly as always. He unlocked the door, and let himself in.

He had assumed that Billie would be asleep by now, and that he would have to rouse her and get her moving. But he found her wide awake across the room, in her nightgown and negligee, uninterestedly playing solitaire with cards laid out on the coffee table. After he shut the door behind him, she lifted her head and acknowledged his arrival with a small show of surprise.

Quickly, he brought his forefinger to his lips, signalling her to be quiet. He crossed to the radio, which was playing symphonic music, the volume low. He turned up the volume until the music filled the room, then approached her.

Watching him, she said, 'Isn't this a rather odd hour for you to come here?'

'I had something important to tell you,' he said in an urgent undertone.

She put down her pack. 'Any news?' she asked eagerly.

'There is some news, Billie. Not exactly what you've been expecting.'

'Tell me,' she said, searching his face.

'I will tell you. But I don't want you to panic. I'm here to help you. Whatever you feel, remember that.'

'All right,' she said, as if bracing herself. 'Are you going to tell me they're not sending me home yet?'

'Worse. Much worse. They've decided to get rid of you.'

'What?' It was as if she had not quite heard him. 'Get rid –'

'They want to get rid of you,' he repeated.

What he was saying had finally penetrated. She looked stricken. 'Oh, no – no –'

'It's *not* going to happen,' he hastily reassured her. 'But that's what they plan. They want to kill you.'

'Kill me, actually kill me?' she repeated with utter disbelief.

'Tonight,' he said. 'They want to let their Second Lady remain as First Lady. Permanently.'

'But that would never –'

'They think it will.'

'Let me talk to them, explain –' she pleaded.

'No. It would be hopeless. Once they got their hands on you, you'd be finished. There is only one chance. I'm going to help you escape right now. I'm supposed to go to London tonight as a courier. There's a plane standing by for me. I'm going to try to get you on it with me. We've got to move fast.'

He had expected her to react immediately, obey him, jump up, run to the bedroom. Instead, she sat staring at him, a bitter expression on her face. She had regained her composure and picked up the pack of cards.

Bewildered, Razin said, 'Billie, didn't you hear me?'

Concentrating on the cards, she said, 'I heard you. I don't believe you.'

'You don't believe me? Billie –'

She looked up at him. 'No, I don't. You lied to me once, pretending to help me escape. You used me. I won't let it happen again. I know you're a KGB agent. Are you going to deny it? Don't. I saw your ID card.'

Razin stood momentarily speechless.

341

'You're no friend,' Billie continued relentlessly. 'You're one of them. I have no idea what you want with me this time. Maybe *you* want to kill me. Maybe they ordered you to get me out of here without difficulty. Whatever your game is, I'm not playing it again. You're a liar, you can't be trusted, and I want no part –'

Razin went down on one knee before her, gripping her arms so hard she winced. 'Billie, listen. Please listen. Everything you've said is true. I am a KGB agent. I did use you. I was ordered to and I went along. But not now. Not this time. Why would I use you? What reason would there be?'

Shaken, she met his eyes. His intensity made her hesitant. 'How – how do I know?' she said uncertainly.

'Billie, if I was still on their side, I wouldn't dare tell you what I've told you. They are planning to execute you tonight. How could I use you, what could I do to you that's worse than that? What have I to gain?'

'Suppose what you say is true, why bother to help me? Why risk your career, your life?'

'I have my reasons,' he said, rising. 'But there's no time for them now. I repeat, we've got to move quickly. Otherwise we don't have a chance.'

She came to her feet. 'You mean it? They really want to kill me?'

'They're going to, I swear.'

She was beginning to look distraught. 'And you – you want to help me?'

'I can only try. General Petrov is coming here tonight to take you away. I don't know exactly when. Maybe later. Maybe any second. We've got to get going. My car's outside. Now do as I say.'

'All right.'

'Get into some clothes immediately –' She was on her way to the bedroom, as he went on. '– and wear the mink outfit.'

She paused at the doorway. 'Mink outfit? How did you –?'

'We know everything about you. Have you forgotten? The mink outfit or ensemble means your brown suit, blouse, brown lizard shoes, and beige mink coat. Get into them. I can probably get you past the guard outside. But I prefer the other route, the trapdoor in the kitchen to the storage –'

'They nailed it down.'

'I know. But I can open it. Now hurry.'

The moment that she rushed into the bedroom, he headed for the kitchen. He kicked aside the mat covering the trapdoor. He knelt. There were eight nails securing the trapdoor. He dug a hand into the pocket of his leather jacket. He brought out the chisel. He began to pry at the nails, loosening each. They were deeply imbedded and it wasn't easy. Five minutes passed. He had two nails out. He worked harder.

Only one thing troubled him. The success of their escape would depend entirely on the time that General Petrov arrived here. If he came soon after they left, found Billie missing, he would suspect Razin and have them arrested at the airport. If they were airborne, Petrov would radio the pilot to turn back. It was the possible arrest at the airport that bothered Razin, not the recall of the plane. If the pilot received an order to turn around, he would also find Razin's pistol at his head. They simply had to get off the ground before Petrov learned of the escape attempt.

Razin yanked out the last nail. With his forefingers, he had a hold on each side of the trapdoor. He worked it loose, and lifted it out of the floor and laid it aside. Beneath him, he saw the steep ladder leading down to the darkened storage room.

Billie must be dressed by now. About to rise and summon her, Razin became aware of a lull in the music and he clearly heard another sound. He heard the grating of a key in the front door. The sound was paralysing. His heart stood still.

Crouched, Razin listened. The door creaked open, then banged shut.

From his angle, Razin could see no one, but there was someone else in the living room. Razin mobilized himself into movement. He rose, backed off quietly against the refrigerator, from which vantage point he could see the rest of the room and the doorway to the bedroom.

That instant, a bulky figure came into view, General Petrov marching past the kitchen towards the bedroom. He was almost across the room, when Billie, swathed in her mink, materialized in her bedroom doorway. She, too, had heard the front door, had come to see what was going on, and now found herself facing General Petrov. Her fright was apparent, although she tried to retain her poise.

Petrov, momentarily disturbed by the resumption of the deafening music, stopped. 'Good evening, Mrs Bradford,' he said, loudly, eyeing her from head to toe. 'Were you planning to go out? The theatre, perhaps? The ballet?'

'N-n-no,' she stammered. 'I was bored. I was trying on clothes.'

Petrov was briefly silent, as if considering her reply, then he spoke, almost cheerfully. 'A happy coincidence,' he said. 'I had just decided to drop by and ask you out.'

Billied appeared to stall. 'Out? Me? Where?'

'A surprise. You shall see. You've been cooped up in here too long. Come with me.'

'I – I'm not sure I feel like going out. I was planning to go to bed.'

'There's plenty of time for sleep. I suggest you join me.'

'Really, I'm not up to it, General. If you don't mind –'

'I do mind,' he said on a harsher note. 'In fact, I insist.'

'Well, if I must –'

'Now,' he commanded.

She teetered uncertainly. 'My purse, let me get my purse.'

'You won't need your purse,' Petrov said gruffly. 'Come on.' His voice was steely. 'Don't make me force you.'

She started into the living room, walked slowly past Petrov not meeting his eyes, continued toward the front door, as Petrov fell in several feet behind her.

From the kitchen, Razin had been watching and listening. The crisis had come to them sooner than he had expected. His mind raced, sorting his options. Of only one thing could he be certain. Petrov was leading the First Lady to her death. He must be stopped by any means. By what means? Razin's right hand had burrowed into his jacket pocket. Petrov must be disarmed, forced down into the storage room below, gagged and bound and left there. He and Billie might be safe before Petrov was found.

The pair was moving out of Razin's line of vision. Razin's hand clasped the butt of his Makarov. He drew the pistol with its silencer out of his pocket and pressed down the safety catch. In a rapid movement, he stepped into the living room, gun held high.

'Petrov,' he called out.

Startled, the KGB chief stopped dead in his tracks. He swung about, his features showing his surprise, his widening eyes staring at Razin.

Razin did not blink. 'Come here,' he ordered.

Obediently, Petrov took a step toward him, beginning to raise his hands in abject surrender, and as he did so, one hand, swift as lightning, darted to his shoulder holster. Even as Razin's pistol took aim, Petrov's gun was free of the holster.

Razin fired first. A cottony swoosh from the silencer. Petrov gasped, the gun falling from his hand, which came up to join his other hand clutching his abdomen. Petrov reeled, staggered forward, went down to his knees, one hand instinctively pushing forward to break his fall. He keeled over flat on his face.

Billie and Razin watched the prone body with fascination, studying it for any sign of movement. There was none. There was blood being blotted up by the carpet.

As if coming out of a hypnotic trance, Razin forced himself to action. With his gun, he gestured for Billie to join him in the kitchen. She, too, had seemed in a trance, but at once she was out of it. She ran past Petrov's unconscious body. Razin led her to the opening in the floor.

'I believe you now,' she whispered against his ear. 'Will we make it?'

'I don't know, but we'd better. I've no place to go but straight ahead.'

Razin was at the wheel, Billie Bradford in the passenger seat beside him, and they were speeding south-west on the high-way that led to Vnukovo airport.

Except for one brief delay, their departure from the Kremlin had been unobstructed. After emerging from the storage room, Razin had advised Billie to cover the lower half of her face by raising the collar of her mink coat. Then, taking her by the elbow, he had walked her unhurriedly toward the yellow four-storey Administrative Building across the way. Nonchalantly, he had waved to the few guards en route who knew him, recognized him, and had waved back.

In the parking area, Razin had guided Billie along the string of big black official vehicles that dwarfed his own Volga sedan. At the sedan, he had helped her into the passenger seat, and gone around the car to settle behind the steering wheel. After backing out, he had driven to the Spasskaya Gate.

A new KGB guard, unfamiliar to him, had barred the way. The guard had peered in through the open car window. 'Identification?' he had demanded of Razin.

Razin had produced his wallet and removed his KGB identity card.

The guard had squinted down at it and up at Razin's face. Satisfied with Razin, the guard had poked his rifle toward Billie. 'And the lady?' he had asked.

'She is a witness in a criminal case,' Razin had said. 'General Petrov wants her at Lubyanka for interrogation.'

'Thank you, sir,' the guard had said. 'You may pass.'

As his sedan moved ahead, leaving the Kremlin behind, Razin had said cryptically, 'One more step to go – a long one.'

She had tried to understand what he meant.

Noticing the curiosity in her expression, he had explained, 'Getting to the airport, before they get to us. Sooner or later, someone will miss Petrov and go to find him. When they question Boris, your guard, they'll know I was in the suite and that we both used the trapdoor. They'll try to stop us at the airport. But that might not happen.'

Billie had shivered. 'What do I do at the airport?'

'Nothing. You will see shortly. Leave it to me.'

Passing through Moscow with his recognizable passenger, at this late hour, he had felt enclosed and threatened. As he sped past Gagarin Square, continuing on Lenin Prospect, he had been able to make out Patrice Lumumba Friendship University, the dim lights of the Sputnik Hotel, and the darkened commercial buildings like the House of Shoes, the House of Fabrics, and the Moscow Department Store. Soon, he had known, he would be free of the city.

Once he had crossed Vernadsky Prospect, he had begun to see stretches of open countryside. Yet, his fear had not diminished. Hunching over the wheel, he had driven in silence, with Billie huddled in the corner of her seat. Along the way, Lenin Prospect had become the concrete four-lane highway named Kiev Chaussée. He had been conscious of every chauffeured limousine, every uniformed motorcyclist, every public bus, approaching or passing him, and he had been wary of every pair of headlights shining out from side roads.

Now, eyeing a sign that told him he was four kilometres from the airport, he eased his foot on the gas pedal, slowed, gradually moved his vehicle to the outside lane of the highway, seeking something in the patches of semi-darkness and the dense forests beyond. Abruptly Razin swung the car off the main thoroughfare and on to a dirt road. A slight decline brought him to a cross street. He drove past it and spun the sedan on to a wide wagon track that disappeared into the dark wooded area. For perhaps 100 metres he zigzagged the car between spruce and birch trees, and finally brought it to a halt in a small clearing.

Dousing his headlights, he turned to Billie. She sat filled with apprehension, wondering.

'The last step,' he said to her. 'You must be prepared to be uncomfortable for a half-hour, maybe an hour. You may be bruised and shaken up and scared. But if all goes well, you'll be alive. Let's hope it works.'

'Let's hope what works?'

He opened his side door. 'In the back of this car, in the

luggage compartment, there's a travelling trunk. You've got to climb into it. I'll lock you in. You've got to curl up in there, and not make a sound. There's a blanket in the trunk. That, and your fur coat, will protect you from being bumped around. There are small holes I made to give you some air. Do you think you can manage?'

'After what I've endured already?'

'Good. Let's get moving.'

They stepped out on opposite sides of the Volga sedan and met at the rear of the car. He unlocked the luggage compartment, and raised the cover revealing the used travelling trunk. He hoped that it was large enough to contain her. He undid the clasps and raised the lid of the trunk.

'Think you can squeeze in there?' he asked Billie.

She appeared doubtful. 'It would be easier if I took off my mink coat.'

He shook his head. 'No. You'll need the protection of the fur. Let's find out if you'll fit.' He held out a hand. 'Here, step up on the bumper and I'll help you in.'

Gripping his hand, she stepped up. Taking hold of an edge of the trunk with one hand, she pulled up the coat and skirt above her knees with the other hand, and precariously she put one leg over the side of the trunk, and then the other. She lowered herself to her knees.

'All right,' he said, 'now get on your side, bringing your knees up toward your chin. That's right. Now a little more, if you can.' He bent over the trunk opening, trying to adjust her fur coat around her. 'How's that?'

'Terrible. But more comfortable than a coffin. How long again?'

'A half-hour to an hour at most. Once we're airborne, I'll let you out. Do your best, Billie. Ready? Here we go.'

He brought the top down slowly, then secured the brass clasps, and locked the trunk.

Closing the luggage compartment, he hurried to his car seat. Pressured though he was, he took great care in backing the sedan around, determined not to jostle or injure his charge. The Volga swayed as he drove it back over the wagon track and ascended the road.

Minutes later he was on the highway and heading for the airport.

Only one thought was uppermost in his mind: would Petrov's Praetorian guard, his execution squad, be waiting for them?

No one appeared to be waiting for them, and Razin breathed easier.

Approaching the terminal itself, which he had visited only a short time ago, Razin was momentarily confused. He found himself confronting not one airport building, but two. To the right was a small, obviously old, cream-coloured stucco structure fronted by steps and a porch. To the left, separated from it by a gap of ten or fifteen feet, rose a newer, higher, more imposing building, its exterior a glass curtain design, three rows of glass set in aluminium frames. Above the roof, a floodlighted sign at least five feet high read: VNUKOVO.

This newer building, he decided, was not the one where he was expected.

He curved his sedan in before the older building and, ignoring the parking spaces across the way, drove alongside the broad sidewalk, pulled up ahead of a metal 'No Parking' sign set in the concrete of the sidewalk, and parked his car against the curb. Looking about him, he could see that Vnukovo airport appeared busy even at this late hour, although the older building beside him seemed abandoned. Razin got out of the car hoping to find some night porters who might be on duty.

At that moment, a military officer burst out of the front door of the smaller airport building and strode rapidly toward Razin. He was wearing a KGB uniform, Razin could see. Razin tightened immediately, but then saw the officer was carrying no visible arms. Razin relaxed slightly and waited.

The captain was before him. 'Excuse me, are you Alex Razin?'

349

'I am.'

'I was ordered to watch for you. I'm Captain Meshlauk, KGB. My instructions are to facilitate your departure in every way. First, if you please, your identity card and passport.'

Razin produced both.

Captain Meshlauk glanced at Razin's KGB card and his passport, and nodded. 'Very well. A plane has been assigned to you – a roomy Antonov An-12 transport. You will have it to yourself, except for the crew, of course. There will be a pilot, co-pilot, navigator, engineer, radio operator, but they will be locked up front. Instructions are that they are not to fraternize with you, nor you with them. The plane is ready to take you to London's Westridge airport immediately. He looked Razin over. 'I was told to expect you with a package.'

Razin showed his empty hands and smiled. 'Oh, it's in the back of my car, and it is not exactly what I would call a package. It's a travelling trunk I'm supposed to turn over to Premier Kirechenko in London.'

'A trunk, is it? Well, I suppose some people might call that a package.'

'I'll open the back of my car. I'll need two porters to lug it to the plane.'

'Be right back with them.' He spun away and dashed off into the terminal.

Razin strolled back to the car and unlocked the rear compartment. There was the travelling trunk, with Billie in its womb. He wondered how she was faring. He was tempted to speak to her, but he did not dare.

He stood surveying the area partially illuminated by the night lights. No signs of danger yet. He could only hope that his luck would hold.

He wished Captain Meshlauk would hurry. Then, as if in answer to his wish, the captain reappeared from the terminal with two drably clad, elderly porters at his heels.

Razin met them at the car. 'There it is,' he said, indicating the trunk. 'Handle it with care, great care. There's a leather strap on each end.'

The porters pulled the travelling trunk towards them, each took hold of a strap, and grunting they lifted it out of the car.

'See that they take it to the passenger section of the aircraft,' Razin told the captain. 'I'm supposed to keep it in sight at all times.' .

The captain nodded, and barked out the order to the two porters. 'Take it to the Antonov An-12. Have it put in the passenger section.'

After watching the porters depart, Razin shut the rear compartment of his car and handed the keys to Captain Meshlauk. 'Will you park it? I should be back in about eight hours.'

'I'll be here waiting for you,' said the captain. 'Now we better get you aboard. We don't have to bother about passport control.'

They were entering the air terminal when Razin gripped the captain's arm, restraining him. 'One thing more,' said Razin. 'I'm supposed to report when I'm ready to leave. Where can I find a private phone?'

'No problem. Let me show you.'

The captain guided Razin to a cubbyhole of an office nearby. He unlocked the door, turned up the light, and directed Razin into the room. 'There's a phone on the desk. I'll go see that the porters got your package aboard safely. Then I'll meet you at the exit and take you to the plane.'

Once the captain was gone, Razin felt inside his jacket pocket and brought out Ambassador Youngdahl's card bearing the telephone number of the American embassy in Moscow. Still standing, Razin picked up the phone receiver and dialled the American embassy.

An embassy night operator promptly answered the first ring. He told her that he had to speak to Ambassador Youngdahl, and that his call was expected. 'Tell him it concerns a Mr Guy Parker.'

There was a fifteen-second interval before the ambassador's sleepy voice came on. 'This is the ambassador. Is this Alex Razin?'

'Yes. I have a message to be given to the First Lady directly or through her secretary.'

'I'm ready with pad and pencil.'

'Here is the message.' He dictated slowly. ' "I am en route to London with package. I should be there at daybreak. Come to Westridge airport to meet me. Be sure to wear mink outfit. Since I may be restricted for a time, please come aboard aircraft. I will then instruct you further. Signed, Alex Razin." ' He paused. 'End of message. Is it clear, Mr Ambassador?'

'Not to me. But it may be to the First Lady.'

'Read it back, if you don't mind.'

The ambassador read it back.

'Perfect,' said Razin. 'You will now relay it to Mrs Bradford?'

'Immediately.'

'Thank you, Mr Ambassador. I must go now.'

Hanging up, he realized that he was perspiring. He took out his handkerchief and wiped his forehead and dried his upper lip. Tucking away his handkerchief, he turned off the office light and went into the almost empty cavern of the dimly lit building. At a distance, past the passport counters and baggage check-in desks, near the exit doors, he saw the captain beckoning to him.

Hurriedly, he closed the distance between them and joined the captain, who held open the exit door. 'Everything is in order, sir.'

'Thank you.'

They were outdoors now, and the chill bit into Razin. The officer had jumped ahead, and Razin followed him closely to the giant military turbo-jet rising before them. The jets were whining, blowing up gusts of dust and debris.

The captain began to ascend the movable ramp. With one hasty look behind him, Razin also ascended the stairs. At the plane's entrance, the captain waited and pointed inside. 'Your trunk,' he said above the scream of the jets. 'A row of seats has been installed. Take your choice.' He extended his hand. 'Good journey. See you in the late morning.'

'I'll be looking for you,' said Razin, shaking hands. 'And thanks again for your help.'

Razin made his way deeper into the plane. Glancing back, he saw that the captain had put his head inside the cockpit. A moment later he departed. Now, a member of the crew came out and, without so much as a look at his lone passenger, closed the heavy door through which Razin had entered, securing it in place. Then he disappeared into the cockpit again.

Razin got his bearings. The interior of the Antonov was stripped except for the long benches along the interior walls – obviously intended for paratroopers – and a row of four connecting seats – and the travelling trunk a few feet from the seats.

With a sigh of exhaustion, Razin lowered himself in an end seat. He stared at the trunk. Inside it, the First Lady of the United States. Incredible.

And equally incredible that they had come this far. His mind went to the executioner. Was General Petrov dead or alive? If alive, had he been found by someone?

If alive, if found, there was still jeopardy. Razin patted his pocket. He still had his gun.

He looked out the window. The plane was moving.

The first streaks of dawn were outlining the domes of the Kremlin.

At a curb inside the Kremlin, the elongated dark blue Zil limousine, belonging to the chairman of the KGB, remained parked where it had been since its arrival.

Inside the limousine, the four occupants continued to wait. Behind the wheel reclined Konstantin, the chauffeur, and beside him sat Sukoloff, a photographer. In the spacious rear, two of the three vinyl armchairs held two of General Petrov's most trusted KGB bodyguards, Captain Ilya Mirsky and Captain Andrei Dogel.

Mirsky's sullen misshapen face reflected his impatience. Restlessly, he peered outside. 'It's getting light,' he growled.

'I don't like it. We're way behind schedule. The whole thing was to be done during the night.'

'What difference?' said Dogel.

To Mirsky, there was a difference. A plan was a plan. If people did not adhere to plans, the world, life on earth, would be chaos. Without following plans, things could go wrong, things could not be accomplished. That was one of the admirable qualities about General Petrov. He always planned. He always adhered to what he had planned. He got things done.

To Mirsky, his boss's tardiness tonight was inexplicable.

Now, for at least the tenth time, as an antidote to the boredom of inaction, Mirsky reviewed the delayed plan. They all had their precise assignments, although only he and Dogel actually knew in advance what was to happen. The chauffeur Konstantin had his instructions – once the extra passenger was picked up, he was to drive five kilometres beyond Izmailovo Park to a dense forest of virgin pine that hid an old graveyard. The chauffeur was to stay in the car, and the photographer Sukoloff was to stay with him, until he was summoned to bring his camera into the forest. The passenger, a woman that Petrov had come here to pick up, would be unconscious. The second Petrov had brought her to the limousine, Dogel would have covered her face with a rag saturated with ether, and pushed her to the floor of the car. Mirsky and Dogel would carry her through the woods to the graveyard. An open grave would be waiting. Mirsky was to shoot her in the heart, stay away from her face, until the photographer had taken his pictures. After Sukoloff had made his close-ups of her lifeless face and bullet wound, and had been sent away, Dogel would pour acid on her face to obliterate it beyond recognition. The corpse would then be rolled into the grave and Mirsky and Dogel would use their shovels to fill the hole with dirt, cover it with a layer of sod. After that, they would hasten back to KGB headquarters. The prints of the photographs would be turned over to Petrov, who would hand them over to Alex Razin.

That was the plan – as yet unfulfilled.

Mirsky put a light to his cigarette, puffed furiously, looked down at his watch. 'It's almost three hours,' he said. He glanced outside once more. 'Practically daylight. I tell you, it's not like him.' He crushed out his cigarette. 'I better see what's going on.'

'I don't know,' said Dogel. 'Our orders were to wait. You might break in on him giving the lady one long last fuck.'

Mirsky opened the limousine door. 'I'll take my chances,' he said, and stepped out and strode away.

Walking fast, Mirsky reached his destination in less than ten minutes. Approaching the Bradford suite, he saw the night guard still stationed before the door.

'How are you, Boris?' Mirsky called.

'Fine, sir.'

'Who's inside there right now?'

'Well, sir, the lady, of course. Then Mr Razin –'

'Mr Razin?'

'He's been inside maybe four hours. General Petrov came after him. The general's inside, too.'

'None of them has left?' asked Mirsky. 'They're all still in there?'

'Yes, sir.'

'Well, I'll have to interrupt General Petrov. Will you let me in?'

Boris found his key and unlocked the door to the suite.

The instant that Mirsky pushed the door open, he saw the bulky body of General Petrov – unmistakably Petrov – sprawled on the floor. This was so unexpected that Mirsky's composure, usually stonelike, cracked.

Recovering, he bellowed over the thunderous music, 'Boris!'

Mirsky leaped forward, went down on a knee beside his chief, as the guard Boris ran into the room.

Carefully, Mirsky turned the body on its side, revealing the blood and the ugly bullet wound. 'He's been shot –' Mirsky lowered the body to the floor, reached for Petrov's wrist and felt for the pulse. The beat was feeble. 'He's still alive.' Mirsky looked up at the guard. 'Get an ambulance, fast as possible! Sound the alarm!'

The guard whirled and bounded out of the room.

When his shock had receded, Mirsky came to his feet. Drawing his pistol from its holster, he surveyed the living room. There had been two others in the suite. Where were they?

Mirsky advanced swiftly to the bedroom, and cautiously entered it. The bedroom was empty. He hurried to the bathroom. Both bathroom and shower were empty. Retracing his steps, he looked into the kitchen. Empty. Their prisoner, the First Lady, was gone, and so was Alex Razin. There was no question in Mirsky's mind about what had happened. But how had they got away?

Instantly, he remembered the trapdoor, and the previous effort to escape. He went into the kitchen. The trapdoor seemed in place, but then he realized that the nails had been removed. Tugging off the trapdoor and laying it to one side, he took a miniature flashlight from his pocket, dropped himself to the floor, and poked his light into the hole. The beam showed only a vacant storage room.

Mirsky stood up, putting away his light, certain that the fugitives had fled through the trapdoor. Dusting himself off, he tried to reason out why a trusted, veteran KGB agent like Alex Razin would do such a thing. Had the CIA bought him out? Or had he been a double agent in the pay of the Americans all along? Or had he learned of the First Lady's impending execution and agreed to save her for a reward? In any case, how did Razin imagine he could possibly get the American First Lady out of Moscow and Russia? Razin's behaviour was baffling. It made no sense.

Turning back to the living room, he saw that Petrov's body was surrounded by a medical crew consisting of a physician, two nurses, two stretcher-bearers. Mirsky hung back, until they were taking Petrov from the room. One doctor called out, 'We'll know how serious it is when we get him to the Kremlin Clinic.'

As Mirsky left the suite, he was intercepted by Moscow

police investigators and several fellow KGB officers. Quickly, he recounted what he knew, and then hurried out toward the limousine. He stopped once to watch the ambulance, a white minibus with red cross emblems and a flashing light on the roof, gathering speed as it made its way toward the Borovitsky Gate.

In the limousine, Mirsky commanded Konstantin to take them to the Kremlin Clinic building only a few minutes away, as fast as possible. 'The one just across from the Lenin Library,' he added. While their limousine headed for the hospital, Mirsky told the mystified Dogel and Sukoloff what had happened. When they arrived at the five-storey red granite building, Mirsky concluded, 'Only Petrov can answer our questions – if he lives.' He opened the car door. 'Come on,' he said to Dogel, 'let's find out.'

The small, stifling waiting room was opposite the surgery. In the time that followed, Mirsky, more restless than ever, walked back and forth ceaselessly and chain-smoked steadily, while Dogel sat leafing through a magazine. Neither man spoke. It was more than an hour before the senior surgeon appeared, unfastening his white mask.

'The odds are favourable that, barring unforeseen complications, General Petrov will recover,' the surgeon said. 'I know you gentlemen need information. However, do not expect anything from the general for two or three days. You will be kept informed daily – and privately – of his condition.'

Departing the hospital, Mirsky knew what had to be done next. He must order the driver to get them to KGB headquarters – Petrov's office – immediately.

The flight time from Moscow to London was three-and-a-half hours, and the Antonov transport with its two passengers was over the North Sea, less than an hour from its destination.

Once the plane had been airborne, Alex Razin had not lost a moment in opening the trunk. He had found Billie Bradford curled and compressed inside, her eyes closed, her features etched with pain. She had seemed only half conscious. Hooking his hands under her armpits, he had gently set her upright, lifted her out of the trunk, held her in a standing position beside the seats. Immediately, her knees had buckled and she had collapsed in his arms. He had helped her to a seat and settled her into it.

He had watched over her as she lay there, comatose, unable to speak.

Once, after a half-hour, she had partially opened her eyes.

'Are you all right?' he had asked worriedly.

'I – I don't know.'

'Does anything hurt?'

'Everything.'

'Do you want me to massage you?'

She had nodded weakly.

He had begun by kneading her shoulders lightly, then had gone on to massage her sides and thighs and legs. By the time he had finished, she had been fast asleep.

He had taken the seat beside her, and smoked, and had reflected on his past and speculated upon his immediate future. Then he had dozed off.

Awakening with a start, he realized that two hours had passed, and that she, too, was awake and staring straight ahead.

'How are you?' he wanted to know.

'Much better. Where are we?'

'An hour or so out of London.'

'Are we safe?'

'I think so.'

'Thank God.' She turned her head toward him, and touched his cheek. 'Thank you. I owe everything to you.'

'Including getting you into the whole thing,' he said bitterly.

'And getting me out of it,' she added. 'It was so dangerous. Why did you do it?'

'That's a long story, Billie. I'll tell you all of it before we land. But I think you need a stiff drink first.'

'I think so, too.'

He produced the pint flask of vodka from his jacket, unscrewed the cap, and handed her the bottle. She took a gulp, choked and coughed, and sat up. She took a second swallow, and returned the bottle. 'Potent,' she said. 'I'm awake now.'

He had one drink, then another, capped the flask and put it away.

Her eyes were on him. 'Now tell me,' she said.

'Tell you what?'

'Why you did it. Why we're here. You said it was a long story.'

He smiled. 'I'll try to make it short. Yes, I suppose you should know every detail, because we'll be walking into an extremely awkward and potentially dangerous situation. You know some of what happened already. I should fill you in on the rest.'

Razin started with General Petrov's accidental discovery of the provincial actress, Vera Vavilova, in Kiev, and Petrov's fascination with the fact that Vera looked almost exactly like the wife of one of the two United States presidential nominees. When that wife became the First Lady, Petrov got his Second Lady project under way. At the outset, Petrov had no specific purpose in mind, only the knowledge that several future crises loomed and that a Russian First Lady in the White House might be an espionage coup for the Soviet Union. Petrov spent almost three years, and a fortune in roubles, to convert Vera Vavilova into a replica of Billie Bradford.

'I was in on the project from the beginning,' said Razin. 'Because, as you know, I was acquainted with America and spoke good English. I was put in charge of Americanizing our Vera Vavilova. Along the way, I fell deeply in love with Vera, and she with me. I hated sending her off to Washington in exchange for you, but I had to do so. After that, I had to see that she succeeded, went undetected, not only to protect her but to keep her safe for me.'

Meanwhile, the KGB had put him in charge of Billie during her imprisonment. As Billie now knew, every act he had performed — from assisting Billie in her first escape attempt to preventing her from being punished for it – had been ordered by the KGB. Their biggest problem, he said, had been Vera's need to know how to behave in bed with the President.

'I was assigned to find out,' said Razin. 'I tried to use you. And you tried to use me. Yet, when it was over I came to the conclusion you had tried to mislead me, and so I gambled and instructed Vera to act completely opposite from the way you had acted. I was proved to be right.'

'I was afraid of that,' said Billie.

'My duty,' said Razin. 'But today I forgot duty. I refused to obey them. Somehow, in London, your writer, Guy Parker, found out you were in Moscow and to be executed tonight. He conveyed the news to me using your ambassador in Moscow as an intermediary. Parker guessed I would not permit it. He was right. I would not. The men I had been blindly obeying, all at once I saw them as monsters. I decided to risk my life to save yours. I had two motives. The first was selfish. If you were murdered, Vera would remain the President's mate as long as they both lived – and I would lose her for ever. The other motive was – well, a humane one – but the fact is that I had become genuinely fond of you and somehow come to regard you as Vera's surrogate. The act of killing you was a barbaric act. I wanted no part of it. By saving you, I might restore my honour as well as save the woman I love for myself. There you have it, Billie, all of it.'

Throughout his confession, she had listened mesmerized, her feelings toward him seesawing from anger to affection. Now, more tolerant, accepting the change he had undergone, she appreciated the risk he had taken. She spoke, at last. 'You shot General Petrov to get me out. What'll happen to you?'

'What will happen to me? That is entirely up to you, Billie.'

'Me? What can I do for you? What do you want?'

'I want my life and Vera's,' he said simply. 'Vera will be there to meet our plane. I've arranged that. She'll be extremely upset, even frightened, to see you, but I'll calm her down.

You and Vera will trade places. I've even had her dress as you're dressed to make the exchange easier. Then, to begin with, you must hide us briefly. You should be able to get us out of the airport without any trouble. No one will delay the First Lady and her entourage. You must hide us overnight –'

'I know a place in the West End. A flat that's owned by a widower and his son –'

'Get us American passports. You promised mine from the start. I'll want another for Vera. Under new names.'

'It can be arranged.'

'And find us an out-of-the-way clinic and a plastic surgeon in England. Schedule us for immediate facial surgery. Vera must no longer look like you, or her old self, and I must never be recognized as Alex Razin. This will protect us from being found by the KGB."

'It will be done immediately.'

'Once we are given permanent residence in the United States, help me get a reporting or teaching job and help Vera get back on the stage.'

'I'm sure I can do it.'

'One final thing,' said Razin. 'Never speak publicly or privately about what happened to you. No word of it must get out. Because if it did, if your husband or anyone in the American government ever learned of your abduction, of your double, well, then the United States and the Soviet Union –' He showed her his despair. 'Friendship and peace would be impossible, and their relationship would become a nightmare.'

Billie fully understood. 'Tempted as I might be, Alex – the desire for revenge is a powerful emotional force – I'll try to keep my head. No Alex, don't worry. I promise you I'll never speak of this.'

He smiled slightly. 'Then you will have repaid me.' He looked out the window. 'It's getting light now.' He sat back and his brow furrowed. 'I wonder what's happening in Moscow?'

At KGB headquarters near the Kremlin, Mirsky stood behind General Petrov's desk, all of the previous evening's memorandums and notes and decoded wireless messages from London spread out before him. Gathered across from him were Dogel and three other KGB officers who had known about Project Second Lady.

For a last time Mirsky reviewed General Petrov's papers. The fuzzy picture of what had taken place was now sharply in focus. Not all of it, to be sure, but most of it, enough of it.

The significant fact was that, after the Premier had ordered Mrs Bradford liquidated, and after Alex Razin had been assigned to take a package (containing photographs of the corpse) to London, Razin had by some means learned of the pending execution. He had, for whatever reasons, undertaken to rescue Billie Bradford and bring her to London on the plane assigned to him.

Once this had become clear to Mirsky, he had telephoned Vnukovo airport and spoken to a Captain Meshlauk. Mirsky had been informed that the Antonov transport with Razin aboard had left for London more than three hours ago.

'This Mr Razin, did he have a lady with him?' Mirsky had inquired.

'No, there was no one with him. He got aboard alone with his package – well, actually a large travelling trunk.'

'Ah, a trunk, a large travelling trunk.'

At once, Mirsky had seen the horrendous inevitability of what would follow. The KGB had its First Lady, Vera Vavilova, safe in London. Shortly, the real First Lady, Billie Bradford, would also be in London. The confrontation between the two First Ladies would blow the KGB plot sky-high. The resultant exposure, and its consequences, were beyond calculation.

Mirsky shook his head and looked up at his colleagues. 'I guess we know what's taken place. The question is – what can we do about it?' He fixed his gaze on Dogel. 'You are absolutely sure that plane cannot be recalled?'

Dogel turned both thumbs down. 'Impossible. There's not

sufficient fuel for the round trip. The plane was to refuel at Westridge. Besides, we know Razin has a gun.'

'Well,' said Mirsky, 'that leaves us just one thing to do. We must notify Premier Kirechenko immediately. He's on the scene. He's the only one who can save us.'

At Claridge's Hotel in London, Guy Parker was picking up Nora Judson in her office, and leading her through Dolores Martin's office, on the way to an early breakfast, when the President's scrambler phone started ringing. Mrs Martin came to her feet and ran for the phone.

Parker held Nora back at the door. 'This could be for one of us.'

Mrs Martin already had the phone to her ear. 'Oh, hello, Mr Ambassador ... Well, I don't think she's up yet, but Nora Judson is here. Do you want to speak to her?' She listened, then cupped her hand over the phone. 'Nora! It's Ambassador Youngdahl calling from Moscow. He wants to speak to you.'

Nora gave Parker a meaningful look. 'Coming!' she called back to Mrs Martin, and hurried into the President's office, signalling for Parker to join her.

She took over the telephone. 'Hello, Mr Ambassador. This is Nora Judson. Would you like me to wake Mrs Bradford?'

'No, you'll do.'

'Very well.'

'First of all, tell Parker I did as he instructed me. I located Alex Razin and passed on the message. I did it in person and then left him. Later, I heard from Mr Razin briefly. He had a message for the First Lady, for Mrs Bradford.'

'I'll be happy to pass it on to her.'

'I have it written down. Let me read it to you. Ready?'

'One second.' Nora snatched a pad of paper, placed it before her, and picked up a pencil. 'Go ahead.'

'All right,' said Ambassador Youngdahl. 'The message: "I am en route to London with package. I should be there at daybreak. Come to Westridge airport to meet me. Be sure to wear mink outfit. Since I may be restricted for a time,

363

please come aboard aircraft. I will instruct you further. Signed, Alex Razin." That's the complete message.'

'I'll convey it to Mrs Bradford as soon as she's available.

'Sorry to be so late with it. I would have got it to you hours ago, but there was a telephone breakdown. Now everything's working again. Anyway, you've got it now. Give my regards to Mrs Bradford.'

'Thank you, Mr Ambassador.'

Dropping the receiver in the cradle, Nora tore the message off the pad. 'Razin's on his way. He wants Billie to meet him at Westridge airport. I'd better give this to the First Lady.'

Parker looked worried. 'Won't Billie be concerned about your knowing an American First Lady is going to meet a Soviet citizen at —'

'I'll just play it dumb, Guy. Say this came for her, makes no sense to me, and leave it at that.' She paused. 'One good thing. I won't have to wake them both. She's sleeping alone in another bedroom. She was afraid he was catching a cold, and she wanted none of it.'

Parker was frowning. 'One second, Nora.' He plucked the message from her fingers and read it. He reread it and stared at Nora, a stricken look on his face. 'Razin's coming with a package. That was what he was assigned to bring here, a package with photographs of Billie's corpse. And no word about Billie.'

'He couldn't mention Billie. This is for Billie, remember?'

Parker glanced at the message again, and returned it to Nora. 'Does that mean — Razin wasn't able to save her?'

'I don't know what it really means, Guy. Razin couldn't say much dictating this to our ambassador.'

'Then why does he want to see Vera at the airport?'

'I haven't the faintest idea,' said Nora.

'It must mean he couldn't save Billie. He has the photographs of her body. He wants to let Vera know right away that she is the First Lady from now on in.'

'Don't keep saying that. We just don't know. Listen, I'd better wake Vera and give her this message. She's still our First Lady. Will you be here?'

'No,' he said starting to leave the President's office.

'Guy, where will you be?'

'At Westridge airport,' he said, dropping his voice. 'I've got to find out whether Billie is dead or alive — and which First Lady we're going to live with.'

Premier Dmitri Kirechenko was in an ebullient mood as he climbed the stairs to the Terrace Suite of the Dorchester Hotel.

The breakfast at the embassy of the Soviet Union in London had gone well. He had dined with most of his staff and discussed the agenda for what he hoped would be one of the last Summit meetings at the American embassy tomorrow morning. Until now, he and his delegation had employed delaying tactics at each session. But by tomorrow he expected to be able to announce a definite decision on the Boende non-aggression pact.

That tough little whore, Vera Vavilova, had kept him dangling. She had high-handedly withheld her precious information. Well, since he was in a good mood, he could be reasonable about it, and reasonably, he could not blame her. She wanted a guarantee of safety. Now she would have it. By now, the Bradford woman would have been executed. Within the hour, Razin would arrive with the photographic evidence. The minute this was shown to Vera, he would have the information he needed. If it was favourable, he would bring the Americans to their knees tomorrow.

As he reached the top of the staircase, he realized that Razin might have arrived early, and in that case Vera would be ready to talk. Otherwise, why would General Chukovsky have called him away from the embassy breakfast twenty minutes ago? Chukovsky had telephoned to ask him to return to the Dorchester immediately on a matter of great importance, nothing he could discuss on the telephone.

Well, here he was. He acknowledged the saluting guards, and cheerfully, filled with anticipation, entered the Terrace Suite.

The uniformed, bemedalled Chukovsky was pacing in the

centre of the room. Premier Kirechenko took in the room. There was no sign of Vera Vavilova. Puzzled, the Premier crossed over to the desk and sat down heavily.

'All right, Chukovsky, what is this matter of great importance?'

Chukovsky did not reply. Instead, he pulled a paper from his pocket, unfolded it, and laid it out before the Premier. 'This wireless message just arrived from Moscow, Comrade Kirechenko. It's been decoded.'

Premier Kirechenko picked it up, began to read it. His scowl deepened. He murmured key words as he continued to read. 'Petrov shot . . . Razin escaped with First Lady. . . . Took plane you assigned to London . . . .' Kirechenko's face was aflame as his rage mounted. He crumpled the wireless message in his fist, his eyes rolling and his features contorted as if he were in the throes of an apoplectic fit.

Then he began cursing in Russian. 'How in the hell could this happen?' he shouted.

Chukovsky recoiled. 'I – I don't know, sir. All I know is what you have seen in the message. Razin seems to have learned about the execution. He would not let it be carried out. He appears to have shot Petrov and got away with the First Lady. He has Mrs Bradford with him on the courier plane. He is bringing her here alive.'

'An impossible situation!' roared the Premier, banging his fist down on the desk, making the empty inkwell turn over. 'It can absolutely destroy us, destroy everything we worked for. Vera will be exposed. We will never get her information – and if the Americans find out – impossible!' He jumped to his feet. 'We must do something.'

'As you read, it is too late to return the plane to Moscow.'

The Premier was thinking. 'But not too late for something else,' he said slowly. He stared down at his wristwatch. 'They will be landing shortly.' He looked up, gnawing his lower lip. 'All right. We did not execute the First Lady in Moscow. But we *can* execute her right here.' He slapped the flat of his hand down hard on the desk. 'Yes. That's it. We must do it here.' He glanced at his watch again. 'Not much time left. But we can do it. Who's our best man for the job?'

'Baginov, without question.'

'Bring him to me at once!'

13

Stationed inside Westridge air terminal, at a picture window that looked out over the field and the landing strips, Guy Parker maintained his watch for the expected plane from Moscow. He had been here for a half-hour, and he was becoming more anxious with each passing moment.

Leaving London, after Ambassador Youngdahl's phone call, Parker had driven his rented Jaguar at breakneck speed in the darkness over the increasingly desolate highway, and then following the road sign had branched off the main highway toward the Westridge airport. Once the lights of the small abandoned RAF airfield came into view, Parker had slowed down, spotted the parking lot opposite the terminal and steered into it.

Crossing the street to the terminal, he had seen only one glass door open. Flanking this entrance were two unarmed British immigration officers, standing casually, smoking. Politely, one of them had asked Parker for identification. He had displayed his White House credentials. One immigration officer had called his name to the other, who had punched it out on the keys of a portable computer. Apparently, what had showed up on the screen had been satisfactory, for Parker had been admitted. He presumed that when the First Lady – or alleged First Lady – arrived from Claridge's, she would not have to undergo similar verification.

Striding over the cracked concrete floor, Parker had reached the exit doorway to the field. Two armed Soviet guards had been posted there. One had said in broken English, 'No one allowed on field. You must wait by window.'

Obediently, Parker had strolled along the window, and thirty feet from the exit had taken a position that gave him a better view of the runways. In the immediate foreground, there had been space for two airplanes. One space was filled by a huge helicopter which Parker recognized as a Mil Mi–6, used for transport and cargo. Alongside it, perched on a mobile platform, a single ground-crew technician in navy blue cover-alls was servicing some malfunctioning part, using a flashlight from his tool cart as he tinkered away. The parking space next to the helicopter had been empty, with two other Soviet technicians idle at the portable boarding ramp as they awaited the arrival of the special plane from Moscow.

That had been more than a half-hour ago.

Now, with the growing dawn, Parker could see the night lights going out. The empty space, meant for the second plane, was still waiting to be filled.

Lighting his pipe, Parker shifted his weight from one leg to the other, and tried to resist the fatigue that came from lack of sleep. Once more, he examined his reason for coming here. He knew that Vera would be arriving momentarily to meet the Moscow plane and Alex Razin. How she intended to get away from the President at this hour, Parker could not imagine. Then he remembered that Nora had told him. Vera was sleeping alone in another bedroom tonight. She would have no trouble getting away.

For Parker, the question that demanded an answer – and his presence here – was simple: was Razin arriving alone with the package that contained photographs of Billie's corpse or was he arriving with Billie herself, alive and well? Of course, Vera would not know of this last possibility. Her single-minded purpose would be to see the photographs, reassure herself that Billie was gone and that she, herself, was safe as the only First Lady. Also, secondarily, her purpose would be to get Razin past immigration and into London where she could change his status from undesirable alien to accepted visitor. She, of course, would have the power to effect this change. Her next move would be to call secretly upon Premier Kirechenko, and reveal to him what she knew about President Bradford's Summit plans.

Distracted by his thoughts, Parker had missed the arrival and landing of the Soviet plane. But he could make out the plane now, the four single-shaft turbo-props, the red band along its fuselage, and the red star on its high rear fin. He watched it gradually begin to slow on the cement landing strip. This must be it, he told himself, the expected aircraft that would resolve the enigma of Billie Bradford's fate.

He had turned to glance at the terminal entrance, wondering when Vera would get here, when he caught sight of her coming swiftly through the doorway. She was wearing her well-know beige mink coat, the collar shielding most of her famous face. A slender, dapper man had her by the arm, and after a few seconds Parker was able to recognize him. He was Fred Willis, the protocol chief, the American traitor.

Willis had brought Vera to a stop, and whispered something to each of the British immigration officers. Both had looked at Vera, and each gave a short deferential bow to her. Now Willis was speaking to Vera, and she was nodding. Abruptly, Willis left her and left the terminal for what looked like an Austin at the curb. Vera resumed walking across the departure lounge.

As his gaze followed her, Parker caught another sight from the corner of his eye. The newly landed Soviet plane was growing larger through the window, taxiing slowly, and wheeling into the empty space beside the helicopter. Two crewmen started rolling the portable ramp toward it.

After averting his face for a moment, Parker's eyes went back to Vera. She had dropped her mink collar slightly, and smiled at the two Soviet guards at the exit. Both bowed their heads respectfully. Vera continued out on to the field.

The huge Soviet plane had halted. The workmen were pushing the portable ramp into place against the plane. Vera waited at the foot of the steps. When the door of the plane, high above, began to open, Vera hurriedly ascended the steps, climbing toward the doorway.

Parker held his breath, wondering what would happen next.

During the last forty-five minutes, the ground technician on the platform alongside the helicopter had kept his back to the terminal window and to the newly arrived airplane in the neighbouring space. He had not seen the transport arrive, although he was aware it was there. He had not seen the portable staircase rolled up. He had not seen the arrival of Vera Vavilova nor had he seen her disappear into the plane.

He had seen as little as possible, because he, himself, did not wish to be seen – and described by someone later.

Now, with the passengers sure to be leaving the plane any second, Baginov turned around fully for the first time. Wiping his broad countenance with a dirty hand, he had a glimpse of the tall man at the terminal window and the Soviet guards at the exit. Turning further, he saw the two crewmen who had left the portable ramp and several other Soviet workmen assembling beyond to look over the plane.

Unobtrusively, he dismounted from the platform, laid his flashlight in the tool cart, and began to push the cart away from the helicopter. He was on the wrong side of the just arrived Antonov. But he had known it would be that way, and he was prepared. Rolling his cart at a snail's pace toward the front of the Antonov, he advanced in the direction of the repair shed attached to the side of the terminal.

As he passed under the nose of the big plane, Baginov raised his eyes. The portable ramp was in view from bottom to top. He could see that the door of the plane above was wide open. There was no one leaving through the doorway, and no one visible inside the opened door.

Perfect, Baginov told himself, perfect timing.

He continued to push his cart ahead. At a distance midway between the foot of the portable ramp and the tool shed, he brought his cart to a stop. Casually, he reached into the cart for a small box inside. He opened the top of the box, then set the box atop the cart as he rubbed the palm of his right hand against his cover-alls to be certain it was dry.

He faced the portable stairs, his eyes intent on the opening above.

He waited.

Vera Vavilova had come breathlessly through the plane door, turned and hastened towards the empty interior, expecting to be met by Alex Razin. At the edge of the main cabin, she stood bewildered. Alex was not there. No member of the crew was there. The section was empty.

That instant she heard footsteps and spun around. Alex Razin, who had opened the plane door and remained partially behind it, was coming toward her. Seeing him again, her knees felt like jelly. It seemed ages since she and Alex had been together, and here he was so handsome, so masculine, so comforting – and yet, surprisingly, so strangely grim.

Arms out, she rushed to him. 'Oh, Alex!'

She was in his arms, her own arms hugging him tightly. She wanted to cry with relief.

'Vera,' he whispered, 'I love you.'

Their lips pressed together as she clung to him. But soon she became aware that his hand was against her shoulder, and that he was making an effort to push her away.

She let go, and stepped back, puzzled.

'Vera, there's something –' he began to say.

'Alex,' she interrupted, 'you are here, you are safe. Everything will be arranged. You will stay. I've worked it out.' She paused. 'The photographs. You have them? I must see them before –'

'There are no photographs,' he said flatly. 'There is something else.' He half turned, and beckoned to someone in the rear of the plane.

From out of the unlighted section of the plane, someone was emerging, someone was coming forward.

A woman was coming forward.

Vera's eyes widened, her mouth fell open, and involuntarily she let out a strangled cry of disbelief.

The woman in front of her, facing her, was Billie Bradford.

Vera stared. She stared at her own hair, her own eyes, nose, lips, chin, bosom, even her own fur coat. For spinning seconds she thought that she was seeing herself in a full-length mirror. Vera looking at Vera. But, no – she was looking at Billie Bradford in the flesh, and she struggled to hold on to her senses, to realize that this was the real thing and she, herself, was the counterfeit.

Then the implications of this terrible encounter struck her. Frightened, her wild eyes sought Alex. He had come between them. 'You know about each other,' he said quickly.

Vera, chilled to the marrow, began to tremble. 'Alex, I – I don't understand –'

'I had to do it,' said Alex. 'I had no choice. I did it for you, for us, believe me.'

Vera's fear tripped her anger. 'No, you stupid fool! It could have been worked without this. But now – you've destroyed me – sold out our people – ruined everything.'

'Stop it!' Razin commanded, grabbing Vera by the shoulders. 'It had to be this way. We are not murderers.'

'You've murdered me,' said Vera, her voice going hollow.

For the first time, Billie Bradford spoke. 'You will be safe, Vera, I promise that. Don't blame Alex. He is a man of conscience. He did not want to see me die, and he did not want to lose you. No matter what was done to me, I still owe my life to Alex. In return, I will help you both. We have it planned –'

Vera felt her self-control slipping from her. 'No – no, no, no – nothing can help.'

Billie stepped nearer to Vera, taking her arm. 'You have my word, Vera, I can help you and I will. As First Lady –'

'First Lady,' Vera echoed, horrified, shaking her head.

'I've suffered, and survived,' said Billie. 'Now you are suffering – but will survive.'

As if hypnotized, Vera could not take her eyes off Billie, trying to understand the reassurance being offered. In the long silent seconds that followed, Vera sought to take hold of herself, tried to consider her mirror image more objectively. Realization of what had been done to this other woman, realization of her own fall from power and her sudden helplessness, gradually made her abject. 'I – I am sorry,' she murmured, 'deeply sorry about what was done to you –'

'I know what you had to do,' Billie interrupted. 'I forgive you. Alex had to do what he did today – for you – for me. Everything will work out.'

'Can it?'

'It's happening right now,' said Billie. 'One thing. If I can be objective, as your severest critic –' She summoned up a wan smile. '– you have undoubtedly given the single greatest performance ever given by any actress in history.'

Vera's mingled hostility and fear began to melt. She felt a touch of respect for this woman.

Billie was addressing her again. 'You will have another role to perform now.' Billie paused. 'Since what happened had to be, let me add something that may sound strange. Thank you for deceiving my husband and – and caring for him and living out my image, so that I can resume as of today. And – thank you for Alex – and his ultimate decency.'

Razin had found his voice. 'All right, now we must move. There is much to do.' He stepped between them, linking one of his arms in Vera's and the other in Billie's. 'We will leave the plane now. To prevent rumours and gossip, both of you bring your collars up, hide your faces. We will leave quickly. You have a car, Vera?'

Vera nodded. Willis would be at the wheel, waiting. He would not know there would be two of them. But considering his own position, he would never dare to speak of it.

'After we're on our way,' said Razin, 'Billie will take over. Now, let's go. Which of you wants to go first?'

Guy Parker stood rigidly at the picture window, his gaze focused on the portable staircase standing at the open doorway of the Soviet plane. No one had emerged yet. Parker held his breath and watched.

He knew the numbers, and he knew what the totals would mean.

If one, and only one, First Lady emerged, it would have to be Vera, it would mean Billie was dead and the Russians had their victory.

If two First Ladies emerged, it would mean Billie was alive and the Russians had suffered defeat.

Parker kept his eyes on the empty doorway.

Suddenly, a beautiful woman in a mink coat, face partially concealed by her collar, materialized, framed by the open doorway of the aircraft. Gracefully, holding one rail, she began to descend the portable steps. Seconds later, a dark-haired, broad-shouldered man, wearing a leather jacket, came through the doorway and started down the steps. This was Razin, Parker's distant collaborator.

Parker kept his gaze fastened on the open doorway, hoping for another to appear.

He realized that his heart was beating harder and faster.

A short distance from the foot of the portable staircase, Baginov busied himself with his tool cart as he kept the staircase in view. Baginov's eyes followed the woman down the steps as she descended with the Soviet agent, Razin, right behind her.

Baginov watched her foot touch the last metal step, with Razin at her heels. Now one foot came off the metal step, then the other. Having reached the ground, she hesitated to allow Razin to draw up alongside her.

Holding them in sight, Baginov's hand snaked across the top of the tool cart, dipped into the open box, clutched the light metal fragmentation bomb. Encased in the metal was deadly gelignite. As he swiftly brought the bomb to his side, Baginov remembered the first time he had seen it tested on a range thirty kilometres from Moscow. The Red Army had used a live political prisoner, a Czech. The device had exploded at his feet, and when the dust had cleared the Czech was gone. The largest piece of him found had been a two-inch patch of skin.

Baginov saw them – the woman in the mink, the man

named Razin – resume walking away from the bottom of the portable staircase.

Now, he told himself.

His thumb triggered the near instantaneous timing device. Eight seconds to detonation. He raised the bomb above his shoulder, reared back and whipped his arm forward, flinging it in a high arc toward the pair. As the bomb left his fingers, and he followed its trajectory, ticking off the seconds in his head, he caught the flash of movement in the doorway at the top of the portable staircase. Another woman was emerging from the plane, ready to step down on the platform of the staircase. She was identical, as far as he could make out, to the woman before him on the ground – same hair, eyes, mink coat. For an instant he was immobilized and numbed by confusion.

But the count in his head had just reached six seconds. Instinctively, he spun away and threw himself to the ground beside his cart.

Seven . . . eight . . . and the gelignite blew sky-high with a deafening roar.

The earth beneath him heaved, and the smoke choked him, and the debris showered down upon him.

Ears ringing, momentarily blinded, Baginov found strength to rise to his knees. He began to crawl, faster and faster, toward his pre-arranged escape hatch, the Soviet repair shed. He reached the broken door, pushed it inward, started to crawl inside. But before disappearing, he wanted to be sure he could report success.

He glanced over his shoulder, trying to pierce the screen of dense grey-black smoke. Something was burning. He could make out the damaged belly of the plane, the void where the staircase had once been, the other woman above thrown against the side of the doorway. As the smoke lifted, thinned, in the place where the mink-clad lady and Razin had been walking – there was no one, there was nothing. The pair had been totally obliterated, wiped off the face of the earth.

Baginov had seen all he needed to see. He offered himself a grimy, congratulatory smile. Then the smile left him. The other woman. She had not been part of the plan. Something had gone wrong, he sensed. He had done his job precisely and well. But there was something wrong.

He ceased crawling, staggered to his feet inside the dark shed, and stumbled to the exit that would lead him to safety.

Guy Parker lay stunned and bleeding on the floor of the air terminal.

The tremendous explosion had completely shattered the window at which he had been standing. The force of the detonation had knocked him flat on his back. The blood on his right cheek and neck had come from shards of flying glass.

He sat up, groggily trying to recover his senses, and understand what he had seen.

The first thing that he recalled was that there had been two of them, two women, just before the blast. He was positive he was not mistaken. There had been one woman at the foot of the portable staircase, and another coming out of the plane door at the top, and at least from a quick look they had appeared to be the same. This meant that Razin had managed to save Billie and had escaped from Moscow with her. This meant that Billie and Vera had confronted each other inside the plane, before leaving it.

Rising to a knee, Parker took a snap survey of the air terminal. The two Russian guards at the exit to the airfield were still down, dazed, one lying on his side, the other sitting up. At the entrance, the two British immigration officers had left their posts, one heading for the field, the other going to a telephone. Beyond them, Fred Willis had left his parked car and was running to the terminal entrance.

With effort, Parker brought himself to his feet. Tentatively, he took several steps. His legs were wobbly, but he remained upright. He attempted a few more steps. He could walk. He turned to the shattered window. He found a large gaping hole. He started for it, hesitated, then stepped through it onto the cement area of the airfield.

Stopping, he tried to make order out of the disaster. Off

to one side, a number of Russian ground crewmen were aimlessly wandering about in shock. Nearby, a dazed Russian in military uniform was staring at the twisted pieces of metal of the portable staircase that had been blown away and widely scattered. One British immigration officer had just come breathlessly through the exit shouting in English that the assassin must be found.

Ignoring them all, Parker had eyes for only one object. Through the thinning smoke rising from the bomb's crater, he squinted up toward the scarred fuselage of the airplane, concentrating on the doorway. There was a woman there and he recognized her. The First Lady had survived and was struggling to her feet and limping back to the plane's doorway. She stared down at the empty space beneath her and then off at the shredded remnants of the portable staircase that littered the field below. In those fleeting seconds, Parker could discern other human figures above, two, now three, members of the Soviet plane crew materializing behind her.

The First Lady, Parker told himself with relief, alive and unharmed.

He knew he must act. Someone must help her.

Bringing his handkerchief to his nose and mouth, Parker ducked his head and raced into the smoke, side-stepping the huge crater, trying to ignore the small strips of charred mink and the grisly portion of a human ear.

He burst out of the column of smoke, coughing, and stumbled across the cement until he was directly below the plane's doorway and the First Lady.

He waved up to Billie, to catch her attention. 'Here, Billie!' he shouted. 'It's me!'

She had heard him, and her head bobbed.

Parker stretched his arms up toward her. 'Come on, drop down! It's not far! The crewmen will help you! Just drop down! I'll catch you!'

Without a word, she turned, offering her hands to two of the crewmen. Each took one of her hands, as they flanked her, gripping the sides of the doorway. She sat on the edge, her legs hanging free. She eased away, and was out of the plane as they held her tightly. They lowered her gradually, and for seconds she dangled in space.

Parker reaching higher, was able to touch her ankles.

'Let go!' he called.

She let go, falling away, plummeting towards him, and Parker caught her, his arms around the lower half of her mink coat. The impact staggered him, sent him reeling backwards, until he lost his footing and went down on the cement with her body sprawled on top of him.

They lay in a heap, while he shook his head, and began pushing her off. With effort, he squirmed out from under her, and rising, helped her to her feet.

'Are you all right?' he wanted to know.

She nodded dumbly.

From a distance, he heard a siren, and then another and another.

He grasped her hand. 'You've got to get out of here,' he said.

Quickly, he led her away, circumnavigating the smoke, hurrying her to what was left of the terminal window. At the gaping hole, he gestured her into the building. She stepped over the jagged remnants of glass and was inside. He followed her, pointing toward the entrance.

That moment, he saw someone in the middle of the room, frantically beckoning to her. It was Fred Willis.

'Mrs Bradford!' Willis cried. 'Hurry!'

She broke away and ran towards Willis.

Parker watched her come up beside Willis, saw the protocol chief take her by the arm, watched them hasten to the entrance. About to go through the entrance, she half turned and waved her thanks to Parker.

Slowly approaching the door, Parker could see Willis helping her into his car, and then dashing around to the driver's side and swinging into the seat. The car started, and catapulted away.

Parker stood in the entrance, eyes on the receding vehicle.

In that instant he remembered something almost forgotten.

There had been two of them.

Now there was only one.

'What?' bellowed Premier Dmitri Kirechenko, bolting out of his chair and advancing toward KGB agent Baginov. 'You say there were two of them – *two* of them? And they looked alike?'

Nervously, Baginov backed up a few feet towards the centre of the sitting room of the Dorchester suite, nodding his affirmation. 'Yes,' he gulped to the Premier. Then to General Vladimir Chukovsky, on his feet behind the Premier, Baginov added, 'Two of them. One on the ground. One on top, about to leave the plane.'

'And they looked the same?' demanded the Premier.

'Like identical twins,' said Baginov.

'You're sure of that?'

'I – I had only a glance at the second one, but – yes, Comrade Kirechenko, I am positive.'

Premier Kirechenko stood stock-still, his steely blue eyes fixed hard on his KGB agent.

'Let met get this straight,' the Premier said. 'You blew up the First Lady, the one on the ground?'

'And the man with her.'

'Razin,' muttered the Premier. 'Good riddance. But you got rid of the First Lady totally?'

'Totally. Those bombs blast a person into thousands of pieces. Whatever is left cannot be identified.'

'And during this you saw another woman emerge at the top of the stairs?'

'Absolutely.'

'Another lady. You recognized her?'

'Yes, sir. She looked exactly like the one below, like the First Lady.'

'The two looked the same – two First Ladies?'

Baginov nodded vigorously.

Premier Kirechenko's countenance was crusted in a deep frown. 'All right. What happened to her, the one above? Was she blown up, too?'

'No,' said Baginov firmly. 'I had only a glimpse before

escaping. She was knocked sideways and backwards by the explosion. But she was not killed. The one on the ground died. The one on the plane lived.'

The Premier seemed to reflect on this, and when he spoke, it was almost to himself. 'So,' he said, 'Vera, the bitch, went to the plane. She and the Bradford woman saw each other. Now one is gone, and the other survives.' He took a step toward Baginov, and pushed a finger against his agent's chest. 'Baginov, think carefully. Which one died?' He held his breath, and exhaled. 'Which one lived?'

'I don't know, Comrade,' Baginov said hurriedly. 'I don't know at all. They were one and the same. I don't understand it. I followed orders, sir. Get rid of the First Lady. I saw her. I got rid of her. Then, to my surprise, there she was again. It made no sense.'

The Premier gave a heavy sigh. 'Never mind. Thank you for doing your job. You can go now.'

He waited for the KGB agent to leave. When the door was closed, he slowly turned and made his way to the chair before the desk, and absently lowered himself into it. He sat very still, his face a mask staring blankly across the room. After more than a minute, he twisted his chair around to confront General Chukovsky.

'Well,' said the Premier, 'what do you make of it?'

'Naturally, I don't like it.'

'We may have killed theirs all right,' the Premier mused. 'Or we may have killed our own.'

General Chukovsky nodded. 'But I think we shall find out soon enough. If our Vera was the one killed, then of course their First Lady will not come to us. But if their Billie was killed, then Vera will show up and all will be well.'

The Premier pushed himself to his feet, and circled the nearby coffee table, lost in thought. He stopped in front of the general. He shook his head. 'No, General, you are wrong. No one will show up. If our Vera was the one killed, she couldn't show up. If their Billie was killed, and our Vera survived, she won't show up. Not now. Because now she does not have to. Now she *is* the First Lady – we can't prove she isn't. We don't dare to approach her because she may be the real one, she may be Billie Bradford.'

The Premier drifted to the coffee table, contemplated the fruit bowl, and found himself a green apple.

'Who in the hell got Vera to go to that plane?' he asked himself, polishing the apple with his bare hands. 'That is what ruined us.'

He studied the apple and took a loud bite of it. Chewing, he said with a shrug, 'There is an American expression. You win some, you lose some. This time we lose. We will never know if the Americans are bluffing in Boende. We can't risk testing them. We have to play it safe and wait for another time. For the present, we have to give in, agree with the Americans on the non-aggression pact. To the world, we, too, will be peace lovers. Some day, ten, twenty years, a half-century from now, there may be another opportunity, even another and better Vera. But not now. Thanks to Vera, we lose one.'

He walked to the desk. 'I'll call the President, tell him we've reached a decision, arrange for an emergency session at their embassy this afternoon.'

He set the apple down in the ashtray, and pressed the buzzer on his telephone. He looked at the general with a crooked smile. 'I wonder,' he said, 'who will be sleeping with the President tonight?'

The following day, Air Force One was high over the Atlantic, winging its way back to Andrews Air Force Base and to Washington DC.

Parker and Nora Judson sat low in the reclining chairs of the staff section, as Parker shared the front page of this morning's London *Telegraph* with her.

The biggest headline hailed the successful climax of the Summit Conference, the non-aggression treaty agreement, peace in Africa, a new era of detente between the United States and the Soviet Union. A smaller headline was devoted to the mysterious killings at Westridge airfield, where an unknown right-wing assassin had bombed and murdered a

Russian stewardess and the Russian navigator of a Soviet military plane just arrived from Moscow.

Finally, Parker cast the newspaper aside, and with Nora watched the excitement up ahead. There was an air of festivity and celebration inside the plane. The President and the First Lady had come out of their suite to join staff members in a victory toast. President Bradford, grinning, a drink in one hand, an arm around the smiling First Lady, was cheerfully chatting with White House staff members. The President, flushed by his triumph, was confident about his re-election.

The First Lady, glancing around the cabin, noticed Parker and Nora. Separating herself from the President, carrying her highball, she came up the aisle toward them. 'There you are,' she said approaching them. 'I wanted to thank you two for everything.'

Parker tried to rise, but the First Lady's free hand on his shoulder held him firmly in place.

The First Lady lifted her glass. 'And I wanted to propose a toast.'

Parker and Nora raised their drinks to salute her back. 'To the successful Summit,' Parker said.

'To that, of course,' said the First Lady. 'But actually, the toast is to both of you, if what I hear is right. I hear you're planning to marry.'

Nora nodded, smiling broadly. 'We are, Billie. Thank you. I intended to tell you when things calmed down.'

'It couldn't happen to two nicer people,' said the First Lady. She sipped her drink. 'The best I can wish you is that you'll be as happy as Andrew and I have been these past years.'

'We could wish for nothing more,' said Parker.

'Listen, don't get her pregnant right away, Guy,' said the First Lady in a mock scolding tone. 'I need Nora for our second term. And I'll need you, too. Anyway, congratulations and best wishes.'

With that, she turned from them and went to rejoin the President and his cluster of staff members.

Parker's set smile followed her. After a while, his eyes fell on the discarded newspaper. He fingered it thoughtfully, rereading the front-page story on the mysterious killings at Westridge airfield. When he finished, he looked up to find Nora staring at him.

'Well?' she asked.

The smile vanished from Parker's face. 'There must be some way we can find out.'

'How?' said Nora simply. 'We thought of everything we could last night. Nothing worked out. Her gynaecologist is a vegetable in a sanitarium now. Her dog in California was accidentally run over by an automobile a week ago. Vera must have telltale plastic surgery scars, you said. I told you Billie once had plastic surgery, her big secret. So we have nowhere to go, unless you find out something when you go on with her autobiography.'

'I doubt if that'll ever turn up anything.'

'Then where does that leave us? Do you think we'll ever find out?'

'I'll tell you what I really think,' said Parker. 'I think no one will ever know the truth. Not the President. Not the country. Not the world. Only one person knows.' He paused. '*She* knows.'